EDWARD MARSTON was born and brought up in South Wales. A full-time writer for over forty years, he has worked in radio, film, television and the theatre and is a former chairman of the Crime Writers' Association. Prolific and highly successful, he is equally at home writing children's books or literary criticism, plays or biographies.

www.edwardmarston.com

By Edward Marston

PERIL ON
THE ROYAL TRAIN

EDWARD MARSTON

Allison & Busby Limited
12 Fitzroy Mews
London W1T 6DW
www.allisonandbusby.com

First published in Great Britain by Allison & Busby in 2013.
This paperback edition published by Allison & Busby in 2014.

A CIP catalogue record for this book is available from
the British Library.

10 9 8 7 6 5

ISBN 978-0-7490-1249-6

Typeset in 10.5/15 pt Sabon by
Allison & Busby Ltd.

The paper used for this Allison & Busby publication
has been produced from trees that have been legally sourced
from well-managed and credibly certified forests.

Printed and bound by

CPI Group (UK) Ltd, Croydon, CR0 4YY

CHAPTER ONE

Spring 1858

Jamie Farr held the body in his arms and ignored the blood that was dripping onto his smock. The corpse was still warm. It was the third victim in a month and it left him at once saddened and enraged. Others might say that it was an unfortunate accident but, in his eyes, it was nothing short of brutal murder. He could still hear the killer, thundering unseen on its way to Glasgow, leaving smoke and tragedy in its wake. Farr hated railways. A tall, wiry lad with a shepherd's protective love of his flock, he viewed steam locomotives as ruthless enemies, ugly iron monsters that invaded the southern uplands of Scotland, terrorising livestock and mangling to death any animals who caught their feet in the rails. Compensation was difficult to squeeze out of the railway companies and often inadequate when it was paid. They argued that it was the responsibility of farmers to keep their cattle, sheep, pigs and horses away from danger. That only served to anger the young shepherd even more. How could anyone afford to build fences or walls of dry stone that ran for miles? In any case, he asked, why should such beautiful countryside be turned into a place of lurking menace?

Farr shook with impotent fury. He didn't even feel his leg being rubbed. It was only when Angus barked that he realised what the sheepdog was doing. Angus wanted a pardon. It was not his fault that the lamb had scampered down the hill towards the line, then frozen with fear as the train bore down on him. The flock was too large for one dog to manage. Farr understood what the animal was trying to say. When he'd put the remains of the lamb gently to the ground, he gave Angus a reassuring pat. Relieved of guilt, the dog barked in gratitude. One ewe and two lambs had been slaughtered in the space of a month. No matter how vigilant they were, Farr and his dog couldn't guarantee that the rest of the flock was safe. Sheep were inclined to wander. They loved freedom of movement. Nobody had told them about train timetables or warned them about the hurtling speed of the locomotives.

Other shepherds had been forced to accept the coming of the railway. Some had even been heard to concede that it had benefits. Farr's own father, a shepherd like him, took a philosophical view, albeit one that was spiced with strong language. Railways were there to stay, he said. You had to get used to them. Along with foul weather, foxes and rustlers, they were just one more threat with which a shepherd had to live. Jamie Farr didn't share his father's attitude. He was too young and too headstrong. He'd never acknowledge the railway's right to torment livestock and kill indiscriminately. As he gazed down at the tiny lamb, crushed obscenely and now being sniffed by its grieving mother, he was overwhelmed by a sense of injustice. A heinous crime had been committed. They shouldn't be allowed to get away with it. A lust for revenge swelled up inside him. There had to be a way to strike back.

* * *

'Look at it, will ye?' said Dougal Murray. 'There's no' a soul in sight out there.'

'Aye,' agreed Jock Laidlaw. 'I can see naething but empty fields and hills. I like it tha' way, Dougal.'

'It doesnae appeal to me. I want to see toons and people and things going on.'

'Ye'll get your share of tha' farther up the line.'

'But there's still too much countryside to go through yet.'

'A body can *breathe* out here,' said Laidlaw. 'I dinna feel shut in by hooses and factories and the like. Too many people make my heed spin, ye ken. I always feel lost in a big city.'

The two men had to raise their voices over the hiss, roar and clatter. Laidlaw was the driver of the goods train and Murray, his fireman, stood beside him on the footplate. They were taking a mixed cargo from Carlisle to Edinburgh, rattling along at a good speed and seeing all that the billowing smoke allowed them to see of their surroundings. Laidlaw was bigger, older and more compact than the stringy Murray. They were friends as well as colleagues, enjoying leisure time together. Not that their rota on the Caledonian Railway permitted them much leisure. They worked hard for very long hours. Laidlaw was a jovial man, experienced and easy-going. Murray always looked to him for advice.

'What d'ye think Alan will be doing?' he asked.

Laidlaw smiled wryly. 'Can ye no' guess?'

'The mahn will be fast asleep by now, I reckon.'

'Tha', he will – and wi' a pipe stuck in his gob.'

'Alan took a fair bucket of drink last night.'

'So did we, Dougal, but you'll no' find us dozing off at work.'

'It'd be the death of us if we did.'

Alan Grint was their guard, the man who was nominally in charge of the train and who occupied the brake van at the rear, separated from the locomotive by an endless row of wagons. Never without his pipe, Grint was inclined to nod off in his little van where nobody could see or challenge him. Whenever they reached a station, however, he was miraculously awake and alert. Laidlaw and Murray knew the truth. Since they were fond of Grint, they overlooked his weakness and never for a moment considered reporting him.

As the train rumbled on, it approached a point where it had killed a lamb a week earlier. Driver and fireman were unaware of what had happened. It was different when they hit a cow or a horse. Large animals could derail a locomotive but a spring lamb offered no resistance. It had been sliced open effortlessly.

Laidlaw waited until Murray had shovelled some coal into the firebox.

'Have ye set a date yet, Dougal?'

'It isna down to me,' said Murray, gloomily.

'Well, has your lassie set a date?'

'If it were left to Annie, we'd have been wed years ago. It's her mother who's dragging her heels. She says that Annie's too young to marry.'

'When a lassie has a shape on her like Annie Bray,' said Laidlaw with a chuckle of approval, 'then she's good and ready. Take ma word on that. Ye'll have to run off to Gretna with her.'

'Dinna think it hasnae gone through my mind.'

'What's stopping ye, mahn?'

'I need to save a wee bit more first.'

'Marry now and save later.'

'That's a fine thing for ye to say, Jock,' said the fireman, jabbing him with a grimy finger. 'No woman has managed to get *ye* down the aisle. Yet ye keep on at me to get wed.'

'Ye *need* a wife, Dougal. I don't. I'm no' the marrying type.'

'Wait till you've met the right woman.'

'Och,' said Laidlaw with a lecherous grin, 'I've met ma share of those along the way, believe me. I love wummen – always have. I just don't love them enough to take one as a wife.'

'Do ye no' want to raise a family?'

'It'd be too much of an ordeal. Look at Alan, will ye? He's got a wife and four bairns. When he goes home at night, he's up to his armpits in family life. No wonder the puir mahn is fair exhausted. Coming to work is the only rest he gets. Be warned, Dougal. Too many bairns can be the death of ye.'

'We havna thought that far ahead,' admitted Murray.

'Then it's high time ye did.'

Laidlaw was about to explain why but the words died in his throat. They'd just come round a bend and expected to see a clear line ahead of them. Instead, they were confronted by a large pile of rocks. Surging towards it, the locomotive was doomed. There was no time to slow it down, still less to stop it. Laidlaw and Murray didn't even have the presence of mind to jump from the footplate. Disaster was only seconds away and they stood there transfixed. When it came, the impact was deafening. Cast iron met solid rock in a fierce collision. The locomotive was instantly derailed, rolling down an embankment and dragging the wagons after it, their loads scattered willy-nilly across the ground. Driver and fireman were killed outright, pinned beneath tons of metal and wood. There'd be no wedding for Murray now and Laidlaw wouldn't be able to pass on any more advice to his friend. Their futures had been cruelly obliterated. When hot coals spilling from the engine started a fire, flames licked hungrily at their bodies.

Back in the brake van, Alan Grint fared no better. The guard never even woke up. The sheer force of the impact flung him across the van so hard that he dashed out his brains against the unforgiving

9

timber and collapsed in a heap, his pipe still held grimly between his teeth. Ahead of him, dozens of wagons snaked and bucked and fought a losing battle to stay on the rails. It was a scene of accelerating destruction. Nothing escaped. From locomotive to brake van, the goods train contracted violently until it was almost half its original length, its power gone, its timetable cancelled, its cargo flung far and wide, its destination for ever beyond reach. Both sets of lines were impassably blocked. Traffic on that stretch of the Caledonian Railway had come to a decisive halt. Wheels of upturned wagons rotated pointlessly in the eerie silence that followed the pandemonium. All was lost.

From the top of the hill, someone looked down with quiet satisfaction.

CHAPTER TWO

'Let them sort out their own mess,' said Tallis, peremptorily.

'But they asked for our help, sir,' argued Colbeck. 'More specifically, they requested my assistance by name.'

'You're needed here in London.'

'I'd say that Scotland has a greater need of my services.'

'Damn you, man! I decide where you go and what you do.'

'Are you going to refuse their appeal?'

'I have to,' said Tallis, slapping the telegraph down on his desk. 'It's a question of priorities.'

'What can possibly take precedence over a train crash?'

'I don't want you gallivanting north of the border when we live in the capital city of crime. There's more than enough to keep you occupied here.'

'My instinct is that I should go, sir.'

Tallis snorted. 'I'm a martyr to your instincts,' he said, rolling his eyes. 'You're forever relying on guesswork instead of on cumulative evidence. We don't even know if foul play was involved. The crash could have been caused by a random fall of rock. It may not be a police matter at all.'

'I can see that you're not familiar with the Caledonian Railway,' said Colbeck, icily calm in the face of provocation. 'The engineer who surveyed the terrain was Joseph Locke. The contractor who actually built the line was Thomas Brassey, a man whom I had the privilege to meet when investigating a case in France. Locke and Brassey are renowned experts in their respective fields. They'd never construct a railway that was likely to be imperilled by falling rock. That accident was contrived,' he went on. 'The three men were murdered.'

'How can you possibly know that?'

'Would you care to accept a wager on it, Superintendent?'

Edward Tallis smouldered in his chair. Colbeck met his hostile glare with a challenging smile. It was at moments like this that the underlying tension between the two men came to the fore. While they shared a degree of mutual respect, they also had grave reservations about each other. A former soldier, accustomed to unquestioning obedience, Tallis resented the fact that his inspector always teetered on the brink of insubordination. The resentment was shored up by envy and disapproval. Tallis was jealous of the praise that the so-called Railway Detective routinely garnered at the end of a successful investigation, while he – technically in charge of the case – was usually given short shrift in the press. Then there was the question of the inspector's private life. Having lectured Colbeck on the importance of having no distractions, the superintendent was mortified when he chose to get married, fearing that it would weaken his effectiveness.

For his part, Colbeck was ready to acknowledge the time, effort and commitment that his superior put into his job, but the man's single-mindedness was a flaw in his character. Tallis had no existence outside Scotland Yard. That was his kingdom and he

12

liked to rule the roost. He had no understanding of the lives of his officers and treated them with a mixture of strict discipline and distrust. Colbeck could make allowances for the man's envy and shrugged off his disapproval of the recent marriage. But he could not countenance the way Tallis tried to interfere in cases, causing both delay and frustration. Over the years he'd learnt to cope with the superintendent but he still couldn't bring himself to like the man.

'The matter is settled,' decided Tallis, taking a cigar from the box in front of him. 'Forget that you ever saw this telegraph.'

'I'm afraid that I can't do that, sir.'

'You'll do as you're told, Inspector.'

'We can't turn down an appeal like that,' insisted Colbeck. 'Instead of bickering about it, I should be finding out the time of the next train to Scotland.'

'You'll do nothing of the kind.' Tallis paused to cut off the end of the cigar before thrusting it into his mouth and lighting it. He puffed hard then exhaled a cloud of smoke. 'Is that clear?'

'It may be clear, sir, but it also happens to be wrong-headed.'

Tallis bridled. 'Do you *dare* to question my judgement?'

'Ordinarily, it would never cross my mind to do so,' said Colbeck, smoothly, 'because your judgement is usually sound. In this case, I submit, you haven't taken all the facts into consideration.'

'We *have* no facts. The telegraph is terse in the extreme.'

'The word "disaster" is enough for me, Superintendent. That, and the fact that three railwaymen were killed. This is a crisis. We must respond to it.'

Tallis's only response was to jab the cigar between his teeth and puff on it as if his life depended on creating a smokescreen. He was momentarily obscured. It was pure accident that Colbeck even knew about the accident. When the telegraph from the Caledonian

Railway arrived at Scotland Yard, it went first to the commissioner. The man charged with taking it to the superintendent's office happened to bump into Colbeck in the corridor.

'Another case for the Railway Detective,' he'd said, waving the paper.

Colbeck had taken it from him. 'Let me see.'

When he'd read the summons, he acted as the delivery boy, taking the telegraph into Tallis's office and handing it over. Eager to be told to leave for Scotland, he was dismayed when the superintendent wanted to keep him shackled in London. When other pleas for help had come in from different parts of the country, Tallis had been willing to dispatch him instantly. For some reason, he was not going to do it this time.

Colbeck rose to his feet and adjusted his frock coat. He was a portrait of elegance, tall, slim and debonair. It was another thing that Tallis held against him. Colbeck was such a dandy that he made the superintendent feel unkempt. Detectives in the Metropolitan Police Force were not well paid but Colbeck had private means that enabled him to retain the services of a good tailor. That set him apart from his colleagues – as well as from most members of the criminal fraternity. What he and Tallis had in common was an iron will. A collision between them was imminent.

'Perhaps I should take the matter up with the commissioner,' suggested Colbeck with feigned politeness.

'You'll do nothing of the kind!' yelled Tallis, banging a fist on the desk.

'But the telegraph was sent directly to him.'

'It was then passed on to me for consideration. Unfortunately, you had an unauthorised glance at it before it was put in my hands.'

'It was just as well that I saw it, sir. Had I not done so, you'd have rushed into a foolish decision to disregard the summons.'

'My decisions are never foolish.'

'Let's call them rash and overhasty, then.'

Tallis's cheeks reddened. 'You are not going to Scotland.'

'The commissioner may take a different view.'

'And you are not bothering the commissioner,' asserted the other, jumping up and inadvertently flicking cigar ash all down his waistcoat. 'He has empowered me to take whatever action I feel necessary. I expect loyalty from my detectives,' he boomed. 'Try to go over my head and you'll suffer the consequences.'

'The only consequences that interest me are those that emanate from the train crash. They are desperate for my help in Scotland. It would be cruel to deny it to them.'

Tallis was peevish. 'If I sent you up there, you'd only be in the way.'

'That's not the impression I get from the telegraph, sir.'

'They'll have enough people to look into the disaster. The railway police will already be asking questions and the procurator fiscal will launch his own inquiry. If memory serves me, there's also a sheriff who's likely to get involved as well. Then, of course, there's the railway inspector. That stretch of line will be crawling with officers of one kind or another. In short,' concluded Tallis with an air of finality, 'you are redundant.'

'There's something you're forgetting, Superintendent.'

'I very much doubt that.'

'Competent as any investigation will surely be, it's unlikely to be led by someone with direct experience of a railway disaster. That's where Sergeant Leeming and I have the advantage.' Colbeck took a step towards him. 'Do I need to remind you of the catastrophe that befell the Brighton express some years ago?'

'No, you don't – it was one of our greatest successes.'

An express train had been derailed at speed and crashed into a ballast train coming in the opposite direction. The railway inspector had described it as an accident brought about by a serious error by the driver, a man killed on the spot and therefore unable to defend himself. Colbeck had proved that the disaster had been deliberately contrived by someone with an obsessive grudge against the London, Brighton and South Coast Railway and one of its regular passengers.

'Investigating that crash gave us insights that can be put to practical use in Scotland,' said Colbeck, reasonably. 'We know how to avoid the blind alleys.'

Tallis was unmoved. 'You are staying here,' he decreed. 'As you well know, the Detective Department is plagued by an insufficient budget and a shortage of manpower. I can't afford to send two of my best men hundreds of miles away for what may well be a lengthy investigation.'

'You were happy enough to send us off to Devon last year.'

'That's immaterial.'

'I disagree,' said Colbeck, locking horns with him. 'What took us to Exeter was the murder of a stationmaster. Regrettable as it was, it doesn't compare in scope and significance with a calamity like this. Three people have been killed and the damage to freight and rolling stock is immense. We simply must answer the call.'

'Out of the question,' snapped Tallis. 'You could be away for weeks.'

'I'll stay in Scotland for months if that's what it takes.'

'You won't be going anywhere near that benighted country. There's work for you right on our doorstep. A publican had his throat cut in Whitechapel last night. You and Sergeant Leeming are to take charge of the investigation.' He treated Colbeck to the withering stare with which he used to cow rebellious soldiers during his army days. Then he turned his back to signal that the discussion was over. 'The details are in the folder on my desk,' he said, coldly. 'Study them on the cab ride to Whitechapel.'

Colbeck ignored the command. Instead of touching the folder, he reached for a piece of blank stationery and took the quill from the inkwell. When he heard the scratch of the pen, Tallis swung round in disbelief.

'What – in God's name – are you *doing*?' he cried.

'I'm writing a letter of resignation,' replied Colbeck. 'It will take immediate effect. Send someone else to Whitechapel.'

'But I'm giving you an order.'

'You are no longer in a position to do so, sir. We've obviously come to a parting of the ways. My place is on the Caledonian Railway. If you refuse to sanction my departure, I've no alternative but to resign and go of my own accord.'

'But you'd have no authority,' blustered Tallis. 'You wouldn't have the weight of Scotland Yard behind you.'

Colbeck's retort was crisp. 'At the moment, I feel that it's right on top of me and it's a burden I need to shed. As for authority,' he went on, drawing himself up and casting off his natural modesty for once, 'it lies in my reputation and there's not a detective alive who can match my record of solving crime on the railways of Britain. I cannot – and will not – turn my back on this emergency. Now, sir,' he added, motioning the other man back, 'I beg you to stop looming over me so that I sever my links with Scotland Yard in favour of Scotland.'

Tallis was thunderstruck. Colbeck was in earnest. Rather than obey orders, he was going to resign. The superintendent quailed at the thought of having to explain to the commissioner why the finest detective in the department had left them. Blame would fall directly on Tallis. There was a secondary fear. If the inspector did resign, he would not be abandoning the fight against crime. He'd simply continue that fight on a different basis. Instead of being able to utilise Colbeck's rare gifts, Tallis might be in competition with them. Railway companies in dire need would turn first to a man of proven ability. Robert Colbeck, private detective, would be free to choose the cases he took on. It was a terrifying possibility.

There was a final indignity. As he tried to draw solace from his cigar, Tallis discovered that it had gone out. His glowing certainty had also dimmed to the faintest glimmer. His will of iron cracked. He reached out a hand to grab Colbeck's wrist.

'There's no need to write any more,' he said with a note of appeasement, forcing his features into a semblance of a smile. 'Let's talk about Scotland, shall we? You may, after all, have a point.'

CHAPTER THREE

In the wake of the crash, there were two immediate priorities. The first was to recover the dead bodies, a simple undertaking in the case of the guard but a daunting one where driver and fireman were concerned. Their mutilated corpses, blackened by fire, were at the very bottom of the wreckage. Rescue workers strove hard to shift the mounds of debris in order to get the two men out before their relatives arrived. At all costs, they wanted to prevent grieving families from seeing the hideous sight that greeted them on arrival. Jock Laidlaw and Dougal Murray were unrecognisable, their heads smashed to a pulp and their roasted bodies twisted into unnatural shapes. Laidlaw had lost an arm. Both of Murray's legs had been cut off at the knee. Death had been mercifully swift but it had left a repulsive signature.

While a team of men addressed the first priority, another team turned its attention to the second. The line had to be cleared. It was a Herculean task but there were many volunteers. As word spread, people swarmed in from every direction, some carrying spades, axes or other implements, others merely bringing strong arms and a desire to help. They worked with railway employees throughout the evening and on into the night, reinforced by fresh assistance from the surrounding villages and farms. Darkness brought another problem. Fires were lit to illumine the scene and to burn some of the debris but they only cast a fitful glare over the devastation. It meant that the discarded freight was at the mercy of nocturnal predators, quick-fingered thieves who sought to exploit the disaster for their own ends rather than joining the rescuers. Railway policemen were powerless to stop them. They were hopelessly outnumbered and, even with lanterns in their hands, couldn't easily pick people out in the dark.

One of the few wagons that had somehow remained on the track was carrying a consignment of cheese, destined for a wholesaler in Edinburgh. Much of it would never reach him. Once discovered, the wagon became a magnet for the thieves who grabbed everything they could carry, hid it nearby then went back for more. And there were other foodstuffs on hand for those bold enough to steal them, not to mention crates of dead or squawking chickens tossed out uncaringly during the crash and piled up at crazy angles. If something could be carried, it was likely to disappear.

Nairn Craig was disgusted by the reports he received next morning.

'How could any decent man behave like that?' he asked.

'It's human nature, sir,' replied his companion, dourly. 'A tragedy like this brings out the best in some people and the very worst in others. And it wasn't only men involved. I heard the rustle of skirts clearly. Women can pilfer just as well. They and their menfolk swooped down like so many vultures.'

'They should be sent to prison for a long time.'

'That's easier said than done, Mr Craig. How can you arrest

people when you don't know who they are? They were phantoms in the night. By dawn, they'd vanished into thin air. Besides,' he said, raising a meaningful eyebrow, 'they weren't all driven by criminal intent. Wages are low for farm labourers and those out of work have even emptier bellies. There's a lot of desperation in this shire, sir. When they see a chance like this, the needy can't stop themselves.'

'That's no excuse, Superintendent.'

'It's not an excuse – it's an explanation.'

'Theft is theft, whichever way you look at it.'

Rory McTurk gave a nod of agreement. As superintendent of the railway police, he was one of the first on the scene and been appalled by what he found. He was a huge bear of a man with a black beard and bushy eyebrows that all but concealed the deep-set eyes. Relishing his authority, McTurk liked nothing better than ordering people about in his gruff voice. In the presence of the general manager of the Caledonian Railway, however, he was more subdued and deferential. Nairn Craig was a stout man of medium height and middle years with flabby cheeks that quivered as he spoke. Even though he wore the tallest of top hats, he still looked short beside the towering figure of the superintendent.

'Naturally,' he said, surveying the scene with an anxious eye, 'our sympathies must be with the families of the deceased. But we must also concentrate on clearing the track and getting it repaired where it was ripped up. Every hour that we're unable to run trains on this stretch of line is costing us money. More to the point, it's a gift to our rivals. The North British Railway will be rubbing their hands. When our passengers and freight customers are denied uninterrupted traffic on the western route in and out of Scotland, they'll obviously use the eastern route instead. The NBR will profit from our loss.'

'It was the first thing that crossed my mind, sir,' said McTurk, pointedly.

The manager blinked. 'You think that *they* might be responsible?'

'They'd be at the top of my list of suspects, I know that.'

'Well,' said Craig, rubbing his chin, 'they've employed some underhand methods in the past to get the better of us, I grant you, but even they would draw back from something as despicable as this, surely.'

'All's fair in love and war, sir – and we've been at war with the NBR for many years. I'd put nothing past them. When the procurator fiscal launches his inquiry, I'll point in their direction.'

'You must do the same to Inspector Colbeck.'

McTurk was startled. 'What does he have to do with it?'

'He's the man we most need at a time like this, Superintendent. I sent a telegraph to Scotland Yard this very morning. Pray God he answers my plea.' He saw the evident consternation on McTurk's face. 'Colbeck has no peer. You must have heard of the Railway Detective.'

'I've done more than hear about him, sir,' said McTurk, guardedly. 'I've met the inspector. Our paths crossed when I was working in England. A mail train was robbed in broad daylight. It was a crime that I could easily have solved myself,' he boasted, 'but I was severely hampered by Colbeck.'

'I've heard nothing but praise of the man.'

'Oh, he's well intentioned, I'll give him that. But he's too high-handed for my liking. Besides, he knows nothing at all about the operation of the Caledonian Railway. The only person who can get to the bottom of this outrage is someone with local knowledge – someone like me.'

Craig was brisk. 'I beg leave to doubt that, McTurk,' he said. 'This is beyond you. The procurator fiscal will set up an investigation but his men have no experience of dealing with a catastrophe on this scale. Inspector Colbeck does. He solved a not dissimilar crime in Sussex and was feted by the railway company involved. I read reports of it. As for local knowledge,' he continued with a flick of the hand, 'you can provide that, Superintendent. I'm sure that Colbeck will call on your expertise. I look to you to offer it.'

McTurk squared his shoulders. 'I'd do so unwillingly, Mr Craig.'

'Why do you say that?'

'Because this is a Scottish disaster occurring on Scottish soil and only Scotsmen should be entitled to root out the villains behind it. We can do it alone, sir, without interference from south of the border.'

Craig was caustic. 'This is no time for misplaced patriotism,' he said, sharply. 'In my opinion, Scotsmen are much better at committing crimes than solving them. Spend a Saturday night in the rougher districts of Glasgow and you'll see what I mean. I'm proud of being a Scot but I'm also aware of a bellicose instinct that lurks inside many of my fellow countrymen. You're a prime example. You can be quickly stirred to action. That's what makes you such a good railway policeman.'

'I also have skills as a detective,' contended McTurk.

'Confine yourself to your duties, Superintendent. In a situation like this, I want the best man for the task and his name is Inspector Robert Colbeck. My only hope is that he's on his way here even as we speak. Assist him to the best of your ability.'

McTurk's gurgling reply was muffled by his beard. He was seething. He'd not only been put in his place by the general manager, he'd been ordered to cooperate with a man he despised. The only way to assuage his anger was to prove that he could solve the crime on his own account and that's what he determined to do.

After clearing his throat, he spoke obediently.

'Very well, Mr Craig,' he said, 'I'll do all I can to help.'

But he vowed inwardly that Colbeck would get no welcome from him.

For a man who hated railways as much as Victor Leeming, even a small journey was something of a trial. If he couldn't walk somewhere, the detective sergeant's preferred mode of travel was a horse-drawn cab. Indeed, he'd often thought that his life would have been much easier and far less stressful if he'd joined the army of London cab drivers. There was much to be said for serving those citizens who could afford the luxury of a cab. Some of them would tip the driver handsomely. And though he'd be out in all weathers, Leeming would at least see more of his wife and children. As a detective, he was at the mercy of distant crimes. Today was a case in point. Being sent off to Scotland for an indeterminate period was his notion of purgatory. He felt deprived. Seated in a train racing north with a rhythmical rattle, he grimaced and made an already unappealing face look positively grotesque.

'Scotland is a foreign country,' he moaned. 'They speak a different language up there.'

'They speak the same language but with a different accent,' said Colbeck.

'That's not true, sir. When I was in uniform, I worked with a constable from Glasgow and could only understand one in every five words he spoke. If he lost his temper – and he did that whenever drink was taken – then I couldn't hear a word that I recognised. It was probably just as well. Knowing him, they'd have been vile.'

'You'll soon get used to Scottish idiosyncrasies, Victor. It's only if we come up against someone who speaks in a broad dialect that we may have trouble. In any case,' Colbeck went on, 'language difficulties have never deterred you in the past. You managed very well when we had that spell in France.'

Leeming scowled. 'That's not how I remember it.'

Though their investigation had had a successful outcome, it had left the sergeant with some searing memories. He'd not only been forced to endure a choppy crossing of the English Channel in both directions, he'd been pitched into a nation of gesticulating Frenchmen and their bold women, then beaten up so badly by Irish navvies that he'd had to withdraw from the fray and return home to recuperate. Leeming didn't want a repeat of the experience in Scotland.

'At least, we won't have to *sail* anywhere,' he said.

'You never know,' teased Colbeck. 'They have plenty of lochs and rivers up there. We may have to use a boat at some stage. That shouldn't worry you, Victor. After all, you're an experienced sailor now.'

It was a reference to a case that had taken them across the Atlantic Ocean to make two arrests in New York City and to extradite the criminals. It was an episode that still featured regularly in Leeming's nightmares. He was an unashamed landlubber. If it were left to him, he decided, he'd banish sailing ships along with the entire railway network.

Not for the first time, Colbeck seemed to read his thoughts.

'Would you rather travel to Scotland by means of stagecoach, Victor?' he asked. 'It would be tedious, tiring and take us days. Thanks to this express train, we'll be there this evening.'

'But we have no details,' protested Leeming. 'We don't know where the crash actually occurred and what precisely happened.

And we certainly don't have a clue who or what might have caused it.'

'The telegraph mentioned rock on the line.'

'How can we possibly find out how it got there?'

'We follow the obvious guidelines.'

'I didn't know that we had any, Inspector.'

Colbeck smiled. 'That's because you're too busy thinking about Estelle and the children. Forget your family. The sooner we solve this crime, the sooner you'll be reunited with them. Now,' he added, 'what day is it today?'

'Monday.'

'That gives us our first clue, Victor.'

Leeming was baffled. 'Does it?'

'Of course,' said Colbeck. 'If today is Monday, the crash took place on Sunday. Immediate suspects must be rabid sabbatarians.'

'Who on earth are they?'

'People who believe we should observe the Sabbath in every particular. It should be a day of rest on which everyone attends church or chapel instead of riding around on the railways. From the moment the trains reached Scotland, there were demands that they didn't operate on Sundays.'

'Would these sabbatarians actually wreck a train?'

'It's a possibility we have to bear in mind, Victor. Religion can ignite the most violent passions. We've seen it happen before.'

'But if they planned this disaster, they must have known there'd be a risk of death for anybody on board that train. "Thou shalt not kill" is what the Bible tells us. Would they ignore that commandment in order to remind people that Sunday is the day of rest?' Leeming scratched his head. 'That doesn't make sense, sir.'

'I agree,' said Colbeck, 'but extremism has a way of blinding people to such contradictions. They act on impulse. And if lives are sacrificed in pursuit of their cause, they may even see it as a justifiable way to gain publicity.'

When the driver and his fireman went into the engine shed, they were astonished at what they found. Across the full length of their locomotive was a message in large, crude letters – NOT FOR USE ON SUNDAYS. The paint was still wet.

CHAPTER FOUR

Word travelled fast on the railway system. News of the disaster crossed the border and went rapidly down the line. When the detectives stopped at any station where there was time to get out and stretch their legs, they made a point of questioning railway staff about what had happened and they learnt new details from each conversation. They knew exactly when and where the crash had occurred and had been treated to some fevered speculation regarding its cause. At Carlisle, the terminus of the London and North Western Railway, they had to change trains. While doing so they found additional information in a newspaper on sale at the station. Colbeck would have liked an opportunity to explore the ancient city to see its sights but there was no possibility of that. Besides, Leeming was a reluctant tourist at the best of times. It was no use pointing out to him that Carlisle had been an English stronghold for centuries, charged with keeping the fiery Scots at bay. It was now a thriving community of over twenty thousand souls with a variety of industries that had burgeoned since the arrival of the railways. Its long and battle-scarred history fascinated Robert Colbeck. To his companion, however, it was simply a place that was uncomfortably distant from his beloved family.

Passengers had been forewarned of the destruction of the goods train. A fleet of coaches, cabs and other horse-drawn vehicles had been hastily assembled to take them around the obstruction so that they could join a train on the other side and continue their journey north. Those travelling south on the Caledonian Railway were offered the same option in reverse but many were deterred by the prospect of delay and inconvenience. Goods trains were summarily cancelled. There was no way of carrying vast quantities of freight on carts and wagons past the blockage. In some places, narrow roads deteriorated into mere tracks. The important thing, the company felt, was to keep the passengers they still had in motion and to ensure that they went in a wide sweep around the site so that were not disturbed by a glimpse of the carnage there. Informed by telegraph that the line would be out of action for days, freight customers were already looking for an alternative means of sending their goods to and from Scotland. The North British Railway, its main rival, was the first to prosper from the Caledonian's misfortune.

'This crash will cost the company a great deal of money,' observed Colbeck. 'And its reputation for reliability will be badly damaged.' He looked across at Leeming, gazing abstractedly out of the window of the train. 'Did you hear what I said, Victor?'

The sergeant came out of his reverie. 'What was that, sir?'

'You were miles away.'

'Was I? Then I apologise.' He shook his head as if to clear it. 'How much farther do we have to go?'

'We'll soon reach the Lowther Hills at this rate,' said Colbeck with a tolerant smile. 'You've been daydreaming for ages. You didn't even notice that we slipped across the Scottish border. Is something on your mind?'

'It is, Inspector.'

'Go on.'

'I keep asking the same question over and over again.'

'Oh?'

'What on earth are we *doing* here?'

Colbeck was amused by the expression of mild panic on the sergeant's face. It was always the same. Leeming hated venturing out of London, yet, once embroiled in a case, he always acted with commitment and determination. When physical violence was involved, Colbeck had learnt that there was no better man to have at his side. Leeming was a born fighter. It was only before they were really engaged in an investigation that he was morose and homesick. The inspector had his own reason for wanting to bring the visit to Scotland to a speedy conclusion. Married the previous November, he was still enjoying the delights of his new estate and missed his wife every bit as keenly as Leeming was missing his spouse. Detective work, however, took precedence. Madeleine had understood that when she'd married Colbeck and accepted the situation without complaint. Unlike the sergeant's wife, she'd been able to take part in the investigative process in the past, so she had a clearer insight into what it entailed.

'We'll be up against competition,' said Colbeck.

'What do you mean, sir?'

'Well, for a start, there'll be an inquiry set up by the procurator fiscal. It's an office unique to Scotland. Procurator fiscals are public prosecutors who investigate all suspicious deaths and fatal accidents. This crash comes very much under their jurisdiction. They'll institute a form of inquest.'

'Then they don't need us here, do they?' said Leeming, hopefully.

'The railway inspector will also want to decide on the precise cause of the crash. The same thing happened after that disaster on the Brighton line. You'll remember the problems we had with his counterpart there.'

'I do, indeed – he told us that we were wasting our time.'

'We had to disillusion him on that score,' said Colbeck, smiling at the memory. 'Let's hope we have a more cooperative inspector this time. As for the local sheriff, I'm not quite sure how far his powers stretch.' He heaved a sigh. 'Then, of course, there are the railway police. They usually resent us more than anyone.'

'In other words, we could have a lot of interference.'

'I'm certain of it, Victor. The Scots are very territorial. We're unwanted intruders, part of the nation that invaded and subdued them. My guess is that some people will do everything they can to get in our way. Expect a lot of opposition.'

'That's a disappointment,' said Leeming with light sarcasm. 'I was hoping that they'd put the flags out for us and organise a brass band. When are we going to go somewhere where they actually *want* us?'

'We'll simply have to win them over, that's all.'

'The best way to do that is to go straight back to London. It's an idea that would win *me* over as well.' When the train began to slow down, he peered through the window. 'Thank heaven for that!' exclaimed Leeming. 'This journey seems to have taken days. Was it really worth all this effort?'

'Yes, it was,' said Colbeck, seriously. 'Three railwaymen were murdered. The only way to offer consolation to their grieving families is to solve the crime. It will take a lot more effort to achieve that objective but every last second will be worth it.'

* * *

Even in daylight, some of the bolder thieves had returned for more booty. McTurk had laid a trap for them, hiding some of his men near an overturned wagon that had spilt its cargo of meat down the embankment. The superintendent himself was crouched beside a wagon piled high with leatherware from the tanneries of Carlisle, reasoning that it would be less of a target than prime beef and lamb. His instincts were sound. Thinking that everyone there was distracted by the work of clearing the line, a couple of young men in ragged clothing crept furtively towards the crates of meat. It was too big a temptation to resist. When they felt they were safe, the pair of them darted out of cover, ran to a crate and lifted it between them. Intending to scamper away, they were dismayed when three railway policemen appeared out of nowhere.

One of the thieves reacted much quicker than his companion, leaving go of the crate and cleverly dodging the outstretched arms of the policemen before sprinting off down the embankment. His friend was too slow. By the time he made his dash for freedom, a strong hand was already on his shoulder. He was grabbed, overpowered and held tight. McTurk came out from behind the consignment of leatherware to confront the prisoner.

'Hungry, are you, lad?' he asked, curling a lip. 'Take a good look at all this meat. It's the last you'll be seeing for a while. Prison food is like sawdust, only not as tasty. You'll be lucky to get enough grub to keep you alive.'

'We didnae mean to tek it,' said the thief, piteously. 'We only wanted to see what was going on, I swear it.'

'Is that so? Sightseers, were you?' He addressed his men. 'Do you hear that? He and his friend didn't come to steal. They just wanted to see what was happening here – and whether or not our backs were turned. They're as innocent as the driven snow.' There was derisive laughter from the policemen. 'What's the name of your accomplice?'

The thief was defiant. 'I'll no' tell ye.'

'He was a wee bit younger than you and faster on his feet.'

'Ye've got me and it's all ye'll get.'

'Forgotten his name, have you? Then I'll have to jog your memory, won't I?' He took the thief by the scruff of his neck and hurled him against a wagon. It knocked all the breath out of him. 'I can always get people to talk – it's so simple. All I have to do is to kick seven barrels of shit out of them and they sing their heads off.' He lumbered forward and punched the thief full in the face, drawing blood from his nose. 'Has that helped you to remember his name?' he taunted.

Before he could administer further punishment, McTurk heard someone call his name and he saw the general manager waddling towards him. He was annoyed at having to suspend his interrogation but he'd already done enough. Recognising the hopelessness of his position, the thief willingly surrendered the name and address of his accomplice. The superintendent nodded to his men and they hustled the prisoner out of sight. Nairn Craig was panting by the time he finally reached McTurk.

'What's going on, Superintendent?' he asked.

'We caught a thief, sir. His accomplice managed to get away but he won't go far. I persuaded the lad to tell us who he is. When we pick him up at his home, I daresay we'll find a lot of stolen property that disappeared during the night.'

'Good work!'

'We know our job, sir.'

'Our freight customers are already demanding compensation for any losses. They'll be heartened to learn that you're catching some of the thieves. But that's not what I came to tell you,' he went on. 'There's some cheering news. A telegraph arrived at our Glasgow office earlier today. It confirmed that Inspector Colbeck is definitely on his way.' McTurk growled silently into his beard. 'Indeed, he could be here at any time.'

'You know my view. We can sort everything out ourselves.'

'Be realistic, man. You've never led a complex investigation before. That's why we need professional assistance.'

'We already have it,' asserted McTurk. 'Inspector Rae is here at the behest of the procurator fiscal. I've been able to give him the benefit of my opinion.'

'Then you can do the same to the Railway Detective,' said Craig, tartly. 'The other piece of news is that we're offering a reward of four hundred pounds for information leading to the arrest and conviction of those responsible for this outrage. Posters are already being printed.'

McTurk was impressed by the size of the reward. To a man on his wage, it was an absolute fortune. A new element was suddenly brought into play. There was pecuniary gain as well as kudos to be had. McTurk wanted both. He now had an even greater incentive to solve the crime himself and to keep any Scotland Yard detectives in the dark. Supremely confident of his ability, he allowed himself a knowing grin.

'I'll spread the word, sir,' he said. 'That kind of money will loosen a few tongues. We'll find the bastards who caused all this chaos. You have my word.'

It was beautiful countryside and even Victor Leeming was struck by it. After leaving the train at Wamphray station, he and Colbeck had watched the other passengers climbing into a variety of vehicles before setting off on a long curve that would take them past the site of the crash. The detectives, by contrast, were driven directly towards it, travelling through a verdant dale that was ringed with hills. It was a far cry from the narrow streets and abiding stink of London. Shaken out of his apathy, the sergeant forgot all about the discomfort of the long journey.

'I'd love Estelle and the children to see this,' he declared. 'The air is so clean and we can see for miles. It's . . . well, it's wonderful.'

'You must bring them here on holiday,' said Colbeck.

'Ha!' Leeming's face crumpled. 'There's fat chance of that ever happening.'

'Don't be too sure, Victor. Railway companies can be very grateful if we solve heinous crimes for them. Look what happened after our success at that other crash. You finished up with tickets to take the family to Brighton.'

Leeming beamed. 'That's true, sir – and we had a grand day at the seaside. The children keep asking when we can go again. Do you really think I'd be able to bring them here one day?'

'It's not impossible. But,' said Colbeck, adding a rider, 'it would, of course, be conditional upon our finding and arresting the culprits behind the disaster. Put any thought of reward out of your mind until then and simply enjoy the scenery.'

After travelling to Scotland in a first-class carriage, they were now being taken along a winding track in an ancient cart. Seated beside the taciturn driver, they had to hold on tight as the vehicle swayed violently and explored every bump and hollow. In the back of the cart, their luggage bounced all over the place. Colbeck tried to prise some information out of the old man at the reins.

'Have you seen where the accident happened?' he asked.

'Aye, sir.'

'Is it as bad as everyone says?'

'Aye, sir.'

'Do you live nearby?'

'Aye, sir.'

'And where would that be?'

'Dinwoodie.'

'We came past there in the train,' recalled Leeming.

'Aye, sir, ye would.'

'What can you tell us about the crash?' wondered Colbeck.

'Ah'll no' speak of it, sir.'

'Why is that?'

There was no reply. The driver lapsed back into a hurt silence. Colbeck understood. Shocked by what he'd seen, the man was unable to put it into words that would rekindle ugly memories. He was being paid to transport two people to a site further up the line and that's all he was prepared to do. Conversation was too painful for him. If they wanted a description of the wreckage ahead, his passengers would have to wait until they reached their destination.

Wamphray had been over thirty miles from Carlisle and it had been reached at a good speed. The pace had now slowed dramatically. It gave Colbeck time to reflect on what might lie in wait for them and it offered Leeming the opportunity to indulge his fantasies about an extended holiday in Annandale with his family. The railway line was never far away from them on the right and, in normal circumstances, it would be singing under the wheels of trains going in both directions. It was deserted now, useless until the track ahead was cleared. They heard the noise of the rescue operation long before they caught sight of it. Smoke from burning debris rose up into the sky and helped to pinpoint the exact spot. As they got closer, raised voices were audible amid the banging and bumping and clang of metal.

When they finally came round the bend, the driver pulled his horse to a halt.

'Ye'll have to walk now,' he said, averting his gaze from the disaster.

'We could do with some exercise,' said Colbeck, hopping off the cart and retrieving his bag. 'Come on, Victor.'

Leeming was open-mouthed. 'Look at it!' he gasped. 'It's terrible!'

'That's why we mustn't detain our friend here. He wants to get away and I don't blame him.' While the sergeant got down from the cart, Colbeck paid the driver and gave him a handsome tip. It elicited no thanks. 'Goodbye.'

Turning his cart in a circle, the driver went back in the direction from which they'd just come. Leeming had to move smartly to snatch his valise before it set off towards Wamphray. Both detectives surveyed the scene. Many hands had worked to clear the devastation for a period of over twenty-four hours yet they seemed to have made little impact. A huge area was littered with a frightening array of battered wagons and their erstwhile contents. What could not be salvaged had been sacrificed on one of the fires. The locomotive itself lay twisted and forlorn. The damage to the train was colossal but Colbeck also bewailed the brutal punishment inflicted on the embankment. Large holes had been gouged out and runaway wagons had cut deep channels into it. Green swathes had been sullied by discarded coal. An air of ruin and despair hung over the whole landscape.

Colbeck studied the line on the other side of the disaster area.

'A train coming from the south would be bound to hit any obstruction when it came around the bend,' he noted. 'There'd be no time to stop. Trains coming from the north must have the best part of a mile of straight line before reaching the spot. They'd have seen any rockfall and taken measures to avoid it.'

'What does that tell you, Inspector?' asked Leeming.

'The goods train was a specific target.'

'There would have been more victims if they'd waited for a passenger train.'

'But they didn't, Victor. That's an important detail.'

'I don't understand why.'

'Neither do I at the moment,' confessed Colbeck, 'but I intend to find out.'

Light was fading and evening shadows were starting to dapple the scene. The droves of people engaged in the clearance worked on regardless of the time of day. Colbeck raised his eyes to the hills beyond and thought he saw a solitary figure, silhouetted against the sky with an animal of some kind at his side. When Colbeck concentrated his gaze, the figure and the animal had vanished and he was left to wonder if they'd really been there in the first place.

CHAPTER FIVE

The meeting was held at the Glasgow home of Tam and Flora Howie, a middle-aged couple who – like everyone present – were an image of respectability. There were ten of them altogether, seven men and three women. Seated comfortably in the parlour, they were able to study the framed biblical tracts on the wall and the other evidence of a fiercely Christian household. As their leader, Howie spoke first, rising to his feet and gripping his lapels between thumb and forefinger. Of medium height and spare frame, he somehow seemed more substantial when taking the floor.

'You all know why we're here,' he said, crisply. 'In spite of years of protest, the railway companies remain defiant. They insist on running trains on the Sabbath and flouting the teaching of the Good Book. We have protested time and time again but all to no avail. Posters and pamphlets have a limited effect. All that they can do is to express our opinion. They are not enough in themselves to change minds.'

'Tam is right,' interjected his diminutive wife. 'We need to do more.'

'What else can we do?' asked Gregor Hines, a sagging old man with a white beard. 'There are only so many ways of legitimate protest. We've tried them all.'

'That's why we must employ other means,' insisted Howie. 'Some like-minded people have already done that and we must follow suit. We must be ready to break the law to achieve our ends.'

A faint murmur of agreement was swiftly muffled under a concerted growl of dissent. They were pillars of the community, law-abiding people who led lives of moral probity. A few might be prepared to consider taking direct action against the railways but the majority felt that it was a step too far. Of the women, only Flora Howie was in favour of it.

'If we cause trouble,' she argued, 'it not only makes the railway companies aware of the strength of our beliefs, it also gets valuable attention. Look what happened earlier today. Someone who understands the true meaning of the Sabbath painted a warning on one of the Caledonian's locomotives. It was mentioned in this evening's paper.'

'But who saw it?' croaked Hines. 'Hardly anyone, I fancy. Readers would only have been interested in the story on the front page about that terrible crash in Annandale.'

'That was an act of God,' claimed Nell, his wife, a skeletal figure in a black dress. 'It was a warning from on high to all who run trains on a Sunday.'

'It was a warning, certainly,' agreed Howie, 'but it was not delivered by the Almighty. The newspaper report was categorical. That disaster was contrived by human hand. Someone is doing our job for us.'

Gasps of outrage filled the room and Nell Hines spluttered in disbelief. Seeing that he'd gone too far, Howie did his best to retrieve the situation.

'Don't misunderstand me,' he said, calming them down with outstretched palms. 'I don't for a moment condone a strategy that leads to the loss of life. I utterly deplore it. What I applaud, however, is the way that the incident has gained attention. The whole of Scotland is aware of it and it will hurt the Caledonian Railway in its pocket. In short, it achieved its objective. Why can't we do something similar?' he went on, raising his voice above the rumbling discontent. 'Hear me out, friends. I'm not advocating a repetition of what happened. That was a cruel and criminal act. But it does show what consequences flow from a blockage on the line on a Sunday. It would be a wonderful advertisement for our cause.'

'Are you telling us to commit a heinous crime?' asked Hines.

'Shame on you, Tam Howie!' added Nell.

'It's unthinkable.'

'More to the point, it's unchristian.'

'In any case, how are my dear wife and I supposed to block the line? Do you want us to prostrate ourselves across the track like sacrificial victims? Is that the sabbatarian gospel now? Must we spend the day of rest lying horizontally side by side like so many railway sleepers? Away with you, man,' said Hines scornfully. 'You've taken leave of your senses.'

'We must do something more extreme,' declared Howie, eyes blazing with passion. 'It's not enough to write letters and organise petitions. We're on the side of God against Mammon. Our enemies will stop at nothing and nor should we. We must fight fire with fire.'

'Listen to Tam,' pleaded his wife. 'My husband is talking sense.'

'He's talking the whole pack of us into prison,' said Hines, sourly.

'Only if we're caught, Gregor,' countered Howie, 'and we're far too intelligent to let that happen. We've raised our voices for years

41

and we might as well be baying at the moon. Railway companies will always put profit before religious observance. Where voices fail, action can succeed. You must see that.'

The old man shook his head. 'What I see is the road to damnation. You'll not turn Nell and me into common criminals. We'll defend the sanctity of the Sabbath until our dying day but we won't do it by breaking the law or behaving like vandals.'

'Gregor speaks for me,' said Nell, patting her husband on the back.

'And for me,' piped up another voice.

'Let's hear Tam out,' suggested a portly man. 'There may be a kernel of truth in what he says. Let him finish before we condemn his idea outright.'

'Thank you,' said Howie with a nod of gratitude. 'I'm glad that one person is prepared to listen. My plan of action would be this . . .'

But the argument had already been lost. Though his speech was cogent and his conviction undeniable, Howie converted only two of them to his point of view. The rest remained implacably opposed. When a vote was taken, he had to concede defeat. His fellow sabbatarians were always ready to spend time and money on promoting their beliefs. They would happily stand outside railway stations in the driving rain with placards urging passengers to respect the Sabbath but that was the extent of their protest. Taking active steps to prevent trains from running on a Sunday was beyond them. As they trooped out of the house, they bade farewell to their hosts.

Gregor Hines was the last to leave. After shaking Howie's hand, he peered at it with interest then raised an admonitory eyebrow.

'You've still got paint on your fingernails, Tam,' he said, knowingly. 'Since you're far too honest a man to lie, I'll not ask you how it got there.'

* * *

42

Nairn Craig was so pleased to see the detectives that he shook their hands with an exuberance that boarded on physical assault. Fires kept the fading light at bay and allowed Colbeck and Leeming to assess the full scope of the disaster. They looked around with a mixture of dismay and sympathy. Colbeck's thoughts were with the families of the three victims while Leeming dismissed his own family from his mind. To dwell on his absence from them was an act of selfishness. He accepted that now. They'd been right to come to Scotland. What he saw filled him with an urge to catch those responsible for the chaos. It was a crime that yearned for punishment.

'The facts, as I understand them,' said Craig, 'are these . . .'

'There's no need to explain, sir,' said Colbeck. 'We are already well informed about the incident. It was the talk of Carlisle when we changed trains there.'

'I should have known that you'd gather information in transit.'

'It was not only information, sir,' said Leeming. 'We had to listen to a lot of wild guesswork as well. One man claimed that the rockfall was the work of Irish rebels, while another believed that a witch had placed a curse on your company. Then there was the fellow who said that the Caledonian Railway was subjected to the wrath of heaven because of the high prices you charged.'

Craig blenched. 'That's certainly not the case, Sergeant.'

'Rumour is always more colourful than the truth,' said Colbeck.

He went on to give the general manager a succinct account of what they already knew. Amazed at the detail so far gleaned, Craig was unable to add anything of value. Instead he began to talk about accommodation for the detectives.

'Before we discuss that,' said Colbeck, politely interrupting him, 'I'd like to see the exact spot where the collision took place. I take it that you've cleared away the rocks by now.'

'We have, indeed,' said Craig, taking in the whole site with a gesture. 'It may not look like it, but we've made huge strides already. Once the cranes and the winches were brought here, we began to make real progress.'

'That's commendable, sir. What of the procurator fiscal's investigation?'

'It's being led by Inspector Rae. He's an able man but has none of the specialist knowledge that you and the sergeant possess. He's been here for most of the day and will return again tomorrow. You can meet him then.'

'Was he told of our imminent arrival?'

Craig pulled a face. 'Yes, he was.'

'I can see that it didn't meet with his approval,' said Colbeck, amused.

'Inspector Rae does not welcome rivals.'

'Then he should see us in the guise of assistants.'

'What about your own railway police?' asked Leeming.

'They've been working at full stretch,' replied Craig. 'As a matter of fact, I believe that you're already acquainted with our superintendent.'

Right on cue, Rory McTurk emerged from behind an overturned wagon with the dramatic suddenness of a pantomime villain appearing through a trapdoor. The others were startled. It was obvious that he'd been there all along, eavesdropping on their conversation. After glaring at Colbeck and Leeming in turn, he manufactured a cold smile.

'We meet again, gentlemen,' he said.

'I can't say that it's a happy reunion,' muttered Leeming.

'But we must adapt to circumstance,' said Colbeck, veiling his dislike of the man. 'First of all, I must congratulate you on your promotion, Superintendent. When we first met, you were working as an inspector of the LNWR.'

McTurk inflated his chest. 'The Caledonian Railway recognised my merits.'

'The superintendent has given us good service,' endorsed Craig.

'You'll not find me wanting, sir.'

'*We* did,' said Leeming, softly.

'This crime took place on my patch and I want it cleared up quickly.'

'We all share that objective,' said Colbeck, irritated by the man's proprietorial tone, 'but an investigation on this scale is way beyond your jurisdiction and – if I may say so – hopelessly beyond your capabilities.'

'That's not true!' howled McTurk, stung by the criticism.

'Inspector Colbeck has hit the mark,' said Craig, quelling the superintendent with a glance. 'You simply police the railway. Don't stray beyond that remit.'

'That's not to say we don't welcome your help,' resumed Colbeck, offering some balm to McTurk's injured pride. 'You obviously know the area far better than us and are infinitely more familiar with the operation of this railway.'

'I know *everything* better than you, Inspector,' asserted McTurk. 'I was among the first people here after the crash and I worked throughout the night.'

'Your devotion to duty is admirable. I'm sure that Mr Craig realises that.'

'Yes, yes,' said Craig, 'Well done, McTurk!'

'There's no more loyal servant of the Caledonian,' said the giant Scotsman, reaching a hand into his beard as if to extract glowing testimonials of his worth. 'I'll always put it first.'

'We're more interested in the company's enemies than in its servants,' said Colbeck, 'and you must already have formulated a theory as to which of those enemies is culpable for this atrocious crime.'

'It has to be the NBR,' urged McTurk.

Craig was unconvinced. 'That's an allegation based on insufficient evidence.'

'The North British want to cause maximum disruption, sir.'

'But that's not what they've done,' Leeming pointed out.

'Of course, it is, man. Look around you.'

'It's closed the line, I agree, Superintendent. But it could have been worse. Inspector Colbeck was quick to note that there were only three victims. Had a passenger train been derailed, there'd have been many more deaths and you'd be digging out the bodies for days. There'd have been much more disruption.'

'I hadn't thought of that,' admitted Craig.

'We were lucky,' conceded McTurk. 'By the grace of God, a goods train came along the track first and ran into that pile of rock.'

'I hate to disagree with you,' said Colbeck with a disarming smile, 'but luck played no part whatsoever. The goods train was a designated target. It was derailed by someone who knew precisely when it would arrive at the chosen spot. How many people would have access to that information?'

'Good heavens!' exclaimed Craig, clutching at his throat. 'Are you suggesting that someone from *within* the company is behind this?'

'Not everyone is as loyal as Superintendent McTurk, sir.'

'Why choose that particular train?'

'It's one of the many things I intend to find out,' replied Colbeck. 'I'm assuming that a rockfall of that size could only have been engineered with the help of gunpowder? Did nobody hear the blast and raise the alarm?'

'You are showing your ignorance, Inspector,' said McTurk, relishing the opportunity to score a point against him. 'If you knew the area as well as I do, you'd know there was a quarry a mile

46

or so away. The sounds of an explosion are quite normal. Even the sheep are no longer disturbed by it.'

'Thank you for educating me on that point.'

'I suspect that there'll be a lot more schooling to be done before we've finished. But I hold to my claim that the NBR is behind this. More than one former employee of the Caledonian now works for our rival. They'd be aware of the timetables for the movement of freight on this line.'

'That's very astute of you, Superintendent,' said Craig.

'I'm more than a mere railway policeman, sir.'

'There's nothing "mere" about guarding the railway,' said Colbeck, seriously. 'It's a vital job and I salute anyone who undertakes it. As for the NBR, they are, of necessity, potential suspects but no more than that. It would be both wrong and impulsive of us to settle on one of your commercial rivals when you have others, not least among them the Edinburgh and Glasgow Railway.'

'And don't forget the sabbatarians,' advised Leeming. 'It could be them.'

'It could be the work of a dozen or more suspects. We need to look at each and every one of them before we make a final judgement. That will mean a painstaking process of gathering evidence and interviewing an appreciable number of people. Well, now,' said Colbeck, turning to McTurk, 'perhaps we could avail ourselves of your superior knowledge of the actual crash. Please conduct us to the point on the line where it occurred and indicate its salient features.' He stepped back to let the Scotsman pass. 'We're in your hands, Superintendent.'

Basking in his temporary authority, McTurk inflated his chest again.

'Follow me, gentlemen . . .'

* * *

It was a warm night with only the whisper of a breeze to rustle the leaves on the trees. Most of the flock were grazing in the gloom or sleeping in huddled groups. Jamie Farr was checking the pens where the newborn lambs were nestling against their mothers. He was kept busy. One lamb had got its head caught in the fence and had to be rescued while another was trapped beneath the full weight of its mother before being eased out by the shepherd. Angus tripped along beside his master, letting the sheep know that he was in control by poking his head into their little domains and showing his teeth. It was a slow, unhurried patrol and it was repeated at various intervals. The sheep comprised Farr's family and he nurtured them accordingly.

He was the only survivor of five sons. His mother had died trying to bring the fifth into the world. Farr was left alone with his father and, though they worked together, he saw little of the older man during the day and even less at night. It made for a lonely life. Colin Farr had coped with the death of his wife and four children by turning to drink. Whenever he could afford it – and often when he could not – he'd walk the two miles to a village pub. Jamie always braced himself for his father's return. It was never a happy homecoming. Colin Farr was either disgustingly drunk or railing at the world for his misfortunes. If his son didn't have to put him to bed, he had to listen to an hour of pointless ranting.

Sometimes – especially during winter – the father might not be able to get back safely to their tiny stone cottage. He'd collapse on the sodden ground or get caught in a snowstorm. Farr had to rescue him, braving the bad weather to find out where his father was and to carry him back home. He rarely got any thanks for his efforts. When his father came out of his stupor, he was more likely to hurl abuse at his son. Farr had learnt to suffer in silence. For the sake of his mother's memory, he could not protest, challenge or strike back.

It was late when Farr heard the distinctive dragging sound of his father's footsteps. The long-suffering son didn't know what to expect. He'd either have to endure a display of drunken merriment or a bout of maudlin reminiscence. On this occasion, however, it was neither. When he lifted the latch and walked into the room, Colin Farr was almost sober. There was no swaying, no swearing and no threat of violence. He looked down at his son, perched on a stool beneath the lantern that hung from the cobwebbed beam.

'I've news for ye, Jamie,' he said.

'It's time for bed,' suggested Farr. 'I only stayed up till ye came.'

'And ye'll be glad that ye did.'

'Why's that?'

'I've something to tell ye, lad.'

'Save it till t'morrer.'

'This willna keep,' said the father, grabbing him by the shoulder as he rose from the stool. 'D'ye ken what I heerd at the inn tonight?'

'How could I?'

'There's a fortune to be had.'

'What are ye talking about?'

'It was Rab Logan as told us,' said the father, 'but, then, he always did have big ears.' He cackled aloud. 'Rab's got bigger ears than a donkey.'

Farr wrinkled his nose at the whisky fumes. Relieved that his father was not in an abusive mood, he was anxious to go off to bed but he was held in an iron grasp and had to stay where he was. When the father put his face even closer, the son could smell the whisky on his breath more clearly.

'There's been an awfu' crash on the railway,' continued the older man. 'The line is covered wi' broken wagons and the like. Ye must have heerd tell of it.'

'No,' said Farr, guardedly. 'This is the first word I've had of it.'

'Well, it will make someone rich.'

'How?'

'There's a reward, lad,' said the father, slapping him on the back. 'That's the news I brought back for ye. Some villain caused the accident, so he did, and they want to see the devil hanged until every breeth of life is squeezed out o' him. If anyone can tell them who the rogue is, he'll be four hundred pounds better off.'

Farr was astounded. 'How much did ye say?'

'The reward is four hundred pounds. Rab Logan says there are handbills.'

'I'd like to see one.'

'Aye, so would I, Jamie. And I'd love to get ma hands on that money.' He rubbed his palms together. 'Just think what we could do wi' a fortune like that.'

Farr was already thinking the same thing. When he was finally able to go off to bed, he spent a sleepless night. The reward was more than an enticement. It would buy him a whole new life and rescue him from the domination of his father. There had to be a way of earning the money and there would be the additional pleasure of taking it from a railway company he loathed. It was not only a reward. It was compensation for all the animals killed or maimed on the line. That was why Farr deserved it.

CHAPTER SIX

After spending the night at a wayside inn, the detectives rose early so that they could discuss their plans over breakfast. They sat either side of a rickety table in a dank room with an uneven paved floor. A haunting aroma of beer flirted with their nostrils. Leeming chewed his way disconsolately through a bowl of cold porridge but Colbeck actually enjoyed the fare. It was very different from the sort of breakfast that he and Madeleine shared every morning and had the appeal of novelty. Leeming missed his wife's cooking. At the same time, he was determined not to be distracted by fond thoughts of his family. He could only savour their company, he reminded himself, when the case was solved. That, however, was a distant prospect.

'How long will we be here, Inspector?' he asked.

'We'll do what we always do, Victor, and stay until the bitter end.'

'Can you see any hope on the horizon?'

'I'm always hopeful,' said Colbeck with a grin. 'Optimism aids digestion.'

Leeming indicated his bowl. 'I can't digest *this*, sir.'

'It's a good, honest, nourishing meal.'

'I find it hard to swallow. It's nothing like the porridge my wife makes.'

'You'll acquire a taste for it in time.'

'Don't they serve any *real* food?'

Pushing his bowl aside, he looked down at the sketch that Colbeck had drawn of the accident. It showed the exact point of collision. There was a sheer rock face to one side of the track and an embankment to the other. Colbeck had even made a note of the estimated speed at which the goods train had been travelling. Met by a wall of solid rock as it rounded the bend, it had bounced off the track and rolled helplessly down the embankment.

'Now that we've been to the spot,' said Colbeck, studying his handiwork, 'I can see why it was chosen. The crucial factor is its isolation. No witnesses would have been there to see or to interfere. The person or persons we're after are clearly familiar with that stretch of line.'

'If gunpowder was used, where did they get it?'

'It could have come from the quarry.'

'Were there any reports of gunpowder being stolen from there?'

'None, according to Mr Craig.'

'Then it must have been obtained elsewhere.'

'Not necessarily,' said Colbeck, musing. 'There's always the possibility that the culprit had an accomplice who worked at the quarry and who could spirit some gunpowder away without being noticed.'

'Do you want me to visit the place?' asked Leeming.

'Not at this stage, Victor. You've a more important task today. I'm sending you up to Glasgow. That's where the Caledonian has its headquarters.'

'What do I do up there, sir?'

'Find out as much as you can about the three men who were killed. Look into their private lives. If someone had a strong enough grudge against one of them,' said Colbeck, 'he might be ready to sacrifice two other lives to get his revenge.'

'And what will *you* be doing while I'm away?'

'I'll have the dubious pleasure of working with Superintendent McTurk.'

'His only interest is working *against* us.'

'He's an obstructive individual, I know, and he's learnt nothing since the last time we crossed swords with him. Yet he does have knowledge that we need, so we have to suffer his shortcomings.'

'Shortcomings!' cried Leeming. 'The man is a menace in uniform. I didn't like him the first time we met him. He's even worse now.'

'Then you'll be glad to escape his company for a day,' said Colbeck. 'I'll have to cope with both of them alone.'

'Both of them?'

'You're forgetting Inspector Rae, sent at the behest of the procurator fiscal. Didn't you notice how many times McTurk worked the man's name into the conversation? He was letting us know that he and the inspector are birds of the same feather. Neither of them has any time at all for us.'

'Do they hate us simply because we're English?'

'That's part of it,' said Colbeck. 'Study their history and it's understandable. But their antagonism is also grounded in fear. They're terrified that we'll solve the case and show them how it's done.'

Leeming shrugged. 'Does it matter *who* catches the villains as long as they're actually caught?'

'It matters to them, Victor. It matters a great deal.'

'In a situation like this, we should all pull together.'

'Ideally, that's what will happen in due course. But that kind of cooperation may take a long time to achieve. Anyway,' Colbeck went on, picking up the sketch, 'let's get to work. I'll tackle Inspector Rae and McTurk while you enjoy a rare experience.'

'What kind of rare experience?' asked Leeming, worriedly.

'You're going to climb Beattock Bank. That involves a ten-mile ascent into rough country between the Lowther Hills and the heights of Tweedsmuir. How they coped with the steep gradient is a marvel of engineering. I envy you the trip.'

'Then why not make it instead of me?'

'My place is on the crash site,' said Colbeck, 'but I'll be interested to know how you fare on the Bank. You'll pick up the train at the hamlet of Beattock and have the combined power of two locomotives to pull you up to the summit.'

Leeming was uneasy. 'I'm not sure that I like the sound of that, sir.'

'A seasoned traveller like you will love it. When you reach the peak, you'll have a spectacular view before the train plunges down again.' Rising to his feet, he glanced at his sketch again. 'I wish that my dear wife were here,' he said with affection. 'I have no skill with a pencil. Madeleine is the artist in the family. She could have made the scene come alive on paper.'

Madeleine Colbeck was working at the easel in her new studio. It was so much easier to pursue her career as an artist now that she had a much bigger room with far more natural light flooding into it. Her subject, as always, was the railway and she was conjuring yet another locomotive into being on the canvas. When she heard the doorbell ring, she broke off immediately, knowing that it would be her father. Putting her brush aside, she wiped her hands on a damp cloth and left the room. By the time she got to the bottom of the stairs, her visitor had been admitted and shown into the drawing room. Madeleine gave him a kiss of welcome.

Caleb Andrews looked around the spacious, well-appointed room in awe.

'I still can't believe that a daughter of mine can live in a place like this,' he said. 'It must be five or six times the size of our little house in Camden Town.'

'Don't exaggerate, Father.'

'It's true. I just wish that your mother had lived to see it.'

'So do I,' she said, waving him to a chair then sitting opposite him.

'A servant to open the door and a cook to make your meals – it's a different world from the one I know. But you *deserve* it, Maddy. You look at home here.'

'To be honest, I still find it rather overwhelming. Robert inherited the house from his parents so is quite used to living under this roof. After all this time, I still feel like a guest here. I have to keep pinching myself.'

The Westminster residence was in John Islip Street and it had an elegance and luxury she'd never known before. Madeleine had lived happily at the family home in Camden where she was born but had now realised how cramped and utilitarian it had been. Andrews lived there alone but a hired servant came in regularly to perform menial tasks and offer him some company. Not that Andrews was a lonely man. Now that he'd retired after a lifetime's service as an engine driver on the London and North Western Railway, he kept himself busy and had a wide circle of friends. Nothing pleased him more than to spend an evening at a pub near Euston frequented by railwaymen. It allowed him to wallow in nostalgia and to brag about his daughter. He was a short, sharp-featured, sinewy man in his late fifties with a fringe beard taking on an increasingly snowy hue.

'You're like me, Maddy,' he declared. 'We can do anything we set our minds to. It's a gift.'

'I disagree. There are lots of things I'd love to be able to do but I just can't get the hang of them somehow.' Lowering her voice, she glanced towards the door. 'Giving orders to servants is one example. And there are lots of others.'

'You're the most capable young woman I know.'

'I don't always *feel* capable, Father. Anyway,' she continued, 'I didn't ask you to call in so that we could discuss my failings. I wanted to tell you about Robert's latest case.'

'Your note said that he'd gone to Scotland – whatever for?'

'He was needed there.'

'His place is beside his wife in London.'

'You won't think that when you hear what's happened.'

Madeleine gave him the few details she possessed about the disaster on the Caledonian Railway and her father listened open-mouthed. As a former railwayman, Andrews had great sympathy for anyone killed in the course of his duties and, over the years, he'd been to the funerals of a number of colleagues who'd died as a result of serious accidents on the line. In this case, however, the deaths were not accidental. His ire was roused immediately.

'I'd like to drive an express train over the villains who did this,' he said, vengefully. 'It's more than a crime, it's sheer wickedness.'

'They'll get their punishment in a court of law.'

'Hanging is too good for them.'

'Robert was horrified when he first heard what had happened. Superintendent Tallis didn't want him to go to Scotland but Robert insisted. He was right to do so,' she said, 'even though it means that he may be away for a long time.'

'Why didn't you go with him?'

'How could I?'

'You're Mrs Colbeck now, aren't you?' he argued. 'And it wouldn't be the first time you've helped him in his work.'

'I'd only be a hindrance, Father. Beside, any assistance I've been able to give has been unofficial. Scotland Yard would never have approved.'

'Then you make sure that they don't know, Maddy. Keep everything secret. I've got a better idea,' he said, warming to the notion. 'You can go to Scotland and I'll come with you.'

'We can't do that.'

'What's stopping us? We might be able to offer valuable help.'

'Robert would be embarrassed if we suddenly rolled up out of the blue.'

'No, he wouldn't,' he retorted. 'You're his wife and I'm his father-in-law. He'd probably be pleased to see the pair of us. He was delighted when we turned up unexpectedly in Exeter last autumn. We'll get the same welcome this time.'

'I don't think so,' she said, firmly. 'I know him far better than you do. When and if he ever needs us, Robert will send for us. Until then, all that we can do is to watch and wait.' There was a tap on the door and a servant entered. 'Now, then,' she went on. 'What would you like in the way of refreshment?'

Andrews grinned. 'Two train tickets to Scotland.'

Inspector Malcolm Rae was a tall, slender, well-dressed man in his forties with an almost permanent smile hovering around his lips. Where McTurk was inclined to bluster, Rae was softly spoken and approachable. His manner was pleasant and confiding. When he shook the man's hand, Colbeck felt that he could have a proper conversation with him based on mutual respect. Rae, however, wanted to clarify something.

'Tell me, Inspector,' he said in a lilting Edinburgh accent, 'how would you feel if I came to London to solve a crime that occurred on the railway there?'

'I'd feel justifiably annoyed,' admitted Colbeck.

'Then you understand my position perfectly.'

'If, however, you'd been summoned by the relevant railway company, then I'd accept you had a legitimate right to carry out an investigation. I wouldn't *like* it but I'd acknowledge the company's decision to retain your services.'

'Good,' said Rae. 'We now know where we stand with each other.'

The smile blossomed for a second before fading gently away. They were standing at the crash site and the clearance work was continuing noisily all around them. Nairn Craig was pacing anxiously up and down in the background, haranguing some of the rescue crew and wondering when the line would be finally open again. The two detectives reviewed the situation. Rae had clearly been listening to McTurk. When he talked about his instinctive response to the tragedy, he agreed with the superintendent that commercial rivalry lay at the root of the outrage. All too aware of the skulduggery practised by rival companies in England, Colbeck was amazed at the lengths that some Scottish companies had gone to in order to gain an advantage over their competitors. Intimidation, vandalism, vicious fare-cutting and violence had all been used but, so far, nothing on the scale of the crash.

'How will the Caledonian respond?' asked Colbeck.

'That's for Mr Craig to decide.'

'Would he feel obliged to strike back at the company he feels is responsible?'

'I'm sure that the notion would have some appeal to him,' said

Rae, 'but he's sensible enough to know that you cannot atone for one criminal act with another.'

'Yet, from what you've told me, the Caledonian has already committed criminal acts in pursuit of its ambitions.'

'Nothing conclusive has been proved, Inspector. But those of us aware of the antics of railway companies north of the border know that every one of them has sailed close to the wind.'

'That's a strange metaphor to use of a land-based mode of transport.'

Rae laughed. 'Yes, I suppose that it was ill-chosen.' He became more businesslike. 'What do you propose to do next?'

'I'll endeavour not to tread on your toes, Inspector.'

'Thank you.'

'It shouldn't be difficult to keep out of each other's way,' said Colbeck. 'For the most part, I suspect, we'll be looking in different places.'

'But sharing any evidence we unearth, I trust.'

'That goes without saying.'

'I believe that it has to be said,' insisted Rae. 'According to Superintendent McTurk, you have a habit of keeping things to yourself. That, at least, was his experience when you worked together on a previous occasion.'

'Don't rely too much on the superintendent's powers of recall,' said Colbeck, brusquely. 'They are coloured by the fact that he was given a sharp rebuke by his employers when I exposed the derelictions of the men working under him. McTurk did nothing to advance that particular investigation. I hope that he will be more supportive in this one.'

'I find him a source of useful information.'

'Then we must both tap into it.'

'I'm glad that we agree on that.'

In other circumstances, Colbeck felt that he could like Rae and the latter clearly had a grudging admiration for the feats of the Railway Detective. Geography divided them. An English detective was investigating a crime in Scotland. Inevitably, he was seen as an interloper. The relationship between the two men would never cross the border into anything stronger than professional respect.

They were still discussing their plans when Nairn Craig came over to them.

'Good morning, gentlemen,' he said, receiving their greetings in return. 'I have one piece of cheering news for you. The cause of the fatal accident was so obvious that the railway inspector, Major Kean, has already completed his report. Neither of you will be bothered by him.'

'That's a relief,' said Rae.

'Yes,' added Colbeck. 'Two inspectors are enough for any investigation. A third would take us into the realms of overcrowding.'

'What about the sheriff?'

'He wants to be kept abreast of developments at every stage,' said Craig. 'Apart from anything else, he holds a lot of shares in the Caledonian. But I can see why you asked that question, Inspector. You wanted to know if the sheriff was likely to impede your inquiry. He gave me his word that he would not do so and,' he went on with a glance at Colbeck, 'he was thrilled to hear that we'd called *you* in.'

'I'm glad that somebody other than you feels that I have a place here,' said Colbeck. 'It may take longer to convince most people of my usefulness.'

'Oh, I accept that you are useful,' said Rae with a broadening smile. 'What is not so clear is whether your presence is necessary.'

'Indeed, it is,' said Craig, forcefully.

'We shall see.'

'Inspector Colbeck towers above any other detective.'

'I dispute that, Mr Craig. Put us back to back and you'd see that he and I are of roughly equivalent height.' He inclined his head. 'Excuse me, gentlemen. Duty calls.'

After beaming at each in turn, Inspector Rae spun on his heel and walked off to seek out members of his investigative team. His animosity towards Colbeck was largely concealed under a carapace of politeness but it was still there. And it would handicap proceedings. Though Rae had more or less demanded cooperation from him, Colbeck had the feeling that he'd get very little in return. In that respect, the inspector was a sophisticated and clean-shaven version of Superintendent McTurk.

'You talked of sending the sergeant off to Glasgow,' recalled Craig.

'Yes, sir, and he's no doubt already enjoying the pleasure of climbing up Beattock Bank. Thanks to that letter of introduction you kindly wrote, he'll have access to your headquarters.'

'The pair of you can have access to anything you wish, Inspector.'

'That's good to hear.'

'If we have a villain inside the Caledonian, I want him flushed out.'

'Leave it to us, Mr Craig.'

'Meanwhile,' said the other, taking a sheet of paper from his inside pocket, 'I thought you might like a copy of this. Posters have already been put up advertising the reward but I also had these printed for distribution.' He passed the handbill over. 'You never know,' he continued. 'It may be a long shot but somebody might actually have witnessed the disaster.'

Colbeck showed surprise. 'Out here in this pretty wilderness?'

'It's not as uninhabited as it might seem,' replied Craig. 'Most people here work on the land but there are a few of them with jobs at the quarry. They'd have to go right past here to get there. And you're not the first to notice how pretty Annandale is. Walkers often come to appreciate its beauty.' He bit his lip. 'It's just a pity that the beauty has been scarred by the accident.'

'I'm sure that this handbill will produce results,' said Colbeck, reading it. 'Unfortunately, they may not be the results we want. When handsome rewards like this are offered, we always tend to get bogus witnesses. They can make up some very beguiling stories for four hundred pounds.'

No matter how much he concentrated, Jamie Farr could not decipher every word on the handbill. Some of them baffled him. Having walked to the nearest village to collect one, he sat by the roadside with his dog curled up beside him. There was not much call for reading in the shepherd's life and, in any case, he was a poor scholar. What did jump straight at him off the handbill was the amount being offered as a reward. It was a dizzying prize. If he could secure that, he could escape from the long shadow of his father. He might even be able to contrive an escape for someone else at the same time. The thought made him tremble with joy.

Slipping the handbill into his pocket, he leapt up and called Angus to heel. The pair of them set off in the direction of their flock but they didn't take the most direct route. Instead, they made a little detour past a farmhouse in a state of neglect. There was a hole in the roof and the shutters were broken. In one of the outhouses, a door was hanging off its hinges. Small and cheerless, it was home to seven people but only one of them interested Jamie. Her name was Bella Drew. He knew that she'd be there, working at the spinning wheel as she always did. Jamie supplied some of the wool. It was how they'd become friends. Bella would have been left at home with her deaf old mother while the menfolk of the house went off to work.

After ordering his dog to sit, Jamie approached the house with care but nevertheless managed to disturb the chickens. Their squawks brought the lovely face of Bella Drew to the window. It brightened when she saw her friend and she waved to him. Seconds later, she slipped out of the house and trotted across to him. Though she was tousled and wearing a tattered dress, she had the bloom of youth on her.

'What are ye doing here, Jamie Farr?' she asked, brushing back a tuft of hair.

'I came to see ye, Bella.'

'I should be working.'

'Aye,' he said, 'and so should I but I had to ask ye a favour.'

'What do ye mean?'

When he took the handbill from his pocket, he felt a surge of tenderness. He was holding something that might transform their lives if they had courage enough to turn their backs on their respective families. Bella looked up with eyes full of hope.

'Well?' she prodded. 'Are ye going to speak?'

He cleared his throat and ran his tongue over dry lips.

'How well can ye read?' he asked.

CHAPTER SEVEN

Victor Leeming was glad to reach the comparative safety of Glasgow and to stand on solid ground once more. The journey from Beattock had been testing. As the train struggled up the Bank with the aid of two locomotives, Leeming didn't dare to look out of the window. The gradient felt alarmingly steep and his hope that they'd eventually reach the summit was eroded by a garrulous companion who told him scary stories of wheels losing their grip during heavy rain or of the train sliding backwards when the rails were rimed with frost. Scenic beauty held no interest for him. It was only when they arrived at his destination that he felt confident enough to peer through the glass. They'd entered Buchanan Street station and were slowing to a halt. The sergeant gulped with relief. After miles of open countryside, the clamour, bustle and industrial grime of Glasgow were wonderfully reassuring.

The letter of introduction did more than offer him access to the headquarters of the Caledonian Railway. It gained him an unexpectedly cordial welcome and equipped him with a willing guide in the shape of John Mudie, a red-haired young man with a nervous laugh and an affable manner. Charged with offering unlimited assistance to the detective, Mudie did everything that was asked of him. The first thing that Leeming wanted to see was the service record of the three victims of the disaster. Dougal Murray, the fireman, and Alan Grint, the guard, had worked for the Caledonian for years. It had been their sole source of employment. Jock Laidlaw, the driver, had been more ubiquitous. He'd worked for two of the smaller Scottish railway companies before spending four years with the North British. According to Mudie, the driver had been lured to the Caledonian by the promise of higher wages and better working conditions. Laidlaw had been with them for a few years now.

'What else can I show you, Sergeant?' asked Mudie.

'I'd like to hear about any discontented employees who've recently left. Do you keep any record of them?'

'We have a long list of people whose employment was terminated. It goes back over the years.'

'I'm only interested in those who parted company with you in the last six months, say. Does anyone come into that category?'

'Rather too many, I fear,' admitted the Scotsman.

'Give me some examples,' said Leeming.

They were in a small office that reminded him of the pokey room assigned to him at Scotland Yard. The difference was that Mudie's domain was scrupulously tidy. He had Colbeck's predilection for order. Leeming's natural habitat, by contrast, was an amiable clutter. Mudie abhorred disarray. Everything was self-evidently in its proper place. Plucking a ledger from a shelf, he opened it, found the page he was after and ran a finger down a list of names.

'We've had five men dismissed for drunkenness, two for persistent lateness, three for disobeying orders from a superior and one . . .' Mudie paused as he searched for the right words. 'And one was sacked for behaving improperly with a young woman during the night shift. Add to that a couple who resorted to violence.'

'And did all these people work on the footplate?'

'No, no, Sergeant, this also covers station staff and railway policemen.'

'Are any of those dismissals in any way connected with the three people who were killed in the crash?' asked Leeming. 'Or don't you go into such detail?'

'Indeed, we do.'

'Then I'd be grateful if you could check through the list.'

'That's what I'm doing, Sergeant,' said Mudie, going slowly from one name to another. 'I can't see any link at the moment. I wish that I could. Ah – wait a moment,' he added, tapping the page. 'This looks promising.'

'Go on.'

'There *is* a connection, after all.'

'Who is it with?'

'Jock Laidlaw – he was assaulted by another driver some weeks ago and the attacker was dismissed on the spot. Superintendent McTurk was a witness to the assault.'

'Yes,' said Leeming through gritted teeth, 'we've met the superintendent.'

'He'd be able to tell you more about the incident.'

'What was the name of the other man?'

'Lackey Paterson.'

'Do you have an address for him?'

'I can give you his last known address, Sergeant.'

'Thank you,' said Leeming. 'You've been very helpful. We need to eliminate this fellow from our enquiries. If I can't track down Paterson, I'd like the names of employees who might have worked with him and who knew Jock Laidlaw as well. With respect to your ledger, Mr Mudie, it merely records the bare facts. I suspect that there was more to the assault on Laidlaw than appears there. Now, could I have that address, please?'

'You can have more than that,' said Mudie with a nervous laugh. 'I'll take you there. Glasgow is a rabbit warren. You'd never find your way around alone.'

While work to clear the crash site continued in earnest, Robert Colbeck explored the immediate surroundings. Armed with an ordnance survey map, he started at the point immediately above the point of collision and walked due east. What he was looking for was the likely route taken by anyone coming to cause an explosion. A nearby copse offered possible cover and he first investigated that, picking his way through the trees and searching the ground as he did so. It was slow and laborious work but it eventually yielded a dividend. In the shade of a pine tree, he found a depression in the grass that suggested something had been stored there for a while. When he knelt down to examine the flattened-out area, he saw a telltale trickle of powder. Whoever had blocked the line had first hidden small barrels of gunpowder in the copse. He could still see their circular bases described in the grass.

It would have taken no more than five minutes to carry the gunpowder to the edge of the rock that overlooked the line. Colbeck had the feeling that more than one person was involved. To avoid any chance of being seen, they could have stored the gunpowder in place during the night then set off the blast shortly before the goods train was due to arrive. A loud boom from the quarry echoed across the whole area and told him that stone was being harvested for a less lethal purpose. After covering every inch of the copse, Colbeck stepped out into the sunshine and gazed around. Sheep could be seen grazing in the distance but there was no sign of any human beings. Yet he felt somehow that he was being watched. It was an odd sensation.

In his top hat and frock coat, he was an incongruous figure in a rural landscape and might be expected to attract attention. Nobody, however, was in sight. Though he looked in every direction, he failed even to get a glimpse of someone. He recalled the earlier occasion when he felt that he was under surveillance by a figure high above him on the hill. That person – if he were ever there – had melted into invisibility. There were many places to hide ahead of Colbeck. The rolling countryside created dips and hollows where a person could easily be concealed. He walked towards them, expecting that, at any moment, someone would pop up into view. But it never happened. He was utterly alone.

Yet the further he went, the more convinced he became that a pair of eyes was on him. The observation did not feel friendly. He stopped, bided his time, removed his top hat and ran a hand through his hair. Pretending to scan the landscape in front of him, he suddenly swung round on his heel and looked directly behind him. Colbeck was just in time to see someone dive unceremoniously behind a bush. There was no need to speculate on whom it might be. The uniform gave the man away.

It was Superintendent McTurk.

Tam Howie conducted his visitor into his office and closed the door behind him. Ian Dalton had called on a fellow merchant but he hadn't come to discuss business. They were committed members of the same kirk and Dalton had been present at the meeting when Howie had tried to persuade the others to take more extreme action against the railway companies. He was one of the two converts to Howie's cause. Younger and stockier than his friend, Dalton had grown tired of their lack of success in the battle against the desecration of the Sabbath.

'You spoke well the other day, Tam,' he said.

'Not well enough to win the argument, I'm afraid. The rest of them are like Gregor Hines – too old and too frightened to do what's needful. It fair sickens me, Ian,' complained Howie. 'When we have the means at our disposal to strike with real effect, why don't we use it?'

'I couldn't agree more.'

'It's not as if we can't afford it.'

'Quite so, Tam – my pockets are deep enough.'

'And so are mine. What better way to spend our money?'

Both men made a comfortable living by importing and selling goods during the week. On Sunday, however, they transacted no business. That would have been morally wrong on the day of rest. Their Sabbath was devoted to attendance at kirk services and Bible-reading. Their respective children had been brought up to maintain that tradition. Because they were keen market rivals, Howie and Dalton didn't see much of each other socially. What brought them together was a shared purpose.

'You were right,' said Dalton. 'We must do more.'

'Some of us have already moved in that direction,' confessed Howie. 'We'd wait until Doomsday until Gregor and the rest of the old guard finally see sense. I just won't stand by and watch the trains run all over Scotland on the Sabbath.'

'What have you done, Tam?'

'That's between Flora and me.'

Dalton was taken aback. 'Are you saying that your *wife* is involved?'

'Aye – she's involved right up to the hilt.'

'Good for her!'

'Flora is as passionate a devotee of the cause as I am.'

'We're lucky to have two such people in our midst,' said Dalton. 'The others may not want to follow your example but I certainly do. If there's work for my hands, just tell me what it is.'

'That depends on how far you're prepared to go, Ian.'

'I'll go all the way.'

'Even if it means breaking the law?'

'Even then, Tam – you have my word. After all, Jesus broke the law when he felt that it was right to do so. We only follow where he led. You can count on my unqualified support.'

'Thank you,' said Howie, grasping his hand and shaking it vigorously. 'We need help, Ian. There's a limit to what Flora and I can do alone.'

'Rely on me from now on.'

'You do realise the risk that you're taking, don't you?'

'I'm a businessman. I take risks all the time.'

'But you don't usually flout the law when you're doing so. Very well,' he went on, 'let's take a little time to mull this over. Each of us can decide what we prefer to do to make the railway companies sit up and take notice. Be bold, Ian,' he said, bunching a fist. 'This is no time for faint hearts.'

'I can be bold when the need arises,' boasted Dalton.

'Then let's leave it at that. Flora will be delighted by the news. We had the feeling that you inclined towards us.'

'It's the only way to show how serious we are in our beliefs. If we cause embarrassment to the railway and – if at all possible – wreak havoc, people will pay heed to our point of view.'

'It's not people whom we have to convince,' said Howie. 'It's the Caledonian and the North British and the Edinburgh to Glasgow and all the other companies who need convincing. We have to make them think that it's too dangerous to run trains on a Sunday. That will mean a long and bitter campaign.' His eyes glinted. 'Are you with us, Ian Dalton?'

'I'm with you every step of the way,' promised the other.

Victor Leeming was accustomed to seeing poverty and deprivation in the teeming rookeries of London. Even so, he was shocked by what he found in the Gorbals. Back-to-back tenements offered drab accommodation to families with what seemed like armies of children. The streets were alive with them, playing, arguing, threatening, fighting or learning how to steal. Stray cats and dogs abounded. Street vendors were getting short shrift from penniless housewives. The noise was deafening and the stench overpowering. Leeming was glad that he had a guide but it was John Mudie who was the more grateful. Venturing into the Gorbals was like stepping into a swamp for him. Whenever anyone brushed against him, his nervous laugh turned into a squeak of fear. Leeming saved him from physical assault and from the depredations of pickpockets. The sergeant fended off trouble at every turn.

The address they had took them to a tenement on the corner of a lane. It was a larger building than the average and there was less filth on the pavement outside. A woman was sitting outside the door on a stool, dandling a baby on her knee. From a distance, she looked quite old. When they got closer, however, they saw that she was barely out of her twenties, with the remains of a dark prettiness. It was the rounded shoulders and air of weariness that added years to her. She looked up at them with dull eyes then nursed the baby as it began to cry.

'It's no' the day for the rent,' she said, rancorously.

'We're not here to collect anything,' explained Mudie. 'Well, as a matter of fact, we are but the only thing we're after is information.'

'We're looking for Mr Lackey Paterson,' said Leeming.

'And who might ye be?' she asked.

'We're acting on behalf of the Caledonian Railway.'

'Ha!' she said with contempt. 'Dinna mention them to me.'

'Why is that?'

'I'm Lackey's wife. It was the Caledonian as sacked him.'

'That's what we came to discuss, Mrs Paterson. Where can we find him?'

'Your guess is as guid as mine.'

'Does he have a job somewhere?'

'If he does,' she said with vehemence, 'he'll no be telling me about it. Lackey's no' ma mahn any more. He doesnae live wi' me now. I've to bring the bairn up on ma own.'

As if it heard what she said, the baby's howl became so piteous that Mudie felt obliged to put a hand into his waistcoat pocket and take out a few coins. When he thrust them into her hand, he got no thanks. She simply glared at him.

'Is your husband a violent man?' asked Leeming.

'I told ye. He's no' ma husband any more.'

'Was he likely to get into fights when he was here?'

'In a place like this, ye have to fight to get by,' she said, ruefully. 'Lackey was as ready wi' his fists as any of 'em. I should know. I felt 'em often enough.'

It accounted for the scar over one eye and for the strange lump on her temple. Mudie had to master the impulse to give her more money to assuage his feeling of guilt. The woman was poor, helpless and abandoned. It was a life of drudgery.

Leeming probed. 'Have you any idea – any idea at all – where your husband might be, Mrs Paterson? It's very important that we find him.'

She turned her head away. 'What's tha' to me?'

'We're ready to pay for information,' said Mudie, recklessly. He dug some more coins from his waistcoat pocket. 'You must have some notion of where he is.'

'I do, as it happens,' she conceded, tempted by the promise of reward. She opened her palm and he dropped the money into it. 'I can only tell ye what I've heerd,' she warned. 'The rumour is that Lackey left for a job further south.'

'And where would that be, Mrs Paterson?'

'It's in a quarry.'

Many men had toiled to clear the line and their efforts had finally borne fruit. The debris had been shifted, fresh ballast and sleepers had been installed and new lengths of rail were being put in place. Within the hour, trains would be running normally again. There was still an immense amount of work to do, burning shattered wagons or reclaiming those that could be repaired. Some freight still needed to be salvaged but the interruption to services had at last been corrected. To meet the needs of the crew on site, an improvised kitchen had been set up, serving food and drink to the men during brief moments of respite. It was near the kitchen that Colbeck met up again with Inspector Rae. They exchanged greetings.

'We're almost done here,' said Rae, looking around. 'They've worked well.'

'Do you feel you've learnt everything there is to learn here, Inspector?'

'Yes, I do. The villains have long since fled the area. We must search elsewhere. I'll start looking for them among employees of the North British.'

'I wish you well,' said Colbeck.

Rae smiled. 'I can't believe that you mean that.'

'Indeed, I do. If you can track down the culprits, I'll be the first to congratulate you. It's just that I believe you are looking in the wrong place.'

'Oddly enough, I could say the same about you. This crash has nothing to do with the personal lives of any of the three men on that train.'

'We must agree to differ.'

'You've sent Sergeant Leeming on a wild goose chase. He'll find nothing of value at the headquarters of the Caledonian.'

'You seem very well informed,' said Colbeck.

'I make it my business to be so.'

'Is that why you set spies to watch on us? In future, I'd suggest you choose someone more skilled at the trade than Superintendent McTurk. When he trailed me this morning, I sensed at once that he was there.'

'Well, it was not at my behest,' said Rae, seriously. 'If he followed you, he did so off his own initiative. It may just be that he was hoping to pick up a few tips from a famous detective. McTurk is very ambitious. He doesn't intend to spend the rest of his life as a railway policeman.'

'I don't think he's capable of anything else.'

'That's not his opinion, Inspector. He told Mr Craig that he can solve this case without help from either you or me. You have to admire his confidence.'

'I'd call it arrant folly.'

'Be fair, now – the fellow does have some talents.'

'Then they should be confined to supervisory work on the railway,' said Colbeck. 'If he was intent on catching the people behind this crime, he'd have taken the trouble to search the area above us. In a copse nearby, I found clear evidence that gunpowder had been stored there. It never occurred to McTurk to look for it.'

'And, by implication, you're saying that it never occurred to me either. I felt it unnecessary,' said Rae. 'It was less important to find out where the gunpowder was stored than where it came from. The first thing I did when I arrived here was to make enquiries at the quarry. I asked Mr Craig to pass on the information that nothing had been stolen from that source.'

'He did so, Inspector. But I still think that my search was productive.'

'Why – the villains are never going to come back here, are they?'

'Perhaps not,' admitted Colbeck.

'Lightning doesn't strike twice in the same place.'

'But it may strike again. Knowledge of the *modus operandi* of the culprits is therefore valuable. Don't you agree?'

'No,' said Rae with emphasis. 'This was an isolated attack, intended to cause disruption and to divert custom from one railway to another. I understand the politics of the situation in a way that even you can't grasp.'

'That may be so, Inspector. Then again . . .'

Colbeck left the sentence unfinished but he was clearly not persuaded by Rae's argument. When he surveyed the scene, he did so with a pang of remorse. Hard work would eventually rid the site of its remaining debris but the gaping wounds in the embankment would remain. It would take Mother Nature a long time to repair them. Every time a train went past, it would be reminded of the gruesome event that occurred there. Until the malefactors could be brought to justice, there would always be the lingering fear that – in spite of Rae's opinion – it might happen again. The only way to still public apprehension was to make arrests.

'Have the posters and handbills had any effect yet?' asked Colbeck.

'Two men have come forward,' replied Rae.

'Did they have anything useful to tell you?'

'If their evidence had been true, it would have been very useful.'

'But it was not, I suspect.'

'The first man claimed to have witnessed the whole thing,' said Rae, 'and gave a very plausible description of what had happened. My hopes were raised. Then it emerged that on the day in question, he was staying with relatives in Edinburgh. He was nowhere near this place.'

'What about the second man?'

'He demanded the reward before he even gave his information. When we refused, he became obstreperous and had to be restrained. We later learnt that he'd been put up to it by friends at a pub. They got him drunk then dared him to tell us a tale that would charm the money out of us. He's now in a lock-up.'

'It was ever thus,' said Colbeck. 'Some people will fabricate any story if a reward is on offer. I still doubt if a genuine witness will ever come forward.'

Superintendent McTurk was urinating behind some bushes when he heard someone coming. He quickly finished what he was doing and buttoned up his flies. Emerging flustered from his hiding place, he was confronted by a young man with a crook in one hand and a sheepdog at his heels.

'What the devil do you want?' demanded the policeman, reddening.

Jamie Farr held up the handbill that bore details of the reward.

'I've come aboot this, sir,' he muttered.

CHAPTER EIGHT

John Mudie was unable to identify particular friends of Jock Laidlaw and Lackey Paterson but he did direct Victor Leeming to a place where the two men would be well known. The Railway Inn was only a short distance from the station in Glasgow and a natural venue for off-duty employees to gather. Feeling that his guide had given all the help that he usefully could, Leeming sent him back to his office and ventured into the inn alone. His top hat and frock coat immediately set him apart from anyone else there, though it was countered by his ugliness and by the solidity of his frame. He looked, if anything, like a working man in stolen apparel that didn't quite fit him and which made him very uncomfortable. When he opened his mouth, his London vowels estranged him even more and the news that he was a detective silenced a number of tongues instantly. Most of those there confessed that they knew both Laidlaw and Paterson but very few were prepared to offer much information about them. Even the promise of a free drink couldn't coax anything out of them. When Leeming pressed them, they simply shrugged and drifted out of the door.

Treating himself to a glass of beer, he retired to a table in a corner and pondered. After the gushing helpfulness of Mudie, he'd come up against a barrier. It was disappointing. Yet his cause was not entirely hopeless. An old man was watching him with interest. After a while, he got up with difficulty, removed his cap so that he could scratch his bald head, then ambled across to the newcomer. Sighing at the effort it cost him, he lowered himself creakily onto the seat opposite Leeming.

'My old bones will be the death of me,' he complained.

'Can I get you a drink?' asked Leeming, hopes rising.

'Thank ye, kind sir. I'll have a wee dram.'

Leeming got up to order the drink then brought it back to the table. The old man thanked him with a wheezing chortle then took a first sip. Sitting down again, Leeming waited patiently as his companion seemed to drift off into a reverie. The latter came out of it with a start.

'I'm no' like the others,' he said, nodding sagely towards the door. 'I'm retired from the railway, ye ken. They cannae touch me if I speak out o' turn.'

'Is that why the others kept silent?' asked Leeming. 'Were they afraid there'd be repercussions if they talked to me?'

'That's part of it.'

'And what's the other part?'

'You're a Sassenach. That's someone who's no' a true Scotsman.'

'But I'm trying to *help* the Caledonian Railway.'

'Your face doesnae fit heer, ma friend.'

Leeming took a long sip of his beer. 'Do you know the people I was asking about – Jock Laidlaw and Lackey Paterson?'

'Oh, ar, I ken them both. When I was a driver, Lackey was my fireman.'

'What can you tell me about him?'

'He was a lad wi' too much fire in his belly.'

'He had a temper, then?'

'That he did and it got him into trouble. But he wasnae a bad mahn, for a' that. Lackey was guid company even though he could be a bit wild when he'd drunk too much. That's no' a crime in my book. A mahn's entitled to his drink. What else is there to cheer us up in this wicked world?'

Leeming was about to say that a wife and family were more likely to provide cheer but he didn't want to interrupt the old man. He let him ramble on, telling many anecdotes about Paterson's antics at the Railway Inn and realising that the sacked driver had been quite popular there. When his companion paused for breath, Leeming shifted the conversation to Jock Laidlaw. He got a very different response.

'Jock was a cocky bugger,' said the old man with disapproval. 'He'd strut around in heer like a rooster. Anyone'd think he was the only person who'd ever driven a train. Jock was always bragging about how guid he was.'

'How did he and Paterson get on?'

'They kept out of each other's way.'

'Why was that?'

'They'd nothing in common.'

'Yet they ended up fighting.'

'Aye,' said the other, sadly. 'It were the end for puir Lackey. He threw the first punch, I heer, and out he went.'

'Do you know what caused him to attack Laidlaw?'

'He must have been fed up wi' all that bragging.'

'Was there no other reason?'

'None that I ken. I told ye that Lackey was hot-blooded. It'd only take a spark to set him off. Jock must've gi' it to him.'

Leeming thought about the woman with the scar and the lump on her temple.

'Were you aware that Paterson has left his wife?' he asked.

'I was shocked when I heerd it,' said the old man, eyes widening in sympathy. 'Puir woman is left alone wi' a bairn. Margaret, that's her name – and she was the pride of the Gorbals as a lassie. Every mahn who saw her was jealous of Lackey. But having the bairn changed her, they say. She's no' the lovely creature she was.'

'We spoke to her earlier today. She was bitter about being left by her husband. She told us that he knocked her about sometimes.'

'Ye have to show a wife who's in charge.'

Leeming was indignant. 'But you don't have to do it with your fists.'

'Ye do it *your* way – Lackey did it his way.'

'Well, it's a cowardly way, if you ask me. Mrs Paterson would have been defenceless against him.' He waited until his ire had subdued. 'Why did he leave his wife? Was he so unhappy with her?'

'The only person who can answer that is Lackey himself. I dinna ken why. It's a mystery. If ye find out the truth, I'd like to heer it. I'll tell ye this,' the old man added. 'I'd never walk out on a lassie as fine as Maggie Paterson. I think that Lackey must've taken leave of his senses.'

Rory McTurk flattered himself a good judge of men. Suspicious when Farr first made his claim, he questioned him closely about his work as a shepherd and gradually came round to the view that he might, after all, be telling the truth. Someone who looked after sheep all day would have good eyesight and sharp instincts. Taking a notebook from his pocket, McTurk licked the end of a pencil.

'Now, then,' he began. 'You say that you saw two men with a horse and cart.'

'Aye, sir.'

'And how close did you get?'

'I was close enough to have a guid look at them.'

'Did they see you?'

'No,' replied Farr. 'If they had, they'd have turned tail and gone. They were looking over their shoulder a' the time.'

'You mean that they were furtive because they were up to no good?'

'I think so, sir.'

'Can you describe them?'

'Aye, that's why I'm heer. They were about the same age, mebbe ten years older than me. And they were ma height, only broader. They wore dark clothes and hats and . . . well, sir, they just didnae *belong*.'

'They were townsfolk out in the country – is that it?'

'Aye.'

'What was on the cart?'

'Some rope, a pile of empty sacks and an ould tarpaulin.'

'And where exactly did you see them?'

Farr pointed in the direction of the crash site. McTurk went over the details again and squeezed even more out of him. No matter how much pressure he put on the shepherd, the latter didn't flinch. In the policeman's judgement, his informant was not clever enough to make up the tale. He had seen someone on the eve of the disaster and it could be highly significant. McTurk was excited, sensing that this was the breakthrough he needed.

'Who else have you told?' he asked.

'Nobody – I've only spoke to ye.'

'Then let's keep it that way. This is between you and me. You understand?'

'Aye, sir – when do I get the money?'

'I'm not sure that you've earned it yet.'

Farr's face clouded. 'But I've told ye the truth.'

'I believe that you have, lad, but there's no guarantee that these two men are in any way connected with the crime. Even if they were, they'll have to be tracked down and interrogated. Read the handbill,' he instructed. 'It says that the reward is for information leading to the arrest and conviction of the villains responsible. Not a penny will be handed over until we get a guilty verdict in court. And you,' he went on, 'will be there to act as a witness.'

The shepherd gave a visible shudder. He hadn't realised that there would be such complications. His naive hope had been that his story would be accepted and that the money would be handed over. With such a fortune in his possession, he knew that he could persuade Bella Drew to run away with him. It was his dearest wish. Instead, he was being forced to wait and might have to bear witness in court, an eventuality that filled him with dread.

After noting down where he could find the shepherd, McTurk closed his book.

'And remember,' he warned. 'Your lips must be sealed.'

'Aye, sir, they will be.'

'What you've told me is useful but not conclusive.'

'It's *them*, sir, I'm sure it was them.'

'Then why were they carrying so little on the cart? Answer me that. You can't cause an explosion with a load of sacks and a tarpaulin. Where was the gunpowder? I think you're getting ahead of yourself, lad. There's a lot still to unravel.'

'Oh, I see.' Farr's head dropped to his chest.

'I'll be in touch,' said McTurk, dismissively.

'Can ye no' even gi' me *some* of the money?'

'You'll get nothing until we've gathered more evidence.'

'But I *need* it,' said Farr, plaintively.

McTurk roared with laughter. 'We *all* need money,' he said.

'There's nothing special about you. Be patient, lad. I'll get back to you in the fullness of time.'

'Is that a promise, sir?'

'My word is my bond.'

But even as the solemn assertion came out of his mouth, McTurk rescinded it in his mind. He wasn't going to let four hundred pounds be wasted on a simple shepherd. All that Farr had done was to see something of possible interest. It was McTurk who'd act on the information and – if it proved crucial – who deserved to profit from it. Stroking his beard, he watched the shepherd trudge off with his dog dancing around him. It was pure accident that he'd chosen to relieve himself there. It was a moment of destiny. Thanks to what he'd been told, he might well end up with four hundred pounds and the satisfaction of having got the better of the renowned Railway Detective.

McTurk grinned all the way back to the crash site.

Robert Colbeck sat back and enjoyed the view. Unlike Leeming, he relished every moment of the train journey to Glasgow, marvelling at the ascent of Beattock Bank and the work of the navvies who'd laboured to build the track in such unpromising terrain. Nairn Craig was his travelling companion but he soon fell asleep, leaving Colbeck to stare out of the window and appreciate some of the delights of Scotland. When they neared their destination, Craig suddenly woke up, profuse in his apologies.

'I'm so sorry that I dozed off, Inspector,' he said. 'Train journeys always send me to sleep. I'm a walking paradox, a man who runs a railway yet can't keep his eyes open when he travels on it.'

'You must be very fatigued. This business has kept you up all hours and the sheer anxiety of it all must be draining.'

'Oh, it is – never was a truer word spoken.'

When he dispatched Leeming to Glasgow, Colbeck had warned him that he'd be joining him there later in the day. His work at the site was complete and he felt that he needed to be close to the headquarters of the company. Craig was less confident that anything could be gained by looking into the private life of the three dead railwaymen. To him, they were random victims.

'I doubt that the sergeant has found anything of moment,' he said.

'Don't underestimate him,' cautioned Colbeck. 'He has a gift for burrowing away until he gets what he wants. Victor Leeming seldom returns empty-handed.'

'I hope that proves to be the case now.'

'What plans do you have regarding compensation, Mr Craig?'

The general manager twitched. 'Compensation? For whom, may I ask?'

'Why,' said Colbeck, 'for the families of the victims, of course. Their grief is sharpened by the loss of their wage earner. They will surely struggle. I assumed that a benevolent man such as you would insist on making a gesture of some kind.'

'Yes, yes,' said Craig, pretending that that had always been his intention. 'It's a matter to which I've given some thought. There will be some form of remuneration. After all, they died in the service of the Caledonian. That fact must be respected.'

Without his mention of the subject, Colbeck surmised, it would not even have crossed the general manager's mind. The company employed a large staff at set wage rates. Whatever the circumstances, they were not in the habit of making unscheduled payments to their families. Colbeck made a mental note to pursue the issue until it was resolved. The unnatural deaths of Laidlaw, Murray and Grint deserved some recompense.

When they reached the station, John Mudie was waiting

to welcome Craig to bring him up to date with what had been happening. Colbeck was glad to be free of the general manager. Though a keen supporter of the detective, he was starting to question his methods and that was irritating. Pushing his way through the crowd with his luggage, Colbeck's attention was drawn to a figure on a bench. The man was reading a newspaper so his face was completely covered but the creased trousers and the unpolished shoes disclosed his identity. It was Leeming.

'Hello, Victor,' said Colbeck, going across to him.

The sergeant lowered the paper. 'I didn't expect you this early, sir.'

'Normal service has been resumed. I caught the train from Beattock.'

'Don't mention that climb to me. It was a nightmare.'

'You'll be going down it next time so you can keep your eyes open. Still,' said Colbeck, sitting beside him. 'That can wait. How has the day gone?'

'I'd like to think I made some progress, sir.'

'Good – let's find somewhere a little more private and you can tell all.'

They adjourned to the waiting room and found it half-empty. Taking seats in a corner, they were able to talk without being overheard. Leeming gave a full account of his movements in Glasgow. Colbeck was intrigued to hear about the disappearance of Lackey Paterson in the wake of his assault on Jock Laidlaw. It gave credence to his theory that personal enmity might lie behind the train crash.

'We need to find the man,' he said, 'and do so quickly.'

'Don't send me off to the quarry,' pleaded Leeming. 'I don't think I could face another train journey.'

'I wouldn't dream of sending you, Victor. I'll retrace my steps.'

'What am I to do meanwhile?'

'You can take our luggage to the hotel where Mr Craig has kindly reserved rooms for us. He's been very attentive to our needs. I just wish he'd been equally attentive to the needs of the families of the victims. If I hadn't nudged him in that direction,' recalled Colbeck, 'he wouldn't have considered offering compensation to them for their loss.'

'But that's such an obvious thing to do, sir.'

'It's an additional expense and Mr Craig was anxious to avoid it.'

'What about the reward money?'

'That's an unavoidable outlay.'

'I know that, Inspector. What I'm asking is this – if we solve the crime, do *we* get the reward? By rights, we ought to.'

'I agree, Victor. Anyway,' Colbeck went on, getting up, 'you take a cab to The Angel Hotel and wait for me there. I have an appointment at the quarry.'

'Be careful, sir. Paterson has a temper on him.'

'Then I'll take pains to provoke it. There's no better way to learn the true character of a man than by making him lose his self-control.' He chuckled. 'I do it all the time with Superintendent Tallis.'

It was not until early evening that Tam Howie returned home. After a busy day at the office, he could turn his mind away from commerce and concentrate on something else. The visit of Ian Dalton had been a bonus. They now had another pair of hands at their disposal. It would enable Howie and his wife to be more enterprising in their battle against the railways. Having grown up at a time when the Sabbath was sacrosanct, he was determined to return it to that state. Rail services on a Sunday were an insult to God. They encouraged people away from their kirks and other places of worship, solely in the name of profit. Howie was well acquainted with the need for profit but there were six other days when it could be pursued with vigour. In his view, that was enough for anybody. He remembered the occasion when Jesus turned the money changers out of the temple. That, in essence, he felt, was what he was trying to do, expelling the unrighteous and restoring respect for the Almighty.

The cab dropped him off outside his home in one of the more prosperous districts of the city. The maidservant admitted him and his wife gave him a token kiss of welcome. When they adjourned to the parlour, he told Flora the news about their new recruit. Her pleasure was tempered with caution.

'Ian Dalton is a good man,' she said, 'but how far can we trust him?'

'He's a willing volunteer. That's enough for me, Flora.'

'I'm not sure that he's altogether discreet.'

'Don't trouble yourself on that score,' he said. 'I've impressed upon him the absolute need for discretion. Secrecy is our main weapon. Dalton appreciates that.'

'I'm worried about his wife.'

'Morag will take no part in it.'

'Perhaps not but she'll be aware that her husband is up to something. What if she objects or lets the cat out of the bag?'

'Stop fretting,' he advised. 'Dalton's marriage is very different to ours. He doesn't have a wife like you who is passionate about the causes in which she believes. Morag Dalton is a little mouse of a woman with nothing to say. That's why he was so astounded when I told him that *you* were involved.' He smiled quietly. 'Dalton just couldn't believe that a woman would be prepared to take action against the railway companies. It's something that *his* wife would never even contemplate.'

'Morag doesn't have enough spirit to fight for anything.'

'Forget the woman, Flora. The point is that we have a convert.'

'True – as long as he doesn't get cold feet.'

'Oh, I don't think so. Dalton's got nerves of steel.'

'Does he realise what he might have to do?'

'He knows that we'll be acting outside the law.'

'Have you told him how far you and I have already gone?'

Howie shook his head and put an affectionate hand on her arm.

'It was too soon for that,' he explained. 'I didn't want to shock him and run the risk of frightening him off. Let's draw him in first. When he's fully committed, we can spring our surprise on him.' His smile verged on the triumphant this time. 'I think he'll be full of admiration at what we've so far achieved.'

The visit to the quarry entailed a train journey to Wamphray and a bumpy ride in a trap. Colbeck enjoyed the first and used the second to prise information about the locality from the driver. He arrived at the quarry with a clear idea of its extent, its workforce and its operation. He also learnt that it did not cease its output on a Sunday. Because it was so isolated, the quarry felt able to stay in production and gather more rock with the aid of gunpowder. The driver was asked to wait in order to take him back to the railway station. Colbeck, meanwhile, took a look at the vast hole excavated out of the ground. Stone was being quarried and loaded onto carts for transportation. As if to acknowledge his presence, a deafening blast was set off and the noise reverberated around the hillsides. A thickset man with a wispy beard came out of a hut to approach him. Colbeck introduced himself and learnt that he was talking to the supervisor.

'How can I help ye, sir?' asked the man.

'I believe that you employ a fellow named Lackey Paterson.'

'We employ a large number of people, as you can see. I cannae remember all their names. But I do ken we've more than one Paterson here.'

'Is there some way of finding this particular man?'

'Aye, sir. We keep a record of who's working where on each day. It may look like a mess when ye stand heer but we've a proper system.'

'Then I'd be grateful if you could tell me where Paterson might be.'

'I will, sir. Excuse me a moment.'

The supervisor stepped into the hut to consult a ledger. He was away for a couple of minutes. When he emerged, he was bristling with anger.

'Lackey Paterson is no' heer,' he said.

'Are you sure about that?'

'The work record doesnae lie. If he was at the quarry, there'd be a tick against his name but there's only a cross. The wretch hasnae been heer since last Saturday. I'll no' put up wi' that. I'll no' let Lackey Paterson or any other mahn under me take time off when it suits him. He's done for at the quarry,' he said with venom. 'If ye find the lazy guid-for-nothing, tell him to stay awa'. He's no' got a job heer any longer.'

Colbeck was not dismayed. Discovering that Paterson had left on the eve of the crash made his journey to the quarry worthwhile. Evidently, the quarry worker had no intention of coming back. Colbeck would have to look elsewhere.

CHAPTER NINE

Madeleine Colbeck tried to cope with her husband's absence by throwing herself into her work but it didn't always preoccupy her. Her thoughts kept drifting uncontrollably to Colbeck and she felt pangs of loneliness. She kept telling herself how lucky she'd been. Since their marriage, he'd always worked on cases that kept him in or near London. Madeleine had been spoilt. She'd been able to see him every day and take an interest in what he was doing. All that had changed. He was now hundreds of miles away, leading an investigation about which she knew almost nothing. She felt excluded, cut adrift from something she'd taken for granted. Even with the servants there, the house felt empty and the marital bed felt even emptier. It was at night that she missed him most but it was something she had to endure as best she could because the Railway Detective's work would take him all over the country.

Unable to paint without natural light, Madeleine put her brush aside as the evening shadows started to lengthen. She was surprised to hear the doorbell ring. Not expecting a visitor, she wondered who it might be and opened the door to listen. The distinctive sound of her father's voice came up from the hallway. Madeleine wiped her hands on a damp cloth and went swiftly downstairs. Caleb Andrews was standing there with his cap in his hand.

'Father,' she said, brow wrinkled in curiosity, 'what are *you* doing here?'

'I was hoping for a better welcome than that, Maddy,' he replied with mock irritation. 'Have I caught you at a bad moment?'

'Not at all – you've come in time to dine with me.'

'But that's not why I'm here.'

She smiled fondly. 'It is now.'

She nodded to the maid who went off to pass on the information to the cook. Madeleine took her father into the drawing room. When she sat down, he remained on his feet. She could tell that he was excited.

'Has something happened?' she asked.

'No, no,' he replied, airily. 'Nothing ever happens in my life.'

'You can't fool me, Father.'

'I don't know what you're talking about.'

'You came here with a purpose. I recognise that look in your eye.'

'There's no deceiving you, Maddy, is there?' he said with a cackle. 'You can read your old father like a book. I could never keep a secret from you.'

'So what is it that cheered you up so much?'

'See for yourself.'

Reaching inside his coat, Andrews took out a letter and handed it over to his daughter. Madeleine read it with a mixture of interest and delight. It was from Archibald Renwick, general manager of the London and North Western Railway, the company for which her father had worked throughout his life. In recognition of his long service, Andrews – along with other retired drivers – was

91

invited to a celebratory dinner. Madeleine could understand why her father was so elated. He would be part of an exclusive group. Only one thing puzzled her.

'The invitation is for this week,' she said. 'Why not give you more notice?'

'Who cares? If it was tomorrow, that would be notice enough for me.'

'This is a real honour, Father.'

He thrust out his chest. 'It's no more than I deserve.'

'You've always admired Mr Renwick.'

'He's a man who knows his job,' said Andrews with approval. 'He also has an eye for something that's rather special – and I'm not only talking about me.'

'Who else?'

'A talented young artist named Madeleine Colbeck – except that you were Madeleine Andrews at the time when you painted a picture of an engine named "Cornwall". It was one of the first I drove for the LNWR. I can still tell you the exact diameter of its driving wheel, its boiler pressure, its coal and water capacity and its traction power.' He beamed nostalgically. 'Oh, I had some good times on the footplate of Cornwall.'

'Why do you pick out that painting?'

'Because it's the one that Mr Renwick owns,' he replied. 'Yes, my daughter's work is hanging in his house. Isn't that wonderful? I only learnt about it today. It was quite by chance. When I showed that letter to some friends earlier on, one of them said he'd actually been to Mr Renwick's house for some function or other. He told me that our general manager had bought Cornwall – that's the painting, of course, not the county.' He glowed with pride. 'What do you think of that?'

'I think that I ought to be very cross with you,' she said, sternly.

Andrews was aghast. 'When I've brought you such good news?'

'I'd like to have been the *first* to hear about your invitation but you had to boast about it to your friends over a pint of beer, didn't you? In other words, they were more important than me. However,' she added, reproach fading from her voice, 'you did find out something very gratifying. I'm so flattered that Mr Renwick thinks my work is good enough to buy. I loved putting Cornwall on canvas.'

'It's one of your best paintings, Maddy.'

'When you meet him, do thank Mr Renwick on my behalf.'

'There's no need. You can do that yourself.'

She blinked. 'What do you mean?'

'Read that letter again,' he suggested. 'You'll see that drivers and their *wives* have been invited. Since I don't have a wife, I'll take my daughter along instead. Oh, it will be such a night for you, Maddy,' he went on, rubbing his hands together with glee. 'You're not only an artist whose work Mr Renwick loves. When he realises that you're married to the Railway Detective as well, he'll insist that you sit right next to him.'

Glasgow was a city of contrasts. Victor Leeming now understood that. Having seen the horror of the Gorbals, he was enjoying accommodation at the other end of the social scale. Standing in an avenue of palatial houses, The Angel Hotel offered a luxury he'd never known before. It made him feel as if he were trespassing, especially as some of the staff kept looking at him with suspicion. Leeming was completely out of his depth. Robert Colbeck, on the other hand, adapted easily to the new surroundings and settled gratefully into them.

'Mr Craig is feather-bedding us,' he observed. 'We've never stayed in a hotel as lavish as this.'

'My room is enormous,' said Leeming. 'I won't be able to sleep in there.'

'Why ever not?'

'It just doesn't feel *right*, sir.'

Colbeck laughed. 'Oh, I don't think you'll have any difficulty dozing off, Victor. It's been a long day and you've worked hard. Make the most of this place while you can. We may never see such opulence again.'

'I'm glad about that.'

'Can't you take *any* enjoyment out of it?'

'No,' confessed Leeming. 'The truth is that I feel so guilty. Why should we have people waiting on us hand and foot while most ordinary people live in the sort of tenements I saw in the Gorbals?'

'There's always a huge chasm between the rich and the poor. It's at its most marked in a city like Glasgow.'

'It's so *unfair*, sir.'

'I couldn't agree more,' said Colbeck. 'Unfortunately, we're not in a position to do anything about it. But you've touched on something I meant to ask you about.'

'What's that?'

'Why did Lackey Paterson live in such straitened conditions? Engine drivers are relatively well paid. Look at my father-in-law. You've seen the house he was able to buy. Paterson should have had something equivalent to that.'

'Yet he didn't – he lived in a slum.'

'It's one more question we'll have to put to him.'

They were in the hotel lounge, relaxing in well-upholstered armchairs. Other guests were chatting over a drink or summoning waiters with a snap of their fingers. They all looked supremely at home. Leeming didn't envy them. He just wondered what they'd done to deserve a life of such extravagance. Colbeck was practical.

'We could easily have stayed in more modest accommodation,' he said. 'The money could have been better spent, not on us but on the families of those three victims of the crash. They'll be in despair.'

'Yes,' said Leeming, sadly. 'Dougal Murray, I discovered, was engaged to be married. Think how his bride-to-be must be suffering.'

'I feel sympathy for anyone touched by this disaster. It's one of the reasons I'm so eager to solve the crime. If Paterson *is* behind it – and evidence is beginning to point that way – he needs to be caught and hanged. However,' said Colbeck, 'we must continue to explore other avenues as well. Paterson may be quite innocent.'

'You wouldn't think that if you'd seen his wife, sir. He was guilty of beating the poor woman and leaving her to bring up their child alone. In my opinion, they're appalling crimes. What about his marriage vows? Well, you took them yourself at your wedding and you know how solemn they are.'

'I do indeed, Victor.'

'A husband should respect his wife.'

Leeming was about to expand on the theme when he saw someone walking towards them. Inspector Rae had his familiar smile in position. After handing his hat to a passing waiter, he sank into a chair opposite the two detectives.

'May I join you, gentlemen?' he asked.

'Please do,' rejoined Colbeck.

Rae looked around. 'Well, this certainly does give lie to the belief that all Scotsmen are skinflints. This hotel is oozing with wealth. Money is being poured away like so much water.'

'That's what worries me,' said Leeming.

Colbeck ordered a drink for the newcomer then told Rae about his visit to the quarry. The latter was interested to hear about the disappearance of Paterson.

'It may or may not be a coincidence,' he decided. 'What else have you learnt?'

Leeming described his visit to the headquarters of the railway company and his subsequent activities. Rae seemed quietly pleased that they had made no apparent progress. At the same time, however, he had to concede that he and his detectives had unearthed no significant new evidence. What he had brought to show them was a letter from the general manager of the North British Railway, categorically denying that the company had anything whatsoever to do with the train crash. Colbeck read the missive before handing it back.

'I think the gentleman doth protest too much,' he remarked.

'I'll interview him tomorrow,' said Rae, 'and question this spirited denial. It's come far too soon. He's pleading the NBR's innocence before it's been accused.'

'Suspicion is bound to fall on a close rival, Inspector. He realises that. I daresay you'll have similar letters from other railway companies before too long.'

'The NBR remains my main source of interest.'

'Is that because Superintendent McTurk believes it to be the prime suspect?'

'No – I came to that conclusion of my own volition. But I'm glad you mentioned McTurk,' said Rae, smile disappearing. 'When I left him earlier on, he was behaving strangely.'

'In what way?' asked Colbeck.

'He'd suddenly become rather secretive. Until then, I couldn't stop the man from talking. He was giving me advice on every aspect of the case. Something has happened to stop him gushing forth.'

'Have you any idea what it might be, Inspector?'

'I can only guess,' said Rae, 'but there was a smugness about him that I thought indicative. It's almost as if he knows something that the rest of us don't. McTurk has picked up a scent that's eluded our nostrils. We're not just in competition with each other, Inspector Colbeck. Unless I'm very much mistaken,' he warned, 'we have a rival with a black beard and a firm resolve to embarrass the pair of us.'

Convinced that he was on the trail of the culprits, Rory McTurk rode to the nearest inn to enquire if two men had stayed there recently. When he drew a blank, he went on to a tavern near Beattock. That, too, was unable to assist him. Riding further afield on his bay mare, he came to The Jolly Traveller, a wayside inn with a spectacular view of the dale. It was a case of third time lucky. The landlord, a portly man in his sixties with a mane of white hair, was able to supply valuable information.

'Aye, sir,' he said. 'That's reet. Two men stayed heer on the Saturday afore that terrible crash on the railway.'

'How old would they be?'

The landlord grinned. 'Oh, a lot younger than either of us.'

'Thirty or thereabouts, perhaps?'

'How did ye know that?'

'Never ye mind – am I right?'

'Ye are, sir.'

'Describe them.'

'They were tall and well built with long, dark hair. Ye'd no' call 'em handsome. They were rough-looking and could both have used a razor. In my job, I weigh people up at a glance and I didnae like them one bit. They were no' people ye'd ever trust.'

'And did they look alike?'

'Aye,' replied the landlord, 'but that's no' surprising, is it?'

'I don't follow.'

'They were brothers.'

McTurk's interest quickened. The landlord was confirming what the shepherd had seen. The two men did exist and they had stayed in the locality prior to the crash.

'Did they tell you their names?' he pressed.

'No,' said the landlord, 'they went straight up to their room. We saw neither hide nor hair of them. But ma daughter heerd what they called each other when they'd an early breakfast on the Sunday.'

'Well?'

'One of 'em was Ewen and t'other was Duncan.'

'Ewen and Duncan,' repeated McTurk, committing the names to memory.

'That's all I can tell ye. They paid the bill and I unlocked the stable.'

'Did they have a cart with them?'

'Aye, sir, they did and they were very partic'lar aboot it. If I'd not been able to lock it safely away, I doobt if they'd have stayed at The Jolly Traveller.'

'Why were they so concerned? All they had on the cart was some rope, a pile of sacks and an old tarpaulin.'

'Who told you that, sir?'

'Isn't it true?'

'No,' said the landlord, clicking his tongue. 'They'd quite a cargo on board. It was under the tarpaulin and tied down wi' the rope. I couldnae see it but it was obviously something worth having. That's why they were fretting aboot it so much.'

McTurk made him go over the details again then gave him a few coins by way of thanks. He was now certain that he'd identified the men responsible for the crash. All that he had to do was to track them down.

'When they left here,' he asked, 'did they say where they were going?'

'Not to me, sir, but my daughter overheard them talk about going home.'

'Where were they heading?'

'Glasgow.'

McTurk was thrilled. The men lived in a city he knew well. Armed with their Christian names and a description of them that tallied with the one given by the shepherd, he believed that he had enough information to go off in pursuit. He was not going to share the evidence he'd just gathered. It belonged solely to him. He wanted all the glory for himself. Striding out of the inn, he mounted his horse. As he cantered away, he could almost feel the four hundred pounds reward in his hand.

When he took the train to the nation's capital next morning, Colbeck was able to travel on lines owned by another company. The Edinburgh and Glasgow Railway, connecting Scotland's two main centres, was a thing of magnificence with impressive viaducts, deep cuttings and three long tunnels. It had easier curves and gentler gradients than the Caledonian. Colbeck marvelled at the genius of its construction. At the invitation of Inspector Rae, he was going to meet the general manager of the North British Railway. Though he didn't believe that the men they were after were in the pay of the company, he was nevertheless pleased to make the acquaintance of Alastair Weir and to learn more about the politics of running railways in Scotland.

They met in a private room at a small hotel near the station. Weir was a cold, impassive man of middle years who kept fiddling with the watch chain that dangled from the pocket of his waistcoat. After introductions had been made, he went on the attack at once.

'This meeting is quite unnecessary,' he said. 'My letter should have been enough in itself to quash any suspicions you might entertain. Nobody in our employ has any link whatsoever with the unfortunate incident on the Caledonian.'

'How do you know that, sir?' asked Rae, levelly.

'We have no criminals in the NBR.'

'That's patently untrue, Mr Weir. Like every other railway company, you suffer at the hands of pilferers. Many of them are your own employees. Instead of sitting in your ivory tower of an office, you should do what I did and study the record of dismissals from the NBR.'

'Don't you dare presume to tell me how to do my job,' growled Weir.

'Inspector Rae is only pointing out what is the bane of any major enterprise,' said Colbeck, striking a note of appeasement. 'When you have a large number of people on your payroll, the law of averages comes into play. It's inevitable that you'll have a few bad apples in the barrel – it's the same for the Caledonian and for the Edinburgh and Glasgow.'

'Petty crime is very different from engineering a train crash.'

'I agree.'

'And so do I,' said Rae, 'but that doesn't absolve the NBR. The simple fact is that you stood to gain from any disruption on a rival line. Now, I'm not for a moment suggesting that you deliberately hatched a plot to disable the Caledonian. You'd never dream of doing that,' he added, absolving Weir of any personal blame. 'But someone else might, someone with the interests of the NBR at heart, someone with a financial stake in the company.'

'That's a monstrous allegation!' snapped Weir.

'Calm down, sir. This is not an attack on you.'

'I speak for the company and I'll defend it against malicious slander.'

Colbeck lifted his shoulders. 'I've heard no slander,' he said.

'And none has been intended,' said Rae with an emollient smile. 'We do, however, have to face facts. The NBR and the Caledonian have been at each other's throats for years. Apart from anything else, both of you have been fighting to take over the Edinburgh and Glasgow.' Weir glowered at him. 'Is that correct, sir?'

'The NBR is always looking to expand,' admitted the other.

'But your methods of doing so are not always gentlemanly.'

'I can see that you're not a businessman, Inspector.'

Rae smiled. 'It's something for which I'm eternally grateful.'

Colbeck took little part in the conversation. He was content to sit there and watch Inspector Rae joust with the pompous general manager. It was not long before Weir's expressionless face was animated, eyes flashing, hair tossing, lip curling and cheeks turning a bright shade of crimson. Colbeck learnt an immense amount about railways north of the border. While they were built predominantly with English capital, they were run almost exclusively by Scotsmen like Alastair Weir, though they tended to keep token Englishmen on their respective boards.

They also retained the services of tame members of parliament who could advance their interests at Westminster. As Colbeck knew, this was also standard practice in England. Railway companies were monumentally expensive to set up. Rather than risk the loss of their vast initial outlay, boards of directors made sure that they had sympathetic voices in the House of Commons to smooth the progress of any bill. Colbeck was well versed in the political infighting that took place in parliament over rival plans. What he'd not encountered to the same degree before was the naked aggression between railway companies. Weir described it as fair competition but it went well beyond that. Colbeck watched with admiration as Inspector Rae probed away until the general manager was virtually frothing at the mouth. When there was a lull in the storm, Colbeck stepped in.

'Did you know that the driver of the train used to work for you?' he asked.

'No,' grunted Weir, 'I did not.'

'If the NBR is the wonderful company you describe, why did Jock Laidlaw turn his back on it?'

'I don't know and I don't care.'

'But you ought to care, sir. He's not the first driver to defect to the Caledonian and he won't be the last unless you divine the cause of the exodus.'

'It's not an exodus,' snarled Weir. 'Drivers leave for all sorts of reasons and not only from us. We employ men who used to work for the Caledonian. Why don't you ask Mr Craig why they fled from his company?'

'They're the very people that interest me,' said Colbeck. 'They'd know about the way the Caledonian was run and be aware of the timetabling of its freight.'

Weir exploded. 'Don't *you* start hurling unfounded accusations at the NBR as well. I've had enough of that from Inspector Rae. I came in the hope of receiving an apology, yet all that I've got so far is a string of insults.'

'They were not intentional,' Rae told him.

'Be that as it may,' said Weir, hauling himself out of his seat. 'I've stayed long enough. My time is money. This conversation is over.' He snatched up his top hat and headed for the door. 'Good day to you, gentlemen.'

Colbeck waited until he'd left the room before turning to his companion.

'I thought you treated him with just the right amount of polite disrespect.'

'Thank you, Inspector,' said Rae, 'but I'll pay for it. As soon as he gets back to his office, he'll dictate a letter of complaint about me to the procurator fiscal. In the mood he's in, he might even send one about you to Scotland Yard.'

'Criticism never hurts me,' said Colbeck, suavely. 'I've had so much of it over the years that I've become inured to it. As a rule, it comes from people I've upset because they have something to hide.'

'What do you think Mr Weir was hiding?'

'He was trying to conceal his fear that you might, after all, be right. It's not inconceivable that there *is* a connection between the NBR and the crash. Needless to say, the crime was in no way prompted by Mr Weir, but he can't be certain that someone on his payroll didn't take the law in their own hands. That's what was behind all that righteous indignation,' argued Colbeck. 'A seed of fear has been sown. Mr Weir is terrified that one of us will find proof that the NBR is implicated, after all. If it is – and I know you incline to that view – it may well cost him his position.'

Victor Leeming was glad of an assignment that took him out of the hotel and relieved him of his discomfort in its sumptuousness. His task was to begin the search for Lackey Paterson. If the man had left the quarry, there was a strong possibility that he'd return to the city where he was born. At Colbeck's suggestion, Leeming first sought the help of the police. While the rank of detective sergeant had real status in England, it did not impress his Scottish counterparts. They claimed to be the oldest police service in the world, having been set up almost thirty years before the Metropolitan Police came into being.

Before he had any actual assistance, Leeming was treated to a brief history of the Glasgow force and learnt that, over ten years earlier, it had merged with the Gorbals, Calton and Anderston Burgh Police to form a single unit comprising some three hundred and sixty officers. Four divisions existed. The men looked smart enough in their top hats and three-quarter-length dress coats with their standing collars and nine shiny buttons but, as in London, their numbers were wholly inadequate to police such a large and populous city. Having listened to the lecture with good grace, Leeming was rewarded with some advice about where he might start the search for Lackey Paterson. The inspector to whom he spoke also promised to spread the word among his officers that Paterson was wanted for questioning.

The task that confronted Leeming was disheartening. He was looking for a man he'd never seen before in a city he didn't know at all. It was like searching for a particular grain of sand on a very large beach. What drove him on was the recurring image of Margaret Paterson, a pretty woman sullied by circumstance and destined for a life of drudgery. Touched by her plight, Leeming was determined to find the husband who'd beaten and abandoned her. The description he'd picked up of Paterson seemed to fit dozens of the men who walked past him in the street. What he'd been given at the police station was a list of haunts favoured by railwaymen. Many of the pubs – including the one already visited by Leeming – would be well known to Paterson. They'd be his natural habitat. Since the majority of them offered cheap accommodation, he might have taken refuge at one of the pubs.

Leeming had second thoughts about the advice. If Paterson had been involved in causing the train crash, he reasoned, would he seek out the company of railwaymen or would he go to ground elsewhere? The latter course of action seemed more likely. Instead of trailing around a sequence of pubs, therefore, Leeming decided to go back to the Gorbals as a first port of call. While he knew that

Paterson had left his wife for good, he hoped that she – aware of his habits and inclinations – might give him more reliable guidance. There was another reason that drew him back to the tenement. He wanted to see her again.

It was the same as before. As he walked through the stink and squalor of the slums, his top hat and frock coat excited a lot of jeers from undernourished children and outright abuse from unemployed men idling on corners. The sense of destitution and hopelessness made Leeming feel ashamed to be staying at The Angel Hotel. There was nothing angelic about the Gorbals. It was closer to the seventh circle of hell and, as such, more familiar territory for him. Leeming's career as a policeman had begun in uniform, pounding the beat in some of London's most run-down and crime-ridden districts. The Gorbals seemed like a darker version of the rookeries of St Giles.

When he located the house, it was some time before Margaret Paterson came to the door. She was not pleased to see him and shrank back, pulling the baby against her chest and enfolding it in protective arms.

'What're ye after?' she demanded, shrilly.

'There's no need to be alarmed, Mrs Paterson,' he said, trying to calm her with a smile. 'I simply need your help. We've been to the quarry where your husband used to work and he's no longer there. We believe he may be back in Glasgow.'

'Then ye can keep the devil awa' from me.'

'I don't think he'd come back here. What we need is some help in finding him. Does he have any relatives in the city, people he'd go to if he needed somewhere to stay? What about his parents, for instance?'

'They're both dead.'

'Does he have any brothers or sisters?'

'Aye, but they'd turn him away as soon as look at him.'

'Perhaps he has friends who'd offer him shelter.'

Her laugh was scornful. 'Lackey was guid at making friends,' she said, 'but even better at losing them. Nobody would take him in. He'd be too much trouble.'

'So where might he go?'

'Why should I care?'

'Please, Mrs Paterson,' he said as she tried to turn away. 'This is very important. I wouldn't have come here otherwise. I know you must be angry at the way your husband treated you and I deplore what he did. But I still think you're the one person who might be able to help. You know him better than anyone. Put yourself in his position. Where might he go?'

Her manner softened. Leeming's plea was sincere and heartfelt. He'd not come to harass or threaten her. He simply wanted information.

'There is one place . . .' she murmured.

'Yes?'

'He spent a lot of time there in the ould days. Sometimes, he'd stay the night and go to work from there the next morning.'

'Where is it, Mrs Paterson?'

'It's a pub called The Stag in Marigold Street,' she said with asperity, 'and I wish I could burn it to the ground. It was a gambling den. Lackey was there a' the time. It's where he lost his money and had us turned out o' our home. We didnae always live heer, ye ken. We'd a proper hoose once. It was gambling that sent us down into this foul pit.' She bit her lip. 'I've to go now, sir.'

'Wait,' he said, moved by the insight into her life and wanting to relieve her predicament in some way. 'I'm sorry I had to bother you again but what you've told me is very helpful and deserves a reward.' Fumbling in his pocket, he took out some coins and thrust them at her. 'Thank you very much, Mrs Paterson.'

Taking the money, she smiled for the first time and looked at him afresh. He was kind and generous. Her hostility melted into something closer to pleasure. As she studied his face, she wondered if she might earn more from him. Straightening her back and brushing her hair away from her forehead, she took a step closer to him.

'If ye'll gi' me a moment to put the bairn down,' she said, 'I'll invite ye in. It's no' a nice place but I'll make up for tha', sir, I promise.'

Leeming was shocked. During his time in uniform, he'd been offered favours by prostitutes many times and had found them easy to resist. This was different. Margaret Paterson was a respectable woman with none of the practised wiles of a streetwalker. Reduced to the situation she was in, however, she was desperate to make money by any means. Leeming felt embarrassed on her behalf.

Thrusting more money at her, he turned on his heel and marched away.

CHAPTER TEN

Work as a shepherd gave Jamie Farr ample time for reflection. While roaming the hills with his flock and his sheepdog, he was able both to do his job properly and reflect on his sudden change of fortune. He felt profoundly cheated. When he first spoke to the bearded railway policeman, he believed that he was in possession of information worthy of the advertised reward. In his ignorance, Farr hadn't realised that there were several stages to go through before the money was his. Despite their combined efforts, he and Bella Drew had been unable to read the handbill in its entirety. The lack of education which had bonded them had also let them down at a critical moment. Farr regretted having given his evidence before he fully understood what would happen to it.

Something else troubled him. The policeman had given him no guarantees. He'd simply gobbled up what the shepherd had to say then disappeared with it. Farr had disliked the man on sight, partly because he was employed by a despicable railway company but mainly because he inspired no trust. There was something mean and guileful about him. Farr sensed that he could be tricked out of the reward that was due to him. While the policeman knew how to find him, the shepherd had no idea how to make contact with McTurk. How would he ever know what use had been made of his evidence? If the policeman exploited it for his own purposes, Farr would be none the wiser. The notion that he'd been robbed continued to gnaw at his brain with sharp teeth.

At least he knew the name. When he saw that they were still clearing the debris from the site, he asked some of the men about the big policeman with the black beard and was told that he was Superintendent Rory McTurk. From the way they talked about him, he gathered that McTurk wielded his power with full force. He was not a person to cross. Farr paid no heed to the advice. In order to get what he felt was due to him, he was prepared to take on anyone. His problem – and it made him simmer with frustration – was finding a way to go about it.

A bark from Angus alerted him but there was no trouble with the sheep. What the dog had warned him about was a visitor. When he saw who it was, Farr went gambolling down the hill to intercept her. Bella Drew was striding along with the sun gilding her hair and the wind blowing it into cobwebs of spun gold. While his master was away, Angus patrolled the margins of the flock.

'What're ye doing heer?' asked Farr when he reached her.

'I wanted to see ye, Jamie.'

'Thank ye. I'm glad ye came.'

They stood in silence for a full minute, basking in the unspoken affection between them. Though neither understood it, they each felt a commitment to the other that excluded everything else. Bella tried to control her hair with a hand.

'It's windy up heer,' she said.

'I like it that way.'

'Aye, it makes you feel guid.'

He wanted to tell her that it was she who made *him* feel good but he lacked the confidence to say so. Instead, he settled for gazing at her with a blank smile.

'What happened to that thing ye showed me?' she wondered.

'Do ye mean the handbill?'

'Aye, I do.'

'I gi' my evidence to a p'liceman.'

She was thrilled. 'So ye'll get the money?'

'I hope so, Bella.'

'Just think what ye could do with it!'

'It's no' mine yet,' he said.

'But it'll come one day, won't it?'

Farr was cautious. 'It may or it may not.'

'You don't sound as if ye expect to get it,' she said, face falling.

'Ye never know.'

'What do ye have to do?'

The question was like a pinprick and it made him wince. It was the most worrying aspect of the situation. Even if his evidence led to the arrest of the wanted men, there'd be no prospect of any reward until they'd been tried and convicted. Farr would have to appear in court and the very thought made him shudder. As a key witness, he'd be questioned closely. He wasn't at all sure that he could survive the ordeal. McTurk, by contrast, would be very accustomed to judicial procedure. He'd have appeared in court as a witness many times. What was to stop him pretending that Farr's evidence was really his own and reaping the benefit accordingly? It was the kind of deception of which he'd looked capable. Farr felt the gnawing sensation in his brain once more. Standing beside Bella, he vowed that he wouldn't let anyone deprive them of their future together. When he made his decision, he blurted it out.

'I've to go to Glasgow,' he said.

When he walked into Nairn Craig's office, Colbeck was immediately reminded of Edward Tallis. The office was the same size as that of the superintendent and the furniture was practically identical. Most telling of all was the box of cigars on the desk. The only thing missing was the hectoring voice of Tallis himself.

'I gather that you and Inspector Rae have been busy,' said Craig.

'Yes,' replied Colbeck. 'We spoke to Mr Weir of the NBR.'

'I'm surprised that you could get a word in edgeways. Weir likes the sound of his own voice. His idea of conversation is an extended monologue.'

'Oh, to be fair, he did hear us out.'

'How did he respond?'

Colbeck gave him an attenuated account of the interview with the other general manager. Craig was simultaneously amused and annoyed, diverted by a description of the way that Weir had lost his temper and infuriated that the man had issued a robust denial of any involvement in the crime by NBR employees.

'While we were trying to repair the track,' he complained, 'the NBR was taking business away from us. They *must* have blood on their hands.'

'Inspector Rae and Superintendent McTurk support that view.'

'Do you still think that this fellow, Paterson, is a more likely culprit?'

'Why else would he give up his job in the quarry on the eve of the crash?'

'I wish I knew, Inspector.'

'Not that we must place too much emphasis on Paterson,' said Colbeck. 'Other possibilities must be looked into. It could be the work of some other disgruntled former employee of yours or it might even be someone with a rooted objection to railways. That's what prompted a train robbery we once investigated. The man behind it had an obsessive dislike of the whole system. Rightly or wrongly, he blamed the railway for the death of his wife.'

'This whole business is so maddening,' said Craig. 'We have too many potential suspects. Before we know it, there'll be other names to add to the list.' He picked up a sheet of paper and offered it to his visitor. 'We must include the author of this charming little billet-doux.'

Colbeck took the letter. It was unsigned. Written in bold capitals, it ordered the company to cease running trains on a Sunday. The crash had been designed as a warning. If the Caledonian persisted in polluting the Sabbath, worse was to come.

'It's not the only anonymous threat we've had,' said Craig. 'Some have been so vile that I tore them up and threw them away.'

'That's a pity,' said Colbeck. 'They might have been useful evidence.'

'They were the work of cranks, Inspector.'

'How do you know?'

'They were couched in language so wild and extreme.'

'And what about this?' asked Colbeck, holding up the letter. 'Do you consider this to be the work of cranks?'

'No – it smacks of misguided sabbatarians.'

'Have they given you much trouble in the past?'

'They've caused us a lot of inconvenience, principally at stations like Glasgow and Edinburgh. At first it was limited to demonstrations – dozens of people waving banners in the faces of our passengers every Sunday. More recently, however, it's taken a rather disturbing turn.'

'Oh?'

'Someone has climbed inside the sheds and daubed the engines with slogans. They're a devil to clean off. We have nightwatchmen on duty but it nevertheless goes on. These people are fanatics, Inspector.'

'Have none of them ever been caught?'

'Not as yet – that's why they're getting bolder.'

'Are they bold enough to cause a train crash?'

Craig shivered. 'I've a horrible feeling they soon will be.'

Ian Dalton was astonished at what he saw. After luncheon at the home of Tam and Flora Howie, he was taken to a shed at the bottom of the garden. It was protected by two large padlocks. When Howie used keys to open them, he flung open the door and let his visitor view the display. It was not the many tins of white paint that made Dalton gasp in surprise. It was the collection of items stolen from railway premises. Station signs, fire buckets, shovels, baskets, posters and dozens of other things were there in abundance. There was even a porter's trolley. Howie and his wife were clearly accomplished thieves.

'Where did you get it all?' asked Dalton, examining a trunk.

'We picked it up wherever we found it,' said Howie. 'I used the trolley to purloin that trunk. Flora distracted the porter while I did so.'

'That's my role,' she said. 'I take the attention away from Tam. It always works.' She patted the trunk. 'Whoever owned this would have complained bitterly about its loss and the porter would have taken the blame for the disappearance of the trolley. You've no idea how easy it is to steal things in a crowd.'

Dalton gave a half-laugh. 'I don't know what to say,' he told them. 'I suppose that I ought to condemn theft as a crime but your activities have been in a good cause. That excuses it, in my opinion.'

'You're not disgusted, then?' asked Howie.

'On the contrary, I'm full of admiration.'

'We have a small museum here.'

'It doesn't just irritate the railway companies,' said Flora. 'It spreads confusion. When there are no signs there, passengers don't know which way to go. Instead of taking them, Howie has tried a new trick now. He changes them over to cause even more chaos.'

Dalton surveyed the collection and let out a whistle of amazement.

'It must have taken you ages to accumulate all this,' he said.

'We've been at it for months.'

'When do you do it?'

'Most of the time, it's in broad daylight. Well,' she said, spreading her arms, 'do Tam and I *look* like a pair of unscrupulous thieves?'

'No, you look exactly what you are – decent, honest, law-abiding citizens who wouldn't dream of committing a crime.'

'It's not a crime to defend the Sabbath,' asserted Howie.

'Quite so – the end more than justifies the means.'

'We decided that a long time ago, Ian.'

'So it seems. I'm sorry I've been so tardy in reaching the same conclusion.'

Howie put a warning finger to his lips. 'The rest of the congregation must never know, mind you.'

'Oh, no – they'd never believe what I'm seeing.'

'Gregor Hines would have a heart attack if he were here,' said Flora.

'I disagree,' said her husband. 'He's made of sterner stuff than that. Gregor would run to the nearest police station and betray us. We'd be drummed out of the kirk even though we're fighting on its behalf. He's an old fox, cunning enough to suspect that I might have been leaving messages in white paint on locomotives. That, I fancy, might just be acceptable to him, but not *this*,' he added with an expansive wave of the arm. 'He'd see our booty as the fruit of unpardonable criminality.'

'I see it as a lesson in how to strike effectively,' said Dalton.

'We're glad that you approve, Ian.'

'It's quite remarkable. Both of you have shown such bravery.'

'It's not bravery,' said Flora. 'It's a simple case of belief. Tam and I are guided from above. I'm sure it's the main reason we've never been caught. God has pointed the way and we've taken it.'

'The question is this,' said Howie, gazing into Dalton's eyes. 'Have we scared you off or are you ready to assist us?'

'I can't wait to start,' declared the other. 'Just tell me what to do.'

'Come back tonight, Ian. We'll see if you have any artistic gifts. When it's dark enough, we'll slip into an engine shed and leave a few messages in white paint. That's as good a starting place as any.'

Dalton laughed. 'This is so exciting – we're on a mission!'

Leeming took an age to find the right place. Language was the problem. Unable to translate the thick Glaswegian accents of the people whose advice he sought, he didn't know where to go. He learnt that there was more than one Marigold Street in the city and several pubs called The Stag. When he finally stumbled on the place he was after, he collapsed into a chair and ordered a pint of beer and a meat pie. Sustenance came before detection. Besides, he decided, he wanted to settle in before he began asking questions.

That had been his mistake at the pub near the railway station. He'd shown his hand too early and disclosed his identity. He wouldn't mention that he was a detective this time. His enquiries needed to be more casual.

As he ate his pie and washed it down with sips of beer, he thought about Margaret Paterson. Compassion welled up in him. When she'd offered him her body, she'd done so with the clumsiness and diffidence of someone who'd never done such a thing before. She'd been reacting to force of circumstance. What had driven her to live in the Gorbals was her husband's addiction to gambling. Leeming was sitting in the very place where, reportedly, Paterson had lost a lot of money. Yet the visitor could see no sign of any card games or other form of gambling. It looked like any other pub, a large room furnished with tables and chairs at which patrons could sit. Several were simply doing what Leeming himself was doing, eating, drinking and minding their own business. Others were engaged in lively discussions. Nobody gave him a second glance.

When he finished his meal and emptied his tankard, he drifted across to the bar. He was in luck. Instead of having to interpret what he felt was an alien tongue, he could talk in his own language. The landlord hailed from Devon and his voice had a pleasing West Country burr. It enabled Leeming to open the conversation.

'You sound as if you're a long way from home,' he said.

'I am,' returned the other. 'I married a girl from Dundee. We decided to move there but we only got as far as Glasgow. What about you, sir?'

'Oh, I'm just a visitor. But you must like it here.'

'It's a big city. It's got everything we want.'

The landlord was a short, barrel-chested man in his forties.

Though he was smiling benignly, he was already harbouring suspicions about Leeming.

'Where are you from?' he asked.

'I live in London.'

'What brings you here?'

'I've always wanted to come to Scotland,' lied Leeming, 'and take the opportunity of looking up a few old friends. In fact, that's why I popped in here. I was told that one of them used to come here quite often.'

'Oh – and who might that be, sir?'

'Lackey Paterson.'

The landlord pursed his lips. 'I've never heard of him.'

'But he came here regularly.'

'So do lots of other people. There'll be a hundred or more in here this evening. I can't keep track of all their names. We had a Will Paterson but we've not seen him for months. What does this other man look like?'

As he tried to describe him, Leeming realised that he was giving himself away, claiming to be a friend of someone whom he'd never met and was therefore unable to describe in convincing detail. He clutched at a defining characteristic.

'Lackey was very fond of a game of cards,' he said.

'Is that so?' replied the landlord, now on the defensive.

'He came here to play. You must have a room set aside for that.'

'You're mistaken, sir. I don't allow gambling in here. It leads to fights.'

'I'm certain that this was the place.' Leeming looked upwards. 'Do you have any accommodation here?'

'Were you looking for somewhere to stay?'

'I was just wondering if, by chance, Lackey Paterson had taken a room.'

117

'Don't you have an address for him, sir? It seems very strange that you'd come such a long distance to see someone you didn't know how to find.'

'I've been to his address,' explained Leeming, 'but it seems that he's left his wife. It was she who gave me the name of this place.'

'Well, he's not here,' said the landlord, bluntly. 'I can't help you.'

Leeming knew that the man was holding something back and he cursed himself for being caught out so easily. Since he could get nothing out of the landlord, he decided that the sensible thing to do was to beat a retreat and keep an eye on the place from a safe distance. If Lackey Paterson was not already there, he might come later. It was a possibility in which it was worth investing time.

Although he was a long way away, Edward Tallis nevertheless insisted on having regular reports about the progress that his detectives were making in Scotland. He needed proof that sending them there was necessary. Colbeck therefore penned an account carefully tailored to give the impression that they were making headway. He did, however, warn that the investigation still had some way to run. It was enough to placate the superintendent. In the same mailbag would be a letter to Madeleine. That, too, contained an outline description of the case. Colbeck missed her badly so early in the marriage. Being apart from her for the first time let him see just how much he'd gained in making her his wife. It had given his life more stability, more purpose and an unlimited stock of love on which to draw.

Yet as soon as he'd finished his letter to her, Colbeck dismissed Madeleine from his consciousness. He needed to concentrate on the case in hand. He was making use of the office that the general manager had put at his disposal at the Caledonian headquarters. It was small and nondescript but more than adequate. The only problem was that John Mudie kept interrupting him to offer his services. Colbeck turned him politely away each time. He was disappointed that Leeming hadn't returned with news of Lackey Paterson but knew that the sergeant wouldn't abandon the hunt until he had something to report.

As he reviewed the case, the unappealing countenance of Rory McTurk rose up before him. Though he disliked the man, Colbeck accepted that he was not without ability. If the railway policeman had, in fact, acquired some crucial evidence, he was duty-bound to pass it on to Inspector Rae as well as to Colbeck. Yet no word had come. Rae was certain that McTurk knew something of import. It was time for Colbeck to confront the man. At last having something for John Mudie to do, he asked him to locate the bearded superintendent. Mudie was delighted to be given the task and bounded out of the building. Within half an hour, he was back again.

'He's not at work, Inspector Colbeck,' he said, apologetically. 'It seems that Superintendent McTurk has taken the day off.'

McTurk was sorry to remove his uniform. It gave him a sense of status. But he needed to move about the city with some anonymity. Accordingly he wore a suit and a hat. The easiest way to track down the two brothers would be to involve the police. They would have the resources to mount a proper search. But it would allow them to take credit for something that McTurk wanted to keep for himself. His reasoning was simple. If the two men who stayed the night at the wayside inn had indeed been responsible for the train crash, they were unlikely to be raw newcomers to the world of crime. They'd be hired for their experience and their expertise.

It was more than possible therefore that they were known to the police. Even if they hadn't been convicted, they'd have brushed against the forces of law and order.

That belief took McTurk off to visit his uncle, Toby, a grizzled veteran in his sixties who was retired from the Glasgow police and who spent his days reminiscing about what he considered to be his many triumphs in uniform. They met at the uncle's house. Though the older man looked frail and had a nasty cough, his faculties were still intact. After an exchange of pleasantries, McTurk asked him how good his memory was. His uncle insisted that he recalled every villain with whom he ever dealt. In fact, he was renowned for his encyclopaedic memory.

'Then let me see if you remember two brothers,' said McTurk. 'I don't know their surnames but they're called Ewen and Duncan. They'd be no older than thirty and they'd be the kind of ruffians who'd do anything if there was money in it.'

He went on to describe the two men but his uncle soon stopped him. Unlike his nephew, his Glaswegian vowels hadn't been softened by long years of living in England. He bared his few remaining teeth.

'Ask me something really hard,' he croaked.

McTurk was pleased. 'You *know* who they are?'

'I ken two brothers wi' the names tha' gi' me.'

'Who are they, Uncle Toby?'

'Ewen and Duncan Usher – I arrested the bastards for filching apples from a greengrocer's. It was all o' fifteen years ago. Even at tha' age, they were vicious little brutes.' He looked at his visitor. 'Why do ye want 'em, Rory? Have they been stealing things from the railway?'

'Yes,' replied McTurk, 'something like that.'

* * *

Jamie Farr was in a quandary. Needing to go to Glasgow, he was not at all sure how to get there. His first instinct was to walk but that meant tramping over sixty miles. It was an impossible distance. Riding there on a horse was also out of the question. Farr was a poor horseman and, in any case, had no access to a mount. A horse would never get him there in one journey. He'd have to stay overnight and press on the next day. That would be asking too much of his father, keeping an eye on his son's flock. Only one mode of transport was viable and that was the one he hated. Ironically – if he could overcome his prejudices – it could actually solve his problem. A train from Wamphray would take him all the way to Glasgow.

After much deliberation, he agreed to compromise. He was grateful that he'd done so because the stationmaster was very helpful. He told the shepherd that the best way to find Superintendent McTurk was to go to the headquarters of the Caledonian Railway. He even provided him with an address. Yet the information didn't make him look more favourably on the railway. He still remembered the way that some of his flock had been crushed to death under the wheels of a train. Their murder had been unforgivable. He'd rejoiced in the train crash which had halted traffic on the line close to him and felt that he had a kinship with those who caused it. Faced with the prospect of gaining a huge reward, however, he was ready to trade evidence that would lead to their arrest. Bella Drew came first.

As the train came into the station, he stepped back apprehensively. Belching smoke and hissing steam, the engine frightened him. The carriages swayed and rattled alarmingly. He feared for his safety. Yet he had to go through with it. Having told Bella where he had to go, he couldn't draw back now. Climbing into a carriage with trepidation, he selected a seat and perched on the very edge of it, back upright and body tense. When the train set off again, he was clenching his teeth. It was not until they were halfway there that he began to relax. While he couldn't bring himself to enjoy the journey, it no longer troubled him so much. He was able to think for the first time about what he had to do when he reached his destination.

Farr was lost in Glasgow. Wearing his shepherd's smock and a look of total bewilderment, he didn't know where to turn. There were so many people and such pulsating noise. Having spent all his life on lonely hillsides, he felt completely at sea in the maelstrom of a big city. It was another stationmaster who came to his rescue. When he heard what Farr wanted, he gave him instructions. The shepherd was able to find his way to the building he was after. At first nobody believed his story and they tried to turn him away but he threatened to stay at the door indefinitely until he was allowed to see Superintendent McTurk. In the end, it was John Mudie who sensed that the lad had something of importance to say. Inviting him in, he took Farr along to the office occupied by Colbeck. The shepherd was left alone with the Railway Detective. Facing the man in charge of the investigation, Farr was at first tongue-tied.

'Why don't you sit down?' invited Colbeck with a smile. 'There's no rush. Speak when you're ready and not before.'

Farr lowered himself onto a chair. 'Aye, sir. Thank ye.'

'If you've come all this way, it must be important.'

'It is. I need to talk to the p'liceman wi' the black beard?'

'Do you mean Superintendent McTurk?'

'Aye, sir, that's the mahn.'

'What business do you have with the superintendent?'

In response to Colbeck's genuine interest in what he had to say, Farr's nervousness slowly ebbed away. He explained about the

122

meeting he'd had with McTurk and repeated the evidence he'd given earlier. Colbeck immediately saw a connection between the information and McTurk's absence from work. The new evidence had the ring of truth. Straying outside the boundary of his duties, the railway policeman was apparently acting upon it.

'He told me I'd no' get the money till they were behind bars,' said Farr.

'Yes, that's right,' agreed Colbeck.

'But I'd a feelin' he'd keep the reward for hi'self.'

'Oh, he won't be allowed to do that, I promise you. If what you've told me *does* lead to the conviction of those responsible for that crash, then the reward should rightly come to you. We've had lots of people offering us information,' said Colbeck, 'but you're the first one who's been completely honest.'

'I only told ye what I saw, sir. I've guid eyesight.'

'I'm grateful for that. Now, then, let me take down the details of how to find you.' He reached for a notebook and pencil. 'I daresay that coming to Glasgow must have been a nightmare to someone like you.'

'Aye, sir. It's like a madhoose.'

'Then I'll send you straight back to the serenity of the countryside.'

Colbeck made a note of his name and address then shook his hand in gratitude. Farr was reassured. Unlike McTurk, he felt, the man could be trusted. He hadn't tried to hassle the shepherd or to make false promises. About to leave, Farr turned to him.

'Will you tell Superintendent McTurk that I came here?' he asked.

'Oh, yes,' said Colbeck with a meaningful glint. 'The superintendent and I will be having a very long talk.'

* * *

123

Victor Leeming had been there for hours now and his legs were aching. He'd shifted his position at regular intervals so that he could keep The Stag under observation from different angles. People came and left the pub but none of them fitted the description he had of Lackey Paterson. The landlord had recognised the name. There was no doubt about that. Why was he shielding the man? And why did he deny that no card games took place under his roof when Paterson's wife had called it a gambling den? Lamps were lit in an upstairs room. Leeming wondered if that was where Paterson had gambled away so much of his wages. Some of it had also gone on drink. Very little of the money seemed to have found its way to Margaret Paterson. It was no wonder that she was so embittered.

Light was slowly being drained out of the sky, enabling him to lurk in the shadows. The Stag was doing brisk business and, even from a distance, he could hear the sounds of jollity. His vigil eventually bore fruit. A man walked past, his face momentarily illumined by a street lamp. In every particular, he fitted the description Leeming had of Lackey Paterson. The sergeant tensed himself for action. He watched the man go into The Stag with the air of an habitué of the place. Leeming walked slowly towards the pub. Before he got close to it, however, he saw the man put his head outside the door to look in both directions. When he caught sight of Leeming, he took to his heels and raced off down the street. The detective went after him.

It was a hectic chase. What gave Leeming extra speed was the conviction that he'd at last found Paterson. Apparently, the man had come to the pub, been warned by the landlord that someone was after him and decided to run for cover. Leeming reasoned that, if he had nothing to hide, he'd have no reason to bolt from a stranger. Knowing the area, his quarry was able to take him on a twisting journey through the backstreets. Their hasty footsteps echoed in the gloom. Leeming got closer and closer, calling on all his reserves of strength and lung power. Breathing heavily, the man ahead of him was slowing down and clutching at his side. Unable to outrun the pursuit, he turned to face Leeming and reached inside his coat for a knife. He had no time to use it. Diving at him with full force, Leeming knocked him to the ground and slammed his head against the hard pavement. The knife rolled into the gutter.

'Got you!' gasped Leeming with a grin of triumph.

CHAPTER ELEVEN

McTurk was jubilant. Thanks to his uncle, he'd identified the two men he was after and, after a diligent search, found out where they lived. At that point, he was forced to accept that he'd be no match for two strong young men. They would be dangerous. If they were ruthless enough to commit such a terrible crime, they surely wouldn't surrender without a fight. And they might well be armed. He needed help and – more important, in his mind – he needed his uniform. That always instilled confidence in him. As a railway policeman, his powers were circumscribed and he always yearned to go beyond them. This was his opportunity. He could secure two arrests, solve a heinous crime and win plaudits from the press. What he'd savour most was the moment when Nairn Craig handed over four hundred pounds. A little of it would be passed on to his uncle. None of it would ever reach Jamie Farr.

He had no qualms about casting the shepherd aside. The youth had provided vital evidence but, on his own, he'd never have been able to make proper use of it. McTurk had done the detective work alone and that, in his opinion, entitled him to be the sole recipient of the reward. Farr would be kept in complete ignorance, tending his flock and waiting in vain for word from the railway policeman. He'd never know the true outcome. In any case, McTurk believed, a dim-witted country lad didn't deserve the money. He'd have no idea what to do with it. McTurk, however, knew exactly how to put it to good use. It would transform his life and raise his expectations. All that he had to do was to make two arrests and he'd achieve instant fame.

As he turned into the street where he lived, he lengthened his stride and whistled cheerfully. His success would have many beneficial consequences, none more satisfying than his proven ability to do what the Railway Detective had failed to do. He longed to see the look of dismay on Robert Colbeck's face when he heard what had happened. In the event, he saw the face much sooner than he anticipated. When he let himself into the house, his wife was in the passageway in a state of high anxiety. Standing behind her was the very man about whom he'd just been thinking.

'Welcome back,' said Colbeck with an icy smile. 'We need to talk.'

When he handed the man over at the police station, Leeming was disappointed. His captive was not, after all, Lackey Paterson. He was a petty criminal, wanted for a string of thefts. Tipped off by the landlord of The Stag that a detective was hanging about nearby, the man had flown into a panic and left the pub. When he saw Leeming, he'd hared off in the opposite direction, only to be overhauled after a long chase. He'd not only been arrested, he was nursing a head wound that throbbed incessantly. The fact that he'd been prepared to use a knife would tell against him in court. From the effusive way in which the police thanked Leeming, he could see how glad they were to have the man in custody at last. A prolific thief had been taken off the streets of Glasgow.

Leeming blamed himself for his folly. In alerting the landlord of the pub, he'd lost all chance of catching Lackey Paterson. If the man *had* been staying there – or had turned up later – he would have been warned that an English detective was on his tail. Instead of taking a decisive step in the investigation, Leeming had wasted his efforts on someone who had no connection whatsoever with it. In flattening his man to the ground, he'd scuffed his own trousers and torn his coat. His top hat had gone flying down the street. The chase had not only exhausted him. Leeming had been left with a general feeling of discomfort and a face that glistened with sweat. The euphoria of the arrest had been utterly dissipated.

To continue his surveillance of the pub was clearly futile. Paterson would never be caught there. Nor was a raid on the place advisable. All that he could do was to establish that gambling took place there and he already knew that. Leeming had no grounds to arrest the landlord and every reason to keep away from him. He'd get nothing but blank resistance from that quarter. It was time to admit defeat and renew his efforts on the following day. There was the vague hope that the police might help to find Paterson for him but he wasn't at all sure that they'd be looking for the man with any commitment. They already had enough on their hands, trying to police a violent city with insufficient men to exert any real control.

Shoulders sagging and knees still smarting from the contact with the pavement, he left the police station and looked for a cab to take him back to The Angel Hotel. He suddenly felt lonely and bereft. He desperately needed Estelle and the children but the joys of family life seemed a million miles away.

'Where have you been?' asked Colbeck, watching him shrewdly.

'I went out for a walk,' replied McTurk.

'I'm pleased to hear that you're well enough to do so. The

excuse you gave for taking a day off was that you were unwell. I see no signs of illness.'

'I improved as the day wore on.'

'I wonder why that was.'

The sardonic note annoyed McTurk. He was aggrieved that Colbeck had dared to come to his house to interrogate him and resolved to tell whatever lies were necessary. His wife – a short, stringy woman with a wrinkled face and wayward brown hair – knew nothing of what her husband had been doing and couldn't unwittingly betray him. McTurk simply had to maintain a solid front.

'What right have you got to come here?' he demanded, taking the initiative.

'I wish to solve a crime,' said Colbeck.

'So do I, Inspector. We all want the villains arrested.'

'You misunderstand me. The crime that takes precedence at this moment is one of theft, compounded by fraud. I'm talking about evidence being stolen from one source then passed off as your own.'

McTurk goggled. 'I don't understand.'

'Oh, I think you understand me very well.'

'Are you *accusing* me of something?'

'Yes, I am.'

'But you've no call to do so.'

'Why waste time?' said Colbeck, wearily. 'Put this pretence aside.'

'There's no pretence involved. I resent you coming here.'

'And I resent your hindering this investigation,' came the stinging retort. 'People have been killed and immense damage has been inflicted on the company that employs you. Yet all that interests you is getting your hands on the reward money by means of deception.'

'I'm sorry,' said McTurk, squaring his shoulders. 'I must ask you to leave.'

'He came to see me, Superintendent. A young shepherd named Jamie Farr told me what he'd first told you.' Colbeck lifted a questioning eyebrow. 'Now do you realise why I'm here?'

McTurk was dumbfounded. He and Colbeck stood facing each other in the parlour of the house. During the stunned silence, McTurk's wife entered.

'Should I offer the gentleman some refreshment?' she asked, tentatively.

'We won't be staying,' said Colbeck, politely.

'Oh, I see – very good, sir.'

Hands waving apologetically, she withdrew to the kitchen. Her husband, meanwhile, was trying to think of a way to extricate himself from an awkward situation. Deprived of his uniform, he felt completely powerless. For his part, Colbeck was interested to see the man in a domestic setting. McTurk was so wedded to his career as a railway policeman that it never occurred to the detective that he had a wife and two small sons. Once she'd admitted the visitor, Mrs McTurk had hustled the boys upstairs. Since they were unusually obedient for their age, Colbeck deduced that McTurk ran the home with a rod of iron. His wife certainly had the beaten look of a woman who'd never challenge her husband.

Hands behind his back, Colbeck fixed him with a penetrating stare.

'What do you have to say for yourself?' he asked.

'You've been misinformed, Inspector.'

'Are you claiming that the shepherd lied to me?'

'No, no,' said McTurk, 'I'm sure that he spoke as honestly as he could. I took him for a good, reliable witness. Where he led you astray was in his belief that I intended to deprive him of his reward, because I swear to you that I had no such intention. Once the men had been caught, I'd have insisted that the money went to young Jamie.'

'Then why did you say nothing to Inspector Rae and to me?'

'I wanted to clarify certain details before doing so.'

'You went in search of two men and four hundred pounds,' said Colbeck, glaring at him, 'and you weren't prepared to share the glory or the money with anyone else.'

'You can't prove that.'

'The proof is standing right in front of me.'

McTurk attempted to brazen it out but Colbeck knew too much. He was also extraordinarily intimidating in the narrow confines of the parlour. McTurk was bigger and broader but he seemed to shrink into insignificance. Before entering the police service, Colbeck had been a barrister and knew how to grow in stature during a cross-examination. Without saying a single word, he exerted intense pressure on the railway policeman. McTurk eventually capitulated, eyes closing and head dropping.

'Right,' said Colbeck, 'let's hear the truth, shall we?'

When he got back to the hotel, Leeming felt even more uncomfortable. His dirt-spattered trousers and torn coat made the staff look at him askance. Before he could repair to his room to change, he was handed a note from Colbeck. It summoned him as a matter of urgency. Forgetting all about his appearance and his annoyance with himself, he signalled another cab and headed for the Caledonian headquarters. The note had revived him. Colbeck would not have sent for him unless there'd been a dramatic development in the case. The capture of Lackey Paterson no longer dominated his mind and might even prove to be irrelevant.

Reaching his destination, he went to the room used by the inspector as an office and found that Nairn Craig and Rory McTurk were also there. At first, Leeming didn't recognise the railway policeman because he was not in uniform. A suit robbed the man entirely of his power and dignity. Craig was beaming with delight but McTurk was scowling. Colbeck explained the situation.

'The superintendent has been doing our job for us,' he said with a sideways glance at McTurk. 'He's not only identified two suspects, he's established their whereabouts.'

'Oh,' said Leeming without artifice, 'congratulations to you, Superintendent!'

'Thank you,' muttered McTurk.

'Congratulations are not entirely in order,' warned Colbeck, 'but let that rest for the moment. The point is that the superintendent has provided information that may turn out to be crucial. For that reason, I felt that he was entitled to be there at the moment of arrest. Apart from anything else, we might need him.'

'How many arrests are we likely to make, sir?' asked Leeming.

'We are after two brothers – Ewen and Duncan Usher.'

'Do we *know* that they were behind the crash?'

'There's a strong possibility that it was orchestrated by them.'

'Are they in league with Lackey Paterson, by any chance?'

'I've no answer to that.'

'We can start asking questions once we've got them locked up,' said Craig, barely able to contain his excitement. 'Acting on evidence received, we've finally got a chance to solve the crime. Good luck, gentlemen!'

'Thank you, sir,' said Colbeck.

'Are you sure you don't need more men?'

'Three against two puts the odds very much in our favour, Mr

Craig, and we do have the element of surprise. That's why I didn't want the police involved. The sight of a uniform is a warning signal to any villain.'

'Ah,' said Leeming, 'so *that's* why the superintendent is in a suit.'

'Yes,' observed Colbeck, 'and I'm bound to say that it's a little smarter than your own attire, Sergeant. Patently, there's a story behind the torn coat and scuffed trousers. You can tell it to me on the way.'

'Arrest these monsters,' urged Craig. 'Show them no mercy.'

'Don't raise your hopes too high, sir.'

Nothing could dampen the general manager's joy. 'The evidence is quite irrefutable,' he said. 'These brothers are plainly guilty. The sooner they're both in custody, the better.'

Though Ewen Usher was the older of the two brothers, it was Duncan who made the decisions for the two of them. He had more intelligence and far more imagination. Ewen had strength and daring on his side but little native cunning. He relied on his younger brother to plan their crimes and to handle any money resulting from them. They were tall, muscular men in their late twenties with faces half-hidden by straggly beards. Ewen Usher had been drinking heavily. As his brother counted out the money into two piles, he leant over him and belched.

'Ye've more than me,' he complained.

'I *deserve* more, Ewen.'

'But I took the risks. I could've been killed.'

'Ye made sure that ye *weren't*,' said Duncan, sitting back in his seat. 'Ye've too much to live for – guzzling beer and chasing lassies. What's the name of tha' latest wee thing?'

'Never ye mind,' said Ewen, sourly.

'But I do mind. When ye've done wi' her, pass her on to me.'

'When I've done wi' her, she'll be half-dead.'

They shared a crude laugh. Ewen had a coarse charm that somehow excited young women and he took full advantage of it. Duncan was less appealing to the fair sex and, in spite of many attempts, failed to emulate his brother's success. They lived in a terraced house in one of the rougher districts of the city but their activities were not restricted to Glasgow. In search of prey, they roamed much farther afield.

'Where do we go next?' asked Ewen.

'It'll take us time to spend this money first.'

'I'll drink ma way through it in a fortnight.'

'No, ye won't,' said Duncan, firmly. 'I need ye sober and so do the lassies. Ye dinna want to get a name for brewer's droop, do ye?'

'Beer doesnae affect ma cock.'

'It affects your brain, mahn, and tha' needs to stay clear.'

Ewen was interested. 'Ye've another plan, haven't ye?'

'Aye, I have.'

'Is it to do wi' the railways again?'

'It is, Ewen. There's more rich pickings to be had.'

'Where will it be next time?'

'Wait and see.'

Having counted out all the money, Duncan scooped up his share of it.

Before he gave the signal to move in, Colbeck took time to study the position of the house. It was halfway down a narrow street. At the rear of the houses was a tiny garden terminated by a lane. It gave the dwellings two points of entry and exit. Having sent Leeming down the lane, Colbeck waited until he was in place before walking down the street itself. McTurk had been told to approach the house from the other end. They met in the middle of the street. Colbeck rapped on the door. The response was immediate. A face appeared momentarily in the front window then vanished. They heard raised voices inside the house then another face looked out of the window before withdrawing at speed. Colbeck banged on the door with an authoritative fist but there was no hope of being admitted. In fact, a bolt was pushed home in open defiance. Colbeck nodded to McTurk.

'You know what to do,' he said.

The brothers argued vociferously. Having courted danger for so long, they'd always known that their luck would run out one day and that the police would hound them. The burly man outside their front door was an image of law and order. The dandy beside him would never venture into their district unless he came on official business. Fearing arrest, they debated what to do.

'Let's stay and fight,' cried Ewen, pulling a cudgel from a drawer.

'No,' said Duncan, 'we'll make a run for it.'

'Are ye scared o' two men?'

'There may be more of them.'

Ewen waved the cudgel. 'I'll smash all their heeds in.'

But it was their front door that was about to be smashed in. A first kick made it rattle on its hinges. A second one splintered the timber. The bolt that Duncan had pushed home went sailing down the passageway as a shoulder hit the door with thunderous force. It resolved the argument.

'Ger oot of heer, ye fool!' yelled Duncan.

'Aye,' said Ewen, gathering up his money from the table and thrusting it into his pocket. 'I'll meet up wi' ye later.'

Dashing to the back door, he let himself out into the garden. Duncan chose a different mode of escape, running up the stairs and locking himself into his bedroom. The assault on the front door continued.

It was Colbeck who delivered the final kick. Aiming for the lock, he used his heel to jab at it as hard as he could. The lock gave way and the door swung open. As he rushed in, Colbeck saw that the back door was ajar.

'One of them fled into the garden,' he said. 'Go and help the sergeant.'

'What about you, sir?'

'I heard footsteps on the upstairs.'

'Don't you want my assistance?' asked McTurk.

'No,' said Colbeck, grimly, 'he's all mine.'

Ewen Usher didn't get far. Moving the bolt on the garden gate, he expected to make his escape down the lane but someone was waiting for him. As he hurried out, he was tripped up by the outstretched leg of Victor Leeming. Falling heavily, Ewen hit the ground with a thud and unleashed a torrent of expletives. Before he could get up, he found himself held from behind in a vice-like grip. In spite of his power and the rage that fuelled it, he couldn't dislodge his assailant. Leeming slowly increased the pressure until resistance began to fade. McTurk came lumbering through the garden door and took in the situation.

'Can I be of assistance, Sergeant?' he said.

'Yes – help me to get the handcuffs on him.'

'Which one of the brothers is this?'

Leeming grinned. 'The one I just caught.'

* * *

Colbeck, meanwhile, was confronted by another locked door. Putting his hat aside, he used his shoulder against the timber. After the third blow, the door flew open to reveal an empty bedroom. There was nowhere to hide. The room contained little more than a bed, a chair and a wardrobe too small and rickety to conceal anyone. Covered in filth, the window was shut tight. Nobody had tried to climb through it. Colbeck soon realised where the fugitive had gone. What gave him away was the dust on the bed sheet. It had come down like snowfall when the trapdoor in the ceiling had been opened. Evidently, one of the brothers had clambered up there.

Colbeck went after him. Taking off his coat, he stood on the bed so that he could reach the trapdoor, pushing it up and disturbing another flurry of dust. He had to brush it out of his eyes. He then took a firm grip on the sides of the opening and hauled himself up into the roof space. Colbeck found himself in a long, black cavern that stretched in both directions over the adjoining houses. The fugitive might be anywhere. Colbeck waited until his eyes grew more accustomed to the dark. He could hear mice scuttling to and fro. More significantly, he could hear someone breathing.

'I'd advise you to surrender, Mr Usher,' he said.

There was no reply but someone moved slightly to his left.

'I'm Inspector Colbeck of the Metropolitan Police Force and I'm acting on behalf of the Caledonian Railway. I believe that you can help me in my enquiries.'

Still no answer came but a vague shape was slowly emerging nearby. Before he could make it out properly, Colbeck was under attack. Duncan Usher flung himself at the inspector, knocking him backwards and going for his throat. As strong hands tightened around his neck, Colbeck had to fight for his life.

* * *

When they dragged him back into the house, Ewen Usher was still spitting with fury. Holding him by the scruff of his neck, McTurk forced him down into a chair then stood beside him with his hands on the man's shoulders. Leeming was diverted by the commotion from above. He went quickly upstairs and stood in the open doorway of the front bedroom. Noise, dust and grunts of pain were coming from the roof space. He could hear the sounds of bodies rolling over and of heavy blows being exchanged. Wanting to go to Colbeck's aid, he saw that it would be a difficult exercise. He was not as lithe and athletic as the inspector. Getting up into the roof space would take a real effort. Leeming was still wondering how to go about it when the problem was eliminated. Instead of waiting for assistance, Colbeck came down in search of it. There was a loud crash as the ceiling opened wide and two bodies hurtled down onto the bed in an avalanche of lath and plaster.

As they continued to fight, it was clear that Colbeck had the upper hand, grappling with his opponent before delivering a series of telling punches. Leeming stepped in to hold the groggy Duncan face down while Colbeck pulled back the man's arms and snapped the handcuffs on him. Leeming yanked their prisoner to the floor and pinned him down with a foot in the middle of his back.

'Thank you, Victor,' said Colbeck, standing up.

'His brother is waiting downstairs, sir.'

'I hope that he was easier to catch than this one.'

When he stood up, Colbeck was covered in dust and grime. His hair was matted, his face was dirty and his immaculate clothing was smeared with the dust of decades. Leeming looked at the grubby trousers and the torn waistcoat.

'And you had the gall to criticise *me*,' he observed, dryly.

* * *

Inspector Rae was peevish. 'Why wasn't I informed?' he demanded.

'There was no time,' replied Craig.

'You knew where I was. Word should have been sent.'

'Inspector Colbeck felt the need to take immediate action.'

'Well, it should have involved me.'

'That's a matter of opinion.'

'It's a matter of fact, Mr Craig.'

They were in the general manager's office and Rae had just been made aware of the latest development in the investigation. Like Craig, he was disgusted that McTurk had sought to use the information gleaned from the shepherd for his own advantage, ousting both Rae and Colbeck in the process and making them look inept. Spared that embarrassment, Rae had nevertheless been excluded. He was exasperated.

'The villains are in custody,' said Craig, 'and that's the salient point. Why quibble about rights of jurisdiction when the crime has been solved?'

'We don't know for certain that it has.'

'These men are lifelong rogues.'

'That doesn't mean they caused a train crash,' Rae contended. 'Gunpowder was involved, remember. That can be very dangerous in the wrong hands. Did either of these brothers have experience in handling it?'

'One of them must have, Inspector.'

'I beg leave to doubt that. It's a specialist skill.'

'They are the culprits,' said Craig irritably, 'and it was Inspector Colbeck who captured them. The case is closed. I feel it in my bones.'

'Then they're misleading you, sir. I've been a detective too long to make hasty decisions. On the face of it, I agree, these men are worthy suspects but they're no more than that. The evidence is not compelling. And even if they *are* guilty, proving it will present grave difficulties. If they're the deep-dyed villains of report, they certainly won't oblige us with a full confession.'

'Colbeck will drag the truth out of them. They'll be forced to admit that they were hired by the NBR to commit the outrage.'

'Where are they being held?'

'At the central police station – questioning will already be under way.'

Having delivered the brothers into custody, Colbeck took Leeming back to the hotel so that they could clean themselves up and change their clothes. When the two of them returned to the police station, the inspector was as elegant as ever and the sergeant was marginally less scruffy. One of the first things they'd learnt as detectives was that accomplices had to be kept apart so that they couldn't rehearse an alibi or invent a persuasive story together. Ewen and Duncan Usher were therefore held in separate cells, each wondering what his brother would say under interrogation.

Since he'd arrested the older brother, Leeming was given the task of questioning Ewen. The interview took place in a featureless room with bars in the window. Leeming and the handcuffed prisoner sat either side of a table. Two uniformed policemen stood behind Ewen Usher. The door was locked. There was no possibility of escape. Notwithstanding this, the prisoner was not intimidated. He regarded Leeming with a smirk. The sergeant leant forward.

'You know why you're here, Mr Usher,' he began.

'I've no' done anything wrong,' claimed the other.

'Then why did you try to run away?'

'I'm innocent, I tell ye.'

'Innocent people don't assault a police officer,' said Leeming, 'and they don't hurl vile abuse at him from that sewer you call a mouth. We have conclusive evidence that places you near a section of the Caledonian Railway where a dreadful crime took place.'

Ewen's face darkened. 'It's a lie.'

'You and your brother were seen by witnesses.'

'Tha's no' true.'

'One of them is the landlord of the inn where you stayed.' Ewen shifted uneasily in his chair. 'He got a very good look at you and his daughter remembers the names she overheard – Ewen and Duncan.'

'It wasnae us.'

'Who else could it have been?' pressed Leeming. 'You both arrived in a horse and cart with something tied under a tarpaulin? The landlord wouldn't dream up a thing like that. Other people at that inn remember you well. The description they gave of you tallies in every detail. You were there on the night before you committed that horrible crime.'

Ewen stiffened. 'What're ye talking aboot, man?'

'You know full well.'

'It's a pack o' bleedin' lies.'

'You're the liar, Mr Usher. Do you deny that you stayed at that inn?'

'Aye, I do.'

'And do you deny that you travelled with your brother in a horse and cart?'

'Aye, I do!' shouted Ewen.

'Witnesses will be called in court to identify you,' said Leeming. 'What interests me is whether you were acting alone or whether you had some other accomplices. If there were others beside you, they deserve to share your appointment with the hangman.'

The prisoner blanched. 'What's this aboot a hangman?'

'Murder carries the death penalty and what you did led to the

141

death of three individuals. You created chaos. Who paid you to do it? Who told you to block the line so that the train would crash into it? Come on,' said Leeming, 'the game is up now. You might as well tell us the truth at last. Who was behind the disaster, Mr Usher?'

The prisoner had heard enough. Maddened by the accusation, he jumped up and launched himself across the table, butting Leeming hard in the chest and knocking him from his chair. As the sergeant struggled to push his attacker off, Ewen was overpowered by the two policemen and held tight. He continued to yell abuse at Leeming and to plead his innocence.

'I'm no' a killer!' he howled in despair. 'Duncan and me've never murdered a soul! I'll swear it on the holy Bible. Ye must believe me!'

CHAPTER TWELVE

Colbeck adopted a different approach. Having heard from Leeming what had occurred during the first interview, he decided not to provoke Duncan Usher into a similar rage. More might be gained from a calm discussion. Though he used the same room, Colbeck had no policemen present. He and the prisoner were quite alone. Duncan glowered at him. He still bore the marks of Colbeck's fists. There were livid bruises on his face and one eye was half-closed. What made the stabbing pain more intense was the fact that the inspector seemed to have come through the encounter unscathed. Still in handcuffs, he sat at the table. Colbeck took the seat opposite.

'Does the name Lackey Paterson mean anything to you?' he asked.

'No,' said Duncan.

'Are you quite sure?'

'Aye.'

'What about the name of Jock Laidlaw?'

'I've never heerd o' the mahn.'

'And I suppose you've never heard of Dougal Murray and Alan Grint either.'

Duncan frowned. 'Who are these people?'

'The last three were victims of a train crash on the Caledonian Railway.'

'So? What's tha' to do wi' me?'

He was more cautious and watchful than his brother. Taking care not to raise his voice, he answered the questions straightforwardly. Colbeck pressed on.

'Let me take you back to Saturday night,' he said.

'Why?'

'If you don't mind, Mr Usher, *I'll* ask the questions.'

Duncan glanced towards the door. 'What've ye done wi' my brother? I heerd Ewen shouting.'

'You're much too sensible to do that,' said Colbeck, 'because you know that you'll gain far more by cooperation. Your brother denied everything. That was silly. We have reliable witnesses. Their evidence will stand up in court.'

He gave the prisoner time to absorb what he'd said. Duncan's expression gave nothing away. He knew that he was in serious trouble and was careful to say nothing to make his predicament even worse.

'Do you remember an inn called The Jolly Traveller?'

'Aye, I do.'

'Have you and your brother ever stayed there?'

'Aye, we did – last Sat'day.'

'Why did you drive all the way from Glasgow?'

'We didnae do tha'. We took the train to Elvanfoot and hired the cart there.'

'Why?'

'Ewen and me'd heard tell how beautiful it was around there. We'd a mind to find out if it was true.'

'Why not hire a trap? It would have been more comfortable than a cart.'

'Aye, we found tha' oot.'

'The Jolly Traveller is some distance from Elvanfoot.'

'We drove around for a long time.'

'Did you buy anything on your way?'

Duncan drew back warily. 'What do ye mean?'

'The landlord of the inn claims that you had something on the back of your cart, hidden under a tarpaulin and roped tight.'

'Aye,' replied Duncan, easily, 'it was a rocking chair we bought for our granny in Carstairs. There was a market in a village we went through.'

'What was the name of the village?'

'It's slipped my mind.'

'And I suppose that your granny's address has slipped your mind as well.'

'No, no, I'll gi' it to ye. She was fair delighted wi' the chair.'

He spoke with such confidence that Colbeck was momentarily checked. The prisoner was unperturbed by the thought that the police could visit the grandmother to confirm the claim. The old woman clearly had received the gift.

'What else was under that tarpaulin?' resumed Colbeck.

'Why do ye ask tha'?'

'Could it, for instance, have been two barrels of gunpowder?'

Duncan laughed. 'Gunpowder!'

'It was used to cause a blockage on the railway line.'

The prisoner's laughter died in his throat and a look of fear came into his eyes.

'Ewen and me had nothing to do wi' tha',' he said, earnestly.

'So why did you spend the night at The Jolly Traveller?' asked Colbeck. 'You might as well tell me the truth. If you don't, you and your brother will be charged with causing a train crash that led to excessive damage and to the deaths of the three men on a goods train. I've no need to tell you what the penalty for those crimes will be.' He looked hard at the man. 'Do you really *want* to go to the gallows?'

Duncan Usher's mouth had gone completely dry. As he contemplated the prospect just offered to him, he began to shudder. During some arrests, he'd been able to talk himself out of trouble. That was not an option here. Colbeck was too astute to be fooled. There was only one thing left to do.

After licking his lips, the prisoner told his story.

Deprived of the opportunity to earn the reward by capturing the brothers on his own, McTurk at least had the satisfaction of taking part in the arrests. When he went to his local pub that evening, there were some other off-duty railway policemen enjoying a drink. McTurk joined them. The talk inevitably turned to the investigation and he was able to tell them that he'd been instrumental in catching the two malefactors. After a pint of beer, he portrayed himself as a hero who'd overpowered one of the brothers then saved Sergeant Leeming from being beaten by the other. After a second pint, his tongue ran away with him and his audience grew in size. McTurk added colour to his narrative, inventing details to show himself in a good light.

'They'd never have found the house without me,' he boasted. 'I sent the sergeant down the lane to cut off any escape through the garden then I kicked in the door and got into the house. One of them ran away but the other attacked the inspector and I had to pull him off. I knocked seven barrels of shit out of the bastard and put the handcuffs on him. Then,' he went on, taking a drink from his third pint, 'I heard this noise from the lane so I charged out there. Ewen Usher was sitting astride the sergeant and punching him. Grabbing him by the neck, I hauled him off. It was then that he pulled a knife on me. I was unarmed, of course, but I didn't care. I wasn't going to let him escape. So I whipped off my hat, threw it in his face and kicked him in the balls before he knew what was happening. He went down in agony.'

There was general laughter. Newcomers urged him to tell the story again and McTurk added further embellishment. As a fourth pint was handed to him, he'd really come to believe that he'd caught the brothers single-handed. What he didn't realise was that among the large crowd now gathered around was a man who spied the chance of a profit. Such a stirring tale deserved wider circulation. Finishing his drink, the man left the pub and headed for the offices of one of Glasgow's main newspapers.

McTurk, meanwhile, was still sailing on a wave of imaginary valour.

'Remember my name,' he told them. 'When Ewen and Duncan Usher go to their deaths, remember that it was I who put the rope around their scrawny necks.'

Nairn Craig was still in his office when word came through from the police station. He read Colbeck's neat hand with growing disappointment. The contents of the letter were not what he'd expected. In view of what had happened earlier, he felt duty-bound to pass on the information to Inspector Rae even though it meant calling on the man at home. Surprised to see him, Rae gave him a guarded welcome and conducted the general manager to his study. They settled into high-backed leather armchairs.

'Well?' asked Rae.

'I've come to eat some humble pie, Inspector.'

'That sounds promising.'

'I was too ready to believe that we'd caught the devils at last.'

'Whereas, I suspect, the prisoners are not guilty.'

'Oh, they're guilty enough,' said Craig, 'but they didn't commit the crime for which they were arrested. Inspector Colbeck's letter gave me a detailed account. Ewen and Duncan Usher denied having any involvement in the crash. What took them to the area on the day before was another crime altogether.'

Colbeck had extracted a full confession from Duncan Usher. He and his brother were thieves who'd widened their field of operation by stealing from goods trains. Their work called for planning and audacity. Duncan chose stretches of the line where freight was slowed down by a gradient. Armed with a pile of sacks, his brother would leap into a wagon, stuff items into a sack and throw it into the grass. He was agile enough to move from wagon to wagon in search of booty, choosing things that would not break and which were easy to sell. Duncan's task was to follow the train with the cart and pick up the stolen goods. Since they took only small amounts from the total cargo, the thefts went largely unnoticed. That emboldened them to strike more often and to venture further away from Glasgow. Under the threat of facing a murder charge, Duncan Usher had even volunteered the whereabouts of the shed where the brothers kept the proceeds of their crime until they could sell them.

'So,' said Craig, gloomily, 'we've rid the Caledonian of a pair of vultures but we haven't found the people behind the train crash.'

Rae smiled wryly. 'In short,' he remarked, 'you've caught a sprat instead of a mackerel, let alone a whale. Don't be so downhearted. Now that you're aware of how easily your freight can be pillaged, you can guard against it. Inspector Colbeck should be praised for bringing the practice to light.'

'I'd much rather he did what I brought him here for.'

'Does that mean you're losing faith in him?'

'No, no,' said Craig, quashing the idea at once. 'I back him to the hilt. He showed his true mettle during the arrest of those brothers. According to McTurk, both Colbeck and Leeming were fearless.'

'Unfortunately, they were apprehending the wrong men.'

'They were apprehending the *right* men for a different crime. I suppose that there's some solace in that. But,' he went on, rising out of his chair, 'I'm sorry to disturb you so late in the evening, Inspector. I'll take my leave.'

Rae was on his feet at once, waving his visitor back to his seat.

'You'll do nothing of the kind, Mr Craig. I can't promise that we can provide any humble pie but I've an excellent malt to tempt you. Wait here while I fetch some glasses. There's nothing like whisky for stimulating the brain,' he added, moving to the door. 'It will help us to find the answer we seek.'

'What answer is that?'

'If these brothers are not, after all, the culprits,' said Rae, 'then who is?'

It was after midnight when they approached the engine sheds and their dark clothing made them all but invisible. Tam Howie carried a lamp that could give some degree of illumination when the shutter was opened. Ian Dalton had the pot of paint. It seemed extraordinarily heavy, his sense of guilt adding weight to it. Dalton was having misgivings. Inspired by what Howie and his wife had done, he believed that it would be easy to follow suit. In fact, it was a nerve-racking exercise. It was only when they crept across the railway lines that he realised just how much was at stake. If caught, he stood to lose his freedom, his job and his reputation. Whatever happened, there'd be uneasiness at home because, in order to explain his absence at that hour, he'd been forced to lie to his wife for the first time in their marriage. She would never dare to tax him on the subject but their relationship would undergo a subtle change.

'Stop!' ordered Howie, crouching down.

'What is it?' whispered Dalton, quaking slightly.

'The nightwatchman is doing his rounds.'

They stayed low for several minutes. Dalton's legs were aching and there was a searing pain across his shoulders. When he heard footsteps pass within yards of them, he almost fell over. Howie waited until the coast was clear before nudging him. As he tried to follow his friend, Dalton discovered that the paint pot had doubled its weight and was biting into his hand. He was grateful when they eventually slipped into the engine shed and he was able to put it down.

'Are you nervous?' asked Howie.

'That's putting it mildly, Tam.'

'It will soon pass. Flora and I felt the same the first time.'

'When was that?'

'Oh, it was a long time ago.'

Howie risked opening the shutter on the lamp so that he could pick his way along the shed. When he reached a locomotive, he stopped and pointed.

'There's your canvas,' he said. 'Leave your signature on it.'

Dalton didn't believe that he'd be able to hold the brush steady, let alone scrawl a message. His hands were shaking too much. He steeled himself to go on, reminding himself why they were there and what higher purpose they served. Instead of thinking of himself, he needed to focus on the damage that the Caledonian had done to the purity of the Sabbath. This was his chance to punish it. Opening the paint pot, he dipped in the brush and wrote the first giant letter on the side of the boiler. It gave him a strange thrill. Once he'd added a couple more letters, his fears began to evaporate. He even started to take pleasure in what he was doing. When the slogan had been finished, Howie ran the lamp along its full length and beamed with appreciation.

'Well done, Ian!' he said, grasping his arm. 'You're one of us now.'

'Thank you, Tam. I was glad of the chance to do it.'

'There'll be lots of other chances, don't worry.'

'Now that it's over, I feel so excited.'

'You've struck a blow for the Sabbath.'

'Is it true that Flora has actually done this?'

Howie chuckled. 'Oh, she's done a lot more than paint slogans,' he said, proudly. 'You wouldn't believe how daring my wife is, Ian. Nothing daunts Flora.'

Madeleine Colbeck read the letter three times before putting it down. Couched in loving terms and written in lucid prose, it gave her details of the investigation in which her husband was engaged. Though she was pleased to have more information about the case, she was distressed to learn that it might keep Colbeck away from her for some time. When she called on her father that morning, she told him what she'd learnt about the train crash. Andrews was troubled by the details.

'It could have been *me*, Maddy,' he said, soulfully. 'Not that I'd ever have worked for the Caledonian, mark you, but you know what I mean. It could have been me or Gideon Little or Jonas Marklew or any other driver in that goods train. A deliberate blockage of the line could have killed any one of us. My heart goes out to the driver – and to the fireman and guard, of course. I'm bound to think that there, but for the grace of God, go I.'

'There's no need to be morbid about it, Father.'

'Driving a train means taking a risk. That's all I'm saying.'

'You don't have to tell me that,' said Madeleine, recalling the time when her father was assaulted by train robbers. 'I'm glad all that risk is behind you.'

'What pleases me is that Mr Renwick appreciates our work.'

'And so he should. You were a loyal servant to the company.'

'I learnt my trade properly and I taught it to dozens of others. It's only fitting that I should be invited to the dinner this week.'

'That's one reason I came to see you. I'm not sure what to wear.'

'Whatever it is, you'll look beautiful in it, Maddy.'

'Thank you.'

'The other drivers will be there with their wives,' he told her, 'and all of them are as wrinkly as prunes.'

'Father!' she protested.

'I take that back. Horace Oldfield's wife is as fat as a pig without a wrinkle on her. You'll outshine every woman in the room.'

'Well, I expect you to show more respect to the ladies there.'

'I will, Maddy. I'll be on my best behaviour. Thanks to what you've just told me, I expect to be the centre of attention.'

'Why do you think that?'

'We'll be in a room full of railwaymen,' he said. 'What else will they talk about but the crash up in Scotland? They'll be agog for news. And *I'll* be in a position to tell them exactly what's going on in the investigation.'

Summoned to the general manager's office, Superintendent McTurk believed that he was about to receive praise for his part in the arrests. Back in uniform and with his brass buttons polished to a high sheen, he knocked on the door before opening it. Nairn Craig was standing behind his desk. Colbeck was also on his feet.

Their manner was not welcoming. McTurk closed the door behind him.

'You sent for me, Mr Craig?' he asked.

'Yes, I did,' said the other. 'I require an explanation.'

McTurk was puzzled. 'An explanation for what, sir?'

By way of reply, Craig lifted up the newspaper on his desk and handed it to him. McTurk saw his name in the headline and quailed. The article applauded his bravery in capturing the two men responsible for the train crash and it made much of the fact that a Scotsman had outshone the much-vaunted Railway Detective. Words that McTurk had uttered while in his cups were quoted in full.

'Did you say all this?' demanded Craig.

'No, no, I didn't.'

'You'd obviously been drinking at the time.'

'I may have had one drink, sir, but that was all.'

'Does that mean you were completely sober when you made these ridiculous claims?' asked Colbeck. 'That would be even more reprehensible.'

'This is a tissue of lies,' said McTurk, passing the newspaper to Craig.

'And *you* were the person who told them,' said Colbeck.

'Did it never occur to you,' said Craig, 'that discretion is needed at a time like this? You should have had enough experience to keep your mouth shut. The press feed off things like this. Someone who heard you boasting in that pub obviously sold the story to a newspaper. Once they established from the police that suspects by the name of Ewen and Duncan Usher were indeed in custody, it gave credence to what you were bragging about. The villains had been caught by you,' he added with sarcasm. 'Three cheers for Superintendent McTurk!'

'There's been a misunderstanding,' said McTurk, writhing in discomfort.

'There has indeed,' agreed Colbeck, taking over. 'Overlooking the fact that Sergeant Leeming and I actually fought with the two men, there was a serious misunderstanding on your part. Ewen and Duncan Usher were not, after all, behind the disaster on the line. They had nothing whatsoever to do with it.'

McTurk's jaw dropped. 'But I thought—'

'No, Superintendent, you didn't *think*, you merely *assumed* and that's fatal for any self-appointed detective. Granted,' said Colbeck, 'the evidence was stacked heavily against the brothers but it turned out to be misleading. Before you told your cronies in the pub that you had effectively solved the crime on your own, you should have waited until you knew the outcome of the interviews we had with Ewen and Duncan Usher.'

'But they *seemed* so guilty, sir. They resisted arrest.'

'Most criminals resist arrest, as you well know. As it turns out, there's a whole string of offences for which they can be charged but they do not – contrary to what that newspaper article is telling its many readers – include wanton destruction on the Caledonian. You've made us all look rather stupid, Superintendent.'

'None more so than yourself,' said Craig, bitterly.

McTurk was mortified. He remembered trying to impress his friends in the pub but he hadn't anticipated that his words would travel all the way to a local newspaper. In trying to harvest some glory for himself, he'd told outrageous lies, cast aspersions upon the skills of Colbeck and Leeming, embarrassed the company for whom he worked and accused two men of a crime that they didn't commit. His brass buttons might be shining but his face was darkened by guilt.

'I don't know what to say . . .' he began.

'You've said far too much already,' declared Craig, tossing the newspaper aside. 'It wasn't enough for you to steal information provided by someone else and to pass it off as your own. You also had to be the courageous man who caught the two most wanted men in Scotland. Your talents are clearly wasted here,' he continued with withering scorn. 'A man of your supreme abilities needs to spread his wings. Well, you'll have the chance to do so.' He pointed a finger. 'You're a disgrace to that uniform, Superintendent. You no longer have the right to wear it. I'm not only dismissing you so that you can no longer contaminate the Caledonian with your odious presence, I'm demanding that you send Inspector Colbeck and Sergeant Leeming a written apology for the way that you tried to sully their reputations. Then you can go to the offices of the newspaper and explain why you supplied so much false information.' McTurk stood there dithering. 'Get out, man! And change out of that uniform immediately.'

Hurt and humiliated, McTurk left the room with his tail between his legs.

'You were justifiably hard on him, sir,' said Colbeck. 'You reminded me of someone at Scotland Yard.'

'He deserved it, Inspector. He'll never work for the Caledonian again.'

'I was pleased that you mentioned the way that he made use of the evidence that came from that young shepherd. That was unscrupulous. However, while it didn't lead to the capture of the men we're after, the information did have a positive result. The Usher brothers have been robbing your freight traffic for months. They made a lot of money out of items stolen from your wagons.'

'That's right,' conceded Craig. 'You did make important arrests.'

'Don't you think that that fact should be recognised, sir? I'm thinking about Jamie Farr. Thanks to him, we've sent two villains to prison for a long time. I fancy that calls for a reward of some kind.'

The general manager's brow crinkled and he gave a loud sniff.

'Let me mull it over, Inspector.'

After the excitement of the two arrests, there came a worrying lull in activity. Nothing happened for two days. The investigation continued but it was fruitless. No new evidence came to light and no fresh suspects were unmasked. Leeming became increasingly restive. Staying in a hotel that unnerved him, he was trapped among people whose voices were often incomprehensible and he was in a city he'd grown to dislike more and more. As a result of their investigation, three criminals had been taken into custody but none of them had any link to the train crash. Whoever had brought a stretch of the Caledonian to a standstill seemed to have disappeared off the face of the earth. Hopes of finding them diminished with each day.

Leeming's principal task remained the arrest of Lackey Paterson. As other suspects were ruled out, the former railwayman sparked off additional interest. His work at the quarry placed him within easy reach of the crash site and his sudden disappearance aroused understandable suspicion. If he was indeed back in Glasgow, Paterson would by now be aware that the police were looking for him. Given the chance, the landlord of The Stag would certainly have warned him. Yet knowing that he was wanted, Paterson had failed to come forward to clear his name. Leeming reasoned that that either meant he was not in the city or that he'd gone to ground there. In a community that size, the number of hiding places was unlimited. A stranger like the sergeant could hunt for years without ever finding him.

He was alone in Colbeck's temporary office when Inspector Rae called.

'Ah,' said the visitor, 'I'm glad that I caught you.'

'I'm afraid that Inspector Colbeck isn't here. He went off to catch a train.'

'You're the person I was hoping to see, Sergeant. Let me say straight away that I didn't believe for a second what that newspaper said about you and the inspector. I felt certain that you'd used appropriate force to make those arrests and needed no help. It was vindictive of McTurk to claim credit for catching those men.'

'The superintendent has paid for his mistake,' said Leeming, 'and he sent me a written apology. The matter is closed as far as I'm concerned.'

'Quite so – it's time to move forward.'

'Why did you wish to see me, Inspector?'

'I wanted to correct a false impression you may have.'

'I'm not sure that I understand.'

'Well,' said Rae with his familiar smile, 'I know that the Glasgow police seemed less than cooperative when you first approached them. You must have felt that they were keeping you at arm's length.'

'They simply let me know I was encroaching on their territory.'

'And on mine, of course, but I bear you no ill will. Lest you think that the police ignored your request for assistance, I've come to tell you that they did what they promised and kept their eyes peeled for a certain person.'

Leeming's interest was kindled. 'Are you talking about Lackey Paterson?'

'He's definitely back in Glasgow.'

'Do you know where he is?'

'All I know is that he was spotted by an alert constable who'd read the description of him. As soon as he called out the man's name, Paterson fled. To my mind, that confirms his identity. It was the person you're after.'

'And where did this sighting take place, sir?'

'It was in the Gorbals.'

Leeming's hopes rose. The man had gone to see his wife and child.

Days had passed since his visit to Glasgow and Jamie Farr had heard nothing. It eroded his belief in Colbeck. The shepherd had placed little faith in the railway policeman to whom he'd given his evidence but he'd been convinced that the inspector would deal more justly with him. Colbeck had promised him that he'd be informed when arrests had been made as a result of the information supplied by the shepherd. No money would be paid over at that stage but at least Farr would know that the process had been set in motion. Ignorant of the slowness and complexity of a major police investigation, he'd expected almost immediate results. In the wake of the crash, many of the looters had been caught within a day. He knew some of them. They'd barely had time to eat their stolen food before police swooped down on them. Why couldn't they catch those who caused the crash just as speedily?

As he sat on the hillside, munching a piece of cheese, he was resigned to the fact that he would get no reward whatsoever. Colbeck was simply a more polite version of McTurk, someone who brushed the lad aside with a false promise. Farr had no access to a newspaper and – even with the help of Bella Drew – no ability to read it properly. For all he knew, the case had been solved and the English detectives had returned to London. He'd never hear of them again. The most dispiriting aspect of it was that Bella would feel he'd let her down. When he came back from his trip to Glasgow, he'd been buoyed up by what he'd been told. He'd finally found someone he could trust and told Bella that the money was as good as his. Unable to take in the enormity of it all, she'd burst into tears and he'd held her in his arms. That little moment had sealed the bond between them. It might now be ripped apart.

Going to Glasgow had been a terrifying experience but it had seemed worthwhile at the time. Taking the train to London was out of the question. Farr couldn't find the time or the courage to travel all that way. Even if he did, the chances of his ever getting to meet Inspector Colbeck again were decidedly slim. He had to accept that he'd been tricked once again, cheated out of his reward and, as a possible consequence, robbed of the girl he loved. What would Bella think of him when he confessed that he wouldn't get a penny? Their plans for a future together would crumble into dust. Farr was embittered. The railway was to blame. It not only killed his sheep and disturbed the calm of the countryside. It had led him astray, holding out a promise that would never be fulfilled. From an accident in which he'd rejoiced, he sought to make profit and it had seemed at one point that he might actually be successful. Then a long and ominous silence had descended.

The ugly truth had to be faced. Farr had been cast aside and forgotten. He'd never hear from Colbeck or from anyone else involved in the investigation again. He'd been sent back to the obscurity from which he came. Seething with anger, he hardly felt the nose of his dog nuzzling against him. To get his attention, Angus had to give him a gentle bite on the arm. Farr pushed the dog away.

'What did you do that for?' he said in annoyance.

Regretting his anger at once, he reached out to give the dog a pat of gratitude. Angus had only been trying to warn him that someone was coming. A well-dressed man was driving a trap towards them. When he recognised Colbeck, the shepherd leapt to his feet and ran towards him, arriving almost breathless.

'Have ye brought my money?' he asked between gasps.

'Not exactly,' said Colbeck, 'but I have come to tell you that we acted on the information you gave us and arrested two men.' Farr was elated. 'Before you let your excitement get the better of you, you must know that neither of them had anything to do with the train crash.' The shepherd's joy turned to anguish. 'They were, however, criminals, thieves who'd been robbing goods trains on the Caledonian. Since it was your evidence that led to their arrest,' said Colbeck, putting a hand into his pocket, 'the railway company decided – on my advice – that some sort of reward was due. It won't be the four hundred pounds advertised, I'm afraid, but I hope that this will be some sort of consolation to you.'

Colbeck handed over the money. Farr was thrilled. It was only thirty pounds but that was a substantial amount to him. It was something on which he and Bella could build their plans. Having expected nothing at all, Farr was overcome with emotion. Tears in his eyes, he shook Colbeck's hand.

'Ye came all this way to see me,' he said in surprise. 'I can't thank ye enough.'

'I keep my promises, Jamie.'

Farr looked at the banknotes. 'Is this all for *me*?'

'You earned it,' said Colbeck. 'Your information put two criminals behind bars. Keep those sharp eyes of yours peeled. You never know what they might see.'

CHAPTER THIRTEEN

Victor Leeming had learnt his lesson. On his two previous visits to the Gorbals, he'd worn his customary clothing. His top hat and frock coat made him stand out like a beacon in the darkness. Before he set off a third time, therefore, he changed into rougher garb that enabled him to merge with his surroundings. Baggy trousers, crumpled jacket and dirty cap lent him invisibility. Colbeck had taught him the value of having such a disguise at hand, though he was reluctant to put it on himself because he took such pride in his appearance. Leeming was untroubled by vanity. Dressed as a labourer of some sort, he felt very comfortable. The only problem was that he had to leave the hotel in his new incarnation and he was immediately pounced on by a vigilant manager who blocked his path.

'Excuse me, sir,' he said. 'May I ask what you're doing here?'

'I'm staying at the hotel,' replied Leeming.

'I very much doubt that.'

'Inspector Colbeck and I have rooms here.'

The manager peered at him. '*You* are Sergeant Leeming?'

'I am indeed,' said the other, removing his cap to prove it. 'If you'll stand aside, I have somewhere to go.'

'Yes, yes – I do apologise, Sergeant.'

'It's not necessary. I take it as a compliment.'

Leeming put on his cap and walked out of the hotel. His disguise worked. If it could convince the manager of The Angel Hotel, it could fool anybody. His confidence surged. It soon buckled slightly. When he tried to hail a cab, none of them would stop for him because he didn't look like the sort of customer who could afford the fare. In the end, he walked to a cab rank and brought out a handful of coins to show that he had money. Settling into a vehicle, he was taken on the long ride to the Gorbals.

It was early evening when he got there and the streets were as drab and malodorous as ever. But he was no longer jeered at by children or given hostile stares from windows and doorways. When he found the tenement he was after, he banged on the door and waited. There was no response. He raised a hand to knock again.

'She's no' there,' said a voice.

At first, Leeming didn't hear it because it was muffled beneath the stabbing music of a hurdy-gurdy. The wizened old woman, barely strong enough to hold the instrument, was turning the handle. She paused in order to repeat the warning. Leeming swung round to face her.

'Maggie went oot a wee while ago,' she said.

'Do you know when Mrs Paterson will be back?'

'No.'

'I was really looking for her husband.'

'Lackey doesnae live heer any more.'

'I know that but I thought he might have come back to see his wife.'

'Mebbe he did,' said the woman. 'I've only been in the street for twenty minutes or so. Maggie was leaving as I got heer.'

'Have you any idea where she went?'

'I thought it was Lackey ye was after.'

'It is,' said Leeming, falling back on an excuse he'd thought up earlier. 'We worked in a quarry together but he left the job last weekend. He told me to look out for him when I was next in Glasgow. This was the address he gave me.'

'Then he's led ye astray. He left months ago.'

'But he's back in the city. I know that much.'

'Then ye ken more than me,' said the old woman. 'Walking these streets every day, there's no' much I miss. I've no' seen Lackey since Christmas. Tha's when he left Maggie and the bairn on their own.'

Leeming studied her. She was a true denizen of the area. In spite of her age, the woman seemed to have keen eyesight and a good memory. Having worked there all her life, she was a walking encyclopaedia of the Gorbals, knowing the names, faces and domestic arrangements of hundreds of people. As she brought a little music into their lives, she was permitted to step over the bounds of privacy. She was known, liked, trusted. Leeming had found a reliable source.

'Perhaps you could help me,' he said, hopefully.

'How much is it worth? I'll no' earn a farthing if I talk to ye any longer.' When some coins were pressed into her palm, she held them tight. 'Thank ye, my friend. Ye've just bought ma attention.'

'Where would he go?' asked Leeming. 'If Lackey came back to Glasgow, where would he stay?' The woman was lost in thought for over a minute. Leeming prompted her. 'Mrs Paterson gave me the name of a pub in Marigold Street but he wasn't there. Yet he must lay his head somewhere. I promised to buy him a drink but I can't do that if I can't even find him.'

'He could be at Telfer's, I s'ppose,' replied the other.

'Is that another pub?'

'No, it's a place where ye go when ye've little money and need a rest. Lackey's been there in the past, I ken that. It's no' a hoose ye'd stay in unless ye had to but, if Lackey's gi' up a job, mebbe it's all the mahn can afford.'

'Where is Telfer's?'

Leeming's eagerness caused her slight alarm. She narrowed her eyes.

'Ye're no' a p'liceman, are ye?'

'No, said Leeming, 'I hate the peelers.' He spat on the ground to attest his credentials. 'That's what I think of them and I know that Lackey felt the same. I just want to see him. If he's short of money, I may be able to lend him some.'

'Then ye'll never see a penny of it back,' she warned.

Stepping in close to him, she subjected Leeming to a long, searching stare. All that he could do was to stand there patiently. At length, she decided that she could trust him but wanted more payment. When she thrust out a hand, he slipped some more coins into it. Turning the handle of the hurdy-gurdy, she produced a penetrating sound that made Leeming's ears ring. She raised her voice to speak over it.

'I'll tell ye where Telfer's is . . .'

A dozen of them assembled at the restaurant. Six of them were retired drivers but only five had brought their wives. Caleb Andrews was the odd one out. Having arrived with his daughter on his arm, he enjoyed the look of wonder on the faces of the others when he introduced Madeleine as the wife of Inspector Colbeck.

They'd all heard of the Railway Detective and were eager for news of his latest case. Andrews dispensed what information he had as if he was directly involved in the investigation. There was general sympathy for the victims of the train crash. Every driver there had a tale about coming off the line because of an obstruction. They'd killed farm animals of every kind and one of them had hit a cart that had broken down on the track.

The dinner was due to be served in a private room with a whiff of luxury about it. It was the sort of place to which they could never ordinarily afford to come. Drinks were served on arrival and everyone chatted amiably. What surprised them all was that there was no sign of their host and his wife. In fact, it was half an hour after the advertised time that Archibald Renwick and his wife arrived. They apologised for their lateness and tried to join in the spirit of the occasion but Madeleine noticed how tense the general manager was and how forced his wife's smile appeared to be. Isobel Renwick was a plump woman with a large bosom and spreading midriff putting her red velvet dress under strain. Her husband, noticeably older than her, was a tall, erect, poised man with an air of distinction about him.

When they met Madeleine, they were fulsome in their praise.

'We love the painting,' said Renwick, giving her a congratulatory handshake. 'As soon as I saw it, I knew that I had to have it.'

'Yes,' added his wife, 'I couldn't believe it when my husband said that he wanted to hang a picture of a steam locomotive in our dining room. They're such ugly, noisy things and they belong on a railway line. When I laid eyes on it, however, I was won over at once. You turned it into something beautiful.'

'Cornwall *was* beautiful,' Andrews piped up. 'I should know. It was a joy to be on the footplate. I was the one who told Maddie she ought to paint Cornwall.'

'Then we have to thank you as well,' said Renwick.

'In fact – now that I'm retired – I may take up painting myself.'

'I'll be interested to see what you produce.'

'Maddy must get her artistic skills from somewhere.'

Madeleine smiled, knowing full well that she didn't inherit those skills from her father. The only painting he'd ever done was on the walls of the kitchen and he'd made a complete mess of it. She made no reference to the incident, not wishing to let him down in front of Renwick and in front of the other drivers who obviously held Andrews in high esteem. It was lovely to see her father in his element, basking in the general manager's praise and trading reminiscences with his friends. Madeleine also liked the curiosity she aroused because of her husband's fame. It helped to ease the pain created by his absence.

A table plan had been drawn up and Andrews was disappointed that he was not placed next to Renwick. Never one to be cowed in the presence of someone more senior in the LNWR, he'd hoped for the opportunity to tell the general manager how he might improve the running of the company. Madeleine was grateful that her father wasn't allowed to foist his advice on Renwick. Having heard his trenchant opinions many times, she didn't want the evening to be spoilt by his litany of complaints. At a celebratory event like that, there was no place for argument. It would destroy the mood of happiness.

The meal was excellent, the service brisk and the wine plentiful. Everyone seemed to be enjoying themselves with the exception of Renwick and his wife. The general manager was quite unable to relax and the speech he made in honour of the retired members of his staff, though generous and well meant, was strangely muted. Instead of coming from the heart, it came word for word from the piece of paper on which he'd written it and which he read without ever lifting his face to his audience. Yet if he seemed uninvolved in the proceedings, Isobel Renwick was even more detached. She kept looking over her shoulder as if expecting someone to creep up on her and, when her husband introduced some weak humour into his speech, she had to wrench her features into a smile.

Madeleine was so worried about the woman that she took the trouble to have a quiet word with her. As the guests began to exchange their farewells, Andrews finally managed a private chat with Renwick. The general manager's wife hovered near the door, anxious to leave yet afraid to go through the door alone. She stood back to let others go out, nodding politely as they went past. Madeleine went over to her.

'I'm sorry that you haven't enjoyed the evening, Mrs Renwick,' she said.

'Not at all,' insisted the other woman. 'I loved every moment of it. Meeting people like your father is a pleasure. My husband always says that it is drivers like him who are the backbone of the LNWR, hence this dinner in honour of them.'

'My father was very touched to be invited.'

'I was looking forward to seeing you, Mrs Colbeck. That painting of yours opened my eyes to the sheer beauty of a locomotive. Archie calls them a triumph of engineering and I'm finally seeing why.'

She kept tossing glances in the direction of her husband but he was still deep in conversation with Andrews. Wanting to know why the woman was so nervous, Madeleine didn't feel that she could press her on the subject. Instead, she bade her adieu and made to move way. Isobel grasped her by the wrist.

'I must apologise for my rudeness,' she said.

'I was unaware of it, Mrs Renwick.'

'You were quite right. I wasn't able to take full enjoyment from this evening and neither was my husband. The truth is that we had a rather distressing incident at home and it's been preying on our minds.'

'Oh,' said Madeleine with sympathy, 'I'm sorry to hear that.'

'The house was burgled last night.'

'That must have been frightening.'

'It was, Mrs Colbeck. We were in bed at the time and didn't hear a thing. Neither did any of the servants but, then, they sleep in the attic rooms. The thief came and went like a ghost. It made us feel so vulnerable,' said Isobel, chewing her lip. 'All the doors were locked yet somehow a burglar got in and managed to open the safe.'

'Was very much stolen?'

'As it happens, he only took the money that was there. But that's not the point. If he'd taken nothing at all, we'd still have been upset. Our home was *invaded*. We'll never be able to feel safe there again.'

'It must have been dreadful for you.'

'It was,' said Isobel, wringing her hands. 'I was horrified that he might have stolen my jewels but, for some reason, he left them in the safe. Archie was even more worried than me. There were some important documents in there, including some that related to Her Majesty the Queen. Thank heaven the thief didn't spirit those away!'

Telfer's turned out to be a dingy lodging house, comprising four adjacent buildings knocked into one and filled on three levels with an array of beds, bunks and noisome mattresses. Accommodation was cheap and included free soap, razors, pen and ink, salt and pepper, and a newspaper. Few of the guests had the time or energy to read the daily news. They tumbled into bed at an appointed hour and, when they tumbled out again to go to work, someone immediately took their place. Telfer's was a place of continuous occupation, a male dormitory that stank of dirty sheets and unwashed bodies. Leeming had seen similar establishments in London. It was a house of last resort and that told him something about Lackey Paterson.

Once again, he had to buy information. Ebenezer Telfer was a white-haired old man with one arm but it didn't seem to impede him in any way. Though his guests ebbed and flowed throughout the day and night, he knew who they all were and how many hours they'd bought in one of his unappetising beds. Leeming learnt that Paterson was not due back until later that evening and so he took up a position outside the house. Various men shuffled past him, either going in or coming out. His disguise kept inquisitive looks at bay. Sorry for anyone compelled to live in such a way, he had no sympathy for the man he was tracking. Paterson had beaten his wife and deserted her. She'd been left in the utmost misery. Her husband didn't merit compassion. All that was due to him was contempt.

The wait took longer than he'd expected and Leeming began to wonder if he'd either been given the wrong information by Telfer or if one particular guest had decided to spend the night elsewhere. After another half an hour, Leeming was ready to abandon his vigil altogether. Then he saw someone approaching with a drunken sway. As the man walked beneath the gas lamp opposite, he was caught in the spill of light. Leeming got a good look at him and felt sure that it could be his quarry. He let him get as far as the door before accosting him.

'Lackey Paterson?' he asked.

'Who're ye?' grunted the other, sizing him up.

'I'd like a word with you, Mr Paterson.'

'Get oot of ma way.'

When he tried to push his way past Leeming, he found his arm being grabbed and that ignited his temper immediately. Swinging a fist, he caught the detective on the side of the head and sent him reeling. He then staggered off in a forlorn attempt to run away. Once he'd overcome the shock of the blow, Leeming went after him and soon caught up with him. Paterson tried to hit him again but he was too slow. His punch was blocked and a fist explored his stomach. It took all the fight out of him. Bent double, he moaned in agony.

'Let's have that word now, shall we?' said Leeming.

Time meant nothing to Colbeck when he was absorbed in a case. He stayed at the desk in his office until late evening, sifting through the available clues once again then poring over the ordnance survey map that included the crash site. He picked out the location of Jamie Farr's cottage and wondered what the shepherd would do with the reward he'd received. He was still scrutinising the map when there was a knock on the door and it opened to reveal Inspector Rae.

'I saw a light under the door,' he said. 'Am I disturbing you?'

'No, no, come on in, Inspector.'

'The trail has gone cold.'

'I fear that it has,' admitted Colbeck.

'You should go home.'

'I'm not ready for the comforts of The Angel Hotel just yet.'

'I wasn't referring to the hotel,' said Rae, smiling. 'I meant that you should go home to London. Your work is done here. For once, you failed.'

'I disagree. I'll only acknowledge failure when someone else succeeds and I don't see any visible progress in your inquiry.

Superintendent McTurk sought to steal a march on both of us but only managed to get himself dismissed. Like you, he believed that the NBR was behind the crash but neither of you has made a convincing case for that supposition. The meeting with Mr Weir yielded nothing.'

'That's not true, Inspector. It yielded a great deal of huffing and puffing.'

Colbeck grinned. 'Yes, the gentleman was something of an expert at that.'

'I didn't simply challenge the fellow,' said Rae, 'I recruited him. In enraging him, I turned him into a detective. He might have denied that the NBR was in any way implicated but the notion would have pecked away at him. When his fury abated, the first thing he'd have done is to initiate an inquiry of his own, searching through the employees of the NBR to see if any of them – from whatever motive – was in some way linked to the crash. He doesn't want evil men in his employ. In other words, Alastair Weir will have done what neither you nor I could have contrived. In the course of his hunt, he'll turn the NBR upside down.'

Colbeck was impressed. 'That was very clever of you, Inspector.'

'My opinion is unchanged. This was the work of a commercial rival.'

'Why limit your interest to the NBR?'

'I haven't done so. Other companies are also under suspicion.'

'What about Lackey Paterson?'

'I'm inclined to discount him. He's the man on whom *you* pin your hopes.'

'I wouldn't go so far as to say that,' returned Colbeck, 'but he remains a figure of interest. We can place him near the site of the crash and the fact that he worked at the quarry means that he'd have access to gunpowder.'

'On that score, I must correct you. I'm sorry to muddy the waters of your theory but you'll have to abandon it. Paterson did not steal gunpowder from the quarry – in fact, he didn't steal it from anywhere.'

'How do you know that?'

'A report came in from Perth,' said Rae, relishing the chance to unsettle Colbeck. 'The gunpowder was taken from an army barracks.'

They talked under a lamp post less than fifty yards from Telfer's. There was no danger of another escape attempt from Paterson. He was too drunk and too exhausted. Paterson was in a deplorable state, filthy, wild-eyed and unshaven. Leeming found it hard to believe that the man had once been entrusted with the difficult job of driving a train. Since his days with the Caledonian, Paterson had clearly gone into decline. After introducing himself, Leeming got him to confirm his name.

'Why did you run away?' he asked.

'I thought ye were one of 'em.'

'Who are you talking about?'

'They're after me for money,' confessed Paterson. 'I ran up some debts. It was no' ma fault. It just happened tha' way. It was the reason I left Glasgow.'

'We know that you went to work at a quarry.'

'Aye, I did. I liked it there.'

'So why did you leave?'

'I had some rotten debt collector on my tail,' said Paterson. 'He followed me a' the way there. Since I was earning a wage again, he wanted money for one of my bleedin' creditors. He demanded a lot more than I owed.'

'There was a train crash not far from the quarry.'

'Aye, I read aboot tha'. It was terrible. They've a newspaper at Telfer's if ye're lucky enough to get hold of it. Before ye read it, ye've to make sure that nobody's used it to wipe his arse.'

Leeming was taken aback. Paterson had not become evasive at the mention of the crash. His pity seemed genuine. Crumbs of bread were embedded in the bristles on his chin. He reeked of beer. His clothes were ragged. Leeming wondered what sort of twilight world the man inhabited.

'I believe that you knew a man named Jock Laidlaw,' he said.

Paterson sneered. 'Aye, I ken the cocky devil.'

'He was killed in the crash.'

'It was the one guid thing to come out of it.'

'Did you dislike the man that much?'

'No, Sergeant, I *hated* the swine. I'm glad he was killed. I hope Jock Laidlaw died in agony. I'm just sorry I wasnae there t'enjoy it.'

'You had a fight with him once, I gather.'

'I tried to,' said Paterson, ruefully, 'but that big bugger, McTurk, dragged me off him and reported me. It was unfair – Laidlaw kept his job and I was kicked out.'

'Did that make you angry with the Caledonian Railway?'

'No, it made me even angrier with Laidlaw. I wanted to tear out his black heart and stuff it down his throat.'

'Yet you used to work together at one time. Why did you fall out?'

Paterson lowered his head. 'That's ma business.'

'You wanted revenge against him for some reason, didn't you?'

'Aye, I did.'

'And since you'd been a driver as well, you knew his shift patterns.'

'Ye're talkin' nonsense, man.'

'You knew he'd be on that particular train at that particular time.

That's why you developed a scheme to block the line and cause that crash. You admitted it a moment ago,' reminded Leeming. 'You said you were *glad* he was killed. Because that was the whole point of the crash, wasn't it? You could get your own back.'

It slowly dawned on Paterson that he was being accused of murdering the man he detested. He shuttled between anger and fear, furious that he was considered a suspect and afraid that the police would concoct false evidence against him. Having no means to defend himself, he fell back on honesty.

'I'll tell ye what happened,' he said, visibly simmering. 'I'd a lovely wife.'

'I've met the lady,' Leeming told him.

Paterson was maudlin. 'Maggie meant everything in the world to me.'

'That's not the story I heard. According to Mrs Paterson, you gambled away most of your wages and got turned out of your house. You ended up in the Gorbals then walked out on her – but not before you used your fists on her.'

'Ye don't understand what she did to me.'

'She didn't offer you violence, I know that much. How could she?'

'Ye met her, ye say?'

'I went there twice. She had the baby in her arms. You should be *proud* of your child, Mr Paterson. *I* would be, in your shoes.'

Paterson lurched forward. Summoning up all his energy, he swung a fist at Leeming but the latter ducked beneath the blow with ease. He moved quickly to turn Paterson round, slam him against the wall and put handcuffs on him. His captive was contrite. When he faced Leeming again, his eyes were full of tears.

'Ye shouldn't have said it, Sergeant.'

'Said what?'

'It was cruel of ye, mahn.'

'What did I say to upset you?'

'Can ye no' guess?'

'I showed sympathy for your wife's plight, that's all.'

'Maggie brought it on hersel', I tell ye.'

'No wife deserves that kind of brutal treatment.'

'Are ye married, then?'

'I'm very happily married.'

'And do ye have bairns?'

'Yes,' said Leeming, 'we have two children.'

Paterson suddenly thrust his face inches away from Leeming's nose.

'How do ye ken they're *yours*?' he asked with a wicked grin. 'How can ye prove that ye're their father?'

Insulted by the question, Leeming was about to punch him. What stopped him was the realisation of what Paterson was trying to tell him. The man was not party to the train crash at all. Contriving such a thing was beyond him. But he did have reason to rejoice over the death of one of the victims.

'Aye,' confirmed Paterson. 'When ma back was turned, Jock Laidlaw came callin' at my hoose. Now d'you see why I wanted him dead? The bairn you saw Maggie holding was no' mine. It was Laidlaw's bastard.'

When the cab dropped him off at his house, Andrews was still in a state of high excitement. It had been a wonderful evening and he'd been feted. After he'd kissed his daughter goodnight, he waved off the cab and let himself into the house. The wine had flowed freely and he'd had more than his fair share of it. Andrews felt that he'd earned every last sip. He'd dedicated his working life to the LNWR and it was fitting that the general manager should pay tribute to that. Other drivers were there but he felt that he held the whip hand over them. Not only did he have a daughter who'd become an artist of note, he was the father-in-law of a well-known detective. As he collapsed into his favourite chair, he realised how lucky he'd been.

Piece by piece, he began to reconstruct the evening, starting with his arrival at the restaurant and his deferential treatment by the staff. It had been good to meet his fellow drivers, men who understood the hardship and the risks of working on the footplate in all weathers. Then there was the meal to savour once more. He'd not eaten so much good food since his daughter's wedding. Though he hadn't been seated near Renwick, he had been able to give the general manager some advice at the end of the evening even though it seemed to go largely unheard. All in all, it had been an occasion to look back on with utmost satisfaction and Andrews knew that it would vibrate in his memory for a long time.

The evening had concluded with a ride home in a cab during which he'd boasted about the way he'd been tacitly acknowledged as the finest engine driver in the room. Madeleine had told him something about Isobel Renwick but he'd only half-listened. He tried to cudgel his brain to remind him what she'd said but only a few words emerged. They were enough to make him sit bolt upright. There'd been a burglary. Something was left in a safe. Andrews got to his feet and stumbled to the kitchen. Running the tap, he sprinkled cold water on his face. It brought him to his senses. After drying his face, he headed quickly for the front door.

Madeleine had also been reflecting on the evening and deciding that it had not really fulfilled its promise. Given what she'd been told by Isobel Renwick, it was not altogether surprising. It was up to the general manager and his wife to set the tone and they'd been lacklustre and preoccupied. Luckily, her father hadn't noticed and had been able to luxuriate in the occasion. Madeleine was grateful for that. He had been an honoured guest and she'd never seen him happier. She suspected that he would be talking about the event for several years.

As it happened, he wanted to talk about it there and then. Before she could retire upstairs to bed, she heard someone ringing the doorbell persistently. A servant admitted Andrews and he bustled into the drawing room.

'Thank God you're still up, Maddy,' he said.

'What's the trouble, Father?'

'Tell me what you told me in that cab.'

'I simply said that it was a very pleasant evening.'

'No,' he went on, 'it wasn't that. You talked about a burglary.'

'Yes,' she recalled. 'I spoke to Mrs Renwick. She told me that someone broke into the house the night before and opened the safe.'

'That was the bit I meant. Repeat it for me.'

'I just have.'

'There was something else,' he insisted. 'It was about what was *in* the safe.'

'Oh, yes,' said Madeleine. 'They thought it rather odd that the thief only took the money. He left Mrs Renwick's jewellery even though that was probably worth a great deal. Her husband was relieved that nothing else was taken. He had some important documents locked up in there. One of them was something to do with Her Majesty the Queen.'

He snapped his fingers. 'I know what it must be, Maddy. The royal family go to Balmoral every spring. You must remember the time when your old father had the privilege of driving the royal train as far as Carlisle.'

'Yes, I do. I was so proud of you.'

'In the interests of safety,' he said, breathlessly, 'details of the date and time of departure are kept secret until the last moment. Because the train will be travelling on LNWR track for much of the journey, Mr Renwick is informed well in advance.'

'Calm down, Father. There's no need to get so agitated.'

'But there is, Maddy. Can't you hear what I'm telling you?'

'Frankly,' she admitted, 'I can't.'

'What if the burglar came in search of that document from the palace?'

'That's impossible.'

'Is it? Just think for a moment.'

'The only thing taken was the money. All the documents were untouched.'

'I wonder,' he said, enlarging on his theory. 'The burglar wanted to make it *look* like a robbery when it wasn't. That's why he stole the money. He didn't need to take the document about the royal train because that would've given the game away.'

Madeleine was still mystified. 'What game are you talking about, Father?'

'The royal family could be in danger.'

'You're letting your imagination run away with you.'

'Hear me out,' he begged, taking her by the shoulders. 'As the general manager, Mr Renwick would have details in that safe of when the royal train was due to leave. The burglar must have known that. He came in search of the information. And he didn't need to steal the document,' he pointed out. 'If he had, then they'd change the date and time of the royal visit to Scotland as a precaution.'

'My God!' she exclaimed. 'I begin to see what you mean.'

'All that the burglar was after was a look at the details. Once he had those, he'd got what he came for. In other words, he knows exactly when the royal family will be heading for Balmoral.' He beamed at her. 'Wasn't it clever of me to work that out, Maddy? It comes from having a son-in-law who's a detective.'

'Oh, I do hope you're wrong, Father.'

'I'm sure I'm right. I've driven the royal train, remember. I know the precautions they take. A pilot engine travels fifteen miles ahead to make sure that the line has been kept clear. That's how careful they are.'

Madeleine was alarmed. 'Her Majesty the Queen and her husband will be on the royal train with their children,' she said. 'Is someone planning to harm them?'

'I'm afraid they want to do more than that, Maddy.'

'That's appalling!'

'There are some wicked people in this world. It won't be the first time that one of them has tried to kill the Queen.'

'Robert must be told,' she cried. 'I must get word to him somehow.'

'There's one sure way to do that,' he said. 'This is an emergency. Tomorrow morning, we'll catch the first train to Glasgow.'

CHAPTER FOURTEEN

Nairn Craig was unfailingly polite to his visitors but doubts were beginning to form beneath the surface. When Colbeck and Leeming called on him in his office that morning, he hoped that they had some progress to report. Instead, they had to tell him that their belief that Lackey Paterson might have been involved in the crime had been unfounded. Cornered at last by the sergeant, he'd explained why he'd assaulted Laidlaw and why he'd had to flee from his job at the quarry. One more name could be crossed off the list of suspects. Craig was disturbed. The detectives he'd brought all the way from London had simply gone down a series of cul-de-sacs.

'Will we ever catch the villains behind this?' he asked, mournfully.

'I remain sanguine, sir,' replied Colbeck.

'That's more than I do,' said Leeming to himself. Aloud, he tried to sound more positive. 'These are still early days, Mr Craig. Other clues will soon come to light. They always do.'

'The sergeant is quite right. An investigation like this is bound to be protracted. We can't just wave a magic wand and solve the crime. We have to piece information slowly together.'

'I understand that,' said Craig, 'but I'm bound to be worried when you keep arresting the wrong people.'

'I didn't actually arrest Paterson,' said Leeming, defensively. 'Once I'd got the truth out of him, there was no point in doing so. As for the man I earlier mistook for Paterson, he was wanted by the police so I was right to arrest him.'

'We were equally right to apprehend the Usher brothers,' argued Colbeck. 'I regard their arrest as an incidental bonus. Had they not been caught, they'd have continued to plunder your freight unhindered. And while Paterson turned out to be innocent,' he went on, 'I think we should applaud Sergeant Leeming for his tenacity in tracking him down.'

Craig nodded. 'Yes, yes, I'm full of admiration. What was the name of the place where you found him?'

'It was a lodging house called Telfer's,' said Leeming. 'It's a hellhole for the poor and needy. There are plenty of those in this city, alas.'

'It was ever thus.'

Though the general manager tried his best to hide it, Colbeck could see how disappointed he was in their work. He wished that he could talk about some more productive lines of inquiry but none had so far emerged. In time, he was confident, they would. He turned to the parallel investigation.

'How is Inspector Rae faring?' he asked.

'No better than you, I fancy,' said Craig, 'though I daresay that he'll have a laugh at your expense when he hears that Paterson had no link with the crime.'

'A lot of people have had a laugh at our expense, sir.'

'Most of them are now in prison,' Leeming interjected.

'That won't be the case with the inspector, of course, but I think he'll be more respectful of our efforts in due course. That article in the newspaper exposed us to derision as well,' said Colbeck. 'I was glad when they printed an apology.'

'Yes,' grumbled Leeming. 'The trouble was that we were sneered at on the front page and the apology was tucked away inside the newspaper. They didn't even mention that Superintendent McTurk had been dismissed.'

'That's another incidental bonus,' noted Colbeck. 'We got rid of a man who tried to wheedle that reward money out of you by false pretences. I think that the Caledonian will be far better off without him.'

'I've already forgotten McTurk,' said Craig, looking down at some papers on his desk. 'I've got other things to worry about. There's a whole pile of demands for compensation for goods stolen or damaged in the crash. Sadly, people are much more concerned about their freight than about the three men who died hideous deaths. Then I've got an estimate of how much money we lost when the line was blocked. It made my eyes water. There was also a loss of goodwill, of course, but you can't put a price on that. Financing a railway company is a continuous nightmare. The crash has only made it worse. Never run a railway, gentlemen, unless you want an early grave.'

'You could say the same of the police service, sir,' said Leeming. 'It's full of danger. None of us can count on a long life.'

'Policemen don't have to cope with the financial burdens of the railway industry. Competition is intense and our rivals are merciless. It was only in recent memory, for instance, that we managed to knock some sense into the heads of those running the Edinburgh and Glasgow. Until then, they were conducting a ruinous price war against us.'

Colbeck had heard a different version of events. The Scottish shareholders of the two companies had looked on in despair as income slumped as a result of lower fares. In the end, tiring of the state of affairs, the English shareholders of both companies had convened a meeting in London and reached an agreement to work for a common purse for a period of ten years, the Caledonian taking over two-thirds of it. Craig was claiming credit for something forced upon him.

The general manager snatched up a letter from his desk.

'And here's another demand from the sabbatarians,' he went on. 'Their campaign has taken on fresh impetus. They've not only been daubing slogans on our rolling stock, they've used their artistry elsewhere.'

'In what way?' asked Leeming.

'There are reports of things being painted on station walls, bridges and above the entrance to tunnels. They've even been busy with their spades. Apparently, there's an embankment near Rutherglen into which they've carved SAVE THE SABBATH. They must have worked at night to cut that into the turf.'

'Will it have any effect, sir?'

'None at all,' said Craig, stiffly, 'beyond causing lots of annoyance, that is. We can't entertain the idea of suspending our services on a Sunday. If you're in business, you're subject to the laws of supply and demand. Passengers *want* to travel on the Sabbath. In some cases, it's the only day when they're able to do so. If we don't meet their needs, another railway company will.'

'One has to admire the sabbatarians in a way,' said Colbeck.

Craig grimaced. 'Don't ask me to applaud their activities.'

'I'm not applauding them, sir. Apart from anything else, they're trespassing on your property and defacing it with their slogans. But it takes courage to do that. While I don't hold with religious militancy, I think we should remember that it's prompted by a commitment to biblical teaching.'

'Where in the Bible does it say that you have to paint your demands on walls or dig up embankments to make your point?'

'Nowhere, sir,' conceded Colbeck, 'but the Good Book is full of inspiring stories about people who stay true to their faith even if they're persecuted for it.'

'The Caledonian is persecuting nobody.'

'But I can see what the inspector means,' said Leeming. 'These people are not ordinary criminals. They're devout Christians. We should remember that.'

'The only thing *I* remember,' said Craig with controlled vehemence, 'is what it costs us to clean up after them. These people are a menace. They need to be caught and convicted before they do something really serious.'

Tam and Flora Howie were pleased with the way that their new disciple had behaved. Any doubts they had about him had been swept away. Ian Dalton had not only done exactly what was asked of him, he had – overcoming his initial nervousness – found that he had a flair for it. He'd been out with the paintbrush three nights in a row and had decorated pieces of railway property with relish. Even though his nocturnal absences upset his wife, Dalton pressed on. When they finally achieved their objective of stopping trains on the Sabbath, he believed, he would confide in her and she'd be proud of her husband. For the time, however, she was told nothing.

Over luncheon together, Howie raised the subject of their new recruit.

'I think he's ready,' he decided.

'It's too soon to tell, Tam.'

'You should see him at work. He loves it.'

'But he hasn't been asked to do anything really dangerous yet.'

'We're pioneers,' said Howie. 'That's what Ian likes most. Others are following in our wake because they've seen what can be done. Someone has left a message on an embankment near Rutherglen, apparently, and station signs have been stolen from Edinburgh and Glasgow. A cross was painted on the windows of carriages belonging to the NBR. People have obviously heard what we've been doing to the Caledonian. We've started a movement, Flora.'

'The more, the merrier.'

'It's not really merriment. We're deadly serious.'

He speared the last potato with his fork and popped it into his mouth. They ate in silence for a while. A grandfather clock chimed in the hall.

'I must hurry,' he said. 'I promised to be back in the office at two.'

'What about Ian Dalton?'

'He's coming here tonight at the usual time.'

'Do we tell him?'

'Of course – he deserves fair warning.'

'What if we frighten him off?'

'He's gone too far to pull back now, Flora. My guess is that he'll jump at the opportunity and we do need him. If we went ahead without Ian, I think he'd be very upset. He's like us. He'll want to see the report of it in the newspapers.'

'Publicity certainly helps our cause.'

'It's been the making of it.'

'Until people know what we're doing, they can't copy us. It's only since they started to write about us in the newspapers that we've built up a following.'

'Momentum is vital.'

'That's why we must keep it up,' she said.

'We'll go on shouting at the railway companies until they finally listen to us. It's a contest between profit and the prophets,' said Howie, pleased with the phrase that tripped off his tongue and vowing to use it again. 'They want to make money – a laudable objective for any businessman – and there are six days in which to do it. That's enough for anybody. Set against the ungodly, there are people like us, who hold with the law of the prophets. We must protect the Sabbath and maintain Christian values in Scotland.'

'When do we strike?' she asked.

'Very soon.'

Flora rubbed her hands with glee. 'I can't wait.'

No expense was spared. Since they'd be in a train for over twelve hours, Madeleine and her father travelled first class. Leaving the bustle of Euston station, they went off on a journey that Andrews had taken many times when he worked for the LNWR. It made him highly critical of the driver, complaining that the man should have learnt to ease the train smoothly into a station instead of bringing it to a sudden halt that jolted them out of their seats. Madeleine had brought a book to read and was soon lost in the ordered world of Jane Austen. Though her father had bought a newspaper at the station, he fell asleep before he had time to finish it. The early morning departure that had taxed him somehow refreshed Madeleine. Dying to be reunited with her husband and to pass on their information to him, she remained fully awake.

When she took a break from a novel, there was always something interesting to see out of the window. Some of the countryside that scudded past was inspiring to a Londoner trapped in an urban landscape all day. But it was not a continuous story of scenic delight. There was ugliness as well. As on a previous visit, she was revolted at the sight of the thick industrial haze over Birmingham and its environs yet she experienced a thrill of joy when the train stopped – more gently, for once – in the station. It was the city in which Colbeck had proposed to her and where, in its justly famed jewellery quarter, he'd bought her a beautiful engagement ring. She looked down at her left hand to admire it once more, nestling, as it now did, against the solid gold band of her wedding ring. Her father chose that moment to wake up.

'Where are we?' he asked.

'We're in Birmingham,' she replied.

'Is that all? If I was on the footplate, we'd be pulling into Preston.'

'Don't be silly, Father!'

'I know how to get the best out of an engine.'

When it resumed its journey, the train powered north with occasional stops of longer duration so that passengers could make use of station facilities and buy some refreshments. Because they always had travelling companions, it was impossible for them to discuss the reason that put such urgency into their desire to reach Glasgow. It did not stop Madeleine from thinking about the perceived threat to the lives of the royal family. She hoped that her father had misinterpreted the information about the burglary and that her husband, considering the evidence, would dismiss their fears as groundless. If that were the case, she'd be very relieved and heartened by the fact that she had at least got to see Colbeck and would be able to spend the night with him. Yet she had the unsettling sensation that there was no mistake. She and her father were in possession of evidence about a potential assassination of the Queen.

After changing trains at Carlisle, they found themselves alone in a compartment at last and were able to talk freely. Andrews, too, had been dwelling on the subject.

'It's happened before, you know.'

'What has, Father?'

'Attacks on the Queen,' he told her. 'The first one was soon after she was married. You were too young to remember it, Maddy. The Queen and Prince Albert were travelling in an open carriage when a young man rushed forward with two pistols. Luckily, he missed with both shots.'

'I remember reading about that somewhere,' she said.

'He was sentenced to death and should have been hanged but he wasn't.'

'That's right. He was declared insane.'

'I think *they* were insane *not* to put a rope around his neck,' he argued. 'He tried to kill our Queen. If a mad dog mauls a child to death, you don't spare his life because he was mad at the time he did it.'

'That's not a fair comparison.'

'It is to me. Then there were some other people who tried to shoot Her Majesty,' he went on. 'One of them got very close to her but his gun wasn't loaded. Even so, he was rightly condemned to death. Then they did it again, the fools. They let him off. Instead of hanging him, they only transported him.'

'I do recall the last time it happened,' said Madeleine. 'The Queen was attacked by someone who hit her over the head with a walking stick. It was frightening. He could have dashed out her brains.'

'Yes, Maddy, and the worst of it was that he was a retired soldier. He'd pledged to fight for Queen and Country, not to try to take Her Majesty's life. There are enemies all round her,' said Andrews, worriedly. 'We've unmasked the latest one, thank God.'

'We haven't unmasked anyone. All that we know – or *think* we know – is that the royal family may be put in jeopardy.'

'I'm certain of it.'

'I keep wishing that you turn out to be wrong.'

'When am I ever wrong?' he challenged, tapping his chest.

'Lots of times,' she riposted with a laugh, 'as you well know.'

'I'd never make a mistake about something this serious. I just wish that I'd heard what Mrs Renwick told you. Her husband should have reached the same conclusion that I did and told someone.'

'I fancy that he was too upset to think clearly. Mrs Renwick said that they were both in a daze. The police came but all they did was to take a statement and look at the safe. They obviously made no connection with the royal family.'

'That's because they didn't know about the visit to Balmoral.'

'I wonder what Robert will make of it all.'

'He ought to shake me by the hand and offer me a job as a detective.'

'You're retired, Father,' she reminded him, 'and you've earned a rest. You're too old to join the police force. Besides, people don't just become detectives. They have to start in uniform as a constable. That means walking through the most dangerous parts of London after dark. How would you like to do that?'

'I wouldn't, Maddy,' he confessed.

'In that case, you can't become a real policeman.'

'Then I'll be a chief advisor.'

'Make sure you only give advice,' she warned. 'Robert is in charge of the investigation. If you try to tell him what to do, he might forget that you're his father-in-law.'

'But I'm an important witness here.'

189

'All that you have is a theory.'

'It's much more than that. I once drove the royal train, remember.'

'Yes,' she said, 'and I was very proud of you for doing so. But all you did was to take it to Carlisle. You didn't leave London in the knowledge that the passengers were in mortal danger.'

The move to the Strathallan Hotel was a success in a number of ways. It was much closer to the headquarters of the Caledonian, it was less expensive and therefore appealing to Nairn Craig and it relieved Victor Leeming of his feelings of inferiority. The Strathallan was perfectly comfortable but it had none of the sumptuousness of The Angel Hotel. It had been Colbeck's idea to move. When Leeming came down from his room, the inspector was waiting in the lounge.

'What do you think, Victor?' he asked.

'I think I'll be able to sleep properly at last.'

'The beds at the Angel were wonderfully soft.'

'That was the trouble with them, sir,' said Leeming. 'I was almost too afraid to get into mine at night in case I creased those crisp white bed sheets. This place is much more suitable.'

'Mr Craig was happy for us to move. It saves the company money and he'll embrace anything that does that. Putting us into the Angel was his way of showing what faith he had in us,' said Colbeck. 'It was our reward for solving the case. He expected us to do that within days.'

'We'll be lucky to do it in months,' wailed Leeming.

'We've made more headway than you imagine.'

'I wouldn't say that, sir.'

'You've learnt a great deal about the geography of Glasgow and I've had a fascinating lesson about the character of Scottish railways – red in tooth and claw. Mr Craig is agreeable enough as a person but I don't doubt that he'd be as ready as any other general manager – Mr Weir of the NBR, for example – to adopt underhand methods to gain an advantage over his rivals.'

'They're all as bad as each other, sir.'

'That's inescapably true,' said Colbeck, 'but the fact remains that we've been retained by the Caledonian and we must do our utmost on its behalf.'

'What's the next step?'

'I've already taken it, Victor.'

'Oh?'

'While you were moving into this hotel, I went to see Inspector Rae. I wanted more details about the theft of the gunpowder from a barracks. He told me something very interesting.'

'What was that, sir?'

'A substantial amount was stolen – far more than was needed to cause the explosion on the Caledonian.'

'So someone somewhere still has the means to do it all over again.'

'I'm afraid so.'

'Have you told Mr Craig to be prepared?'

'No,' said Colbeck, 'I didn't wish to push him even closer to a heart attack. In any case, there's no indication that the Caledonian is under threat. With that amount of gunpowder in their possession, the villains could have caused a much bigger explosion and blocked the line for a week. Yet they picked a time and place when a goods train was due. The consequences were deliberately limited.'

'I wouldn't call the death of three railwaymen a limited result, sir,' said Leeming. 'And think how much freight was ruined. Well, you saw the site of the crash. It was like a battlefield after the fighting was over.'

'But supposing it had been a passenger train.'

'Then there'd have been hundreds of dead or badly wounded victims.'

'Yet there weren't,' said Colbeck. 'That's very singular.'

Leeming was bewildered. 'Are you trying to tell me that the people behind this outrage had consciences, after all?' he asked. 'They settled for killing three people when they could actually have murdered a large number?'

'No, Victor, they don't have a shred of sympathy for the loss of human life. They did exactly what they set out to do and that was to strike a telling blow at the Caledonian. But that's all they did. Horrific as the scene of the disaster was, however,' said Colbeck, 'it was much smaller in scale than it could have been. They caused havoc when they could have inflicted utter devastation.'

'What conclusion do you draw from that, sir?'

'I'm not entirely certain, Victor.'

'Well, I've been completely baffled from the start. My guess is that we'll never catch these villains. They've disappeared without trace.'

Colbeck was confident. 'Oh, they'll be back one day.'

'How do you know that?'

'Think it through,' he advised. 'They limited the disaster on purpose. That suggests to me that it's not an isolated phenomenon.'

'Then what is it, sir?'

'I fancy that it might simply be a precursor.'

Leeming started. 'There's going to be *another* crash?'

'They're saving that gunpowder for some reason. What we witnessed at the site was an experiment. They wanted to see if they could contrive a railway accident without going too far. In short, it was a rehearsal.'

'A rehearsal for what, sir?'

Lips pursed and teeth gritted, Colbeck inhaled deeply through his nose.

'I dread to think,' he said.

Bella Drew had never beheld so much money. It was only a fraction of the advertised reward but that didn't trouble her. It was cash in hand and Farr had earned it. She brushed aside his apology that he didn't have the full amount he'd promised. In her eyes, he was a hero who'd helped to catch two criminals. They met on the hillside and shared a meagre repast. While he munched his bread, she held the banknotes and stared at them in awe. Farr was beset by guilt.

'I shouldnae have done it,' he said.

'Why not?'

'I hate railways. If people steal from 'em, I ought to wish 'em guid luck and no' help the p'lice catch them.'

'But ye thought they'd caused tha' crash, Jamie.'

'Aye, I did.'

'It was right to tell what ye'd seen.'

'That wasnae why I did it.'

'Why else?'

'It was for ye, Bella.'

It was the closest he'd ever get to a declaration of love but it had an instantaneous effect. The unspoken and unresolved affection that had been lying dormant for years now came bubbling to the surface. She flung herself into his arms and kissed him on the lips. He responded at once, mutual passion atoning for their clumsiness and lack of experience. They held each other tight for a long time. Feeling excluded, Angus began to whine. Farr released her and patted the dog. Bella looked down at the money again.

'We could buy a wee cottage wi' this,' she said, covetously.

'We could buy a lot more with four hundred pounds.'

'There's no' a hope of getting tha', Jamie.'

'There is,' he said. 'They've no' caught them as set off tha' explosion. Inspector Colbeck told me to keep ma eyes peeled – and ye must do the same, Bella. There may be clues still lying aboot. We might even catch sight of the men the p'lice are after. Someone has to get tha' reward. Why no' us?'

By way of an answer, she kissed and hugged him again. Farr eased her down onto the grass. Angus's protest went unheard.

Not for the first time, Madeleine felt a surge of admiration for her father. She was exhausted by what seemed like an interminable train journey yet she was in the relative comfort of a first-class carriage. When her father had spent lengthy periods on a train every working day, he'd been standing on the footplate. His strength and endurance had been remarkable. Once they'd crossed the border into Scotland, his gaze had been fixed on the window, taking in the glorious sights that floated past and showing a particular interest in the ascent to Beattock Summit. It set off a series of reminiscences about steep gradients he'd had to negotiate on the LNWR. While half-listening to his commentary, Madeleine had been capturing memories of her own in her sketch pad, attempting landscapes for once then drawing quick sketches of a station whenever they pulled into one. It helped to pass the time and to distract her from the increasing discomfort.

When they reached Glasgow, they asked for directions to the headquarters of the Caledonian and went there by cab. Though it was mid evening, John Mudie was still on duty there and told them where they might find Inspector Colbeck and Sergeant Leeming. Another cab ride took them to the Strathallan Hotel and they arrived in time to see the detectives emerging from the dining room. Dropping her valise, Madeleine ran across the lounge on her toes.

'Robert!' she exclaimed.

He took her in his arms. 'Where did you come from?' he asked in amazement.

'Aren't you pleased to see me?' she teased.

'I'm delighted.'

'And so am I,' said Leeming. He nodded to her father who'd walked over to join them. 'Good evening, Mr Andrews.'

'Do they serve a decent beer here?' said Andrews.

'I can recommend it.'

When he heard that they had some important news, Colbeck took his visitors to an unoccupied reading room. After drinks had been ordered, they sat in a corner. Madeleine and her father took it in turns to tell their story. The detectives had met Archibald Renwick in the course of a previous investigation and they were intrigued to hear about the burglary at his house. Andrews wanted his moment of fame.

'I was the one who realised the danger,' he insisted. 'Maddy was about to go off to bed without a second thought. It was me who saw the connection with the royal family. That's why I went straight round to the house and why we caught the earliest train to Glasgow.'

'We're very grateful to you,' said Colbeck.

'Does that mean we were right to come?' asked Madeleine.

'Yes, it does – though I'm surprised that you didn't take the easier alternative of passing on your concerns to Superintendent Tallis.'

'If we'd gone to Scotland Yard, I'd never have seen *you*.'

'And I'd never have had the chance to go up Beattock Bank,'

said Andrews. 'I've heard so much about it over the years.'

'I went up with my eyes closed,' admitted Leeming.

'Then you missed a treat, Sergeant.'

'Going back to what you've told us,' said Colbeck, 'I can't thank you enough for what you've done. Especial thanks must go to my father-in-law, of course. If he hadn't been such an exceptional driver, he'd never have been invited to that dinner with the general manager and wouldn't therefore have even heard of the burglary.'

'There you are, Maddy,' said her father. 'It was all down to me.'

'Not entirely – it was Madeleine who noticed how uneasy Mrs Renwick was and who elicited the reason. Neither the lady nor her husband divined what might turn out to be the true motive behind the burglary.'

'It *is* the true motive. I'm certain of it.'

'I think you're right, Mr Andrews,' said Leeming.

'Yes,' said Colbeck, 'and you've put invaluable information into our hands. Preventing a crime is far better than solving one after it's been committed and we're now in a position to prevent one of the most unspeakable crimes of all.'

'Are we, sir?'

'Yes, Victor.'

'But we're tied up in Scotland,' said Leeming, 'investigating another crime. We'll have to pass on what we've been told to Superintendent Tallis.'

Colbeck smiled. 'Have you forgotten what we discussed earlier?'

'No – we discussed what to have on the menu.'

'I'm talking about gunpowder.'

'Oh, that. Yes, of course. I see what you're getting at now.'

'I'm afraid that I don't,' said Madeleine.

'Nor me,' added Andrews.

'How could you?' said Colbeck. 'The explosion that brought us to Scotland in the first place was caused by gunpowder stolen from an army barracks. I'm informed that an appreciable amount was taken, far more than was necessary for the scheme in hand. Why did the thieves take more than they needed?'

'They made a mistake.'

'No, Mr Andrews, they didn't. People who know how to handle gunpowder don't make mistakes because they have a tendency to be fatal. They know exactly how much to use for a specific purpose.'

'I don't follow you, Robert,' said Madeleine.

'They retained enough to commit a secondary outrage.'

She was a horror-struck. 'Do you mean what I *think* you do?'

'I'm afraid so.'

'I've just remembered that phrase you used earlier,' said Leeming. 'You said that the train crash wasn't an isolated crime.'

'In the light of what we've heard,' said Colbeck, 'that's palpably true. It was a rehearsal for a bigger and more daring crime. The same people are behind both. What they are planning is an attack on the royal family during their journey to Balmoral.'

'Then there's a simple way to foil it,' said Madeleine.

'Yes,' said Andrews. 'Pass on the warning and they can cancel the trip. The royal family would be perfectly safe then.'

'But they wouldn't,' Colbeck pointed out. 'These people are determined to achieve their aim. If they're baulked this time, they'll plan another assassination. As long as they're at liberty, the threat over the royal family will remain.'

'I agree with the inspector,' said Leeming. 'The arrangements must stay in place. They must take the train to Balmoral on the day already decided.'

'But that would expose the royal family to an attack,' protested Madeleine. 'You'd never want to do that, surely?'

'It may be the only way to catch these villains,' reasoned Colbeck. 'They're unaware that their plot has been uncovered and that gives us a huge advantage. We must find out when the royal train is due to leave and ensure that it does so without any danger to its illustrious passengers.'

CHAPTER FIFTEEN

Edward Tallis had his faults but nobody could question his devotion to duty. He always arrived early at Scotland Yard and departed late, sustaining himself throughout the day with frugal meals and an occasional cigar. His stamina was legendary. As younger men began to flag, he carried on with unabated gusto. It was just as well because crime was never-ending in the capital. A string of cases passed ceaselessly across his desk and, with so few detectives to deploy, he had to decide which of the crimes merited intervention from Scotland Yard. Once he'd initiated an investigation, he liked to keep abreast of it and his desk always had a pile of progress reports on it. One of them had come from Robert Colbeck and, when Tallis reached the end of another day, he picked it up and read it once more through jaundiced eyes.

Taken on its own terms, it was a shining example of how a report should be written. It was concise, highly literate and blessed with legible calligraphy. As a rule, Tallis enjoyed reading anything sent to him by the inspector. This time, however, there was a problem. A letter had arrived that morning from the general manager of the Caledonian Railway and its tone was markedly different. Putting the letter beside the report, Tallis picked out the discrepancies. Where Colbeck was optimistic, Craig voiced his serious disappointment. The report talked of valuable evidence yet the letter claimed there was a dearth of clues. And so it went on. Studying them side by side, it was difficult to believe that they referred to the same case.

Reaching for a cigar, Tallis bit off the end and spat it into the wastepaper basket. He lit the cigar and puffed hard, intensifying the glow until the flame got a purchase. He was soon wreathed in comforting smoke.

After reading the report one last time, he used the cigar to set light to it.

'What are you up to, Colbeck?' he growled.

The shock of seeing his wife appear out of nowhere had given way instantly to a sense of overwhelming pleasure. Colbeck was ecstatic. Madeleine had not only banished his feeling of being hopelessly cut off from her, she and her father had provided evidence that moved the investigation on to a different level. As so often in the past, chance had contrived what hard work and an acute analytical brain had failed to supply. Colbeck was duly chastened. He had toyed with the notion that the crash was only one part of a much bigger criminal enterprise but it had never entered his mind that what he was actually investigating was a plot to kill Her Majesty, the Queen and her family en route to Balmoral. What seemed incredible at first glance took on more and more certainty as he weighed the evidence.

For the time being, however, even so monstrous a crime as assassination could be held in abeyance until he was in a position to take active steps to prevent it. The reunion with Madeleine took precedence. As they lay together in bed, entwined in each other's arms, they were in Elysium. It was Colbeck who eventually broke the silence.

'You came a day too late.'

'We only found out about the burglary yesterday evening.'

'I know that, Madeleine,' he said, squeezing her gently, 'and it's not a criticism. Twenty-four hours ago, Victor and I were staying at The Angel Hotel which is the nearest thing to a palace in which *I'll* ever sleep. Had you been there, you'd have had a bed fit for a queen.'

'This bed is comfortable enough for me,' she said, snuggling up to him.

'When we're together, *any* bed is perfect.'

She kissed him. 'What a sweet thing to say!'

'It happens to be true.'

'Why did you leave the other hotel?'

'It made Victor feel that he had to walk on eggshells.'

Madeleine smiled. 'He's always uneasy in the presence of wealth.'

'It's not envy with him. It's a deference I've tried to talk him out of many times. Victor is much happier here. Well,' he added, 'as happy as he could be when he's away from his wife and family.'

'Has he been moping?'

'He has, Madeleine.'

'And I hope that you've been moping as well,' she said.

Colbeck was tactful. 'I did brood from time to time.'

'I did nothing else from the moment you left home. Father kept saying that I should have gone with you.'

'That would have been wonderful had it not been so impractical.'

'Don't you want me here?' she asked, poking him in the ribs.

'I thought that I'd already answered that question.'

They shared a marital laugh and pulled each other even closer.

'I'm so glad that our journey was not in vain. On the way here, I must confess, I began to lose confidence. I thought you might regard the evidence we brought as far-fetched and irrelevant.'

'It's neither of those things, Madeleine. It's a revelation.'

'That made the rigours of the long ride somehow more bearable.'

'You'll have to endure that long ride again, I fear.'

'Yes – but this time my dear husband will be with me.'

'Is it going to become a habit?' he asked. 'Following me whenever I leave London, that is. When we were in Exeter last year, you made a surprise appearance and you've done it again in Glasgow. If this pattern is repeated, Superintendent Tallis will be very angry. You know his opinion of the institution of marriage. He'd never countenance the idea of a female detective.'

'We *had* to tell you what we found out at that dinner.'

'You were right to do so. I can't thank you enough.'

'Don't let that stop you doing it,' she said with a smile. 'What happens next? You'll have to alert the royal family, obviously, but what then?'

He kissed her tenderly. 'Ask me in the morning.'

It was getting more difficult. Alarmed at the spread of vandalism, the Caledonian Railway increased the number of its policemen on night duty and there was a corresponding increase in nightwatchmen. With so many more eyes and ears to contend with, the sabbatarians had to exercise greater care. When Ian Dalton set out with his paintbrush on another nocturnal excursion into crime, he came very close to being caught. His new-found boldness worked against him. Trying to paint some letters across the stationmaster's office, he made too much noise and aroused a passing railway policeman. Had it not been for Tam Howie's quick thinking, they might both have been arrested. Dalton had to abandon his paint pot and run. Howie grabbed him by the arm and rushed him to a hiding place behind the ticket office. They stayed in their place of refuge for half an hour before it was safe to leave.

On the cab ride back home, they were able to compare notes.

'I failed,' said Dalton, dejectedly.

'We're bound to have a setback now and then, Ian.'

'I shouldn't have been so cavalier.'

'It was moving that bench out of the way that caused the trouble,' said Howie. 'It scraped along the floor and gave the game away.'

'I lost the paint pot.'

'That's easily replaced.'

'I blame myself, Tam. I'm very sorry.'

'We escaped. That's what matters.'

Dalton was grateful to him. Expecting a rebuke, he was only getting support.

'Thank you for being so tolerant with me,' he said.

'You've been a godsend to us, Ian, but I think we learnt a lesson tonight. We have to hunt outside the city where the patrols are not so regular. And we must preach our gospel in a more deafening way. In fact,' Howie went on, 'that's something I meant to broach with you.'

Dalton was eager. 'Go on. I know you and Flora have bigger ambitions.'

'You may not agree with what we propose.'

'I've followed in your footsteps so far.'

'Yes, but we're about to take giant strides. Let me say at the outset that if you disagree with our project – or if you feel unable to take part – we'll quite understand. It's a lot to ask of anybody. All that we've done so far,' said Howie, 'is to gain attention. It's made no difference to the Caledonian. Trains continue to be run on the Sabbath. We need to do something that will change their minds.'

'And what's that, Tam?'

'It's a plan that involves a lot of reconnaissance.'

Leaning closer to his companion, Howie outlined the scheme that he and his wife had dreamt up. It had already been touched on at the meeting they held with members of their congregation but nobody – Dalton included – believed that they would carry out such an audacious plan. Yet that was precisely what Tam and Flora Howie intended to do and Dalton had the opportunity to join them. He slapped a thigh in celebration.

'That's brilliant, Tam!'

'We can count on your help, then?'

Dalton grinned. 'You won't be able to keep me away.'

The first thing that Colbeck did after an early breakfast was to visit Nairn Craig to acquaint him with the latest development. The latter was shaken to the core by the notion that his railway would be the setting for an attempted assassination. Colbeck impressed upon him the need to maintain secrecy. If news of the plot leaked out, it would spread quickly and, ultimately, reach the ears of those planning the crime. They would be frightened away and Craig might never discover who had caused the train crash. When he'd controlled his feelings of panic, Craig accepted the wisdom of the advice and promised to say nothing. As a patriotic man, however, he was outraged.

'How could anyone wish to murder our dear Queen?'

'A number of people have already tried, sir,' said Colbeck, 'and they've not all been deranged. I can't believe that anyone would hate Her Majesty enough as a person to want her dead. It's what she represents that attracts enemies.'

'Do you think that this is a foreign conspiracy?'

'It could be.'

'Then it has to be the Russians,' decided Craig. 'They'll never forgive us for winning the Crimean War. This is their revenge.'

'It could equally be the revenge of someone much nearer home,' said Colbeck. 'The Act of Union provoked great opposition at the time and it still rankles with some people a hundred and fifty years later. Deplorable as it is, there are fanatics who'd take their Scottish nationalism to extremes. Then there's something else you must consider,' he went on. 'The Queen may be only an incidental casualty. Her husband will be travelling with her and he has his own detractors. Supposing one of those enemies has designs on Prince Albert's life? Supposing that *he* is the target?'

'The threat is too horrible to contemplate.'

'Forewarned is forearmed.'

'But wait a moment,' said Craig, spying a possible source of relief. 'There's no certainty that the Caledonian has been chosen by these people, is there? The royal train will go all the way from London to Aberdeen. It could be attacked anywhere along the line. Why single out us?'

'Because that's where they held their trial,' replied Colbeck. 'All the elements required were present. They had rural seclusion, a rock face that could be blasted apart and a gradient that slowed the train down. On the journey between Carlisle and Glasgow, those factors are repeated time and again. The logical supposition is that they'll select your railway again, Mr Craig. Why put themselves to the trouble of searching for an ideal location two or three hundred miles south when they already have what they need on a stretch of the Caledonian?'

The general manager's hands went to his head and he emitted a low moan.

'We're doomed,' he said.

'You shouldn't view it in those terms, sir. Instead of seeing this as a plot against the royal family,' said Colbeck, 'regard it as the one chance we have of apprehending the villains behind it – and behind the earlier crash, of course.'

'Must you bait the hook with the royal family to do so?'

'That will be up to them, sir. No compulsion will be involved. They'll be made fully aware of the situation before they agree to take their holiday in Scotland at the appointed time.'

'This is all too much for me,' said Craig, pacing his office and searching for a way out of his dilemma. 'Coming on top of the crash, it's a crippling blow. Imagine what would happen if the Queen *were* assassinated on the Caledonian. We'd bear a stigma for ever.'

'By the same token,' Colbeck told him, 'if the plot is foiled, you'll get your share of congratulation for the way that you helped us. There'll be no stigma, sir. I promise you that it will never reach that stage.'

'Can you guarantee that a calamity will be averted?'

Colbeck measured his words carefully. 'One can never offer an absolute guarantee,' he said. 'What I can pledge is our total commitment to the task of finding and arresting these people before they have the chance to carry out their attack. I have every confidence that we'll succeed, Mr Craig.' He flashed a reassuring smile. 'As you're aware, we have a strange habit of doing so.'

The newspapers that morning were painful to read. Edward Tallis was once again attacked by name. It was not for any fault on his part. The detectives involved in a bungled investigation in

Whitechapel should have been excoriated, not the man who had delegated the task to them. That, at least, was what he believed. It was always the same. The press had chosen Tallis as their favourite target and his relations with them remained hostile. He had even featured in cartoons. Colbeck knew how to deal with reporters. His blend of charm and diplomacy always earned him flattering headlines. The superintendent, by contrast, was characteristically truculent with the press and he paid the price for it. After reading the latest hurtful descriptions of him and his detectives, he put the newspapers in the wastepaper basket and sulked.

The truth of it was that solving the murder in Whitechapel had been beyond the men he assigned to the case. They were too raw and untried, making mistakes at every stage and – worst of all – allowing the chief suspect to flee to Dover where he boarded a ship to France. That constituted an admission of guilt in Tallis's view and in the opinion of the press. The killer would never be brought to justice, it was claimed, because he'd gone abroad where Scotland Yard had no jurisdiction. That would not have deterred Robert Colbeck. In order to solve a murder that occurred on the Sankey Viaduct, he had once followed a trail to France and made significant arrests there. Colbeck would go anywhere in pursuit of the guilty even if, Tallis recalled, it meant crossing the Atlantic.

Unfortunately, Colbeck was unique. Apart from anything else, he seemed to have extraordinary luck. It was something glaringly absent from Tallis's life. He was dogged by ill fortune. The superintendent was certain that Colbeck would have solved the murder of a Whitechapel tailor within a matter of days, whereas the detectives who handled the case spent the whole time in a state of total confusion before letting their chief suspect slip through their fingers. The trouble was that the Railway Detective was still in Scotland when he was desperately needed in London.

Unusually, Colbeck had not so far distinguished himself in his latest investigation, sending an ambiguous report of his activities to mislead the superintendent. That had made Tallis livid. He wanted Colbeck back at Scotland Yard to upbraid him.

Rising from his chair, he stormed out of the room and walked along the corridor to Colbeck's office. There was one thing he could be sure of finding there and that was a copy of Bradshaw's railway timetables. Tallis snatched the volume down from the shelf and flicked through the pages until he found the one he wanted.

'Get back here, Colbeck,' he warned, menacingly, 'or I'll come to Glasgow to drag you back here.'

He snapped the book shut like a steel trap.

On the first stage of their journey, they were fortunate enough to have a first-class compartment to themselves. Colbeck and Madeleine sat with their backs to the engine while Andrews and Leeming faced it. Carlisle was just over a hundred miles from Glasgow and it was there that they'd change trains to travel on the LNWR. Until then, they had both privacy and relative comfort. Three of them settled back to enjoy the journey. Leeming viewed it with dread. Apart from the descent of Beattock Bank, there was half a day on the railway to face. What reconciled him to the trip was the thought that he'd be reunited with his wife and children. It was worth suffering any amount of pain and disquiet. Against that joy could be set the misery of having to return to Scotland before long. It was disconcerting.

For Andrews the train journey was a march of triumph. Thanks to him, he decided, a crime that would have outraged the entire country could be nipped in the bud. His son-in-law had been highly complimentary but the gratitude would not end there. Andrews fully expected to be showered with praise at Scotland Yard and invited to the palace to be thanked in person by the Queen. As he let his imagination flow freely, he saw himself being brought out of retirement to drive the royal train to Scotland. He even envisaged a moment when he would be the subject of glowing tributes in the newspapers, spreading his fame far and wide. A medal might be struck in his honour. He would wear it with excessive pride. The broad smile on his face came in sharp relief to the expression of foreboding on the man beside him.

'When do we come back to Scotland?' asked Andrews.

'Father!' reproached Madeleine. 'We haven't even left it yet.'

'It was a fair question, Maddy.'

'I agree,' said Colbeck, 'but it's based on a false assumption. Victor and I may well be returning north of the border but there's no need to involve you.'

'I'm already involved.'

'That doesn't entitle you to get in the way,' said Madeleine.

'I wouldn't be in the way. I'd be *helping*.'

'You'd do that best by leaving everything to Robert and the sergeant.'

'Without me,' Andrews reminded her, 'the truth would never have come out.'

'Without Madeleine,' said Colbeck, 'you'd never have been in a position to make the deductions that you did. It was your daughter who extracted the information from Mrs Renwick. We are indebted equally to both of you.'

'In any case,' said Leeming, joining in the argument, 'it may not be necessary for any of us to come back to this weird country where most people haven't even learnt to speak English yet. That's my hope, anyway. When the Queen hears about the threat, she'll probably cancel the visit to Balmoral, which will be a pity. If that happens, there'll be no attack on the royal train.'

'But there'll certainly be an attack of another kind. The difference in that case,' stressed Colbeck, 'is that we'll have no idea when and where it will come. We're dealing with people dedicated to a course of action. If one plan falls apart, they won't simply give up. They'll devise another.'

Madeleine shivered. 'That's a frightening thought!'

'So is making this train journey again,' murmured Leeming.

'I still think that you should make use of *me*,' persisted Andrews. 'I have a stake in this investigation.'

'You've done all you need to do,' said Colbeck, 'and we salute you for that. While I'm away in Scotland, however, I take solace from the fact that you'll be in London to look after Madeleine.'

'It's the other way around,' she teased.

'You're interdependent and that's how it should be. There's another drawback to your kind offer, Mr Andrews, and that's our superintendent. He'd never let a civilian take a central role in an investigation. Victor and I are trained to cope with violence and danger. You are not.'

'Nothing frightens me,' declared Andrews.

'The decision must stand.'

'Well, it's a wrong decision.'

'Father!' exclaimed Madeleine. 'Accept it with dignity.'

'I'm sorry, Maddy,' he said, raising a palm. 'My tongue ran away with me. I should have looked in the mirror to remind myself how old I am. I can't go running up these hillsides like a mountain goat. That's for younger men.'

Leeming glanced through the window. '*I'm* a younger man,' he said, 'but I shudder at the notion of climbing some of these crags. I'd get dizzy up there. What I want to know,' he continued, 'is who exactly we're looking for?'

'We're looking for implacable enemies of the Crown,' replied Colbeck.

'But where have they come from?'

'Mr Craig thought that they might be Russians, enraged by the way that they lost the Crimean War.'

'Do you think that's likely, Robert?' asked Madeleine.

'To be candid, I don't. Their language and appearance would mark Russians out at once. And how would they know that details of the royal visit to Balmoral would be kept in Mr Renwick's house? Meticulous planning has gone into this. Advice has been taken from someone with an inside knowledge of the railways.'

'What's your theory?'

'I don't have one, Madeleine. It could be the work of Scottish nationalists or of English people with republican sentiments. And there are an untold number of other possible candidates. Not least among them are Irish dissidents.'

'They're always banging the drum about something,' complained Andrews.

'Some people might say they had just cause.'

'Well, I'm not one of them.'

'What about those sabbatarians we heard about?' asked Leeming. 'Could they turn out to be the devils behind all this?'

'No, Victor,' said Colbeck with amusement. 'Their campaign is against devilry and they see it manifested in railway companies that run trains on Sundays. Sabotage might be within their compass but they'd revere the royal family and do nothing to harm them. One group we can safely forget are the sabbatarians.'

The first thing that greeted him when Tam Howie returned home from work that evening was the sound of the piano. His wife was filling the whole house with the mellifluous strains of a Beethoven sonata. Flora played the organ at the kirk and was at home with any keyboard instrument. Her musical taste was catholic. As the sonata died out, it was replaced by the sound of a Hebridean folk song. After hanging his hat on the stand, Howie came into the parlour and kissed her gently on the head. She broke off at once and turned round.

'Don't stop,' he said. 'I love that tune.'

'I've practised long enough, Tam. My fingers are aching. Did you have a good day at the office?'

'It was much like any other. But what have you been doing with yourself this afternoon – apart from coaxing lovely music out of the piano, that is?'

'I've taken another look at the map,' she said.

'I was hoping you'd do that.'

'Well, we need to make a decision soon.'

Swinging round on the piano stool, she stood up and crossed to the table. A map of south-west Scotland lay open on it, the Caledonian railway zigzagging its way between Dumfries and Strathclyde. A number of crosses had been marked along its route. Howie bent over the table to examine them.

'Do we need to go far from Glasgow?' he asked.

'I think so.'

'There's open countryside much closer.'

'But it doesn't always give us what we want.'

'I don't understand, Flora.'

'Take this place, for instance,' she said, touching one of the crosses on the map. 'It looks ideal and it's less than fifteen miles away. But I discovered that they're cutting down the forest nearby and sending the timber to Carlisle. The area will be crawling with people. If we go there, we're sure to be seen.'

'Someone has been doing her homework,' he said, appreciatively.

'We can't be too careful, Tam.'

'What else have you found out?'

Flora worked her way through the other places marked on the map. All the locations had promise but some were more tempting than others. Her choice fell on a place that looked completely isolated on the map.

'This is the one,' she decided.

'It would take us ages to get there in a trap.'

'Then we take a train to the nearest station and hire our transport. We'd be taken for a middle-aged couple out for a bracing ride in the country.'

'But there'll be three of us,' he reminded her. 'Ian will be there.'

'I'm wondering if that's such a good idea.'

'He's fully committed, Flora. There's not a shadow of doubt about that.'

'We don't need to involve him on Saturday. We can reconnoitre the area on our own and report back to him.'

'Ian would only feel excluded.'

'I'm thinking of his wife.'

'Morag doesn't have a clue what we're up to, Flora.'

'I wonder,' she said. 'When I was out shopping this morning, I met her in the street. Morag was pleasant enough – she always is – but she gave me a strange look. It must worry her that her husband has been out late at night. I had the feeling that she blames us for leading him astray.'

'What if she does? She won't breathe a word about it to anyone else.'

'It might be better if Ian stayed at home with her on Saturday.'

'But he wants to be with us,' argued Howie. 'As for his wife, she'll never challenge him. Morag is as timid as they come. One day – when we finally regain the Sabbath for its true purpose – Ian will tell her the truth. It will be safe to do so when it's all over. If she realised what was going on at this point, the woman would worry herself to death.'

'She's going to worry a great deal if her husband leaves her for a whole day on Saturday. What will Morag think about us then?'

'She'll think what she's always thought about us. I'll be looked upon as a pillar of the kirk and you'll be viewed as the gifted organist you are. In other words, Flora, we're above suspicion.' He put an arm around her. 'Morag is not like you, my dear, able to take a full part in the campaign. You're a woman in a thousand. But I've promised Ian that he'll be travelling with us on Saturday,' he said with firmness, 'and that arrangement must stand.'

Edward Tallis had had a day of unrelieved distress. Having read the unfavourable comments about himself in the press, he had to listen to them again when he was summoned to the commissioner's office and asked to explain why Scotland Yard was being mocked so openly. News then arrived of the collapse of a trial in which Tallis had an interest. By dint of patient surveillance, two of his officers had identified what they believed to be a man who forged official documents for other criminals. His arrest was regarded as a coup and the subsequent trial a formality. Yet the evidence was deemed inadequate by the jury and the judge set the man free to continue his criminal career. Since he had set the original investigation in motion, Tallis felt the setback like a blow in the stomach.

Other disagreeable experiences followed throughout the day, culminating in the discovery that his cigar box was empty. When he dispatched an underling to the tobacconist, the man returned with the news that the chosen brand of cigar was temporarily out of stock. Bruised by harsh criticism and unable to reach for the succour of a smoke, Tallis went on the rampage, touring the building in search of detectives he could berate in order to drain off some of his fury. Much of it still remained, however, boiling inside the cauldron of his brain and seeking someone it could scald and mark for life. Inevitably, the victim selected was Robert Colbeck. He had to take the punishment. Tallis resolved that he'd catch the train to Scotland in the morning and make the inspector's ears burn with shame.

He was seated at his desk, staring at the empty cigar box, when there was a tap on his door. He barked a command that would have sent most people running for safety but his visitor was obviously prepared to brave the tempest. The door opened and Colbeck stepped into the room with a smile.

'Good evening, sir,' he said, affably. 'I knew that you'd still be here.'

Tallis gaped at him. 'I thought you were in Scotland.'

'We decided to come back, sir.'

'Does that mean you *solved* the crime?'

'I'm afraid not,' said Colbeck. 'What we have done is to recognise its true nature. That impelled us to return to Scotland Yard.'

'I had your report,' said Tallis, ready to explode, 'and it was deliberately misleading. A letter from Mr Craig gave a truer picture of events and claimed that your visit to Scotland had achieved practically nothing.'

'Mr Craig doesn't think that now, I can assure you.'

'Why is that?'

'If you'll permit me, sir, I'll tell you.'

'And where is Leeming?' demanded Tallis. 'Did you leave the sergeant in Glasgow?'

'No,' replied Colbeck, 'I sent him off to his family then I took my own wife back home in a cab before I came here.'

The superintendent leapt to his feet. 'Am I hearing this correctly?' he said in disbelief. 'You're in the middle of a major investigation yet you find time to come home to see your respective wives. Is that what you're saying?'

'Let me be more precise. Sergeant Leeming has gone home for the night but I didn't return in order to see my wife. Mrs Colbeck was in Glasgow with us.'

'Good Lord! This gets worse and worse.'

'My wife was there for a purpose, sir.'

'I don't need to be told what that purpose was,' said Tallis with disdain. 'You are a detective, damn you! When you're involved in an investigation, you have no time to be a husband as well. Make that abundantly clear to Mrs Colbeck.'

'I've already done so.'

'Then what – in the name of all that's holy – was the lady doing in Glasgow?'

Colbeck had no opportunity to explain. He was caught in a veritable storm of vituperation. Tallis roared on for several minutes, blaming him for his apparent failure, chiding him for sending a false report of progress, and threatening him with demotion. At the end of his harangue, he sat back in his chair and reached for his cigar box. When he saw that it was empty, he hurled it to the floor. Colbeck retrieved it and set it down on the desk.

'May I be allowed to speak now?' he asked politely.

Tallis was enraged that his visitor was so relaxed and unperturbed.

'You should be cowering with shame, Inspector.'

'There's no reason to do so, sir. What I bring you is news of a far more serious crime than the one we were sent to investigate. It's my belief that the royal family could be in danger.'

'Are you trying to trick me again?' said Tallis, voice thick with suspicion. 'I want no more false reports, Colbeck.'

'This one, I'm afraid, is horribly true. Judge for yourself, sir.'

Having finally got a chance to speak, he didn't waste it. Colbeck gave a succinct account of the evidence gathered by Madeleine and interpreted by her father. He explained how it related to the earlier train crash. Sceptical at first, Tallis soon came to see how convincing the theory was. By the time that Colbeck had finished, the superintendent was ready to admit that he'd been right to return to London.

'Who else knows about this?' he asked.

'Mr Craig is the only person apart from the four of us and you, sir. I told him that the utmost secrecy is required.'

'Quite right – if it becomes public knowledge, the villains will abandon their plan and devise another about which we'll have no forewarning.'

'The commissioner will have to be told, of course,' said Colbeck, 'and he will then liaise with the royal household and its advisors. The decision as to whether or not they travel to Scotland must rest with them.'

'I'm wondering about that document in Mr Renwick's safe,' said Tallis. 'My understanding is that travel arrangements by the royal family are advertised shortly in advance of the nominated day so that the line can be kept clear. The burglar had no need to steal the information.'

'The details he was after didn't simply concern the date of travel. Exact times of arrival and departure at every station on the way were in that document. My father-in-law has driven the royal train. He knows the protocol. And there's another thing that would have interested those behind the attack,' Colbeck went on. 'The document would have told them who'd be on that train and in which compartments they'd travel. They'd know exactly where to hit their target.'

Tallis took a few moments to assimilate all the information. Gone was his blistering antagonism towards Colbeck. In its place was an amalgam of gratitude and admiration. Scotland Yard had been alerted about a crime of grotesque proportions. If it succeeded, the consequences would be incalculable. At the end of a day in which he'd been constantly pilloried, Tallis spotted an opportunity to redeem himself.

'I owe you profound thanks for bringing this to my attention, Inspector,' he said. 'It's a national emergency. That's why I intend to take charge of the case myself. From now on, you and Sergeant Leeming will have me at your side.'

Colbeck quailed. The investigation had just lurched out of his control.

CHAPTER SIXTEEN

Jamie Farr always visited Lockerbie with mixed feelings. It was the home of the largest lamb market in Scotland and, though it was a vital source of income for the landowner who employed him, he never went there with any enthusiasm. Lambs he'd raised with great care were being sold for slaughter and that was bound to cause unease. His father had taught him that sentiment had no place in the life of a shepherd but it was a precept easier to repeat than to obey. Herding lambs into a pen in Lockerbie always troubled Farr. Even when he got a good price for his stock, he returned home with a satisfaction edged with sadness. What he did always enjoy, however, was the opportunity to explore the town. Lockerbie might not compare with the urban sprawl of Glasgow but it was much bigger than the villages and hamlets into which Farr usually ventured. It had well-planned streets, a plethora of shops, a thriving business community and, most recently, its own gasworks. Only twenty miles from the English border, it nevertheless retained its Scottish identity.

On his latest visit to the town, there was something to take his mind off the feelings of loss as he parted with his lambs. Farr was engaged in a search. He had reward money in his pocket and a desire to earn far more. He and Bella Drew had ambitions. They could never be achieved if he remained a shepherd whose father took the greater proportion of what little money came their way. The most he could hope for was to inherit their bare and comfortless cottage and that time might be far distant. Neither he nor Bella could wait that long. The crime was still unsolved. Those who engineered a train crash which resulted in death, destruction and enormous cost had still not been caught. Farr was certain that clues to their identity lay somewhere on the land that he patrolled. It might even be that they intended to strike again. The detective from Scotland Yard had implied that. Why had he told the shepherd to remain on the lookout if he didn't think the railway was still in danger?

Farr went hunting through a number of shops before he found what he wanted. It was in the window of a small establishment that sold second-hand clothing and a vast jumble of curios and other items. What he was after was half-concealed behind a pile of tattered magazines. He went into the shop and picked it up, surprised at its weight and noting that it had acquired a few dents over the years. The shopkeeper, a thin-faced man in his sixties, looked askance at the customer's smock.

'Pu' tha' doon, lad,' he warned. 'It's more than ye can afford.'

'I want it,' said Farr, stubbornly.

'And ye can tak the dog oot of heer. Whatever he breaks wi' waggin' his tail like tha', ye'll have to pay for.'

'Angus!'

The name was enough to make the dog sit down obediently beside his master.

Though the shopkeeper continued to protest, Farr examined the object he wanted, extending it to its full length and gasping in wonder when he applied an eye to one end. It would be well worth the price on the ticket that dangled from it.

Minutes later, he and Angus left the shop with the telescope.

'What time will you be back?' asked Madeleine.

'I don't know.'

'When will you return to Scotland?'

'I can't say.'

'What if the royal train is cancelled altogether?'

'One can only guess at the consequences.'

She was close to exasperation. 'Is there anything you *can* tell me?'

'Yes,' said Colbeck, turning to plant a kiss on her forehead. 'I can tell you that I love my wife more and more each day.'

They were in the hall of their house in John Islip Street. Colbeck had been studying himself in the full-length mirror before putting on his top hat to go out. After the restorative delight of a night in his own home, Colbeck had shared an early breakfast with his wife and was about to depart for Scotland Yard. While she was appalled that anyone should wish to harm the royal family, Madeleine saw that the situation might bring a tangential benefit for her husband.

'Will you get to meet Her Majesty?' she asked with excitement.

'I think it highly unlikely.'

'What about the Prince Consort?'

'That's a possibility,' he replied. 'He acts as Her Majesty's secretary, helping her to make the countless decisions that fall to her and shielding her from intrusion. It may well be that I have the honour of meeting Prince Albert, though, of course, it will not be for the first time.'

She smiled nostalgically. Though he was quite unaware of it, the Prince Consort had actually helped her friendship with Colbeck to develop in its early stages. At the Great Exhibition of 1851 – a project dear to the heart of the Prince – Colbeck had outwitted and apprehended people bent on destroying the vast glass edifice at Crystal Palace. As a result, he'd been thanked in person by the Prince who'd given him two free tickets to the exhibition, enabling him to invite Madeleine to join him on the first of their many outings together.

'The commissioner did well out of the exhibition,' he recalled. 'Because of his success in organising the policing of the event, he was given a knighthood. But I gained even more from the event. Those tickets from Prince Albert changed my life.'

The compliment made Madeleine beam with joy. She adjusted his cravat.

'You must look your best if you're going to meet royalty,' she said.

'It may not be for some time yet,' he said. 'The commissioner will make the initial contact. Indeed, I may not be directly involved in any way.'

'But you *should* be, Robert. It's your investigation.'

'Superintendent Tallis has other ideas. He's taken charge of it now.'

'That's unfair. You've done all the work.'

'He has the power of superior rank.'

'You should complain to the commissioner.'

'I've no wish to get involved in political infighting, my love,' he said. 'The fact is that the superintendent has the right to do what he's done. Like anyone else in the Metropolitan Police, I occupy a place in the structure of command. Those above me can direct my actions. I just hope that, in the superintendent's case, he doesn't hamper this investigation by being overly ambitious.'

'Do you think that he'll make a blunder?'

'I think that his vision is clouded by an unreal hope. This is his opportunity to shine, Madeleine,' he said. 'He's in search of his own knighthood.'

Having faced some biting criticism of late in the commissioner's office, Tallis was now able to approach it with a spring in his step. He had something of great moment to report and expected congratulation. Sir Richard Mayne didn't look as if he was in a congratulatory mood when he exchanged greetings with Tallis. He was still smarting from a recent attack on him in *Punch*, the satirical magazine quick to pillory what it saw as the shortcomings of the police service. The cartoon of him in *Punch* had made the commissioner look old, weary and woebegone. In reality, he was a handsome man who'd not long entered his sixth decade and whose face – framed by luxuriant hair and side whiskers – radiated intelligence. Son of a judge and a former barrister, he had what were deemed to be impeccable credentials when selected to run the Metropolitan Police Force. Joint commissioner with Charles Rowan until 1850, Mayne now had sole command.

After gesturing Tallis to a seat, he regarded him with displeasure.

'What bad news have you brought me this morning?' he asked.

'It's both bad and good, Sir Richard.'

'It's too early in the morning for riddles. Explain yourself.'

'There's a threat to the royal family,' said Tallis, 'but I'm in a position to block it and to arrest those responsible.'

He enlarged on his blunt opening statement, playing down the role of his detectives and giving the impression that the intelligence gathered had been largely the result of his personal intervention. Mayne was not deceived.

'Why wasn't I told this last night?' he demanded.

'I knew that you'd travelled out of London.'

'Then why didn't you come and find me?'

'I had no idea where you were, Sir Richard.'

'Saints preserve us!' exclaimed the commissioner. 'You're a *detective*, man. Was it beyond the bounds of your ability to track me down? As it happens, I was at a dinner in Beaconsfield. You could easily have reached me there.'

'I've reached you now, Sir Richard,' said Tallis with a weak smile, 'and told you everything that's relevant to the situation.'

'I have doubts about that. You've told me about an investigation in which Inspector Colbeck is involved yet you hardly mentioned his name. How did he come by this disturbing information? And why isn't he here to pass it on to me in person? He's far more articulate than you and can give me first-hand intelligence.'

Tallis took a deep breath and considered his reply. He felt that he'd never really been appreciated by Mayne. Of the two original commissioners, he'd much preferred to deal with Rowan, a military hero who'd fought and been wounded at Waterloo. As an army man himself, Tallis had felt an affinity with Rowan. They talked the same language and shared the same attitudes. Mayne was different, more aloof and intellectual, with traits that reminded the superintendent of Robert Colbeck. Yet the man's position had to be respected. An answer was needed.

'This is a matter of the greatest import,' he said. 'I feel that someone more senior than an inspector should be in charge.'

'That's a reasonable argument,' admitted Mayne, 'but my question is still unanswered. How did Colbeck learn of this appalling business?'

'It came to light in the course of his investigation, Sir Richard.'

'Be more explicit.'

'He was informed of the danger.'

'By whom?' pressed Mayne. 'Whom do we have to thank for the warning?'

Tallis cleared his throat. 'It was Mrs Colbeck,' he said, reluctant to yield up credit to anyone else. 'We must thank Colbeck's wife and father-in-law.'

'His father-in-law?' echoed Mayne with incredulity. 'Since when has a police investigation turned into a family matter?'

'It's all rather complicated, Sir Richard.'

'Do you dare to suggest that the intricacies are beyond my comprehension? Let's hear the full story,' insisted Mayne, rapping the top of his desk with his knuckles. 'You should bear in mind that, like Inspector Colbeck, I was a barrister before I joined the police. Grasp of detail is part of our stock-in-trade.'

Tallis gave a fuller account, explaining how a conversation with the wife of the general manager of the LNWR had aroused suspicion. It was painful for him to admit that they owed gratitude to a woman and a retired engine driver, especially as the two of them were related to Colbeck. Mayne had no such reservations. Once he knew all the facts, he praised Caleb Andrews for his perspicacity.

'Have you thanked the fellow?' he asked.

'I've not yet had the chance to do so, Sir Richard.'

'Make sure that you do. But for a stroke of luck, we'd be wholly ignorant of the fact that a conspiracy is afoot against the royal family.' He rose to his feet. 'I must visit the palace at once. They need to be informed immediately.'

'I'll be happy to accompany you,' volunteered Tallis.

'There's no need for that. You can stay here.'

Tallis got up and opened the door for him. 'What am I to do?'

'The obvious thing is to get in touch with Mr Renwick. He needs to know that the burglary at his house had a darker motive than mere theft. And he must be told that secrecy is imperative.'

'I've already sent Colbeck on that particular errand,' said Tallis, hoping that his initiative would be rewarded with approval. 'The inspector has met Mr Renwick before. I dispatched him in case you wanted me to go with you to the palace.'

'Whatever gave you that idea?' said Mayne. 'I need nobody to hold my hand, Superintendent. Still,' he went on, 'you have done something right today. Given the circumstances, Colbeck is the ideal man to talk to Archibald Renwick.'

After a space of several years, Renwick was pleased to see Colbeck again. When his visitor raised the subject of the celebration dinner, the general manager said how much he'd enjoyed meeting Madeleine and her father. Colbeck then informed him that the burglary at his home might be connected with a plot to assassinate members of the royal family. Renwick dismissed the claim out of hand at first. It sounded preposterous. After hearing about the investigation into the train crash on the Caledonian Railway, however, he soon changed his mind. As the truth dawned on him, he took a few steps backwards and rested against his desk for support. Still unsettled by the burglary, he was stunned when it took on a more sinister aspect.

They were in the drawing room in the general manager's house, a Regency mansion set in two acres of well-tended grounds. Renwick was a conscientious man. Colbeck had discovered that when they first became acquainted. A train robbery on the LNWR had brought the detective to the house on that occasion. This time, it was a potential crime of much greater magnitude.

'This is terrifying,' said Renwick, using a handkerchief to dab at his brow. 'My wife will be mortified when she hears about this.'

'Don't tell her, sir.'

'Why not?'

'You'd only make her suffer the torments you're experiencing.

Spare her that agony. There's nothing that Mrs Renwick can do to protect the royal family. Her contribution has already been made, inadvertent though it was. In talking to my wife about the burglary, she indirectly brought this conspiracy to our attention. Grateful as I am, I wouldn't distress Mrs Renwick by telling her so. The time for that will be when the danger is past.'

'I agree,' said Renwick after consideration. 'Isobel has a nervous disposition. Out of kindness, she needs to be kept in the dark. Thank goodness you came to warn me, Inspector,' he continued, visibly sweating now. 'I'll have the royal train cancelled immediately.'

'I'd advise against that, sir.'

'We can't jeopardise the lives of the Queen and her family.'

'We can't catch those behind this plot unless we can lure them out into the open,' said Colbeck, 'and that means allowing the present arrangements to stay in place. If Prince Albert and Her Majesty want to postpone the trip to Balmoral, then we'll bow to their decision but I have a curious feeling that they won't do that.' He took a step closer. 'There's no need to tell you that discretion is everything. The fewer people who know the truth, the better it will be. It's another reason why Mrs Renwick must not be told. Confine the facts to a small circle.'

Renwick nodded before dabbing at his brow again with the handkerchief. He tried to remain calm but his heart was pounding and his brain racing. If he sanctioned the departure of the royal train on the agreed date, he could be sending some of its occupants to their deaths. Guilt coursed through him and made him shudder.

'Why attack the train *there*?' he asked. 'It doesn't make sense. When they reach Aberdeen, the royal party has to travel fifty miles to Balmoral by carriage. They're much more vulnerable to an ambush there.'

'I'm aware of that, sir.'

'Why pick on a stretch of the Caledonian?'

'It's something that's causing anguish to its general manager,' said Colbeck. 'He always believed that that disaster could never occur in the same place twice. Apparently, it can. Mr Craig is bracing himself for the second catastrophe.'

'He can't possibly protect every inch of the line.'

'Quite so – it's far too long. A whole army of policemen couldn't defend it. In any case, their presence would alert the conspirators.'

'Who *are* they, Inspector?'

'We've yet to discover that, sir.'

'Basically, then,' said Renwick with alarm, 'you know nothing whatsoever about these people beyond the fact that their target is the royal family. You don't know where they come from or what their motive is. You haven't any real suspects so there's nobody you can arrest. They can cause a train crash then vanish without trace. More to the point,' he went on, despair creeping in, 'they can enter my house and somehow open a safe and you haven't the slightest idea how they did it.'

'That's where you're wrong, Mr Renwick.'

'They're ahead of you at every stage.'

'Put more trust in us than that, sir,' said Colbeck. 'The burglary not only gave us our first real advance in the investigation, it identified a suspect.'

'How did it do that?'

'Show me your safe and I'll explain.'

Renwick took him along a passageway and into the study, a large room with a mahogany desk, furniture and bookshelves. The shelves were crammed to capacity with matching volumes. On the one bare wall were some family portraits. Colbeck studied each of the bookshelves as if noting the titles.

'How did the burglar know where to *find* the safe?' asked Renwick. 'It's cleverly hidden. Well, *you'd* have no idea where it is, would you?'

'Actually,' said Colbeck, 'I would, sir, because my father was a cabinetmaker and I grew up learning about secret drawers in desks and hidden alcoves in walls. My guess would be that your safe is here.'

Taking hold of the edges of a bookcase, he pulled hard and it revolved outwards on hinges to reveal a large iron safe set into the brickwork.

Renwick was sobered. 'You did that so easily.'

'No more easily than the burglar, sir. Housebreakers know all the favourite places for a safe. The study is one of them. It's where one needs important documents and correspondence at hand. Once inside this room, the burglar would have located the safe in a matter of seconds.'

'But he then had to open it,' said Renwick, puzzled. 'When it was installed, I was assured that it was impossible to open without a key.'

'Then you were misinformed,' said Colbeck. 'There are people – blessedly few in number – who have a remarkable talent for opening any safe, no matter how solid and well constructed it might be.'

'This is a Chubb safe, reputedly one of the best available.'

'It was a good choice, sir, but it's not entirely burglar-proof. Are you familiar with the controversy at the Great Exhibition regarding famous locksmiths?'

'I can't say that I am.'

'An American gentleman named Alfred Hobbs visited the exhibition. He was a notable locksmith and he astounded everyone by picking one of the best Chubb locks in twenty-five minutes. Then there was the famous Bramah lock that had been on display in

229

a London showroom since 1790. Everyone who'd tried to pick it,' said Colbeck, 'had failed. It presented a more difficult challenge to Mr Hobbs but he did eventually succeed after forty-four hours. It wouldn't have taken him that long to open your safe, Mr Renwick. He would have been in and out of this study within ten minutes.'

'Yet you say that this fellow was a legitimate locksmith.'

'Fortunately, he was. On the wrong side of the law, he'd have been a menace. His visit to this country caused uproar among bankers and insurance companies who believed existing locks were perfectly secure. They persuaded the Royal Society of Arts to offer a prize for a strong and utterly reliable lock. The winner of the competition was a locksmith named Saxby,' recalled Colbeck. 'But there was an unforeseen defect in his work.'

'What was that?'

'Alfred Hobbs picked it within three minutes.'

'Dear me!' exclaimed Renwick.

'Fortunately, Mr Hobbs returned to America. But there are other people with similar skills. In some cases, they've worked in the lock trade before turning to crime. That's true of the man I have in mind.'

Renwick's hope stirred. 'You *know* who the burglar was?'

'I could hazard a guess.'

'Who is he?'

'Your house is well protected,' said Colbeck, 'and this is a safe that would test an ordinary cracksman. If I wanted something inside it – and the conspirators obviously did – then I'd hire the best man available.'

'What's his name?'

'Patrick Scanlan. He worked as a locksmith in Willenhall up in the Midlands until he decided that there was more money to be made as a burglar. In the criminal underworld he's well regarded.'

'Then you must arrest him at once,' demanded Renwick. 'I want to see the villain who dared to violate the sanctity of my home. I want him caught and punished.'

'We want him just as much as you, sir,' said Colbeck, 'because he can tell us who hired him. As a rule, he'd never take such a risk in order to retrieve information about a train journey. It would be meaningless to Scanlan. He'd have been paid extremely well to enter your house – and, of course, there was the incidental bonus of the cash that you had in the safe.'

'Why did he ignore my wife's jewellery?'

'Scanlan prefers to work alone. He never steals jewellery because he'd need a fence as an accomplice and that's an unnecessary complication to him. His targets are money and secrets.'

'What kind of secrets, Inspector?'

'He's a blackmailer as well as a thief. Safes tend to contain things of great value to their owner. In addition to valuables, there could be private correspondence intended for nobody else's eyes. Do I need to explain?'

'No, Inspector,' said Renwick, virtuously. 'There was nothing of that nature in my safe, I assure you. If this fellow *is* the burglar, he'll have found no letters with which to embarrass me. How sure are you that Scanlan is the man you're after?'

'Anybody else would have stolen the jewellery as well.'

'Do you know where to find him?'

'I wish that we did, Mr Renwick. We've been after him for some time. The search will be intensified now. The first thing I did when I got to Scotland Yard this morning was to set it in motion. As we speak, Sergeant Leeming is leading the hunt for Patrick Scanlan.'

Refreshed and invigorated by a night in his own bed, Leeming set about his task with enthusiasm. He'd been given a couple of younger detectives to assist him and he sent them off to explore Scanlan's known haunts. Months earlier, a description of the burglar had already been sent to every police station in London and occasional sightings of him had been reported. Scanlan, however, continued to evade arrest. Leeming began his search with two advantages. First, he was back on his home territory. A Londoner born and bred, he was at his happiest and most effective when working in the nation's capital. Second, he'd actually met Patrick Scanlan. Most of those hunting for him were relying on the detailed description pinned up in the police station and Leeming knew how misleading that could be. Scanlan took care to change his appearance from time to time. When he wore a beard, he looked nothing like the man depicted on the noticeboards. A complete change of apparel – and he could afford an expensive tailor – transformed him. Other forms of disguise were also used to keep recognition at bay.

Nevertheless, Leeming was confident that he'd be able to identify the man if they came face-to-face because he'd already got close to the man. It had been a year earlier and Scanlan had made a rare mistake. The police closed in on him and, after wrestling him to the ground, Leeming had handcuffed him. He remembered the feeling of satisfaction as the burglar was taken into custody. Conviction would surely follow and a master criminal would be imprisoned for many years. That, at least, had been Leeming's belief. In fact, imprisonment failed to last one night. Although he'd been searched beforehand, Scanlan had somehow picked the lock of his cell and the locks on the three doors between him and freedom. He'd been at liberty ever since, burgling houses at will and indulging in some profitable blackmail as well.

It was Colbeck who suggested a new line of inquiry. As a result, Leeming set off for a rehearsal room near Drury Lane. It was there that he encountered a man he'd met before and he quailed slightly in front of him.

'What is the meaning of this interruption, pray?' asked Nigel Buckmaster.

'I'd like a few minutes of your time, sir.'

'We are rehearsing *Othello*. It requires all my concentration.'

'You may be able to help us solve a crime,' said Leeming.

'Barging in here like this is a crime, in my opinion. Please depart, Sergeant.'

'Inspector Colbeck sends his regards, sir.'

Buckmaster's manner softened at once. He'd met the detectives in Cardiff when on tour there with his troupe. Colbeck had turned out to be unusually knowledgeable about the theatre and highly appreciative of the actor's skills. The sergeant, however, found those skills intimidating. Buckmaster was a tall, lean, lithe man in his thirties with flowing dark hair and an arresting handsomeness. His voice had a natural authority and his eyes were whirlpools of darkness. Looming over his visitor, he came to a decision and clapped his hands peremptorily. The motley group of actors turned towards him.

'I will return shortly,' announced Buckmaster as if declaiming a speech from the battlements. 'Do not waste time in idle discourse. Learn your lines and rehearse your moves.' With an arm around Leeming's shoulders, he swept him off to the adjoining room. 'Now, then,' he said, eyes flashing, 'how may I help you?'

Leeming blurted out his request. 'Inspector Colbeck wishes to know if you could recommend a good elocution teacher.'

'But the fellow has no need of one,' said the actor in surprise.

'He speaks beautifully. Were he not wedded to the police force, I'd employ him instantly. You, on the other hand, have a voice in sore need of help. Its timbre is unpleasing on the ear and you have the distressing habit of talking out of the side of your mouth.'

'This is nothing to do with the inspector or me, sir.'

'Then why do you come bothering me?'

'Allow me to explain.'

Without mentioning Scanlan by name, Leeming told him about a burglar who'd come from Willenhall to settle in London. What made him stand out among Cockney criminals was his Black Country accent. Indeed, it was his distinctive vowels that led to the arrest in which Leeming was involved. Yet they'd not given him away again and Colbeck suspected that Scanlan had taken the trouble to get rid of them. Money would have been no object. He could pay well for a new voice.

'Who is the finest speech tutor in London?' asked Leeming, respectfully.

Buckmaster drew himself up. 'He stands before you,' he said, striking a pose. 'I've rescued every voice in that rehearsal room. They come to me as gibbering idiots and I turn them into something resembling – and sounding like – professional actors. Needless to say, I only do this for members of my own company. I'd never lower myself to give elocution lessons to members of the public.'

'Do you know anyone who *does*?'

'I know dozens of people – failed actors, every one of them.'

'And who is the best?'

'That's a matter of opinion,' said Buckmaster, wrinkling his nose in disdain. 'Most of them are not fit to carry spears on stage, let alone take a leading role. They'd mangle every iambic pentameter in Shakespeare. That's why the theatre has discarded them as rank failures. So they set themselves up as self-appointed experts on voice instead.'

Leeming was still struggling to work out what iambic pentameters were. As the actor went on to praise his own work at the expense of those driven out of the profession, the sergeant barely heard a word. He suddenly realised why he was there.

'There must be someone you can recommend, sir,' he said.

'Only two of them would pass my rigorous standards.'

'What are their names?'

'Do you have a notebook?'

'Yes, sir,' said Leeming, producing it from his pocket with a pencil.

Buckmaster snatched both from him. 'I can give you their names and their addresses,' he said, scribbling on an empty page. 'Don't mention me, whatever you do. It will only excite envy. While I've soared, they both fell to earth.'

Taking notebook and pencil back from him, Leeming looked at the open page.

'Do they *both* live in taverns?'

'No – but that's where you'll find them. Rejection turns a man to drink.'

'Thank you for your help, Mr Buckmaster.'

'I must return to my rehearsal,' said the other with a grand gesture. 'But do give my regards to Inspector Colbeck. He's an astute theatregoer. He was once kind enough to describe my performance of Othello as masterly. Audiences will be able to feast on it once again at the Theatre Royal. I daresay that you saw the playbills on display as you came past.'

'Yes, sir, a blind man couldn't miss them.'

'And don't despair about your own voice. It's not beyond a cure. If I had you in my company,' said Buckmaster, taking him by the shoulders, 'I could improve it in every way. Instead of talking like a costermonger with a mouth ulcer, you could pass as an aristocrat in six weeks.'

'Thank you,' said Leeming, defiantly, 'but I like my voice the way it is.'

When he got back from market, the first thing that Jamie Farr did was to run to her cottage. As he came over the hill, he saw Bella in the garden, taking the washing down from the line. She looked bored and fatigued. As soon as she noticed him, however, her face was split by a grin and her whole body came alive. After taking the washing indoors, she came out again and raced up the hill to meet him, flinging herself breathlessly into his arms.

'I was hopin' to see ye,' he said.

'How was the market?'

'It was a'right.'

'Did ye get a guid price for the lambs?'

'Let's no' talk about tha'. Come wi' me, Bella.'

'Why?' she asked. 'Where are we goin'?'

'I've somethin' to show ye.'

She was excited. 'Is it for *me*, Jamie?'

'It's for both of us.'

Taking her by the hand, he led her upwards until they crested the hill. They walked along the ridge then stopped to take in the view. It was still afternoon but dark clouds were robbing the sky of some of its light. Farr had a canvas bag slung from his shoulder. Reaching into it, he took out the telescope and held it out to her. He expected a cry of delight but she looked disappointed. It was not the gift for which she'd hoped.

'What is it?' she asked.

'Can ye no' see, Bella? It's a telescope.'

236

'I've heerd tell of them but never seen one before.'

'Hold it,' he invited, thrusting it at her. 'Take it, feel it.'

She did as he bade her. 'It's heavy, Jamie.'

'Put your eye to it.' He laughed when she did so. 'Tha's the wrong end to look into. Turn it round like this.'

He twisted it round for her then urged her to peer into it. When she did so, she let out a gasp of wonder. She let the telescope move slowly across the landscape.

'It's magic,' she said, turning to him with a giggle. 'Everything seems close enough to touch.'

'I bought it for us, Bella. Are ye pleased?'

'I love it. I can see for miles. I could even see the people in tha' trap.'

Farr stiffened. 'What people?' He looked downwards. 'I don't see them.'

'Try lookin' through this,' she advised, handing him the telescope.

He put it to his eye and adjusted it. 'Thank ye.'

It didn't take him long to pick out the figures moving slowly in the distance. The trap was travelling parallel with the railway line. Well off the beaten track, it seemed an odd place for visitors to be.

'Can ye see them now?' said Bella.

'Aye,' he replied, with growing interest, 'I can.'

CHAPTER SEVENTEEN

'How did Mr Renwick react to the news?'

'I think it's fair to say that he was staggered by it, sir.'

'Did it never cross his mind that *that* was what the burglar was after?'

'No,' said Colbeck. 'He assumed that the man came in search of valuables. Why should anyone break into a house to look at a timetable for the royal train?'

'We know the answer to that now,' said Tallis, grimly.

'Until I explained what had happened in Scotland, Mr Renwick refused to accept the truth. He thought it too ludicrous for words at first.'

'I'm glad that he's taking it seriously now.'

'Oh, he is,' said Colbeck. 'There's no question about that. When I finally left him, he was still chiding himself for not seeing a connection between the burglary and the royal family's visit to Balmoral. The one consolation for him, of course, is that the suspected attack is due to take place not on the LNWR but on the Caledonian.'

'What was Renwick's advice?'

'He wanted to cancel the train altogether.'

'That's the sensible thing to do.'

'But it won't be the most productive, sir.'

On his eventual return to Scotland Yard, Colbeck had delivered his report to Tallis in the latter's office. Having been earlier deprived of what he saw as his right to visit Buckingham Palace, Tallis was in a peevish mood. He kept interrupting Colbeck with additional questions, harrying him relentlessly and trying to catch him out so that he could administer a reproach. To his chagrin, he was never given an opportunity to do so. Coping with every demand made on him, Colbeck answered clearly, calmly and concisely. It served to increase the superintendent's irritability.

'And what's taken you so long?' asked Tallis, glancing up at the clock on the wall. 'I expected you back hours ago.'

'Mr Renwick took me to his office,' replied Colbeck, 'and he later invited me to join him for luncheon.'

'Luncheon! You shouldn't have wasted your time over a leisurely meal. I needed you back here. There's a crime to be investigated.'

'Talking to Mr Renwick was an important part of that investigation, sir. I learnt an immense amount from him. Until we went to his office, I hadn't realised just how much planning went into a royal train journey. The detail is remarkable,' said Colbeck. 'Using information about who will be travelling in the royal party, Mr Renwick submits a plan to Buckingham Palace for approval. In this case, the plan was ratified without any correction. A copy of it was kept in Mr Renwick's safe.'

'And it was inspected by the burglar.'

'It would have told him everything he needed to know, including the speed of the train. Did you know that Her Majesty refuses to travel at any speed in excess of 40 miles per hour? That, by the way, is reduced to 30 miles per hour after dark.'

'But that would help the conspirators,' said Tallis, fingering his moustache. 'If the train hared along at full speed, it would be more difficult for them to time their explosion to the right second.'

'They'll strike where a gradient slows the train down.'

Colbeck went on to explain what else he'd discovered during his visit to the general manager's office. Renwick had shown him the plan for the royal train's journey to Balmoral the previous spring. Immediately behind the engine was a brake van with another at the back of the train. Carriages at either end of the train were set aside for royal footmen and attendants. The royal saloon was at the centre of the train with carriages either side reserved for members of the royal family and foreign dignitaries. Queen Victoria had travelled with a large and illustrious party to what she described as the 'dear Paradise' of Balmoral.

'On the way north,' added Colbeck, 'Her Majesty broke the journey at Perth station. When she alighted to retire to her accommodation, there was a huge crowd on the platform as well as a band from a Highland regiment.'

'That was *last* year,' said Tallis, acidly. 'If these villains get their way, the royal train will never even reach Perth. In the interests of safety, Her Majesty would be far better off sailing to Scotland.'

'The railway is much quicker and more comfortable, sir. Bad weather can turn even a short voyage into a harrowing experience. The royal yacht cannot compete with a train or Her Majesty would still be sailing in it by choice.'

'The question is academic until we know what decision has been taken at Buckingham Palace. The commissioner should have returned by now. I've been expecting a summons any minute.'

'In that case,' said Colbeck, seeing a chance to escape and rising from his chair, 'I'll leave you alone.'

'Stay where you are, man. There's something I must remind you about.'

Colbeck resumed his seat. 'What's that, sir?'

'I have taken this investigation into my own hands. You do *nothing* unless it's approved by me in advance.'

'That does rather limit my effectiveness, sir.'

'That's deliberate. You need to be restricted to specific tasks instead of disappearing on impulse to chase something that usually turns out not to be there.'

'I dispute that,' said Colbeck, firmly.

'Dispute what you wish. It's a waste of breath. I'll overrule you at every turn.'

'You're supposed to handcuff *prisoners*, sir, not your own detectives.'

Tallis erupted. 'I'll brook no criticism from you, Colbeck!' he yelled. 'If I have any more carping, I'll have you removed from this case altogether.' There was a knock on the door. 'Come in!'

When the door opened, Sir Richard Mayne sailed in. Colbeck stood up out of politeness and Tallis conjured up a deferential smile. After a nod at Colbeck, the commissioner turned his gaze on the superintendent.

'What's all that bellowing for?' he asked. 'I expected an invitation to enter this office, not an assault on my eardrums. What's going on in here?'

'Nothing, Sir Richard,' said Tallis with a hollow laugh. 'The inspector and I were having a conversation, that's all. It's over now. How did you fare at the palace?'

'I was kept waiting an interminable amount of time. When I finally did have an audience with Prince Albert, it took me ages to convince him that the threat was real.' He turned to Colbeck. 'It was only when I mentioned the inspector's name that he began to listen properly. He has great respect for you, Inspector.'

'That's very gratifying to hear,' said Colbeck, modestly.

'What decision has been taken?' asked Tallis.

'None,' replied Mayne.

'But it can't be left hanging in the air, Sir Richard.'

'I made that point a number of times.'

'Perhaps *I* should speak to His Royal Highness.'

'That's out of the question,' said Mayne. 'Prince Albert wishes to see only Inspector Colbeck and Archibald Renwick. They must present themselves at the palace at ten o'clock tomorrow morning.'

'We'll be there, Sir Richard,' said Colbeck, obediently.

'I should go with you,' asserted Tallis. 'If I am to run this investigation, I must be involved at the highest level.'

'Two people were requested by name,' said Mayne, coldly, 'and you were not one of them, Superintendent. Colbeck and Renwick can manage perfectly well without you looking over their shoulder. Isn't that true, Inspector?'

Colbeck smiled. 'I believe that it is.'

It had been a wearisome day for Victor Leeming. After his visit to the rehearsal room, he went in search of one of the men whose name he'd been given by Buckmaster. It took him to a squalid tavern in a Deptford backstreet. Feeling out of place and blatantly unwelcome, Leeming nursed a pint of beer for over an hour before Orlando Foxe finally turned up. Old, haggard and decrepit, the newcomer nevertheless had a faded grandeur about him. He tossed a mane of silver curls and used expressive gestures. To get his attention, all that Leeming had to do was to invite him to sit at his table and to buy him a drink. Foxe poured it down his throat as if emptying a bucket of water.

'I needed that,' he said, smacking his lips.

'I'm told that you give elocution lessons,' Leeming began.

'I give lessons of any kind that bring in money, my dear friend. What you see before you is a master of his art, a veteran of the theatre, a thespian supreme. I can teach you how to speak properly onstage, sing a sweet ditty, move with true dignity, employ every manner of gesture and handle a sword convincingly in a duel. You will also learn how to wear costumes as if they belonged to you. No aspect of drama is beyond my scope. All that I require is appropriate remuneration.'

'I'm not here on my own account, Mr Foxe.'

'You wish to engage my services for a friend?'

'Not exactly,' said Leeming. 'I'm anxious to track someone down and I believe that he may be a pupil of yours.'

Foxe became wary. 'What makes you think that?'

'This gentleman would want the best teacher and I'm told that that's you.'

'I can't disagree with that,' said Foxe with a lordly wave of a hand. 'My reputation goes before me. Who recommended me?'

'It was an actor by the name of Nigel Buckmaster.'

Foxe gasped. 'Don't mention that foul fiend!'

'But he spoke well of you, sir.'

'Keep that charlatan away from me!' cried Foxe, holding up both arms as if to ward off a blow. 'It was he who ruined my career. I'll never forgive the rogue for that. Treachery, thy name is Buckmaster!' He grabbed Leeming's arm. 'You have just twisted the knife in a very deep wound. I was a leading actor before that bombastic fool first stepped on a stage. My talent is natural while his is artificial. We have nothing whatsoever in common.'

Leeming disagreed. In his view, Foxe and Buckmaster were hewn from the same rock. Both men were imposing, egotistical and blessed with deep, rich voices. Indeed, Foxe might have been

243

an older version of the actor-manager. Evidently, there was intense professional rivalry between them. Not wishing to inflame Foxe again, he changed his tack.

'You must come across many different accents,' he said, casually.

'None as untutored as your own, I dare swear.'

Leeming rode over the insult. 'What's the most difficult to get rid of?'

'That depends on how hard each individual is prepared to work,' said Foxe. 'A good student will shed the most dreadful accent in a matter of months, if not weeks; a bad one is stuck with it for life. Everything comes down to dedication.'

'Some voices must be more difficult to improve. I've just returned from a visit to Scotland. They talk in gibberish there. Could you make a Scotsman speak English in a way I could understand?'

Foxe was fuming. '*I* am a Scotsman,' he declared, one hand to his breast, 'and I resent that slur on my nation. We have the purest vowels and the most decisive consonants in the whole British Isles. If you've come to mock us, begone with you! What gives you the right to sneer at us when you speak as if you have a live crab crawling around inside your mouth?' He jabbed a finger. 'Who *are* you, anyway?'

'My name is Victor Leeming, sir.'

'Then take yourself off, Mr Leeming.'

'I didn't give you my full title – it's Detective Sergeant Leeming of the Metropolitan Police Force.'

A look of terror came into Foxe's eyes and he shrank back in his chair.

'Don't arrest me, sir,' he pleaded. 'I run a legitimate business and my charges are very modest. Ignore any complaints made against me. I'm an honourable man.'

'Your honour is not in question,' said Leeming, trying to soothe him with a smile that only disturbed him even more. 'It's one of your clients who interests me. He's a very *dishonourable* man.'

'Then he is not one of my students. I'm highly selective.'

'His real name is Patrick Scanlan but we know for a fact that he uses a number of aliases. He hails from Willenhall in Staffordshire and you'd have known it from his voice when he first came to London. Someone got rid of his accent for him.'

'So I should hope. It would reek of smoking chimneys.'

'We need to find him,' said Leeming, seriously. 'There could be a reward for the person who tells us where he is.'

Temptation brought a glow to Foxe's face. The promise of money fired his imagination and he began to invent a story about someone who came to him with a Black Country accent. Even as the fictional character formed in his mind, however, he realised that he could not bamboozle Leeming. The sergeant was too experienced to be taken in by a patent lie. Foxe's only option was to fall back on honesty.

'I can tell you, hand on heart,' he said, 'that I've never met the fellow.'

Leeming believed him. Foxe had an actor's prodigious memory. If he'd encountered Patrick Scanlan, he'd remember him. The visit to Deptford had been in vain yet it might still yield something of value.

'Do you happen to know what an iambic pentameter is?' asked Leeming.

Ever since Colbeck had confided in him, Nairn Craig had been stretched on a rack of apprehension. Unable to sleep, he became increasingly fatigued. Unable to tell his wife about the danger to the royal family, he simply claimed that he was not feeling well.

Colleagues at work like John Mudie noticed the bags under his eyes and the shortness of his temper but they knew better than to question him. It would be like thrusting a bare hand into a wasp's nest. Craig had to keep the terrible secret bottled up inside him. It caused him constant discomfort yet he accepted Colbeck's argument that the information could not be voiced abroad. With his company under threat yet again, he became obsessed with finding the most likely spot where any attack would occur. When his visitor called on him, Craig was scrutinising a map on his desk.

'Good day to you,' said Malcolm Rae, cheerily.

'Ah, hello, Inspector – what brings you here?'

'I'm wondering what happened to the Railway Detective.'

'Inspector Colbeck has returned to London.'

Rae grinned. 'Does that mean you've dispensed with his services?'

'Not at all,' said Craig, guardedly. 'He felt that there were lines of inquiry he had to pursue in London. I daresay that he'll be back before long.'

'Did he tell you what these new lines of inquiry were?'

'I was not made privy to that information.'

'I'm intrigued to know what it is.'

'Then you'll have to be patient.'

'Surely he gave you some sort of hint?'

'I've told you all I can,' said Craig, flatly.

He was not taken in by Rae's pretence that he knew nothing of Colbeck's whereabouts. The inspector had come to gloat. He was already aware that Colbeck and Leeming had left Glasgow. Enquiries at the Strathallan had also elicited the fact that Colbeck's wife and father-in-law had spent the night there. Craig had been put in the awkward position of explaining the absence of the man ostensibly leading the investigation into the train crash. It was an odd situation and Rae was exploiting it. Moving to the desk, the inspector stared at the map.

'Is the Caledonian looking to extend its empire?' he taunted.

'Further expansion is always under review,' said Craig, folding the map away. 'But extending a line is an expensive business. Local issues come into play and we always meet with opposition – not least from our competitors, of course. On which subject,' he went on, trying to distract his visitor, 'what have you learnt of the NBR?'

'I've learnt that the general manager has privately admitted that someone in his employ *might* have been party to the accident on your line. The search for suspects is both urgent and comprehensive.'

'And what will Alistair Weir do if he finds that one of his men was involved?'

'I hope that he'll inform the police.'

'He's more likely to promote the fellow and reward him with money.'

'Mr Weir has more sense than that,' said Rae. 'He might rejoice in your disarray but he doesn't want the NBR linked with it in any way. Besides, he knows that my detectives are putting his company under the microscope. He's keen to find the culprit before we do.'

'What if you are looking in the wrong place?'

'I suggest that you put that question to Inspector Colbeck.'

'Why should I do that?'

'On one thing, I fancy, we should all agree. The roots of this crime lie in Scotland. It was conceived and committed north of the border. That being irrefutable,' he added, 'why on earth are Colbeck and his sergeant grubbing around in London?'

'I've already told you.'

'I think you've been misled, Mr Craig.'

'That's arrant nonsense,' retorted the other.

'Your much-vaunted Railway Detective has no new line of inquiry. He simply wants to spend time with his wife. Look at the facts. The man is recently married and we both know what a heady experience that can be. He's still under the spell of his beautiful new wife,' said Rae with a knowing wink. 'She came to Glasgow to fetch him and Colbeck was unable to resist her siren call. One crook of her finger and he deserts you before his work is done.' His smile became a smirk. 'He's left you in the lurch, Mr Craig. Colbeck has run off home to enjoy the delights of the marital couch.'

Madeleine was thrilled. 'You're going to the *palace*, Robert?'

'Mr Renwick and I must be there at ten in the morning.'

'That's such a feather in your cap.'

'I'm not going to receive an honour of any kind,' Colbeck told her. 'I'll simply be there in my capacity as a detective.'

'I should be there as well,' said Andrews. 'I've earned the right.'

'I agree, Mr Andrews. We're indebted to your acuity. It will be brought to the attention of Prince Albert, I can assure you. But this invitation does not, alas, include you.'

'More's the pity!'

'Let Robert finish what he came to tell us, Father,' said Madeleine.

When Colbeck slipped home in a cab that afternoon, he found that his father-in-law was there. It enabled him to tell both Andrews and Madeleine what had so far transpired. Since they'd given the investigation a significant change of direction, Colbeck felt that it was only fair that they should be kept abreast of what was going on.

'What did Mr Renwick have to say?' asked Andrews.

'The first thing he told me was how much he enjoyed meeting

you both at the dinner. I called at his house,' said Colbeck, 'so I was able to see Madeleine's painting hanging on the wall. I was incredibly proud.'

'I was so pleased that he had the urge to buy it,' said Madeleine.

'Mr Renwick loves railways. He has other paintings and prints on display that feature some element of the world in which he works.'

'But none as good as Maddy's,' said Andrews, loyally.

Colbeck kissed her forehead. 'I'd endorse that.'

After recounting details of the time spent at Renwick's house, he talked about his subsequent visit to the man's office. Madeleine was enthralled to hear of the meticulous preparations for a journey by any royal train. Safety was paramount and railway companies went to extraordinary lengths to ensure it. Colbeck's account sparked off a memory for his father-in-law.

'I remember the first time that Her Majesty took the train,' he said. 'It was in 1842 and she made the fatal mistake of choosing the Great Western Railway.'

'You can hardly blame her for that, Mr Andrews,' said Colbeck. 'The LNWR was not in existence at the time.'

'Brunel and Daniel Gooch both travelled on the footplate to reassure her.'

'So did Her Majesty's coachman, it seems. He didn't believe that the train would be safe enough so he insisted on joining the others on the engine itself. I'm told that his scarlet coat got so filthy that he never pushed himself forward again.'

'Driving a train is a dirty job – exciting, maybe, but dirty as well.'

'Her Majesty must have enjoyed that first outing,' said Madeleine, 'or she wouldn't have travelled by train so often since then.'

'She described the event as charming,' said Colbeck. 'Her husband, by all accounts, was less enamoured. "Not so fast next time, Mr Conductor." That's what he's reported to have said.'

'Her Majesty is more gracious,' recalled Andrews. 'On the occasion when I was chosen to drive the royal train, she showed concern for me. Every time we stopped at a station, she'd dispatch an attendant to ask me and my fireman if we were tired. She knew that driving a train was hard work.'

Madeleine was still puzzled by something that Colbeck had said earlier.

'How could you identify the name of the burglar?' she asked.

'Only a highly skilled housebreaker could get in and out of the Renwick abode without arousing those inside,' he replied. 'He then had to open an expensive Chubb safe that would have been a challenge to most cracksmen. Instead of using the tools they'd have employed, he simply picked the lock. That told me that the most likely suspect was Patrick Scanlan.'

'You said that the police have been hunting him for a long while.'

'That's true, Madeleine.'

'How can you be sure of catching him this time?'

'I advised Victor Leeming to take a novel approach,' said Colbeck, 'and I have every hope of success. Instead of looking for a burglar, Victor has gone in search of a missing voice.'

The White Lion was a very different establishment to the one Leeming had been to before. Situated in a lane that branched off Gower Street, it was larger, cleaner and better furnished and it catered for a more discerning clientele. The sergeant aroused no undue interest when he arrived there. It was a promising start after earlier setbacks. Having pursued the wrong man in Deptford, he'd met up by prior arrangement with the two detectives assisting him in the hunt for the burglar. Over a meal together, they admitted that they, too, had been out of luck. They'd called on all the haunts favoured by Scanlan in the past and received the same answer in each case. Scanlan had not been seen for several months. Some claimed that he'd left London altogether but the detectives were not led astray by the information. It came from those with a good reason to protect Scanlan. He was known for his generosity. Whenever he visited a brothel or a gambling den, he paid well for the services offered. That bought him friendship. If the police were after him, people closed ranks.

There was another improvement. The beer tasted better at The White Lion. While he quaffed his pint, Leeming asked after Balthasar Goodfellow and was told that the man was at that very moment upstairs with a student of his. Indeed, when Leeming strained his ears, he could hear stirring speeches being declaimed above him. He reasoned that, if Goodfellow could afford to rent a room in such a place, then his elocution lessons were more profitable than those given by Orlando Foxe. Choosing a table in a corner, Leeming waited until the session was over. Two figures came down the stairs. One was a sleek man in his fifties with a well-trimmed beard. The younger man who followed him was shorter, slimmer and altogether more handsome but he walked with a pronounced limp. Assuming that the older of the two was Balthasar Goodfellow, Leeming got up and approached him, only to learn that he had, in fact, been the client. The teacher was the man with the limp.

Inviting Goodfellow to join him, Leeming bought him a drink. As they sat at the table, he noticed that his guest sipped the beer slowly. Goodfellow was no guzzler like Orlando Foxe. Personable and well dressed, he had an open face and a ready smile. Instead of booming, he talked quietly. There was no sense of the desperation that Leeming had found in his Deptford companion. Nor was he troubled when told that he was talking to a detective from Scotland Yard.

'How may I help you?' asked Goodfellow, pleasantly.

'Someone recommended you to me.'

'May I know the name of my benefactor?'

'It was Nigel Buckmaster.'

'That was uncommonly kind of him.'

'To be honest,' said Leeming, 'he gave me two names and assured me that they belonged to the two best teachers of elocution in London.'

'Who was the other?'

'Does it matter?'

'My first guess would be Orlando Foxe but I know that to be impossible.'

'Then you are wrong because that's the very man he named. I met the gentleman earlier in Deptford. I have to say,' Leeming continued, 'that he shied like a horse when I told him who'd sent me there.'

'That, alas, is not surprising. There's bad blood between Orlando and Nigel. At first they were friends in the same company. Orlando was in his pomp then, taking leading roles and winning plaudits from the critics. He took Nigel under his wing and taught him all he knew.'

'Then why didn't Mr Buckmaster repay him when he formed his own company?'

'You touch on a sore point, Sergeant.'

'He shunned his old friend, then?'

'No,' said Goodfellow with a sigh, 'he did worse than that. He employed Orlando but offered him only supporting roles. It was an insult. When you've eaten a banquet of words onstage every night, you'll not subsist on a diet of scraps. An actor who has played Hamlet feels humiliated if he's condemned to play one of the watch. It was cruel of Nigel. He has many fine qualities but compassion is not foremost among them. In the end, Orlando stormed out. His heart was broken. I doubt if he's worked as an actor since.'

'Yet *you* seem to harbour no grudge against Mr Buckmaster.'

'I owe him thanks for many favours. He not only took me into his company and nurtured my talent, he stood by me after the accident.' He patted his thigh. 'I broke my leg in a bad fall and it was never set properly. This limp is with me for the rest of my days. It might fit me to play murderers and spies and comic characters but who will pay to see a warrior like Henry the Fifth hobbling across a stage, or watch Troilus leaning on Cressida's shoulder for support? Oh, I'm sorry,' he went on. 'You're probably not familiar with the Shakespearean canon.'

'I know what an iambic pentameter is now,' said Leeming, proudly.

'That's all to the good.' Goodfellow shrugged. 'What can I do for you?'

'We're looking for a man who is trying to shed his accent.'

'Then you saw him when he left. That gentleman hails from Newcastle and has a voice that makes Londoners wince. It affects his business adversely so he came to me. I'm slowly driving the north-east out of his speech.'

'What about the Black Country?'

'That, too, produces an accent that lacks any music.'

'Has anyone ever come to you from that part of the country?'

'Two or three people, as it happens.'

'You'd remember this man if you had any dealings with him.'

'What was his name?'

'His real name is Patrick Scanlan and that's on a wanted poster in every police station. He therefore uses other names.'

'Paint a portrait of him, Sergeant.'

Leeming gave him a detailed description of Scanlan, warning him that certain features were liable to change. In order to blend in more effectively in the capital, it was believed, Scanlan would try to remove all trace of Willenhall from his voice. After pondering for a while, Goodfellow gave a decisive nod.

'I fancy that I know the man.'

'Is he still a student of yours?'

'No – he left when he felt my work was done.'

'What name did he give you?'

'Alfred Penn.'

Leeming curled a lip. 'That's an alias.'

'Don't look down on those who use an alias,' warned Goodfellow. 'I did so myself. The name with which I was born was Silas Wragg. Imagine how that would look on a playbill. It was Nigel Buckmaster who christened me anew and gave me my stage name. Balthasar Goodfellow has a ring to it.'

'Let's go back to Alfred Penn. How long did you teach him?'

'It must have been for a few months or more.'

Leeming pointed upwards. 'He came here for the lessons?'

'Twice a week and he was always punctual.'

'Did he give you an address?'

'He didn't, Sergeant, but then I didn't ask him for one. All that I require of my students is diligence and a good fee. I got both from Mr Penn.'

'So you have no idea where he lived?'

'Judging by his appearance,' said Goodfellow, 'it must have been somewhere respectable. There was a suggestion of wealth about him carefully kept in check.'

'Suppose that you wished to get in touch with him again.'

'I've no reason to do so.'

'You may not have,' said Leeming, 'but *we* do. We have a very pressing reason. Can you think of any way in which we might find out where he is?'

Goodfellow scratched his head and took another sip of beer.

'You could always ask Mary, I daresay,' he suggested.

'Is she another of your students?'

'She is indeed and here – another favour he granted me – at the behest of Nigel Buckmaster. Mary Burnell is a promising young actress with an ambition to have a career on the stage. When she came to me,' said Goodfellow, 'she was rather too gauche but she's now starting to blossom.'

'Is she a friend of Patrick Scanlan – or whatever he called himself?'

'It's possible that she might have been more than a friend, Sergeant. I don't know that for a fact, mark you,' he added, discreetly. 'What I can tell you is that he first met Mary when he was leaving my room and she was arriving. According to the landlord, Alfred Penn used to wait down here until she'd finished her lesson. They became acquainted.' His smile was non-committal. 'That's all I can tell you.'

The pleasing odour of progress drifted into Leeming's nostrils.

'Do you, by any chance, have an address for this young lady?' he asked.

'As a matter of fact, I do,' said Goodfellow. 'Mary volunteered her address but Patrick did not.'

'May I have it?'

'Yes, Sergeant, you may. It's in my notebook. Bear with me for a moment and I'll go upstairs to fetch it.'

Leeming beamed. He felt that the burglar was at last within reach.

* * *

It was the gifts that finally won her over. At first, their cost was modest but they always had appeal. Gradually, they became more expensive. What really made her warm to Alfred Penn was the fact that he paid for her lessons with Goodfellow. He not only encouraged her theatrical ambitions, he insisted that she visited The White Lion more often so that she would be ready to fulfil them sooner. Mary Burnell had had many suitors. She was a shapely young woman with an elfin loveliness. Men pursued her in droves but they all had the same base motives. Penn was different. To begin with, he was ten years older than her and infinitely more mature. Even when they were alone together, he never pressed himself upon her. He admired and respected her too much. Mary came to trust him implicitly. She dined out with him and even visited his house. Kind, attentive and charming, Penn had eventually broken down all the barriers between them. Mary loved him.

Today would be very special. He'd promised her the most wonderful gift. A business venture of his had come to fruition and a large amount of money was due to be paid to him. Mary was to share in his good fortune. Trembling in anticipation, she hired a cab and drove to his house. There was no hint of danger in his invitation. On the occasions when she'd been to his home before, a servant had been there. They were never completely alone together. Reassured by that fact at first, she now wished that they *could* be on their own at last. Mary wanted to thank him for all that he'd done for her. She wanted to be free to express her feelings. She wanted him.

Alighting from the cab, she paid the driver then approached the front door. It was a small, neat, terraced house in a good state of repair. A lot of money had been lavished on its interior. When she rang the bell, she expected the servant to admit her but nobody came. A second ring echoed around the empty hallway. Still nobody responded. Mary was perplexed. She had the right day, time and place. Reaching out to ring the bell a third time, her shoulder brushed against the door and it opened slightly. She couldn't understand why it was not locked. Pushing it right open, she stepped into the hallway and looked around.

'I'm here!' she called. 'It's me – Mary. Where are you?'

No answer came and the silence began to feel oppressive. It troubled her. To stiffen her spirits, she told herself that her friend had left the door open for her on purpose. He'd dismissed his servant for the evening and wanted her to come in. They'd be alone at last. Gathering up her skirt, she flitted across the hallway and went into the drawing room, fully expecting to see him with a welcoming smile and a gift for her. It was the moment she'd been looking forward to all day but it was not quite as Mary had envisaged. She came to an abrupt halt and gaped in horror. Alfred Penn, the man she loved, was indeed there but he was not smiling and he had no gift. Lying on his back in a pool of blood, he had the most grotesque expression on his face. It spoke of agony, betrayal and thwarted ambition.

Mary Burnell's scream could be heard in the next street.

CHAPTER EIGHTEEN

As soon as he got to the house, Colbeck took charge. He was pleased to see that a uniformed policeman stood outside the front door to keep inquisitive neighbours at bay. A second policeman was in the drawing room, standing beside the corpse while taking care not to look at it. A third was in the adjoining room, trying to comfort the near-hysterical Mary Burnell. Colbeck bent down to inspect the body. The throat had been slit open from side to side and there were stab wounds in the chest. The crumpled carpet, the overturned side table and the broken vase suggested that there'd been a violent struggle. The victim's contorted features made it impossible for Colbeck to recognise him. Rising to his feet, he turned to the policeman who was clearly still shocked by the discovery.

'Who was the first on the scene?' he asked.

'I was, sir,' replied the policeman. 'Neighbours heard a scream and called me. The door was unlocked. I came in here and found a young lady standing in the middle of the room. She was distraught. Her name is Mary Burnell. It took a long time to calm her down.'

'Did she tell you who this unfortunate gentleman is?'

'Yes, sir – he's Mr Alfred Penn. As soon as help came, I sent word to Scotland Yard. Nothing has been touched in here since I arrived.'

'Good – you did well.'

The policeman gazed at the corpse. 'I've never seen a murder victim before.'

'I've seen far too many,' said Colbeck, sadly.

'Does it get any easier, Inspector?'

'Easier?'

'My stomach was heaving when I first saw him,' confessed the other. 'If I hadn't had the young lady to think about, I'd have been sick on the spot. As it was, when PC Harrison arrived to take her off my hands, I had to go into the garden to get some fresh air. I was shaking all over.'

'That's a natural reaction, Constable, and you shouldn't be ashamed of it. As for it getting easier to cope with, I can't really say. The sight of a life snuffed out by a killer always offends me.' He indicated the body. 'Nobody deserves to die like this. I suppose that my anger always overcomes any sense of queasiness.'

'I'll remember that the next time.'

'I hope that there *is* no next time for you,' said Colbeck. 'You behaved as you should in a difficult situation and should be congratulated. Please wait in the next room with PC Harrison.'

'Thank you, Inspector,' said the policeman, glad to escape.

When the door to the next room opened, sounds of weeping could be heard. After the door closed again, Colbeck examined the body more closely. There was nothing in the man's pockets to identify him and his wallet was missing. What had been left by the killer was an expensive gold watch on a chain. The victim had a good tailor and his shoes were of high quality. While the exterior of the house did not disclose the owner's prosperity, it was very apparent indoors. The drawing room had been recently decorated and contained some exquisite furniture. Small statues, pots and other objects stood on every available surface. On the mantelpiece was an ivory trio of miniature elephants.

The room told him a lot about the character of the man who lived there. A comfortable but relatively modest dwelling had been given a touch of luxury. The thing that interested Colbeck most was the large painting on one wall. It was the portrait of a young actress and he recognised the play at once. It was *Romeo and Juliet* and the eponymous heroine was bending over what she thought was her dead lover. It was a striking study of beauty, anguish and almost unbearable poignance. Colbeck was diverted by the sound of voices outside the front door. A moment later, Leeming came bustling into the room. He stopped in his tracks when he saw the corpse and grimaced at the sight of the multiple wounds. He needed some time to compose himself.

'It's Patrick Scanlan,' he said at length.

'I was told that his name was Alfred Penn.'

'That was the alias he was using, sir. I've just been to the home of a young lady named Mary Burnell. Her parents told me that she was coming here. Scanlan had befriended her.'

'Miss Burnell is in the next room,' said Colbeck, gesturing at the corpse. 'This is what she found on arrival.'

'Have you spoken to her?'

'No, Victor, she needs time to recover first. The policeman who was on guard in here went to join her. When he opened the door, I could hear her sobbing.'

'Scanlan was her sponsor,' explained Leeming. 'She'd dreamt of being a famous actress and was taking lessons from an elocution teacher. Scanlan paid for those lessons. He obviously had faith in her.'

'It was more than faith. He was devoted to her. When we meet the young lady, my guess is that she'll look very much like the actress in that painting.' He moved towards it. 'What do you notice about it, Victor?'

Leeming peered at it. 'It's very well done, sir.'

'Is that all that catches your eye?'

'I don't know much about paintings.'

'Look around the rest of the room.'

'Why?'

'Because you'll see that everything else in here fits perfectly,' said Colbeck. 'The one exception is that painting. It's out of proportion. It's far too big for that wall. What does that tell you?'

'Scanlan should have hung it somewhere else.'

'He needed it in here so that he could feast his eyes on it. He believed he was looking at Mary Burnell. And there's a second reason why it had to be on that wall.'

'What's that, sir?'

'It's hiding something,' surmised Colbeck.

Taking hold of the painting, he lifted it off to expose a safe set into the wall.

'I'd never have known that was there,' admitted Leeming.

'You must learn to think like a burglar.'

'Is that what happened? Somebody came to burgle the house of a burglar and was disturbed? He killed Scanlan in order to escape?'

'Had that been the case,' said Colbeck, 'it would indeed have been a crowning irony. Apart from the theft of a wallet, there was no burglary here. As you can see, the safe is still locked. A more likely explanation is that Scanlan had a visit from his paymaster. Whoever hired him to break into Mr Renwick's house wanted to make sure that he couldn't tell anyone about it. We're dealing with vicious men, Victor. They take no chances.'

'If only I'd got here earlier,' said Leeming in frustration.

'I'm impressed that you got here at all. We've been on the lookout for Scanlan for a long time. You managed to find him in less than a day.'

'That was only thanks to you, Inspector.'

'I wish I'd thought of it before but Scanlan has never been a priority of mine. He only became important to me when I sensed that he might be linked to the train crash. Finding him suddenly took on more urgency.'

'What use is he to us like this?' moaned Leeming as he viewed the dead body. 'Scanlan won't be able to help us now.'

'Miss Burnell might. It depends how close the two of them were.'

'My impression is that they were very close, sir.'

'Then the young lady might furnish some valuable clues.'

'Are you going to take her to Scotland Yard for questioning?'

'No,' replied Colbeck, 'that would be far too intimidating for her. To add to her woes, Superintendent Tallis would insist on being present.'

'We must spare her that, sir. If she saw Scanlan in this state, she's been frightened enough already. We are used to scenes like this – Miss Burnell is not.'

Colbeck was about to hang the painting back on the wall when he spotted something he'd missed earlier. It made him laugh.

'What's so funny, Inspector?' asked Leeming.

'It's this safe,' said Colbeck, amused by the coincidence. 'It's virtually identical to the one in Mr Renwick's study. No wonder Scanlan had so little trouble picking the lock.' After replacing the painting, he was struck by a thought. 'Perhaps I should write to the manufacturer. What better recommendation is there for a Chubb safe than the fact that it was the choice of the ablest burglar in London?'

Tam and Flora Howie were pleased with their excursion. They invited Ian Dalton back to their home for a celebratory drink. Since they were all staunch believers in temperance, only tea was served but it was of the highest quality, part of a consignment imported by Howie from China. Dalton found the taste delicious. Any reservations that Flora had had about him had now been obliterated. She'd seen the strength of his commitment and reproached herself for her earlier doubts. Instead of being shocked by their declared intentions, he'd urged that they took even more extreme steps and they had to point out that there were limits to what three of them could do, especially as one of them was a woman.

'Your presence is the best protection we have, Flora,' observed Dalton. 'Anybody who sees us will imagine that we're out on a picnic.'

'That's exactly what we will be doing, Ian,' she said. 'It will be a long day. We'll need food and drink to sustain us.'

'Is the banner finished?'

'Yes, I painted it yesterday.'

'You've been tireless.'

'We never tire when we're doing God's work,' said Howie, piously. 'It only serves to exhilarate us.'

'It makes my blood race,' said Dalton. 'I love the feeling.'

They chatted about their plan for the following weekend and made a list of things they'd need for the expedition. Howie was supremely confident but there was still a nagging worry at the back of his wife's mind. It was time to address it.

'What does Morag feel about all this, Ian?' she asked.

'I've not breathed a word of it to her,' he said.

'Hasn't she become suspicious?'

'No, not at all.'

'If I went out at strange hours,' said Howie, 'Flora would become suspicious. She'd want to know exactly what was going on.'

'Morag is not like that, Tam. She accepts what I tell her without complaint.'

Howie chuckled. 'If only all wives were like that!'

'Tam!' scolded his wife, playfully. 'You can't believe that.'

'I don't my love. You know full well that I wouldn't change you for the world. What other woman would have your courage to take risks?'

'Morag wouldn't,' said Dalton. 'I love her dearly but I'd be the first to concede that she lacks courage. She's too submissive.'

'As long as we're not putting you in an awkward position,' said Flora. 'In the short time you've been with us, we've made a lot of demands on you. I'd hate to think that they're causing any discord at home.'

'My wife is used to my being away for long periods, Flora. It's in the nature of my business that I have to work long hours and travel away from home from time to time. She knew that when she married me. Well, it must have been the same for you. Tam must have made it clear before the two of you wed that running one's own business is a time-consuming affair.'

'I gave Flora fair warning,' said Howie. 'She knew what to expect.'

She squeezed his arm. 'I have no regrets.'

'What if we're caught next week?'

'There's little danger of that. We've been too careful.'

'Nothing can go wrong,' said Dalton.

'Supposing – just for the sake of argument – that it does?' asked Howie. 'What if there's some unexpected hazard that leads to our being arrested. How would you feel then?'

'I'd have no regrets, Tam. I'd be proud of what I did.'

'So would I,' added Flora, raising her teacup. 'Ours is a noble cause. Whatever happens, I'll feel privileged to be involved in it. Let's drink to success.'

They clinked cups. 'To success!' they said in unison.

When Colbeck introduced himself to Mary Burnell, he could see how distressed she was. It was important to get her away from the scene of the crime to a more neutral and comforting environment. Leeming was left at the house to conduct a thorough search for clues that might lead them to identify Patrick Scanlan's killer. The policemen were charged with removing the body of the deceased. During the cab ride to his house, Colbeck said very little. It was Mary who did all the talking, endlessly repeating the same few sentences about what a wonderful man her friend had been and how he'd encouraged her hopes of a career in the theatre. When the name of Nigel Buckmaster was mentioned, Colbeck tactfully omitted to tell her that he'd met the actor in the course of another murder investigation. What he did promise her was that Alfred Penn's killer – there was no need to sharpen her grief at this stage by telling her Scanlan's real name – would be brought to justice.

As Colbeck ushered her gently into the house, Madeleine came out to meet them. At a glance, she took in the situation and conducted their guest into the drawing room, sitting beside Mary on the sofa with a consoling arm around her. Colbeck introduced the two women then explained to his wife, in an undertone, that Mary had discovered the dead body of her close friend. Reminded of what she'd seen, Mary unleashed a flood of tears and rocked to and fro. Colbeck signalled to Madeleine that he wanted her to take over. A sympathetic woman was likely to get far more out of Mary Burnell than a detective inspector, however skilled in questioning he might be. Leaving them alone, Colbeck slipped quietly out of the room.

Madeleine was patient. She offered Mary a handkerchief to stem her tears but made no attempt to draw anything out of her. It was a long time before their visitor was ready to speak. When she did so, it was with great surprise. She looked around as if realising for the first time that she was in a strange house.

'Where am I?' she asked, apprehensively.

'You're at the home of Inspector Robert Colbeck,' said Madeleine. 'I'm his wife. He did introduce us earlier.'

'Did he? I only half-heard what he said.'

'My name is Madeleine and you're most welcome here. Is there anything you'd like? I could ring for tea, if you wish.'

Mary shook her head. 'I couldn't touch a thing.'

'I'm very sorry to hear about your friend.'

'Oh, he was much more than a friend,' said Mary with passion. 'He was my guardian angel. Alfred was the kindest man in the world.'

'So it appears.'

'Who could have done such a thing to him?'

'Did he ever speak of enemies?'

'He had none,' said Mary with conviction. 'Everyone liked him. How could they not? He devoted his life to helping others.'

'Tell me more about him.'

Out it all came. From the moment she was taken to the Theatre Royal, Drury Lane for the first time, Mary had yearned to be an actress. It had soon become an obsession. Troubled by the

266

rumours that it was a profession with scant moral compass to it, her parents resisted the notion fiercely at first and sought to direct her ambitions elsewhere. But Mary's mind was set on the theatre and they eventually accepted that nothing would stop her. They had therefore secured an introduction for her to Nigel Buckmaster. While he discerned obvious talent, he felt that she needed help with her speech and deportment before she'd be ready to join his company. On the actor-manager's recommendation, she turned to an elocution teacher.

'My father was worried at the outset,' said Mary, 'and insisted on coming with me. When he realised that Mr Goodfellow was utterly trustworthy and that my virtue was not, after all, in danger, I was allowed to attend lessons without a chaperone. It was at The White Lion that I met Alfred and my life changed completely.'

Madeleine was a good listener, allowing Mary the freedom to talk at will without interruption. It was a touching story and not without a parallel in her own life. Like Madeleine, Mary Burnell had met a somewhat older man and moved gently through the stages of acquaintance, companionship and close friendship until she surrendered to unconditional love. Alfred Penn had financed Mary's ambition to become an actress. Colbeck had identified and developed Madeleine's talent as an artist. Beyond that point, there were profound differences. While Madeleine had found marriage and fulfilment, Mary's dreams had been irreparably shattered.

'Alfred bought a painting because it reminded him of me,' said Mary. 'It was the scene at the end of *Romeo and Juliet* when Juliet finds Romeo and thinks that he's dead. Alfred told me that I'd take the role onstage one day and that it would make me famous. I never realised that I'd play the part in real life as I did earlier this evening. I know just how Juliet must have felt,' she wailed. 'I want to kill myself.'

'Don't say that, Mary.'

'It's true – I've nothing left to live for!'

Dissolving into tears, she flung herself into Madeleine's arms.

The search was fruitless. Though he went systematically from room to room, Leeming could find nothing that confirmed Patrick Scanlan's real name or that gave any hint as to who might have killed him. In fact, there were no telltale documents of any kind and he decided that they must be in the safe. Since he had no key – and lacked Scanlan's skill as a cracksman – he was unable to open it. He felt that the one place where something might be hidden was in the main bedroom and he subjected that to the most thorough search, opening every drawer, crawling under the bed and even lifting the carpet to see if anything was concealed beneath the floorboards. Leeming was so engrossed in what he was doing that he didn't hear the front door opening or pick up the sound of footsteps ascending the staircase. He was kneeling on the floor when he felt someone dive on top of him with force and get an arm around his throat. After believing that he was alone in the house, he was now engaged in a frantic fight.

His attacker was strong. The thick forearm was squeezing the breath out of Leeming. He reacted at once, bucking and twisting like an unbroken horse with a rider on his back. When he managed to loosen the hold a little, he suddenly rolled over sharply and dug his elbow hard into the man's ribs. With a cry of pain, the attacker released him for a moment. It was all the time needed for Leeming to sit up and start to pound away with both fists. He could see that he was fighting a sturdy man of his own age with a misshapen nose. Taking punches to face and body, his adversary was also inflicting punishment of his own, flailing away with both fists and landing some stinging blows. It was minutes before the man's resistance slowly faded under Leeming's sustained attack. Both men were bruised, in pain and out of breath.

With a savage blow to the jaw, Leeming finally subdued him.

'Who the devil are *you*?' he demanded.

'I live here,' said the man.

When he saw that Madeleine had drawn all that she could out of their guest, Colbeck took a cab to the address that Victor Leeming had given him. After introducing himself to Mary Burnell's father, he explained that she'd suffered a dreadful shock when she visited her friend. Burnell was horrified to hear the details. On the cab ride back to Colbeck's house, he talked of the trust that he and his wife had placed in the man they called Alfred Penn. They'd found him thoroughly decent, reliable and generous to their daughter. Colbeck didn't disillusion him. Recriminations would come later when Mary and her father learnt Alfred Penn's real name and his true occupation. For the time being, they both needed to be protected from a second thunderbolt. It would have destroyed them.

Reaching the house, they saw that Mary was much calmer than she had been. The sight of her father made her get up from the sofa and stagger over to him. Enfolding her in his arms, he stroked her hair with a soothing hand. Her time with Madeleine had helped her to regain her composure but all that she wanted to do was to go back home. Colbeck escorted them out to the waiting cab and waved them off. He then went back into the house and gave his wife a fuller explanation of what had happened and who the murder victim was.

'He's a convicted criminal?' she said in astonishment. 'Mary talked about him as if he were some kind of saint.'

'Nobody whose house he burgled would subscribe to that view of him.'

'He took her in completely.'

'Evidently,' said Colbeck, 'he was a persuasive man. Yet while he had an influence on her, Mary had made a profound impact on him. One could see that from the painting I just told you about. He was clearly enthralled by her.'

'It's not difficult to see why, Robert. She's very beautiful.'

'Many men would have had designs on her.'

'Scanlan behaved like a perfect gentleman. That's what set him apart from the others. Her parents approved of the friendship.' Madeleine sucked her teeth. 'Both they and Mary will be devastated when they learn the truth.'

'I tried to postpone that awful moment. But tell me what she said, Madeleine.'

'A lot of it was repetition. She was still reeling from the discovery she made at the house. Mary said that it was a special occasion. Her friend was due to receive a lot of money today as a result of a business venture. He'd promised her a gift.'

'The business venture was almost certainly the burglary at Mr Renwick's house,' said Colbeck. 'Instead of being paid by the man who hired him, he was silenced for good. It was unfortunate that she was due there this evening.'

'Were there no servants in the house?'

'I saw none when I was there.'

'So they would have been alone when she got there.'

'That speaks volumes for the amount of trust she had in him.'

'It went beyond trust, Robert,' said Madeleine. 'She worshipped the man. Mary nursed the hope that they might one day marry.'

'At least she's been rescued from that fate. It would have been a marriage built on shifting sand. Scanlan's luck would have run out sooner or later. He'd have been imprisoned and Mary would have seen how ruinously naive she'd been.'

'She'll realise that anyway in due course.'

'I fear that she will,' said Colbeck, 'but it's a question of degree. The unmasking of a dear friend is of a different order to the exposure of a husband in whom one has reposed all one's love and hope. However,' he went on, glancing at the clock on the mantelpiece, 'I must return to Scotland Yard. The superintendent will expect a report on the latest developments.'

'Will you tell him about *my* involvement?'

'I think not, Madeleine. He'd never accept that a woman could be of such value in the investigative process and he'd chide me for not taking Mary Burnell straight to him.' After giving her a kiss, he headed for the door. 'By the time I get there, Victor will have finished his search of the house. I have every hope that he'll have found something of interest to us.'

Leeming usually stayed as far away from Tallis's office as he could and always felt uneasy when summoned there. On this occasion, however, he went willingly because he had a prisoner in tow and could expect praise. The man who'd attacked him at the house was Ned Layne, servant and cook to Scanlan. When he heard that his master had been murdered, he refused to say anything. After handcuffing him, Leeming hauled him off to Scotland Yard. Surly and uncooperative, Layne sat on a chair in Tallis's office while Leeming and the superintendent stood over him. When they fired questions at him, they got no response.

'Withholding information from the police is a crime,' said Tallis, 'and you are in enough trouble as it is. You're the accomplice of a notorious villain.'

Layne gave a dismissive shrug. Being in police custody held no fears for him. It was clearly not the first time that he'd been questioned by detectives.

'Speak up, man!' yelled Tallis.

'May I ask him something, sir?' ventured Leeming.

'It would be a waste of time, whatever you ask.'

'It's worth a try, Superintendent.'

Leeming looked down at him. The fight with Layne had left him with sore knuckles and an ugly bruise on his face but the servant had come off worst. Layne had lost a couple of teeth in the encounter and one eye was half-closed.

'I don't blame you for jumping on me like that,' said Leeming. 'You thought I was an intruder and you tried to protect your master's property. That's what any servant should have done. But, as I told you, Patrick Scanlan was murdered. Do you want the same thing to happen to you?' Layne sat up as if paying attention for the first time. 'Your master burgled the home of a Mr Renwick. Does that name ring a bell with you?' Layne shook his head vigorously. 'Don't lie to us.'

'I've never heard of a Mr Renwick,' said Layne, finding his tongue at last. 'My master never tells me where he's going when he leaves the house.'

'But you know that he's up to no good.'

'I do what I'm paid for.'

'I'm sure that you do,' said Leeming, 'and, in return for your wage, you keep your mouth shut about Scanlan's activities. But this burglary was not the same as the others. It was part of a much bigger crime.'

'That's why your life is in danger,' said Tallis, relieved that they finally got the man to talk. 'Had you been at the house, you'd have been killed as well.'

'I've done nothing!' protested Layne.

'You're an accessory to a crime – to a series of crimes, probably.'

'But the one that concerns us,' said Leeming, 'occurred at the home of Archibald Renwick. Someone was ready to pay a lot of money to your master because they knew of his reputation. But it seems as if they didn't honour their side of the bargain. Instead of getting his reward, he was killed. The man who hired your master will be looking for you now because you could bear witness against him.'

'But that burglary was nothing to do with me,' asserted Layne.

'You *knew* about it. That's enough.'

'All I know is that a man came and offered my master four hundred guineas to break into a house. He gave a deposit at the start and was due to pay the rest of the money today. That's why Miss Burnell was invited.'

'She's the young lady who found the body, sir,' said Leeming to the superintendent. He swung instantly back to Layne. 'Think about this. People who can afford four hundred guineas obviously have a lot of money at their disposal. If they can hire the most successful burglar in the city, they can also hire the most efficient killer. He's already disposed of your master. *You* are his next victim.'

'Unless you help us to catch him first,' said Tallis.

'But I don't know who he is,' bleated Layne.

'You know who came to the house with the offer of money.'

'Yes,' said Leeming, ruefully. 'You wouldn't have treated him the way you treated me, would you? He wouldn't have been assaulted. No, you'd have let him in the front door and overheard what he said to your master. It's not a large house. It would have been easy for you to eavesdrop.'

'What was the name of the man who came?' asked Tallis.

'What did he look like?'

'Did he say *why* he wanted that particular house burgled?'

'Was he alone when he came?'

'How did Scanlan pass on the information he'd gleaned from the safe?'

'Why didn't they pay him there and then?'

'Tell us everything you know, Layne.'

'It's the only way to make sure you stay alive,' said Leeming, meaningfully.

Layne was scared. Though his master was a man well able to take care of himself, he'd nevertheless been murdered in his own home. Being in police custody was no guarantee of safety. If they really wanted Layne dead, it could be arranged somehow. The only way to remove the threat was to help in the search for the killer. Having spent a lifetime hating and avoiding the police, Layne now had to work with them.

'Very well,' he said, morosely. 'I'll tell you what I know.'

The telescope was the most expensive thing he'd ever bought but it had already proved its worth. Having delighted Bella Drew, it enabled him to see something in the distance that he'd have missed with the naked eye. Time spent alone with Bella was too precious to be wasted on anything else but Jamie Farr didn't forget what he'd spied from the top of the hill. Early next morning, therefore, he set off for a walk with his dog. It was not long before he had company. A cry made him turn and he saw Bella struggling to catch up with him. Waving his tail excitedly, Angus went to meet her and ran in circles around her. When she reached Farr, he embraced her warmly.

'I thought ye couldnae get away today,' he said.

'I'm off to my grannie's but I wanted to catch ye first.'

'Well, I'm glad ye came.' The dog barked. 'So is Angus.'

'Where are ye going, Jamie?'

'Can't ye guess?'

'No,' she said.

He held up the telescope. 'Have ye forgotten what we saw yesterday?'

'Ah, ye mean those people oot for a drive.'

'Tha' were no' a drive, Bella.'

'Then why were they there?'

'I'm hoping to find tha' oot.'

Her face brightened. 'D'ye think it's to do with yon crash?'

'Aye, it might be.'

'What do ye hope to find?'

'I ken what I'd *like* to find,' he said, 'and tha's a way to earn the reward. I'm doing this for us, Bella.'

By way of reply, she hugged and kissed him. Then she stepped back.

'I'm away to my grannie's,' she said. 'Guid luck, Jamie.'

'Thank ye.'

He waved her off and she went running off across the grass with her hair streaming behind her. Angus pursued her for the best part of a hundred yards then he responded to the shepherd's whistle and raced back to him. Farr continued his walk downhill until he reached the area where he'd seen the trap. It meant that he had to walk beside the railway line and that soon proved dangerous. He heard the train long before he saw it, its wheels making the rails sing of its approach. When it came, it did so with a burst of speed and an explosion of noise, rattling south with its passengers gazing out of the window at the sight of Farr and his dog cowering only yards away. Suddenly it was gone, leaving smoke, smell and resounding clamour in its wake.

The train had ignited all of Farr's resentment and hatred. He remembered the lamb butchered on the line and the countless times when the fierce passage of a train had terrified his flock. Yet he was helping in the search for those who'd caused the crash. Part of him was still disgusted at that. But his ambition was strong enough to overcome that disgust. He put his hopes of a future with Bella Drew before anything.

With Angus at his heels, he followed the tracks made by the trap on the previous day. They soon veered away from the line and he lost sight of it as he climbed upwards. There were occasional glimpses of it between the bushes but, even when it was invisible, he was aware of its presence. The tracks stopped near a stand of trees and the stony ground beyond bore no marks of it at all. Farr was about to walk on when he heard the dog snuffling among the trees. Angus yelped and the shepherd ran to see what he'd found.

There were ruts in the soft ground but they hadn't been made by the trap. They were too deep and wide. A bigger and heavier vehicle had been there recently. Farr's search had yielded something important. He needed to tell Inspector Colbeck.

CHAPTER NINETEEN

They arrived punctually at Buckingham Palace but they were kept waiting for over half an hour. It gave Colbeck the opportunity to tell Archibald Renwick about the events of the previous day. Renwick listened, open-mouthed in horror. He was still burning with guilt at the thought that he'd indirectly provided the conspirators with information about the royal family that could put them in dire peril. It gave him no satisfaction to hear that the man who'd burgled his house had been murdered. The fate of Patrick Scanlan simply made him realise what they were up against.

'These people will stoop to anything,' he said.

'We'll be ready for them.'

'How can you defend the royal family against such a threat?'

'That's something we must discuss with Prince Albert,' said Colbeck. 'And distressing as the death of Scanlan has been, it has strengthened my belief that he was only a pawn in a much bigger game of which he was totally unaware.'

'I'm pleased that his servant agreed to help you.'

'It was more a case of helping himself, Mr Renwick. Self-interest was what impelled Ned Layne to volunteer information. He's a marked man. Until we catch whoever killed his master, he lives in constant danger.'

'What did he tell you?'

'I was not present at the interview,' replied Colbeck. 'It was conducted by Superintendent Tallis and Sergeant Leeming. It seems that they scared the story out of him. Layne remembered that two men called at the house. He gave a good description of them, though only one of them spoke.'

'Why was that?'

'One can only guess. The other man, who did all the talking, had a Scots accent.'

'What was their proposition?'

'They weren't allowed to make it at first,' explained Colbeck, 'because Scanlan claimed that his name was Alfred Penn and that they'd come to the wrong address. He was naturally suspicious of strangers. When they offered him a large fee for services rendered, however, the temptation was too great to resist. He admitted that he was indeed the man they sought. Before he agreed to go ahead, however, he insisted on visiting your house to see how easy it would be to get inside.'

Renwick was flabbergasted. 'You mean that he went there *twice*?'

'The initial visit was only a reconnaissance. He entered the premises to find out where the safe was located then slipped quietly away into the night.'

'I daren't tell that to my wife,' said Renwick, anxiously. 'Isobel would never sleep soundly again if she knew that this rogue was prowling around our house at will like that. Is there no way to protect ourselves against such a man?'

'Now that he's dead that need won't arise, but I would advise that one of your servants sleeps on the ground floor. Up in the attic rooms, they'll hear nothing.'

'That's good counsel, Inspector.'

'Even if someone *had* been sleeping downstairs,' said Colbeck, 'they might not have been roused by the intruder. Scanlan moved like a ghost, apparently. He told his servant that the task would be relatively simple but his paymasters heard a different story. Scanlan pretended that it would be extremely difficult to open your safe and demanded an extra hundred guineas. They agreed.'

'So this fellow, Layne, met them on two occasions?'

'Yes, he let them in and made sure that he overheard most of what was said. It's a precaution that Scanlan always took when strangers visited the house. He got his servant to listen in case there was any whiff of trouble.'

'Did both men speak on their second visit?'

'No – it was only the one. The same man remained silent.'

'Was he dumb?'

'I can't answer that question,' said Colbeck. 'Interestingly, Layne had the feeling that the silent man was the person in charge. It was he who handed over the first payment to Scanlan.'

'What else did the servant disclose?'

'I think you've heard the gist of it, sir. Layne is not the most articulate of men. Hopefully, when he's had time to think things over, he'll remember more details that will be of use to us. Meanwhile, he's cooling his heels behind bars.'

'I'm disappointed that Sergeant Leeming found nothing at the house itself.'

'It was not for want of trying. He searched high and low – until Layne came in and attacked him, that is. Anything of real use to us is probably locked in the safe.'

'Was there no key?'

'None that we found,' said Colbeck. 'Unfortunately, the man who could have opened it *without* a key was lying dead on the floor. I've sent word to the Chubb factory and given precise details of the safe. I've requested that they send someone capable of opening it.'

'Legally, that is.'

'Indeed, sir.'

'I've rather lost faith in the professed excellence of Chubb safes.'

'You shouldn't,' said Colbeck. 'Scanlan clearly admired them. The curious thing is that he purchased a safe that was virtually the same as yours.'

Renwick sniffed. 'Given the circumstances, I don't find that reassuring.'

'I think you should. An expert cracksman would choose the best.'

Without warning, the double doors opened with a flourish and a liveried attendant came into the room. He gave them a dutiful smile of welcome.

'This way, gentlemen,' he said in a voice dripping with deference. 'His Royal Highness Prince Albert will see you both now.'

It was predictable that Caleb Andrews would complain. He couldn't understand why the invitation to the palace had not been extended to him as well. When he called at the house that morning, he reminded Madeleine that it was he who'd instigated the secondary investigation. For that reason alone, he argued, he deserved to be taken seriously.

'It was not intended as a personal slight to you, Father,' said Madeleine.

'Then why do I feel so hurt?'

'Robert will tell you everything that transpired at the palace.'

'I should be *there*, Maddy. After all, I've met the Queen and

Prince Albert – in a manner of speaking, that is.'

'Driving the royal train is not the same as being introduced to members of the royal family,' she pointed out. 'In any case, the discussion today will be about the security arrangements. You couldn't usefully contribute to that.'

'Yes, I could.'

'How?'

'Well, the first thing I'd do,' he declared, 'is to offer to drive the royal train. That would be a guarantee of safety in itself.'

'It would also be an act of folly.'

'Why?'

'You're too old, Father,' she said with an affectionate arm around his shoulders. 'How many times must I tell you? You've retired from the railway and are entitled to put your feet up.'

'I'd go back on the footplate if I was needed, Maddy,' he affirmed.

'You won't be. Of that, I can assure you.'

Andrews continued to protest until refreshments arrived. As soon as the servant departed, Madeleine poured tea for the two of them and told him about the latest developments in the case. He was shaken when told of the murder and sobered by the account of Leeming's fight with the dead man's servant. While praising the sergeant, Andrews admitted that he couldn't have coped in such a situation. Some things were best left to younger and fitter men.

'I feel sorry for that poor young woman,' he said. 'She was duped.'

'Yet she did gain from the friendship with Scanlan. Thanks to the extra lessons for which he paid, she improved greatly as an actress. When all this is over, Mary Burnell might yet be able to take up the career she wants. Before that, of course,' said Madeleine with a sigh, 'she will have to learn the truth about Patrick Scanlan.'

'And what a terrible truth it is, Maddy. The money he lavished on her was tainted. It was all stolen.'

'That will distress Mary and her parents.'

'How did they let her get involved with such a heartless criminal?'

'They only saw what Scanlan allowed them to see,' replied Madeleine. 'But I don't believe he was heartless. He loved her. There's no doubting that. And while he had many opportunities to take advantage of Mary, he never touched her.'

As he sipped his tea and pecked at a biscuit, Andrews was bound to compare Mary Burnell's experience with that of his own daughter. He sent up a silent prayer of thanks to heaven for sparing Madeleine the ordeal that the young actress was going through. Having to look after him in the wake of her mother's death had given Madeleine a sharper awareness of the ways of the world. Andrews liked to think that she wouldn't have been hoodwinked by a man like Patrick Scanlan.

'What will Robert do next?' he asked.

'That depends on what decision is taken today.'

'Will he go back to Scotland?'

'Oh, yes,' she said. 'That's where the first crime was committed and where the second one is due to take place. Robert expects to travel north very soon.'

'I'll go with him,' volunteered Andrews.

'That wouldn't be allowed.'

'I'd promise not to get in the way.'

'Your place is here, Father – well away from any danger.'

'I can take care of myself, Maddy.'

'Oh, no, you can't,' she said with a smile. 'Having lived with you all those years, I should know. You're too disorganised. When you have such difficulty hunting for the right clothes to wear, how can you hope to track down desperate criminals? It's too big a risk. Remember what they did to Patrick Scanlan.'

'Yes,' he said on reflection. 'Perhaps I am better off in London.'

'If it was left to me, Robert would stay here as well.'

'He must go where he's needed. That's his job. But since you enjoyed your glimpse of Scotland, why not go with him this time?'

'No,' said Madeleine, resignedly, 'that's out of the question. I was lucky enough to be involved on the fringes of this investigation but that's as far as it goes. There's no room for me on the train to Glasgow. I'll leave everything to Robert and Victor Leeming. Unlike me, they'll know what to do.'

It was almost seven years since Colbeck had met him and Prince Albert had changed somewhat in the interim. He was still a tall, arresting man with a handsome face and a full head of hair but his waistline had thickened and strands of grey were starting to appear in his mutton-chop whiskers. What Colbeck remembered most about their first meeting was that he radiated intelligence and was strikingly elegant. As someone who took great pains with his own appearance, he noted the Prince's impeccable attire and footwear with interest.

After shaking hands with both men, the Prince turned to Colbeck. He spoke English fluently but with a guttural accent.

'I believe that congratulations are in order,' he said.

'For what reason, Your Royal Highness?'

'Heavens, have you so soon forgotten that you were recently married?'

'Oh, no,' said Colbeck, stifling a laugh.

'The commissioner told me of your good fortune. This is a remarkable man, Mr Renwick,' he went on, indicating Colbeck. 'As you will know, I conceived of the Great Exhibition as a vast shop window in which we could display British expertise in engineering and in manufacturing skills. We wanted to show that mankind's progress depended on a flourishing international trade. The project had many critics and I had the greatest pleasure in confounding them.'

'The exhibition was a triumph, Your Royal Highness,' said Renwick. 'Over six million visitors came to it. My wife and I were among them.'

'It was the inspector who made the event possible.'

'That's overstating my importance, sir,' said Colbeck.

'Nonsense!' returned the Prince. 'You learnt of a plot to blow up part of the exhibition and you scotched it. I'm eternally grateful to you.'

Prince Albert's gratitude was understandable. He'd been closely involved in the event and stood to lose face if it failed or was undermined in some way. Colbeck had been instrumental in removing a major threat, thereby allowing the exhibition to go ahead. It was a resounding success and much of the credit went to the Prince. The Queen was delighted that her husband's beloved project had stilled the doubters and boosted his reputation.

The visitors waited for the Prince to sit down before they did so themselves. They were in a large, high-ceilinged room with walls covered in gilt-framed portraits. The attendant who'd escorted them there now stood beside the door.

'To business,' said the Prince, briskly. 'The commissioner has explained the situation to me and I'll ask Inspector Colbeck the same question that I put to his superior. Can you guarantee our safety?'

Colbeck was honest. 'Not at this stage, sir.'

'Would you advise us to cancel our visit to Balmoral?'

'Quite the reverse – I'd urge you to abide by the arrangements.'

'I'm still not sure that *I* would,' said Renwick.

'Then we'd lose the chance to catch these people,' argued Colbeck, 'and they'd be free to launch a second attack elsewhere about which we have no foreknowledge.'

'We've survived assassination attempts before,' said the Prince.

'Happily, you did, sir. But they were the work of lone individuals. We are dealing with a group of conspirators with money at their disposal and an ability to plan things with painstaking care.'

'Do you know who they are?'

'No – their identities remain a mystery.'

'Have you made any headway at all in the investigation?'

'It may not *seem* so, Your Royal Highness,' conceded Colbeck, 'but I have a strange feeling that we *are* making progress. That's always a good sign.'

Colbeck gave him a brief account of events at the home of Patrick Scanlan and stressed that they now had good descriptions of the two men who'd hired the burglar to get hold of details of the royal train. He firmly believed that they'd find additional evidence when Scanlan's safe was finally opened. Colbeck went on to say that he'd continue the search north of the border.

'Our intention is to arrest these villains *before* the royal train even sets out on its journey to Balmoral.'

'That would be the ideal outcome, of course,' said the Prince, 'but what happens if you fail? Should the excursion still go ahead?'

'I believe so, Your Royal Highness.'

'You advise it even if we may be put in jeopardy as a result?'

'It's the only way to bring these people out into the open,' said Colbeck. 'And there's a compromise that will remove any direct threat to the royal family. When Mr Renwick showed me the itinerary, I noted that there was a lengthy stop at Carlisle. The royal party can alight there and the train can continue without them.'

'That would put the driver, fireman and guard at risk,' protested Renwick. 'You could be sending them to their deaths.'

'If the conspirators don't see the train coming, they won't show their hand. By that stage, I'm confident, we will have a good idea of where they mean to strike and can move in to overpower them. The train can then return to Carlisle to pick up its passengers and will continue unhindered on its way.'

'*I* wouldn't like to be on that footplate, I know that much.'

'Well, I'd be very willing to offer my services as a fireman,' said Colbeck with a grin. 'In fact, I'd find the idea very appealing.'

'It conjures up an amusing picture, Inspector,' said the Prince, 'but you're far more use to us solving a crime than shovelling coal into the firebox.' He paused to consider what had been said then gave a decisive nod. 'I'll have to discuss this matter with the Queen.'

'Is Her Majesty fully aware of the situation?'

'Oh, yes, I keep nothing from her.'

'May I ask what her initial reaction was?'

'It was the same as mine,' replied the Prince. 'We both trust you, Inspector, and were ready to put ourselves in your hands. In the light of what you've told me, however, that decision may need to be reviewed.'

'I can understand that, Your Royal Highness.'

'The commissioner has promised to remain in constant touch.'

'Sir Richard will report any progress that we make.'

'I'd like notice of that as well,' said Renwick. 'It might stop this feeling of dread that's trying to overwhelm me. The fact is that the royal party will be travelling on the LNWR. We don't want it to be a prelude to disaster.'

'The attack will come on the Caledonian,' Colbeck reminded him.

'That puzzled me,' said the Prince. 'Why have they chosen *that* railway?'

It was something that still puzzled Colbeck and he readily admitted it.

'We don't yet know,' he said, 'but we're determined to find out.'

Even though it had been in existence for a number of years, Victor Leeming was still amazed at the efficiency of the telegraph system. Messages that would once have taken over a day to reach different parts of the country could now be transmitted within minutes. Colbeck's telegraph to Wolverhampton elicited a prompt response. Word came that a locksmith from the Chubb factory was on his way to London. When the man eventually arrived at Scotland Yard, Leeming was there to welcome him.

'I'll take you to the house at once,' he offered.

'Good,' said Wilfred Hounsell.

'Did you have a comfortable journey?'

'No, I didn't.'

'Why was that?'

'I hate railways.'

Sensing that he'd met a kindred spirit, Leeming hustled him out and hailed a cab. Hounsell was a short, thin ferret of a man in his fifties with a long nose and darting eyes. He looked more like a burglar than a man whose job was to defy the criminal fraternity. It was clear that he hadn't been taking elocution lessons from Balthasar Goodfellow. Out of his mouth came the deep, rich, unadulterated sound of a typical Black Country accent. Leeming warmed to him even more.

'What's in the safe?' asked Hounsell.

'We don't know.'

'Why is it so important to find out?'

'We're looking for evidence, Mr Hounsell.'

'Oh, I see.'

'You could be helping us to solve a crime.'

'Ah.'

Hounsell was singularly unimpressed by the news. He seemed more worried about the discomfort of the return journey to Wolverhampton than he was about a police investigation. Leeming saw no reason to give him details of the murder that had occurred. The locksmith was there simply to do a specific task.

The cab deposited them outside Scanlan's house and Leeming introduced himself to the uniformed policeman standing outside it. When the two men went inside, Hounsell showed no interest in the bloodstained carpet. All that he wanted to see was the safe. Leeming lifted the painting off the wall.

'There it is, Mr Hounsell,' he said. 'Open it.'

'It's not as easy as that, Sergeant.'

'Don't you have a key?'

'I have a number of them but this safe also has a combination lock. Why don't you give me a few minutes alone? I'll call you when it's ready.'

Opening the little bag that he carried, Hounsell took out a ring on which a selection of master keys dangled. Leeming left him to it and went outside to talk to the policeman. Since he knew that Ned Layne would now be a target, he asked if anyone had come in search of him. The policeman reported that two men had been looking at the house with some interest but that his presence had kept them at bay. The description he gave of them tallied with that of the two visitors given by Layne. The danger to the servant was real. Leeming resolved to point that out to the prisoner.

He chatted to the policeman for some while before he heard

a shout from indoors. Leeming went hastily into the house and entered the drawing room. He was dismayed to see that the safe was still closed.

'Weren't you able to open it?' he asked.

Hounsell was indignant. 'I know my trade, Sergeant.'

'Then why is it still shut?'

'I thought I'd leave you to open it,' said Hounsell. 'I've no interest in what's inside. The man who bought this safe chose well. What was his name?'

'He was Alfred Penn when he lived here.'

Hounsell chuckled. 'Penn, eh?'

'What's so funny about that?'

'It's a place near Wolverhampton. I was married in the parish church.'

Leeming could now see why Scanlan had used the name as an alias. He expected to find documents in the safe relating to other aliases used by the cracksman. But what he was really after was some indication of who'd employed Scanlan to enter Renwick's house. His expectations soared. Grabbing the handle of the safe, he twisted it and pulled open the heavy steel door. When he peered inside, however, he groaned in disappointment. The safe was completely empty.

Hounsell was outspoken. 'You've wasted my bleeding time, Sergeant.'

Nairn Craig was having another bad day. He was in the middle of wading through a pile of compensation claims from angry businessmen when Inspector Rae called in to add to his discomfort. Rejoicing in Colbeck's disappearance, he saw it as a case of a wounded enemy withdrawing from the field of battle because victory was impossible. It not only meant that Rae's investigation could continue without a rival, it gave him ammunition to use against the careworn general manager.

'How will you justify the expense to your board?' he asked, smirking.

'That's my business, Inspector.'

'I'm inclined to think that it's *their* business as well. The crash has been very costly for the Caledonian. Your colleagues will resent wasting so much additional money on the fabled Railway Detective. Why, they will demand, did you put them in the most expensive hotel in Glasgow?'

'They were entitled to some comfort.'

'Only if they earned it and that – demonstrably – they did not do. Colbeck has failed at last, Mr Craig, and you must take responsibility for funding what can only be described as a doomed enterprise.'

Craig fought back. 'Your investigation is equally doomed,' he said. 'You created a lot of sound and fury but little else. You still have no prime suspect.'

'I'm still here,' emphasised Rae. 'Colbeck is not. My inquiry will blossom very soon. Colbeck's has already withered on the vine. Why is he hiding away in London? One can't solve a crime at long distance.'

'Don't make false assumptions about him.'

Rae's eyelids narrowed. 'You say that as if you know something that I don't,' he challenged. 'Are you party to information that should be shared with me?'

'No,' said Craig, forcefully.

'I hope, for your sake, that that's true.'

Rae continued to bait the general manager but the ordeal didn't continue for long. There was a knock on the door and John Mudie entered with a telegraph.

'This has just arrived, sir,' he said, handing it to Craig.

'Thank you.'

'I think you'll find it cheering news.'

When Craig read the telegraph, his face was suddenly split by a grin.

'Inspector Colbeck hasn't quit the field at all,' he said. 'He'll soon be back in Glasgow to continue the search.'

'It will be as futile as his first attempt,' snapped Rae.

'I'd still back him over you, Inspector.'

'Does that mean you'd pay his expenses out of your own pocket?'

'Yes, I would,' said Craig, goaded into making the commitment. 'He and the sergeant can stay at any hotel in the city and I'll gladly pay the bill.'

'Then you're about to make an extremely expensive mistake.'

On that spiteful note, Rae rose to his feet and swept out of the room.

'Thank you for coming to my rescue, John,' said Craig, flopping back into his chair. 'And thank you for bringing me the news about Colbeck. It enabled me to shake Inspector Rae off my back. He was insufferable.'

'There's other news to pass on,' said Mudie.

'What is it?'

'You have another visitor. He came in search of Inspector Colbeck. When I told him the inspector wasn't here, he insisted on speaking to you instead.'

'Who is he?'

'He's a young shepherd by the name of Jamie Farr. He's been here before.'

'Indeed, he has,' said Craig, roused by the information. 'He was very helpful. Send him in, John. I want to hear what the lad has to say.'

* * *

On the following morning, they caught the early train to Glasgow. Though he braced himself for a punishing journey, Leeming knew very little about it at the outset. Almost as soon as the train left Euston, he fell asleep and didn't wake up until they were steaming into Birmingham. Coming awake with a start, he saw that Colbeck had been writing something in his notebook.

'Ah,' said the inspector, 'you're back in the land of the living.'

Leeming wiped the sleep from his eyes. 'I was tired, sir.'

'Then you did the right thing. You had a refreshing nap and you were spared the discomfort you always feel on a train.'

'I'm not the only one. Hounsell despises them as much as I do.'

'Was he the locksmith from Wolverhampton?'

'Yes,' replied Leeming, 'and he was very annoyed that he had to suffer two train journeys in order to open an empty safe.'

'There was always the possibility that it *would* be empty,' said Colbeck. 'Whoever killed him must have rifled the safe before he left.'

'How could he open it without the key and the combination?'

'I daresay that he got Scanlan to open it for him.'

'Do you mean that he forced him to do it?'

'That wasn't necessary, Victor. There's a very easy way to make someone open a safe.'

'Is there?'

'Of course,' said Colbeck. 'You give him a large amount of money. His first instinct is to lock it away. That's what must have happened at Scanlan's house. We know that he was expecting the rest of the money owed to him. Once it was handed over, he opened the safe to put it inside and was attacked. With Scanlan dead on the floor, all that the killer had to do was to steal everything that was in the safe and lock it behind him.'

'They left us nothing in the way of a clue,' said Leeming,

bitterly. 'Ned Layne told us that there was a lot of money in that safe. It's all gone.'

'Yes, Victor, it's helping to fund the attack on the royal train. Not that the villains are short of money,' he added. 'They appear to have unlimited amounts.'

'Where does it come from?'

'I wish I knew.'

Four passengers joined them at Birmingham so they no longer had the freedom to discuss the case in an empty compartment. Colbeck studied his ordnance survey map and Leeming picked up the newspaper they'd bought from the station bookstall. When he read the report of the murder, he was pleased to see that the victim was referred to as Alfred Penn. His real name would emerge later. For the time being, Mary Burnell and her parents were kept ignorant of it. Any delay would be valuable. It would help them to adjust to the horror of Scanlan's death before they learnt the brutal truth about the man they all revered.

A lengthy stop at Preston station allowed them to get out of the train to stretch their legs. After buying some refreshments, they strolled up and down the platform.

'I saw you looking at that map again, Inspector,' said Leeming.

'Yes – I think I know every inch of that part of Scotland now.'

'There's such a big area for us to cover.'

'Oh, I think we can discount huge parts of it, Victor. My feeling is that the second strike will not be such a great distance from the first.'

'That still gives us miles of railway line to police.'

'I'm afraid that it does,' confessed Colbeck. 'At the moment, we're shooting arrows in the dark. There's something we've missed. It's right there in front of us if we only had the sense to see it. We'll have to start the search again.'

'Where will we begin, sir?'

'*You'll* begin in Perth.'

Leeming blenched. 'But that's even further north than Glasgow.'

'I'm glad to see that you've already mastered the geography of Scotland.'

'Why do I have to go there?'

'It's something we should have done earlier,' explained Colbeck. 'I want you to look more closely at the theft of that gunpowder.'

'I thought it was stolen from a barracks.'

'It was, Victor. The barracks in question belong to the 42nd Regiment of Foot. You probably know them by another name.'

'I don't know much about army regiments.'

'Then this is your opportunity to learn something. The 42nd is better known as the Black Watch, one of the finest and proudest regiments in the British army. In view of that,' said Colbeck, 'I want you to ask them how they allowed gunpowder to be stolen from under their noses and used to cause a train crash. Be warned.'

'Why is that?'

'They won't like the question. You may get a dusty answer.'

The man was very patient. Seated astride his horse, he had an uninterrupted view of the railway line for over a mile as it arrowed its way south. He was sheltering behind some bushes that gave him protection from the wind and cover from prying eyes. In his hand, he held a stopwatch. As each new passenger train came into view, he timed its approach then made a note of it on his pad, estimating the speed as he did so. Goods traffic was of no interest to him. Watching only passenger trains, he counted the number of their carriages as they sped past. Light was fading and the wind was freshening. His work was done. He was about to ride away when another passenger train appeared on the horizon.

Clicking his stopwatch, he could see the seconds tick by as the train approached.

After it had gone, he recorded all the details, glad that he'd waited for one more train. Unlike the others, this one had the requisite number of carriages and was travelling at approximately the right speed. It was a useful guide. The last train had made his long vigil worthwhile and he congratulated himself. What he didn't realise as he rode away was that it was carrying two detectives from Scotland Yard who'd come to arrest him.

CHAPTER TWENTY

Nairn Craig was waiting at the Strathallan Hotel to greet them. He shook their hands with a mixture of relief and desperation. There was a clear smell of whisky on his breath. After giving them time to move into their respective rooms, he took them to the bar and ordered a round of drinks. When they'd settled down at a table, he spread his arms as if imploring help.

'What do you have to tell me?' he asked.

'We've been busy while we've been in London,' replied Colbeck. 'The sergeant had to fight for his life against a strong opponent and I had the privilege of a meeting with Prince Albert.'

'I wish it had been the other way round,' said Leeming, moodily. 'It should have been *your* turn to get into a brawl, Inspector, and my children would be thrilled if they knew that their father had gone to Buckingham Palace.'

'You'll get there one day, I'm sure.'

'Your telegraph said very little, Inspector,' observed Craig.

'That was deliberate. I wasn't certain who'd see it.'

'So what happened while you were away?'

'There have been developments, sir. Isn't that right, Sergeant?'

'Oh, yes,' said Leeming, gulping down his beer. 'I'll vouch for that. I still have some of the bruises from one of those developments.'

Craig rubbed his hands. 'Tell me all.'

Colbeck was unusually prolix, adding details in order to colour the narrative and providing a lot of background information about certain individuals. He explained how the burglary at Renwick's house had sent them off in pursuit of Patrick Scanlan and how Leeming's tenacity had unearthed the burglar's address. Delighted to hear that they'd identified someone involved in the projected crime on his railway, Craig was dismayed to learn that the man was dead. He took little consolation from the fact that Scanlan's servant had provided descriptions of the two men who'd come to the house. They were so general that they could fit thousands of people. In spite of the optimism that Colbeck injected into his voice, the general manager's spirits had been lowered.

'In essence,' he concluded, 'the visit to London was in vain.'

'I wouldn't say that, sir.'

'Nor me,' Leeming chimed in. 'I got to see my family.'

'That hardly advances the investigation,' complained Craig.

'I disagree,' said Colbeck. 'We all need periods of rest to revitalise us. The sergeant is a different man since he spent time at home and I feel inspired after seeing my wife again. We've returned to the fray with new energy.'

'Well, I hope that it's deployed in the right direction.'

'It will be, sir – but I haven't told you about my visit to the palace.'

Craig sat up. 'What's the Queen's position?'

'She and her husband are waiting on events,' said Colbeck. 'I think I persuaded Prince Albert that the royal train must depart on the date set in order to flush out the villains. If we've made no arrests before that day, I suggested that the royal family could leave the train at Carlisle and wait until the coast was clear.'

'Do you intend the train to continue without them?'

'Yes, I do. It's very distinctive and will be seen coming by the villains.'

'What about those still on board it?'

'They'll be made aware of the danger,' said Colbeck, 'but they'll also be told that we're likely to have caught those ready to attack it before they can do so.'

'That word "likely" troubles me, Inspector. I'd want a more definite guarantee. You're asking me to put Caledonian employees into grave danger. They won't have forgotten what happened to that goods train.'

'You're assuming that we'll make no progress in the next few days.'

'We've made little enough so far,' said Craig, 'as Inspector Rae was only too ready to remind me. He's been taunting me ever since you left.'

'What has *his* investigation turned up?'

'Very little, as it happens.'

'Is he still hunting for suspects from the NBR?'

'Yes, he is but he keeps finding time to pester me.'

'Does he suspect that you're hiding something from him?'

'I'm afraid that he does.'

'Too many cooks spoil the broth,' said Leeming. 'We don't want Inspector Rae poking his nose into our business. We had too much of that with Superintendent McTurk.'

'Forget him – he's been sacked. Well,' said Craig, finishing his whisky before getting up, 'I have to admit to disappointment. I hoped you'd bring good news from London with you but it hasn't materialised. That will only encourage Inspector Rae to crow over me once more.'

'He may soon have to replace his scorn with an apology,' said Colbeck.

'I wish I could believe that, Inspector. Good night to you both.' About to depart on that curt note, he remembered something. 'Oh, I had a visit yesterday from the young shepherd who helped us before.'

'What did Jamie say?'

'He insisted on speaking to you, Inspector. For some reason, he doesn't trust the rest of us. He wanted to know when you'd be back in Glasgow.'

'I told him to keep his eyes peeled. Has he seen something of interest?'

'I think so. His story was rather garbled. He refused to give me any details. He said he wanted to show you something.'

'I'll go and see him in the morning.'

'Don't believe everything he tells you.'

'Why not?'

'To be honest, I thought him rather sly.'

Colbeck frowned. 'That wasn't my impression of the lad.'

'He kept on and on about the reward money,' said Craig, irritably. 'I had the feeling that he'd lie his young head off in order to get hold of it.'

The telescope was a wise investment. As well as enabling Farr to scan the horizon, it allowed him to keep a closer watch on his flock. The sheep wandered far and wide and Angus couldn't easily round them all up. Thanks to the telescope, Farr could make sure that none of them strayed near the railway line. If they did, he dispatched his dog to drive them to safety. There was an additional bonus and it was the one that he liked most. With the aid of the instrument, he could see Bella Drew's cottage from over half a mile away. When she came into view, she was tiny and indistinct but he nevertheless took pleasure from simply watching her. If she saw the sun glinting off the telescope, Bella gave him a cheery wave.

His second visit to Glasgow had been disappointing. Overcoming his disgust at the railway, he took the train there and endured another fraught ride. When he got to the offices of the Caledonian Railway the previous day, however, he learnt that Inspector Colbeck had been in London and was unavailable until the morrow. The man to whom he'd spoken was the general manager and he'd been far less pleasant than Colbeck. It was clear that he didn't trust Farr and refused to make any promises about the reward money. Having gone there with high hopes, the shepherd had left dejected because he had no good news to take back to Bella Drew. The undeniable truth was that Craig hadn't taken him seriously. That hurt his pride.

On the train journey back, he came to see that his expectations might be ill-founded. He went to Glasgow in the certainty that he'd made an important discovery yet there was no actual proof of that. Looked at with cold objectivity, his find was not as exciting as he'd thought at first. All that he'd seen were the marks of some cartwheels in a stand of trees. There were lots of reasons to explain how they got there, most of them unconnected with a recent train crash. As for the people he'd seen in the trap, there were several innocent explanations to account for their appearance beside the railway line. He'd been too quick to leap to conclusions and too ready to believe them. More worrying was the fact that he'd made Bella Drew believe them as well. He'd given her false hope.

Sitting down on the ridge, he took out a hunk of bread and a piece of cheese. When he began to munch the food, Angus came to curl up beside him. Farr gave him an absent-minded pat. The railway was out of sight now but he could hear another train hurtling through the dale and leaving its smoky signature in the blue sky. The noise seemed to hang in the air for minutes. It was the dog who saw the trap first. Angus needed no telescope to descry the approach of the vehicle. Farr swung his head round to look. Even from that distance, he could see who the driver was and the telescope confirmed it.

Inspector Colbeck was coming to see him. After swallowing a piece of cheese, Farr wrapped the rest of it up in a piece of cloth with the remains of the bread. He got to his feet with mixed feelings, hopeful that he might, after all, be able to earn the reward, yet resigned to the notion that he'd brought the inspector on a wasted journey. His future was in the balance. Would he be able to celebrate or suffer embarrassment? It was an open question.

Edward Tallis was writhing in annoyance. From the moment he'd taken direct charge of the case, he'd been kept on its periphery. It was Leeming who had the credit for the arrest of Ned Layne and Colbeck who'd been invited to Buckingham Palace in place of his superior. When the superintendent tried to accompany them to Glasgow, he was told by the commissioner to remain at his desk in London because he had no first-hand knowledge of the situation in Scotland and was more likely to be a liability there. That rankled.

Pulling on a cigar from the new box at last provided by the tobacconist, he brooded in silence. He was still dwelling on the slights he'd received of late when there was a loud knock on his door. It was opened by the commissioner who strode into the middle of the room. Tallis hastily stubbed out the cigar in an ashtray. Mayne flicked a hand to disperse the smoke.

'There's a terrible fug in here,' he said.

'I'll open a window,' offered Tallis, getting up to do so. 'There you are, Sir Richard,' he said, facing him again.

'Thank you. This investigation could do with some fresh air in it.'

'I've been thinking about the situation with the royal family.'

'So have I,' said Mayne. 'In fact, that's what I came to talk to you about. As a general rule, I accept Colbeck's advice without questioning it but I'm beginning to have doubts on this occasion.'

'So am I,' agreed Tallis, seizing the opportunity to side with him. 'Colbeck is urging that the excursion to Balmoral goes ahead regardless. I have to say that I regard that as irresponsible.'

'There's too big a risk involved.'

'And there are too many imponderables.'

'Yet the final word lies with Her Majesty, of course, and she listens to her husband. Surprisingly, Prince Albert was won over by Colbeck's rhetoric. We both know how persuasive the fellow can be.'

Tallis pulled a face. 'Sometimes he's too clever for his own good.'

'Let's not belittle his achievements,' said Mayne. 'They are considerable. He's one of the few people in this building who gets a measure of respect out of the press. While he wins praise, you and I are routinely lampooned.'

'It's most unjust, Sir Richard.'

'We have a chance to make amends, Superintendent. The fate of the royal family is in our hands. If we safeguard it, even the most critical newspapers will have to acknowledge the fact. If we fail to do that, however . . .'

'It doesn't bear thinking about,' said Tallis. 'They'll crucify us.'

'That's why we may have to overrule Inspector Colbeck.'

'Do you want me to recall him from Glasgow?'

'No, no,' said Mayne, 'he's there to hunt for the men behind this vile conspiracy. If he catches them, all well and good. The royal train will leave on the date specified. But if he *doesn't* manage to do that, I'm going to urge Prince Albert to delay the trip to Balmoral.'

'You have my full support, Sir Richard.'

'There's always the chance that the Prince will not listen to me, mark you. He's his own man. Nobody can make him do something against his will. We've seen many instances of his obstinacy. But I think that I can marshal a convincing case.'

'I'd be happy to speak up in support of you.'

'You won't be needed, Tallis.'

'But we could present a united front at Buckingham Palace,' insisted the other. 'In terms of age, seniority and experience, we outrank Colbeck completely.'

'This is not a contest between us and the inspector,' said Mayne, sharply. 'It's just a sensible precaution to take. Naturally, my hope is that he will be able to identify and arrest the people involved in this plot very soon. At the same time, I'm aware how difficult a task that is.'

'We have such little evidence to help us, Sir Richard.'

'That hasn't hampered Colbeck in the past. He conjures evidence out of thin air. I pray that he may do so again. It's only by sheer luck that we stumbled upon this conspiracy. Consequently, there's only limited time in which to work.'

'I'm very conscious of that.'

'It's almost as if we have a gun to our head,' said Mayne. 'Incidentally, have you written to Colbeck's father-in-law yet to thank him for providing us with the information that revealed the existence of this plot?'

'I was doing so when you came in, Sir Richard,' lied Tallis.

When he saw no stationery on the desk, Mayne was sarcastic.

'Really?' he said. 'What form of communication did you intend to use? Were you going to ape the Red Indians and send up smoke signals with your cigar? I think Mr Andrews deserves something more tangible than that – don't you?'

Going swiftly out of the room, the commissioner left Tallis squirming in discomfort. The superintendent took out some writing paper then reached for his pen.

Victor Leeming could think of better ways to spend his time than by going on a train journey to Perth. He couldn't imagine that he'd learn anything of practical value to the case. All that the trip meant to him was an extended period of boredom on his least favourite mode of travel. When he reached his destination, the first thing he did was to visit the station hotel to take his bearings and to revive himself with some refreshment. Craig had once boasted that the Caledonian had provided a royal suite of rooms at the hotel, including a retiring room and a dining room. Leeming saw none of them. All that he wanted was a base from which to operate.

Perth was a garrison town on the banks of the River Tay. Known in the past for its fair aspect, it had changed with the coming of the railways and was now an important junction. On the cab ride to the barracks, Leeming saw both of its faces, the pleasant streets and green parks vying with the tumult of industry. When he got to the barracks, he told the driver to wait, not anticipating a long stay. As it turned out, the visit was unduly short. Leeming got no further than the main gate. Two sentries were on duty in the dark uniforms that had given them the name of the Black Watch. As he walked towards them, he tried not to look at the knees peeping out from beneath their kilts. Both men were armed. When Leeming got within five yards, one of the sentries pointed his rifle at the visitor.

'Tha's far enough,' he warned.

'I've come to see your commanding officer,' said Leeming.

'He's no' heer.'

'Then I'll speak to your second in command.'

'Ye've no right to speak to anyone in the barracks.'

Leeming explained who he was and showed a warrant card to prove it but he still didn't get through the gate. Both men glared at him with muted hostility.

'Perhaps you can help me, then,' said Leeming.

'I doot tha', my friend,' replied the sentry.

'I'm investigating a train crash on the Caledonian railway.'

'Then why are ye botherin' us?'

'Gunpowder was used. I'm told that it came from these barracks.'

'It's a bloody lie!' exclaimed the man.

'Aye,' said his companion. 'Where did ye get tha' nonsense from?'

'Are you telling me that it's not true?' pressed Leeming.

'I'm telling ye to be on your way,' said the first man, using his rifle to indicate the cab. 'And ye can stop listening to tales aboot us.'

Leeming looked beyond them at the buildings in the distance. There was a deserted air about them. A few soldiers were visible but there was no sense of a bustling garrison. The place was uncharacteristically silent.

'Where is everybody?' he wondered. 'This place is dead.'

'The regiment's overseas,' said one of the men. 'If ye want to see the colonel, ye'll have to go to India.'

'Ask the cab driver how much it will cost ye,' added the other.

Their mocking laughter pursued him back to the vehicle. Leeming was not dismayed. He'd got the answer for which he came. It had only been possible to steal gunpowder from the barracks because it had a depleted garrison.

Colbeck could see how nervous the shepherd was and wondered what was making him so uneasy. Glad to see Angus again, he patted the seat beside him to indicate that the dog could ride in the trap but the animal preferred to run free and yap at the turning wheels. Farr sat beside Colbeck to act as his guide. He explained how he'd seen someone driving in the same direction even though there was no track. Colbeck told him that he was right to report the incident. He kept Farr talking in the hope that it would instil some confidence in him but the opposite happened. The shepherd seemed to have lost his nerve. Although he'd discovered something, he wasn't at all sure that it was worth bringing the inspector all the way from Glasgow to see it.

'I could be wrong,' he admitted.

'I doubt that, Jamie. You've good instincts.'

'When I first saw it, I was fair excited.'

'And now you're having second thoughts,' said Colbeck. 'Is that it?'

'Aye, Inspector.'

The trap lurched sideways. 'You're right about this being a strange way to bring a vehicle. There are humps and hollows and heaven knows what to contend with. How much farther is there to go?'

'It's up in yon trees,' said Farr, pointing.

They'd lost sight of the railway line and were climbing up the hill between bushes and shrubs. Angus decided that he'd lead the way instead of following and he raced ahead, plunging into the stand of trees then emerging again with his tail wagging and his tongue hanging out. Colbeck snapped the reins to make the horse break into a trot then pulled him to a halt when they reached the trees. He and Farr jumped to the ground. The shepherd nodded.

'In heer, Inspector,' he mumbled.

'Lead the way, lad.'

Farr went into the trees and walked to the clearing where he'd seen the ruts. Colbeck bent down to examine them. They led out of the trees and on to the stony ground beyond where they disappeared.

'These were made recently,' decided Colbeck.

'Aye, tha's what I thought.'

'Who'd want to bring a cart to such an isolated spot?'

'Did I do right to call ye?' asked Farr, hesitantly.

'You certainly did. This would be an ideal hiding place from which to launch a second attack on the railway. It's completely sheltered yet within easy reach of the line. I'll wager that it's overhung by a rocky outcrop that could be turned into a small avalanche.'

Colbeck stood up and walked towards the railway line. Farr trailed behind him. Before they'd gone more than a dozen yards, however, they were stopped by the frenzied barking of the dog. Angus had found something. He was digging his paws in the ground to unearth it. The two of them went back to see what he was doing. Farr thought his dog had found a bone but Colbeck saw something else come into view. It was a steel rim. Kneeling beside Angus, he used both hands to scoop up the earth and toss it away. They were soon looking at the top of a small barrel.

'What d'ye think it is?' asked Farr.

'I *know* what it is, lad. Your dog is a real detective.'

'What has he found?'

Colbeck smiled up at him. 'Gunpowder.'

Tam Howie was making some entries in his account book when he had an unexpected visitor. Gregor Hines was shown into his office. The old man claimed that he'd been out walking and had looked in to pay his respects. As a retired businessman, he knew better than to interrupt his friend during the working day and had therefore timed his arrival at the end of the afternoon. After shaking his hand, Howie offered him a seat. Hines lowered himself slowly into it with a throaty chuckle.

'Thank you, Tam,' he said. 'At my advanced age, there's only so much time I can spend on these old legs.' Offered refreshment, he refused with a gesture. 'If I started eating and drinking, I'll nod off to sleep and then where would you be?'

'I'd leave you alone in that chair overnight,' said Howie, amused.

'I do believe that you would.'

They exchanged pleasantries and asked after each other's wives but Howie knew that it was not a social call. Gregor Hines had come to confront him. It was not long before the old man adopted a stricter tone.

'It was good to see you at the kirk on Sunday,' he began.

'That's where you'll always find me on the Sabbath.'

'But where were you on Saturday?'

'Flora and I went for a picnic,' replied Howie.

'You're not known as a man who likes picnics, Tam.'

'I enjoyed this one.'

'Why did you take Ian Dalton with you?'

'How do you know that we did?'

'The three of you were seen catching a train on Saturday.'

Howie thrust out his jaw. 'Is there any law against that, Gregor?'

'No, there isn't,' said Hines, 'but there ought to be a law against doing it on the Sabbath. However, I don't need to tell you that, do I?' He fixed a watery eye on Howie. 'It must have been an odd sort of picnic that you had.'

'We simply went for a ride in the country.'

'It was just you, your dear wife and Ian Dalton.'

'Yes, that's right.'

'What about Morag? She's a dear wife as well, isn't she?'

'Morag chose not to come.'

'Is that what Ian told you? I wonder if he even bothered to ask her. I kept a close eye on the pair of them at the kirk on Sunday. Not to put too fine a point on it, there was unease between them. Oh, nothing too dramatic,' Hines went on. 'Indeed, most people wouldn't have noticed that anything was wrong. But I've been married for over fifty years. I've learnt to detect the little nuances of connubial bliss and, in the case of Morag Dalton, they were less than blissful.'

Howie's patience was frayed. 'Why don't you say it, Gregor?'

'The three of you are up to something,' asserted the other.

'We went for a picnic. It's possible we'll go for another.'

'Be warned, Tam.'

'Ian is a friend. Flora and I like him.'

'Don't bring disgrace down upon our kirk.'

'That's a terrible thing to accuse me of doing,' said Howie, angrily. 'Flora and I have devoted ourselves to the kirk for many years. We've given money freely and taken on mundane tasks if they needed doing. You'll not find anyone more devout.'

'Your devotion is not the problem,' said Hines. 'I think you've taken it to extremes. Do I need to be more specific?'

There was tension in the air. Hines had thrown down a challenge and backed it up with a piercing stare. Howie fought to control his temper. In a row with the old man, he might say something that gave him away. Besides, he liked and respected Hines. They'd had their differences over the years but it hadn't led to any personal animosity. Hines was acting in good faith. Troubled that their kirk might one day be at the centre of a criminal investigation, the old man felt moved to speak out. Howie accepted his right to do so. But *he* had rights as well and one them was to do whatever he felt necessary to reinstate the Sabbath as a day of rest. Gregor Hines would never condone the action he'd taken so it was best to keep him unaware of it.

Howie sought to pacify him. 'It's good to see you,' he said, patting him on the shoulder. 'And I know that you have concerns about me.'

'My real concern is for Morag Dalton.'

'Don't fret over her. Their marriage is a happy one.'

'It wouldn't be so happy if she lost her husband,' said Hines, 'and I'm not suggesting that a healthy man like Ian is likely to expire before too long.' He raised both hands. 'I've said my piece, Tam. Throw me out.'

'Can't I at least offer you a cup of tea?'

'You can offer it but I'll only refuse for the second time.' With a great effort, he struggled to his feet. 'How's business?'

'It couldn't be better. Unlike you, most people can't wait to drink the tea I import. It's a much healthier drink than alcohol. Nobody ever got inebriated on a cup of China tea.'

'You should say that in your advertisements, Tam.'

'I may just do that,' said Howie with a laugh.

Gregor Hines stumbled across to the door before delivering his parting shot.

'You've a lovely wife, a flourishing business and an established place in the community and the kirk.' His smile was full of sadness. 'Don't lose them all, Howie.'

It was the second time that Caleb Andrews had called at the house while brandishing a letter. Madeleine was so pleased to see him in a state of exhilaration that she didn't mind breaking off from her work. The letter had been delivered by hand and it was full of gracious compliments. Andrews handed it over like a child allowing a best friend to see his new toy. While his daughter read it, he chortled.

'It's from Superintendent Tallis,' she observed.

'He's finally recognised my true worth.'

'This is very gratifying. You must show it to Robert.'

'He'd only be jealous,' said Andrews, jokingly. 'I know that he and the superintendent are not the best of friends.'

She looked up. 'They work well together in spite of that.'

'What do you think of it, Maddy?'

'I think it's overdue. It should have come days ago. You saw something that nobody else would have seen. Scotland Yard is in your debt, Father.'

'That's what I want to ask you about,' he said. 'You've told me that Robert has used informers in the past.'

'The police get information from any source possible.'

'But some people are *paid*, aren't they?'

'Yes,' she replied. 'There are criminals who try to curry favour with the police by helping them and they do expect more of a reward than a letter of thanks.'

'What about me?' asked Andrews.

She handed the letter back. 'Your help has just been acknowledged.'

'It's more than help, Maddy. But for me, the royal family would be setting off to Scotland without realising that someone was waiting to ambush them. Don't you think that deserves some reward?'

Madeleine was shocked. 'You're not expecting *money*, are you?'

'Yes, I am.'

'Father, I'm ashamed of you!'

'I've saved lives.'

'And you're entitled to take some pride out of that,' she said, 'but that doesn't mean you should get paid. It's an almost indecent suggestion.'

Andrews was adamant. 'Robert gets paid for solving crimes. I should be rewarded for uncovering one.'

'Robert is a detective. You're just a member of the public.'

'I'm involved in this case, Maddy.'

'You were, I agree, but you're not any longer. And neither am I. As for claiming all the credit, I think you should remember that this all started when I had a conversation with Mrs Renwick. Some people,' said Madeleine, 'would argue that *I* should have received a letter of thanks. What I would never do is to expect or demand payment. It's unthinkable.'

'*I* think about it.'

'Well, you can stop doing so. It's so mercenary. I'm shocked at you, Father, I really am, and Robert will be shocked as well. This is so unlike you. I don't know what put the dreadful idea into your head.'

Her outburst silenced him and he became repentant. After reading Tallis's letter, he slipped it into his pocket and looked apologetically at his daughter. He hated having upset her so much.

Yet though he wanted to placate her, he was not entirely ready to dismiss the hope of financial gain.

'What about that reward offered by the Caledonian?' he wondered. 'Is there any chance I could have a slice of that?'

On the train journey back, Colbeck saw evidence that the sabbatarians had been continuing their campaign. As they approached Motherwell, over a dozen miles south of Glasgow, he caught sight of another bold message gouged into the turf of an embankment. Colbeck had missed it on the journey south because he'd been seated on the other side of the compartment. Closer to Glasgow, there were other signs of sabbatarian activity. Paint was daubed and banners had been hung. It was costing the Caledonian a lot of money to remove the exhortations to preserve the Sabbath for its original purpose. The campaigners did seem to be concentrating on one particular railway company.

After their earlier meeting, Craig had been despondent when he left them at the hotel. Colbeck was glad to have good news to impart at last. Once they'd found what amounted to buried treasure, they covered it up again and made it look as if the ground had been undisturbed. The conspirators would be back. They had to believe that their hiding place had been undiscovered. Jamie Farr had been elated and Colbeck had had to warn him that there was some time to go before there was a chance to make any arrests. Like Craig, he was irritated by the shepherd's obsession with the reward. Angus had been satisfied with a burst of praise and a congratulatory pat. Farr wanted more. He didn't realise the significance of the find and Colbeck didn't enlighten him. The shepherd would be staggered to learn that something they'd uncovered on a remote Scottish hillside posed a threat to the royal family.

When he arrived back at the hotel, Colbeck saw that Leeming

was waiting for him in the lounge. They'd adjourned upstairs so that they could talk in private. It was Leeming who spoke first, bemoaning the fact that he'd been sent to Perth.

'It's the ancient capital of Scotland,' said Colbeck. 'If you'd taken the trouble to go to Scone Palace, you'd have seen the Stone of Destiny.'

'What's that?'

'It's the place where the king of Scotland was traditionally crowned.'

'But they don't have any kings here now.'

'That's a source of great bitterness in some quarters, Victor. The Scots have long memories. English armies might have subdued them but there are still those who yearn for independence. It's not beyond the bounds of probability that that's what's prompting this attack on the royal family.'

'Well, I couldn't wait to get away from Perth,' said Leeming.

'Why was that?'

'I went a very long way to answer a very simple question. The reason that it was possible to steal that gunpowder from the Black Watch is that the regiment is in India. The barracks was almost empty.'

'To whom did you speak?'

'I got no further than the main gate, sir. The sentries wouldn't let me in. They were very rude to me.'

'I did say that you might get a dusty answer.'

'There was no need for it.'

'Did you tell them we were engaged in a murder investigation?'

'Yes,' said Leeming, 'but they still wouldn't let me in because they claimed that they had no connection with the crime. According to them, no gunpowder was stolen from there.'

'They were lying, Victor.'

'I was about to tell them that but they both had loaded rifles.'

'We mustn't blame them,' said Colbeck, tolerantly. 'They're under orders to deny that the barracks was so vulnerable. It must have been embarrassing for them to have their security breached. But I've just seen incontrovertible proof that the gunpowder did come from there.'

'What proof is that, sir?'

'The name of the regiment was on the barrel.'

Colbeck told him about the visit to Jamie Farr and how the sheepdog had helped them to find the gunpowder. Leeming shook off his boredom at once. He was convinced that one crime had been solved and that another could now be prevented. Since they knew when and where the next strike would be, all that they had to do was to lie in wait for the would-be assassins to arrive then arrest them.

'So the place they chose this time is not far from the original crash,' he noted.

'It offers them the same advantages,' said Colbeck. 'An explosion at that point on the line would cause rock to hit the royal train with destructive effect.'

'They're merciless!'

'They're also clever and resourceful. We mustn't underrate them.'

Leeming grinned. 'They're in for a nasty surprise.'

'We must set the trap with great care, Victor.'

'Mr Craig is going to be overjoyed when he hears the news.'

'It should renew his faith in us. That's been sapped of late.'

'What about Inspector Rae?'

'He never had any faith in us at the start,' said Colbeck. 'When we bring this investigation to a happy conclusion, he'll be enraged that he was not kept informed. But all that he was told to do by the procurator fiscal was to prepare a report on the first crash. He's totally unaware that there's a second, far more serious crime in the offing.' Colbeck became pensive. 'I was just thinking about your comment on Perth.'

'I hope I never have to visit the city again, sir.'

'You said that it was a long way to go.'

'The journey seemed endless,' said Leeming. 'We stopped at every hole in the hedge. I thought that we'd never get there.'

'An obvious question springs to mind, Victor.'

'It's not obvious to me.'

'Perth is some way north of Glasgow yet the train crash was nearly seventy miles south of it. Do you follow my reasoning?'

'I can't say that I do, sir.'

'Why go all the way to Perth to steal gunpowder when they had a supply of it close by at the quarry? Yes, I know that the barracks had only a skeleton battalion there but they'd still have had an armed guard on their arsenal. That wouldn't happen at the quarry,' said Colbeck, developing his argument. 'There'd probably have been no more than a nightwatchman on duty. There'd certainly have been no trained soldiers there to act as sentries. My first question leads on to another. Why raid the barracks in Perth when there are regiments stationed much further south? They'd all have a ready supply of gunpowder.'

'I've no answer to either of those questions,' admitted Leeming, 'but I can add a third one of my own.'

'What's that?'

'Who *are* these devils?'

When they caught the train at Euston, they travelled in separate compartments so that they wouldn't be seen together. While other passengers complained about the long and irksome journey, they held their peace. Had the distance been twice as far, they'd have voiced no protest. They were travelling north for a purpose that fired them so much that all else was blocked out of their minds. Aches and pains were irrelevant. Lengthy delays on cold platforms caused no irritation. They were buoyed up by a missionary zeal. When the train rattled past the site of the earlier crash, they both afforded themselves a quiet smile.

One of them alighted at Beattock. He was stolid man of middle height with curly dark hair and a beard. Tossing his luggage onto the back of a cart, he climbed up beside the driver who squeezed his arm by way of a greeting. The driver was tall, square-shouldered, clean-shaven and with close-cropped hair. Both men were in their thirties. A snap of the reins set the horse off at a trot. Almost nobody saw them leave the station and they were out of the little village within a couple of minutes. They talked with the easy familiarity of cousins.

'It's so guid to see ye again, Callum,' said the driver.

'Aye, it's great to be back on Scottish soil.'

'Did everything go well in London?'

'It went very well,' said Callum Matthews.

'What aboot tha' train timetable?'

'Oh, we ken all we need to ken aboot tha'. And we've *ye* to thank, Davey. It was ye who told us to steal a look at it. We hired a burglar to do just tha' for us.'

'Did he ask why ye wanted it?'

'He was paid *not* to ask questions.'

'The man must have been curious.'

'Aye, he was,' said Matthews, 'but he took his curiosity to the grave. We cut his throat and emptied his safe. Getting what we needed didnae cost us a penny.'

Davey Ure laughed. 'Ye had some fun in London, then?'

'We did what had to be done – nothing more.'

'Well, I've no' been idle heer. I've timed so many bloody trains with my stopwatch that I can tell ye the exact speed at a glance. He's going to be pleased with me, Callum.'

'Everything's gone to plan so far. He's very happy.'

'Where will he get off the train?'

'He'll go as far as Carstairs,' replied Matthews, 'then cross to the other platform and catch the train back heer. By the time ye pick him up, it'll be pitch-dark. Nobody will see ye together.'

'Nobody will see *any* of us together. We'll disappear as if we never existed.' A flick of the wrist made the horse pick up the pace. Ure was excited. 'Not long to go now, Callum.'

'No,' said the other, smirking. 'Queen Victoria and her family will have a warm welcome to Scotland.'

CHAPTER TWENTY-ONE

As he sat in his armchair with a bottle of whisky at hand, Nairn Craig was downcast. He was facing problems of all kinds and their cumulative effect was almost too much to bear. While at work, it was necessary for him to wear a brave face and maintain his composure but there was no such pressure to do that at home. His true feelings were etched into his face. He was pale, drawn and melancholy. Frown lines had deepened and his stare was vacant. His high ambitions for the Caledonian Railway now seemed both ridiculous and unattainable. And the worst, he feared, was yet to come. Even the arrival of his visitors failed to lift him out of his gloom. He assumed that Colbeck and Leeming had come to bring more bad tidings.

A servant showed them into the drawing room where Craig accorded them a lukewarm greeting. He didn't even rise from his armchair. In response to his limp gesture, they sat on the sofa opposite him.

'Forgive us for bothering you at home, sir,' said Colbeck, 'but we have news that we felt could not wait until the morning.'

'What sort of news?' asked Craig, dully.

'It's the very best kind,' said Leeming. 'The inspector went to see Jamie Farr.'

'He's that crafty young shepherd I met, isn't he?'

'Whatever he is,' said Colbeck, 'he's helped us to make the discovery that we needed in this case. He and his dog located the site of the next train crash.'

Craig rallied. 'Are you sure?'

'We found gunpowder hidden there.'

'It was stolen from the barracks in Perth,' Leeming blurted out.

'Let *me* tell the story, Sergeant.'

'I'm sorry, sir.'

Colbeck gave details of his excursion to meet Jamie Farr. While praising the shepherd for showing such enterprise, he also criticised him for asking repeatedly about the prospects of a reward. Colbeck made sure that due credit was given to Angus. The sheepdog was the real hero.

'This is remarkable,' said Craig, animated. 'I should have put more trust in the lad. I misjudged him cruelly.'

'He doesn't know the implications of what he found, of course, and I didn't tell him what they were. I'm not sure that Jamie could cope with the notion that what he found has a direct relevance to the safety of the royal family.'

'No, he's just an ignorant shepherd.'

'You undervalue him, Mr Craig. The lad was clever enough to teach me something. He'd bought himself a telescope.' He smacked his head. 'Why didn't I think of that? It's how he was able to spot that trap going along the railway line. A telescope defies distance,' Colbeck went on. 'We must acquire one.'

'Yes,' agreed Leeming. 'It will come in useful.'

Craig was intrigued. 'How will you catch them, Inspector?'

'We'll arrange an ambush.'

'Won't you need more men?'

'No,' said Colbeck, 'I fancy that the sergeant and I can manage, especially if we're armed. I doubt if there are more than two or three of them. A large gang would be bound to attract attention and they've been careful not to do that. It only takes one person to set off an explosion.'

'I still think it's dangerous. You don't know what you're up against.'

'Neither do they,' said Leeming. 'Because they got away with it the first time, they'll think they can do the same again. They'll be off guard when we pounce.'

'I admire your courage in taking these fiends on.'

'They have a lot to answer for,' said Colbeck, 'so we'll do our best to capture them alive. If that's not possible, I'll have no compunction in pulling the trigger.'

'I'll *enjoy* doing it,' asserted Leeming with almost bloodthirsty relish. 'After the way they killed Patrick Scanlan, they deserve no quarter. We should save the cost of a trial and shoot them.'

Colbeck disagreed strongly. 'We'd never understand their real motives if we did that,' he argued. 'And we'd never know if they were acting on their own or if they were merely part of a much larger movement. No, Sergeant, due process of law must be followed if at all feasible. We mustn't sink to their level.'

'My instinct is to support the sergeant,' said Craig, slapping the arm of the chair. 'These men are vermin. They should be exterminated.'

'It's a task we should leave to the public executioner,' said Colbeck, sternly.

'You'll have to take them alive first.'

'I believe that we can do that, sir.'

Craig got to his feet. 'I knew that it was right to send for you, Inspector,' he said, gratefully, 'and I'm sorry for doubting you. It will give me so much pleasure to taunt Rae for a change. While he's still burrowing around for suspects among NBR employees, you've actually found the culprits.'

'Don't breathe a syllable about this until they're in custody.'

'Rely on me. And excuse my poor hospitality,' added Craig. 'Can I offer you refreshment of any kind?'

'No, thank you, sir,' said Colbeck. 'We dined at the hotel.'

'But a glass of that whisky wouldn't come amiss,' said Leeming, covetously.

Colbeck grinned. 'The sergeant speaks for both of us.'

'Be my guest.'

After finding some glasses, Craig poured each of them a measure of whisky. All three of them were soon relaxing over a bracing drink. The mood had changed completely. Craig's melancholy had been transformed into elation.

'The inspector had an interesting thought,' observed Leeming.

'Oh – what was it?'

'He wondered why the gunpowder was stolen from the barracks in Perth when there was a supply of it at the quarry near the site of the train crash.'

'It *is* odd,' said Craig. 'Do you have an answer to that, Inspector?'

'No, sir,' replied Colbeck, 'but I have a theory about how someone was able to gain entry to the barracks. The man must have been a soldier in the regiment. Who else would know where the arsenal was and what sort of guard was mounted on it?'

'That makes sense.'

'It's highly likely that one of the people we're looking for is a deserter. Nobody still in the army would plot against Her Majesty. They fight for Queen and Country. It would be instructive if we knew the names of any deserters from the Black Watch.'

'I could have found those names for you.'

'You wouldn't even get past the main gate, sir,' warned Leeming. 'The sentries gave me the cold shoulder and sent me on the way. The regiment is in India.'

'I know that, Sergeant,' said Craig. 'They were deployed to Lucknow. My brother went with them. He's a lieutenant colonel in the Black Watch. Had he still been in Perth, he'd have willingly given me a list of deserters.'

Leeming was furious. 'You *knew* that the regiment was abroad?'

'Of course, I did. I'm proud to say that their journey began on the Caledonian. We put out all the flags for them. They were going on a hazardous mission. It wasn't only a deadly enemy they had to face. India is rife with terrible diseases.'

'You could have saved me a miserable journey on the train, sir. Why didn't you *tell* me that you knew that the Black Watch was abroad?'

'You never asked me, Sergeant.'

'That's true, alas,' said Colbeck. 'It was a foolish omission.'

'If you lived in Scotland,' Craig told them, 'you'd know that many of our regiments were sent to India in the wake of the mutiny there last year. Apart from the Black Watch, we waved off the Gordon Highlanders, the Argyll and Sutherland Highlanders, the Seaforth Highlanders, the Camerons and so forth.'

'You seem well versed in troop movements,' remarked Colbeck.

'It comes from having a soldier in the family.'

'Tell me a little more about your brother.'

'Yes,' said Leeming, testily, 'and ask him to give us fair warning next time he's likely to vanish overseas. It would be helpful to know.'

'Listen to what Mr Craig has to say,' advised Colbeck. 'He might be about to solve another thorny problem for us.'

'What's that, sir?'

'Why the Caledonian was singled out as a target.'

Madeleine Colbeck felt that she'd been unduly harsh on her father. She was still appalled by what he'd suggested but decided that she'd reacted too bluntly. In order to repair the rift, she went off to see him the next morning. As the cab dropped her off outside the little house in Camden Town, she looked up at it fondly. It was a treasure trove of memories. Some of them were sad but the overwhelming majority were happy. Born and brought up there, Madeleine would always regard it with affection. At the same time, however, it was a measure of how far she'd gone in the world. Had she not met and married Robert Colbeck, the most that she could have hoped for was to pass the rest of her days in a similarly modest abode. Instead of that, she occupied a fine house in Westminster with servants to relieve her of the routine chores she did when she lived with her father.

Having seen her through the window, Andrews opened the door to greet her.

'I wasn't expecting you, Maddy,' he said, giving her a kiss.

'I thought I'd surprise you.'

'You've certainly done that.'

They went inside the house and sat down. The familiar surroundings enveloped her in a warm hug. Her father had made a few changes to the parlour. New ornaments had appeared on the mantelpiece and he'd rearranged the furniture but the room remained essentially the same.

'I came to apologise, Father,' she began.

'Whatever for?'

'I was too sharp with you yesterday.'

'You weren't sharp enough, in my opinion,' he said, penitently. 'I should be the one saying sorry to *you*, Maddy. It was wrong of me to want money for what I did. I can see that now.'

'It shocked me at the time.'

'I feel ashamed for having such thoughts. When I got back here, I remembered all the times when you helped Robert in an investigation. Yet you never asked for a brass farthing in return.'

Madeleine smiled. 'I got the reward I wanted,' she said.

'Can you forgive me?'

'I'd rather forget the whole thing, Father.'

'So would I.'

'The matter is closed.'

'It would be nice to think that, Maddy,' he said, 'but it's not true, is it?'

'What do you mean?'

'Well, when I went to bed last night, I lay awake thinking about it. I must have spent hours going over and over it. I had this dreadful thought.' He swallowed hard before speaking. 'What if I was wrong?'

'I don't follow you.'

'It was only a guess, after all. When you told me what Mrs Renwick had said to you, I was too quick to jump to a conclusion. That burglar may have had no interest in the timetable of the royal train. He went there after money. It could be that I started a panic for no reason at all.' He reached out to pick up a letter from the table. 'Think how red my face will be if I made a mistake, Maddy. This letter from Superintendent Tallis will have to be thrown away. When he knows that I've misled everybody, he'll send me a much nastier letter.'

'You're talking nonsense, Father,' she said.

His face creased in concern. 'Am I?'

'They found that burglar,' she reminded him. 'He'd been murdered. Robert was certain that he'd been killed because he knew too much. Then there was the dead man's servant. He talked about two strangers hiring his master.'

'But he said nothing about them asking for details of that timetable,' insisted Andrews. 'If the servant had heard about that, Robert would have told us.'

'Robert didn't interview him. It was Victor Leeming and the superintendent who did that and they were left in no doubt that Patrick Scanlan had been dragged into a plot to assassinate members of the royal family.' She went across to put a hand on his shoulder. 'Sleep soundly tonight, Father,' she said. 'You weren't wrong at all. So you can keep that letter from Superintendent Tallis. It's a rarity. According to Robert, he's very frugal with praise yet you've got whole paragraphs of congratulation out of him. That's very unusual.'

'Thank goodness you came, Maddy,' he said, beaming. 'You've taken a load off my mind. As for this,' he went on, holding up the letter, 'I may even frame it.'

After breakfast at the hotel, Colbeck and Leeming scoured the local ships' chandlers in search of a telescope. They eventually found what they wanted. Leeming was struck by its weight.

'This could be used as a weapon,' he said.

'We bought it for a more peaceable purpose, Victor.'

'My children would love to look through it.'

'Perhaps they will one day,' said Colbeck.

They were seated side by side in a cab that was taking them back to the Strathallan Hotel. Their meeting with Craig on the previous evening had given a whole new slant to the investigation.

'At last we have some idea why the Caledonian was chosen,' said Colbeck. 'There's a direct link between the railway and the military. It transported several regiments on their way to India but there was a special connection with the Black Watch. Mr Craig's brother holds a senior rank in it. No wonder they saw the regiment off in such style.'

'Yes,' said Leeming. 'The Caledonian treated them like returning heroes before they'd even left. They spent a lot of money on that farewell.'

'Someone clearly resented that. I think it was a soldier.'

'Could it be that deserter you talked about?'

'It's more than likely. Everyone in the regiment would have known that their lieutenant colonel's brother was the general manager of the Caledonian. It was the reason the Black Watch was given preferential treatment by the company.'

'Why did the soldier desert?' asked Leeming.

'I don't know.'

'And why turn against the Queen he vowed to fight for?'

'That, too, is a mystery.'

'Deserters are usually cowards, aren't they? There were newspaper articles about them during the Crimean War. When they saw how dangerous it was on the battlefield, they ran away in fear. The army executed every one of them caught.'

'People are not only motivated by fear,' said Colbeck. 'The horrors of warfare can disgust them so much that they become pacifists. Or they can be seized by a religious fervour. They might even sympathise with the values of the enemy. It's wrong to brand them all as cowards, Victor. There's a degree of bravery in an action that renders one liable to be hanged summarily if arrested.'

'Cowards are cowards in my book, sir,' said Leeming, brusquely.

'Remind me what Ned Layne said about the two men who hired his master to break into Mr Renwick's house. Could either of them have been a former soldier?'

'It's possible. The one who spoke was a hefty man in his thirties with a full beard. He had a Scots accent, apparently. I suppose that he could easily have once belonged to a Highland regiment.'

'What about the man who didn't say a word?'

'He was short, slight and older – oh, and he was a little swarthier.'

'Did he look foreign?'

'No,' replied Leeming. 'Not according to Layne, anyway – though he did say that there was something peculiar about him even though he couldn't put a finger on what it was.'

Colbeck's smile was bleak. 'I look forward to meeting this gentleman.'

George Hibbard was pleased with the hiding place. It had been well chosen. The three of them had spent the night in a clearing in the middle of the wood. Because it was set on a hill, they had a good view in all directions. It was safe and secluded. Davey Ure had been responsible for choosing the location. He'd erected the tent and brought in food supplies. A nearby stream provided water and he'd even managed to catch a few fish there. Since they were related, there was a faint resemblance between Ure and Callum Matthews and both were muscular. Hibbard, by contrast, was slim and sinewy. He had a European cast of feature but, in the morning sunshine, his dark complexion was exaggerated. He was the acknowledged leader of the trio.

As they ate breakfast, they discussed their plans.

'Everything has gone well so far,' said Matthews, smugly.

'No, it hasn't,' countered Hibbard. 'We weren't able to kill

Scanlan's servant. That was a bad mistake. He saw us and will be able to give the police descriptions of you and me.'

'What does it matter? They might search for us in London but they'd never dream of looking here. We're safe, George. Ye made sure that the servant didn't hear ye speak.'

'I'd still like to have shut his mouth for ever.'

There was a sing-song lilt to Hibbard's voice that partially contradicted his appearance and he made an effort to moderate it. Though brought up by his Indian mother, he'd taken on the name of his English father when he left the country. The older George Hibbard had held a senior position in the East India Company, and – to stave off the boredom of a stale marriage – had strayed outside it. Ure and Matthews made no moral judgements about his parentage. The three of them were united by a common purpose. That was enough.

'D'ye miss the army, Davey?' asked Matthews.

Ure snorted. 'I miss it like a bad tooth that's been pulled out. My army days are over, Callum. Mind you, they taught me a lot. That's why ye spent a comfortable night under canvas. I learnt how to pitch a tent properly.'

Matthews smirked. 'Did they teach ye to steal as well?'

'Tha's a gift that comes naturally.'

'It's served us well,' said Hibbard. 'You stole the gunpowder from your old regiment and just about everything else we needed. Most important of all, I think, was your advice about the royal train.'

'I knew that there was a rigid timetable,' explained Ure, 'because I stood on Perth station more than once waiting for the royal train to arrive. We were soaked to the skin on one occasion because they made us stand out in the rain. To be fair,' he added, 'the train was always on time.'

'It makes our task easier,' said Hibbard. 'We know more or less exactly when our target will come into view.'

'The pilot train will come first, George. The one we want will be fifteen miles behind it, so we'll have fair warning of its approach.' He munched some bread. 'What will ye do when it's all over?'

'I'll sail away from this damned country as soon as I can. I want to go home. What about the two of you? There'll be a lot of money coming your way,' Hibbard continued. 'I honour my promises. You could both afford to go abroad, if you wish.'

'I'm no' doing this for the money,' said Ure, quickly. 'I'm doing it because of what I saw when I was in Lucknow. I don't want to be part of an army that straps men over the end of cannon guns and blows them to bits.'

'And ye'll never get me to leave bonny Scotland,' attested Matthews. 'I'm one of many people here who want to shake off English tyranny. Scotland has been in subjection for far too long. The difference between me and the other rebels is that I'm ready to do something aboot it – at whatever cost.'

Hibbard patted him on the back. 'You're a good man, Callum,' he said. 'And so is your cousin. I found that out when Davey and I travelled together from India. We didn't come all this way to fail,' he declared. 'Thanks to your help, we can set off an explosion that will be heard all over the British Empire.'

Tallis read the report with interest and gratitude, fascinated by its contents and thankful that it had been sent to him and not directly to the commissioner. Being the first to see it gave him a sense of importance. Colbeck had been economical with detail but his advice was clear. Since he'd identified the site of the threatened attack, he would be able to prevent it happening. The royal train should leave on schedule, confident that it would meet with no obstruction north of the border. Tallis took the report straight to the commissioner and handed it over. After studying it, Mayne slapped the top of his desk in approval.

'Well done, Colbeck!' he said. 'I knew that you'd save the day.'

'There's still an element of risk,' argued Tallis. 'I'd feel happier if there were more than the two of them.'

'They know what they're doing, man. You trained them, after all.'

'That's true, Sir Richard. I taught them to temper daring with caution.'

'Judging by this report, they'll need both.' He held up the letter. 'This must be seen by Prince Albert as soon as possible.'

'Will it be enough to convince him to keep arrangements in place?'

'I'm sure that it will.'

'Then I'll leave everything with you, Sir Richard.'

'Wait!' said Mayne, checking his pocket watch. 'I don't have the time to go now. I'm dining with the Home Secretary. We have important business to discuss and Mr Walpole doesn't like to be kept waiting.'

'We can't delay sending this report.'

'I'd never suggest that. Someone else must take it to Buckingham Palace and you are the ideal person to do so. Give my compliments to Prince Albert and tell him that I endorse Inspector Colbeck's advice. But before you go, Superintendent,' he added, reprovingly, 'take a moment to brush that cigar ash from your waistcoat.'

The reproach went unheard. Tallis had been given the responsibility of delivering an important document to Buckingham Palace. Taking the report from Mayne, he straightened his back, glowed inwardly and marched out as if on his way to have a private audience with Queen Victoria herself.

When the day finally came, they caught the train in Glasgow and headed south. Their banner was hidden in a valise and their objective was listed on the poster in Tam Howie's pocket. It was an advertisement for the forthcoming visit of the Queen and her family to Scotland. The timetable for the royal train was laid out with clarity. It gave the sabbatarians an opportunity too good to miss. A full compartment made it impossible for them to discuss what lay ahead. When they alighted and set off in a hired trap, however, nobody could overhear them. Howie drove the vehicle.

'This was a brilliant idea of yours, Tam,' said Dalton.

'I read an article somewhere about the Queen's proposed visit to Balmoral. It's been at the back of my mind for weeks. If the royal train is brought to a halt,' said Howie, 'everyone will see our banner fluttering on the hillside.'

'The beauty of it is that nobody gets hurt.'

'Yet we'll reap a harvest of publicity,' promised Flora. 'Her Majesty is a God-fearing woman. In her heart, she'll applaud our defence of the Sabbath.'

'She's more likely to complain that the train is late.'

'What's a little inconvenience compared to the desecration of Sunday by the very railway company on whose track she's travelling? It will make her think.'

'It will make *everyone* think,' said Dalton.

'Yes,' agreed Howie, 'and that includes Gregor Hines.'

'Has he been badgering you again, Tam?'

'He let me know that he has his suspicions.'

Flora huffed. 'That man was born with suspicions.'

'He's watching us, Flora, waiting for us to make a blunder.'

'Then he's going to wait a long time.'

The three of them laughed. Turning off the track that meandered up the hillside, they drove in the direction of the place they'd selected on their earlier visit. The thick grass slowed them down and the bushes gave them only intermittent glimpses of the railway line below. No human being was in sight. All that they could see was a flock of sheep dotted indiscriminately over the hillside. Eager and confident on the surface, each of them harboured doubts but kept them well hidden, talking continuously to bolster their spirits. Howie had told Gregor Hines that they'd be going on a picnic and they'd brought food and drink with them. Anyone seeing them would assume that they were out on an excursion of some sort. There was an air of collective pleasure about them.

When Howie finally brought the trap to a halt in a glade, they got down to proceed on foot. There were hours to go yet but they wanted to be in position. Besides, they needed to gather brushwood to light the fire that would bring the royal train to a juddering halt and cause the passengers to look through the windows. What they would see on one side of the line was the huge banner that Flora had painstakingly created. **GOD BLESSED THE SEVENTH DAY AND SANCTIFIED IT.** Their message would make the royal family itself take heed.

After tethering the horse in the shadows, Howie tried to lead the way on. Before the sabbatarian had gone ten yards, however, a burly man in a shepherd's smock and a battered hat stepped out to block their way. Howie was livid.

'Stand aside, my man,' he ordered. 'We have somewhere to go.'

'So do we,' said Davey Ure, pointedly. 'Ask my friends.'

Callum Matthews and George Hibbard emerged from the

bushes either side of the three sabbatarians. Both were dressed in the rough garb of shepherds and both had pistols levelled at the newcomers. Flora was alarmed and Dalton began to tremble. Howie stepped forward to confront Ure.

'We mean no harm,' he said, 'so you can tell your friends to put their weapons down. If we are trespassing, we'll pay you well to overlook this intrusion. We had to come here, you see. The royal train will pass close by.'

'Yes,' said Ure, seizing him by the throat. 'We *know*.'

Colbeck and Leeming had also used disguises. Dressed as farm labourers, they looked far less conspicuous in the countryside. Though they were not issued with firearms, there were times when Colbeck felt the need of them and this was one of them. Both he and Leeming therefore carried loaded pistols and a supply of ammunition. Using the telescope to establish that nobody had yet arrived at the place where the gunpowder was hidden, they crept up on it and concealed themselves nearby. All that they had to do was to watch and wait for the moment to surprise the conspirators. Somewhere further down the line, the royal train was on its way north with the most important people in the realm on board. The detectives were determined that it would steam past them unhindered and proceed to Perth.

After the first hour, they merely felt the discomfort. When a second hour slipped by – and when nobody turned up – Leeming's nerves began to fray.

'They're not coming, sir,' he said.

'Be patient, Victor. Give them time.'

'They should have been here by now. They've got to dig up that gunpowder and carry it to the place where they'll set off the explosion. That can't be left until the last minute. We've seen how well they plan things.'

Colbeck checked his watch. 'There's still an hour to go.'

'Where *are* they?'

'Keep your voice down. Sound carries in the open.'

Half an hour later, Colbeck started to have his own fears. Nobody had come anywhere near the clearing. When he used the telescope again, it showed him a deserted landscape. Leeming was agitated.

'They *know*, sir,' he said. 'They know that we're waiting for them and they've called off the attack. That means they'll strike again when we least expect it and when we won't be there to protect the royal family.'

Colbeck was baffled. 'I can't understand it.' He looked at his watch again. 'Time is running out. In thirty minutes, the royal train will be passing near here.'

'It will be quite safe. They're not coming.'

'Oh, yes, they are, Victor.'

'We've scared them off.'

'I doubt that. Put yourself in their shoes. They're bent on assassination and it has to be on the Caledonian. If they miss this opportunity, they'll have to wait until the royal train returns from Balmoral and they don't have full details of that. Her Majesty and her party are capricious,' said Colbeck. 'They'll stay in Scotland as long as they wish. The date of their return may shift.'

'If they're so keen to launch their attack now,' said Leeming with concern, 'why aren't they here? They can't cause an explosion without gunpowder and it's under the ground in that clearing.'

Colbeck was uncertain. 'Is it?'

'You actually saw it, sir.'

'What I saw was a barrel with the name of the regiment on it,' said Colbeck, 'but I didn't check what was in it. Let's do that now.'

Getting up, he led Leeming up the hill towards the stand of trees.

The sergeant was puffing. 'Are you saying there's *no* gunpowder there?'

'I'm suggesting that we might have been tricked. We know that one of the men is a former soldier. He'll understand the importance of strategy.'

'What sort of strategy?'

'Let's be quick about it, Victor.'

Colbeck ran hard with Leeming panting at his heels. They went into the trees and stopped in the clearing. Kneeling down, Colbeck began to shovel the earth away with his hands. Leeming helped him. They were frantic. Time was running out fast. When the barrel came into view, they kept on digging until they'd loosened the earth around its side. It was several minutes before they were able to get a good grip on it. Putting all their energy into the heave, they yanked the barrel free in a snowstorm of earth. It felt suspiciously light. Colbeck used a twig to work away at the bung and it suddenly sprung out. Lifting the barrel, he shook it hard but nothing came out.

'What are they playing at?' wailed Leeming.

'This is a decoy,' said Colbeck. 'We were meant to find it. They knew that the whole area would be searched after that train crash so they made sure that we'd be misled. It's a clever strategy. The royal family is only twenty minutes away and we haven't a clue where the villains will strike.'

Leeming was appalled. 'It's our fault, sir.'

'They've pulled the wool over our eyes.'

'We'll be hanged, drawn and quartered for this.'

'Get back to the horses,' snapped Colbeck. 'We need to move fast.'

* * *

A day that had begun with high ambition had ended in calamity. Instead of being able to proclaim their message to the royal family and, by extension, to a much wider audience, they were trussed up in a tent like three Christmas turkeys. The final insult was that their banner had been torn to shreds to bind them hand and foot. Nobody would see it now. Howie blamed himself for leading them into the dire situation and he could see no way out. He now saw that it had been madness to undertake such a project and wished that they'd never embarked on it. Vowing never to get involved in protest again, he prayed furiously for deliverance.

Dalton, meanwhile, was overcome with remorse. Like Howie, he'd been deceived by their earlier successes into thinking they could do anything. They had now taken a step too far and would suffer for it. There was another strand to his guilt. Having accomplished their work, he'd expected to return to Glasgow where he could take his wife into his confidence at last and tell her what they'd done. Morag Dalton would have applauded him, yet the likelihood now was that she'd never see her husband alive again. He, too, resorted to prayer.

It was Flora who had most to fear. The three men were armed and ruthless. They tied up their captives and stowed them in the tent until they could deal with them later. She knew what they planned. The sabbatarians had merely wished to bring the royal train to a halt whereas the three men intended to cover it under an avalanche. It was an unspeakable crime. Flora and her companions couldn't be left alive to describe the assassins. Their fate was settled. While her husband and Dalton would have a quick death, however, Flora would be kept alive for a while. Her age and respectability were no protection. She'd seen the way two of the men looked at her. Before they killed her, they'd take their pleasure in turns.

Instead of being paralysed by the horror of it all, Flora was prompted to think more clearly than she'd ever done before. Their very survival was at stake. While her companions were pleading for some kind of divine intervention, she was looking for a means of escape. Like the others, she was sitting on the ground with her hands tied behind her back and her feet lashed together. The prisoners were yards apart from each other. Her bonds were biting into her wrists and ankles. No matter how much she struggled, she couldn't loosen them. Yet she was capable of some movement.

'Help me, Tam!' she cried.

'I wish that I could,' he said, tearfully.

'Come towards me.'

'How can I do that?'

Flora showed him. She bounced along inch by excruciating inch then lay back so that she was horizontal. Gathering her strength, she rolled over towards her husband. He was quick to respond, edging towards her in small bounces.

Flora rolled again and got closer.

'Turn round,' she said.

'What are you going to do?'

'Turn round, Tam.'

It took him over a minute to do so. By the time he had his back to her, she was right next to him, manoeuvring her head into position. Howie realised what she was trying to do and moved his hands near her mouth. Lifting her head, Flora began to bite her way frenziedly through the strips of cloth that held his wrists. She drew blood at one point but Howie didn't complain. He could sense that he'd soon be free. Dalton watched in fascination as Flora took one last bite and severed the bond. Howie tossed the bits of cloth away and undid those around his ankles. Then he untied

Flora and hugged her. Dalton was the next to be liberated. All three of them rubbed their wrists and ankles. They might be free but they were also bewildered.

'What do we do now?' asked Dalton.

'I think we should make a run for it,' said Howie.

'They could come after us, Tam.'

'It's a chance we have to take. We can't tackle them. They're armed.'

'But we can't let them set off that explosion,' argued Flora. 'The royal train will have the Queen and her family aboard and it's heading for an ambush. We mustn't just think of ourselves. Somehow we have to raise the alarm.'

'How can we possibly do that?' said Dalton. 'We're miles from anywhere.'

'It's worth a try, Ian.'

'Flora is right,' said Howie, reaching into his pocket. 'We came to start a fire, didn't we? Let's do it. If the blaze is big enough, someone might see it.'

Galloping to a high point, Colbeck reined in his horse and used the telescope to scan the horizon in all directions. He could see nothing suspicious. Leeming joined him, handling his mount with far less skill and worrying about being unsaddled. They were angry at themselves for being deceived and hoped for a chance to make amends. The sergeant's confidence was waning rapidly.

'It's a waste of time,' he said. 'We'll never find them in time.'

'They can't be all that far away, Victor. We know they'll strike somewhere on this stretch of line. We must just keep looking.'

'But we don't know whether to go north or south.'

'Yes, we do,' said Colbeck, peering through the telescope again. 'Take a look along the ridge.'

He handed the instrument to Leeming who did as he was told. About half a mile away, a column of smoke was now curling up into the sky. It was coming from the heart of a wood. Colbeck sensed that it might be a warning signal.

'Let's go,' he said, digging his heels into the horse.

Leeming took a little longer to move. Still with the telescope, he had to hold the reins with one hand. His hopes had been rekindled by the distant fire, however, and he rode with much more purpose now as he followed the bobbing figure of Colbeck ahead of him.

The three of them were standing down by the rocks that overhung the line. Matthews had dug the holes and Ure had filled them with the requisite amount of gunpowder. When it was set off, the explosion would be big enough to knock the train off the rails with the force of a gigantic cannonball. Now that they were so close to achieving their aim, they were almost giddy with the sense of triumph. Because none of them turned round, they didn't see the smoke that was climbing up into the air behind them. Their attention was focused on the line.

'I hope that we kill the whole family,' said Hibbard, licking his lips. 'India has been stripped of all of its riches in the name of the Queen. The East India Company is her tool of repression. It controls the armies.'

'Aye,' said Ure, 'I was part of one and I couldn't believe what I saw. It wasn't the fact that we were made to crush the rebellion. It was the effect that it had on those around me. I'd lived and trained with those men for years. They were my friends until we got to Lucknow,' he went on, 'then they turned into wild animals. What they were doing was inhuman and I wanted no part of it. That's when I deserted.'

'There were outrages on both sides, Davey,' admitted Hibbard, 'but the sepoys and sowars who rose up against the British had good cause. They were poorly paid, badly treated and forced to keep their own countrymen in subjection. They were asked to do things that were against their religion.'

'After what I saw, I no longer *have* any religious beliefs. I just want to stop this monster called the British Empire from killing its way to power.'

'Two of my half-brothers were sepoys. Because they joined the rebellion, they and their wives and children were slaughtered.'

'I ken nothing of India,' said Matthews, 'except that it's been robbed of its resources in the same way as Scotland. Independence is our birthright. This is our chance to grab it with both hands.'

'I agree with ye, Callum,' said Ure. 'All the countries in the Empire should be set free, then there'd be no more fighting. We could all live in peace.'

'It's not peace that I came all this way to get,' Hibbard told them, looking at his watch. 'It's revenge and it's not many minutes away. The pilot train went past a while ago. Callum and I will withdraw to safety while Davey gets ready to set off the explosion. It will be the sweetest sound I ever heard.'

But it was another sound that came into his ears. The drumming of hooves made them turn around. The first thing they saw was the smoke billowing up from what had been their camp. The next second, they saw two horsemen bearing down on them. Hibbard looked at them in amazement.

'Where did they come from?' he demanded.

'And who started the fire?' asked Matthews.

'You carry on, Davey. We'll take care of these two.'

Drawing his pistol, Hibbard went up the hill to meet the approaching riders. Matthews went with him, weapon at the ready. Ure stayed to ignite the gunpowder. He was determined that nothing would stop them.

Colbeck was still in the lead. When he saw that the two men were armed, he tried to zigzag in order to present a less easy target. Leeming was thirty yards behind him, brandishing the telescope and relieved that they'd found the conspirators at last. Throwing caution to the wind, he kicked even more speed out of his horse as it descended the hill. Colbeck headed for the slighter of the two men and braced himself when the man's pistol was aimed at him. But the shot came too soon and was yards wide. The man tried in vain to reload his weapon. Colbeck pulled his horse to a skidding halt and leapt from the saddle. Knocking Hibbard to the ground, he grappled with him and they fought hard.

Leeming's interest was in the second man. When he saw that Hibbard was in difficulties, Matthews went to his aid. Intent on shooting Colbeck, he yelled in pain as Leeming smashed the telescope hard against his wrist. The pistol was dislodged at once. When he'd pulled his horse up, Leeming jumped from the saddle and ran towards Matthews to pull him away from the two threshing figures on the ground. A second fight developed but there could only be one winner. Having tossed the telescope aside, Leeming used both fists to pummel away at the sturdy frame of Matthews. Since his wrist had been broken by the impact of the telescope, the Scotsman could only punch with one hand. It took Leeming less than a minute to overpower him and get his arms behind his back. When the sergeant snapped handcuffs onto his wrists, Matthews howled in agony.

Colbeck's opponent was proving stronger than he looked,

biting, spitting and twisting in all directions. The ferocious contest was brought to a halt when Leeming put his pistol to Hibbard's temple.

'Don't give me an excuse to pull the trigger,' he warned.

Hibbard gave in and Colbeck rolled off him, turned him over and handcuffed him. As soon as he'd done that, he ran down the hill. The royal train could now be heard in the distance. Leeming could see it through the telescope. Colbeck was bent on ensuring its safe passage. When he burst through the bushes, he saw a square-shouldered man kneeling beside a trickle of gunpowder with a tinderbox. Though the man pulled out a pistol, he had no time to aim it because Colbeck dived at his midriff and sent him sprawling. The gun went off and the bullet was discharged harmlessly into the air. The force of the attack made Ure roll uncontrollably towards the railway line, clasped tightly by Colbeck. They got to the very edge of the rocks overlooking the track. The sound of the approaching train was getting louder and louder.

Deprived of his chance to set off the explosion, Ure fought back madly and was a more powerful adversary than Hibbard. He and Colbeck traded blows and each sought to get on top of the other. All the time, the train was getting closer, its royal passengers sublimely unaware of the desperate struggle that was taking place ahead of them. Colbeck put all his strength into his punches but he'd met his match in the former soldier. Whenever the inspector got the upper hand, Ure broke free of his grasp. Both were covered in blood from facial wounds. Colbeck could hear the train getting ever nearer. A second later, he came close to being thrown onto the rails in front of it. Ure landed a blow on Colbeck's chin that momentarily dazed him. He then got up and tried to push the inspector over the edge of the rock.

Before he could do so, however, he let out a cry of anguish and reached for the leg that the sheepdog had just bitten. Having hared down the incline, Angus had arrived just in time to save Colbeck because the royal train was thundering below him on its way to Balmoral. Leeming held his pistol on Ure who was more interested in rubbing his wounded leg than in fighting on. Colbeck dragged himself to his feet and patted the dog in gratitude. Jamie Farr came over to join them.

'We saw the smoke,' he said.

It was not until the following evening that they returned to London. Behind them in Scotland, they left three murderous villains in custody, a delighted general manager of the Caledonian Railway, a chastened Inspector Rae, a happy shepherd and a trio of rueful sabbatarians. Arriving at Scotland Yard, they went straight to Tallis's office. He leapt up from behind his desk to pump their hands in turn.

'I want a full report,' he said, glancing at Colbeck's bruises, 'though your face tells some of the story, Inspector.'

'You can't see *my* bruises, sir,' complained Leeming. 'I never want to ride another horse again. I was saddle-sore within minutes.'

'Nevertheless,' observed Colbeck, 'you proved your point. There are indeed times when a horse is the best way to travel. Without four legs under us, we'd never have been able to save the royal train.'

'Mr Craig's telegraph sang your praises,' said Tallis. 'I'm glad I sent you.'

'With respect, Superintendent, you did everything you could *not* to send me. Had the sergeant and I not gone to Scotland, we would now be reading horrendous stories in the press about the royal train.'

'I encouraged you to go, Colbeck.'

'I remember it differently,' said Leeming.

'Who asked for *your* opinion?' growled Tallis.

'We went because the inspector felt that we had to.'

'Whatever the reason,' said Colbeck, trying to rescue the sergeant from another rebuke, 'we were able to solve the crime. Yet it has to be said that we had assistance from others – Angus among them.'

'Angus?' echoed Tallis.

'He's a sheepdog, sir.'

'He probably saved the inspector's life,' said Leeming.

'Let's go back to the beginning,' suggested Colbeck.

He gave the superintendent an edited account of their second visit to Glasgow and explained how the fire lit in the woods had alerted them. When Colbeck described the clash with the conspirators, Leeming interrupted to say that the telescope had had a double function, guiding them to the site of the explosion and acting as a useful weapon. Tallis wanted to know more about the motives of the three men who would now face certain execution.

'Were they prepared to speak of what impelled them?'

'We couldn't stop them doing so,' said Colbeck.

'Especially the one from India,' added Leeming. 'He was bitter because his English father had disowned him while alive, yet he inherited a lot of money when his father died.'

'He used it to pay all the expenses of the long journey to England and to reward his two accomplices, Ure and Matthews. One was a soldier in the Black Watch, sickened by what he saw in Lucknow, and the other was a dissident with dreams of an independent Scotland. Those dreams won't be realised now.'

'You've both distinguished yourselves,' said Tallis, expansively, 'and I played my part when I delivered the message to Prince Albert that the royal train must leave on time. He was gracious enough to say that he found the way I deployed my detectives as exemplary. I told him that I operated on instinct. I *knew* it was right to send my two best men to Scotland.'

Colbeck and Leeming exchanged a knowing glance. Tallis had already rewritten that part of recent history. Arguing with him would be fruitless. They knew the truth, however. As the superintendent waxed on about the importance of their success, their minds were elsewhere. Leeming was thinking about going home to a rapturous welcome from his wife and children while Colbeck was recalling the look of wonder on the face of Jamie Farr when he discovered the size of the reward he was to be given and learnt the details of the assassination attempt. Most of the people involved in the final confrontation had been losers. The conspirators had been arrested and the sabbatarians had been frightened to death. Apart from the detectives, the decisive winner was a young shepherd with an abiding hatred of railways.

Caleb Andrews relaxed in a chair but his daughter marched up and down the drawing room and kept glancing at the clock on the mantelpiece. Madeleine was at once thrilled and impatient. Andrews was critical.

'You should have gone to Euston to meet him.'

'If Robert had wanted me to do that, he'd have said so in his letter.'

'You're Mrs Colbeck now, Maddy.'

'I'm not likely to forget that,' she said.

'The two of us should have been on the platform to greet him.'

'He'll have to go to Scotland Yard first. The superintendent will expect a report. Until that's out of the way, we must simply sit still and wait.'

'But you're *not* sitting still,' he said with a laugh. 'You've been walking up and down this past hour like a caged animal. Take the weight off your feet.'

'I'd much rather stand up, Father.'

'It won't make him come any earlier.'

She looked at the clock again. 'He should have been here by now,' she said. 'Perhaps the train was late.'

'Not if it's driven by somebody *I* taught,' he boasted. 'We've a reputation for punctuality on the LNWR. If there's a delay, it must have been on the Caledonian.'

'What's *keeping* him?'

As if in answer to her question, she heard the clip-clop of a horse and the rumble of cab wheels. Madeleine rushed off into the hall and flung open the front door. When the cab came to a halt, Colbeck got out with his luggage and paid the driver. Madeleine dashed forward to embrace her husband and receive a kiss. Unable to see his face in the dark, she gasped when they entered the hall and she could look at him properly. She grabbed him by the shoulders.

'What's happened to you, Robert?'

'I had a slight altercation with someone,' he said.

'So you have,' said Andrews, coming out to join them and staring at the bruises. 'Welcome back, Robert.'

'Thank you.'

They exchanged a handshake and a few remarks. Eager to hear about events in Scotland, Andrews accepted that he would have to wait. Colbeck needed to be left alone with his wife. Andrews was in the way. He took his leave, put on his hat and went out of the house. Madeleine closed the door behind him then ran to Colbeck for a second embrace. Arm around her, he led her into the drawing room.

'I'm sorry that it's been so long,' he said.

'It all ended happily, that's my consolation.'

'For some it ended more happily than for others. And Victor and I had some very unhappy moments along the way. Our reward was the satisfaction of knowing that the royal train went through Scotland unimpeded.'

'I'll want to hear all the details, Robert – and so will father.'

'That can wait,' he said, pulling her close. 'I'm back and I'm safe and we're in each other's arms again. What could be better than that?'

'Nothing,' she said, excitedly. 'Nothing at all.'

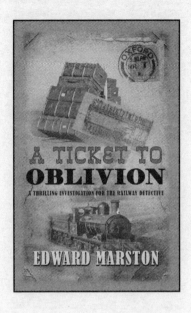

Young Imogen Burnhope and her maid Rhoda board a non-stop train to Oxford to visit her Aunt Cassandra, who waits on the platform at Oxford station where the train terminates, to greet them. Only they never arrive. All the passengers alight but the two women are nowhere to be seen. The train is searched and the coachman swears he saw them board onto first class, but they seem to have vanished into thin air.

Inspector Colbeck and Sergeant Leeming are assigned to the case. Is it a simple case of a run away? Or is there a larger, more sinister conspiracy at work? The Railway Detective must unravel the mystifying web of their disappearance before Imogen and Rhoda vanish into oblivion for good.

To discover more great books and to
place an order visit our website at
www.allisonandbusby.com

Don't forget to sign up to our free newsletter at
www. allisonandbusby.com/newsletter
for latest releases, events and exclusive offers

Allison & Busby Books
@AllisonandBusby

You can also call us on
020 7580 1080
for orders, queries
and reading recommendations